DAVID GIBBINS has worked in underwater archaeology all his professional life. After taking a PhD from Cambridge University he taught archaeology in Britain and abroad, and is a world authority on ancient shipwrecks and sunken cities. He has led numerous expeditions to investigate underwater sites in the Mediterranean and around the world. He currently divides his time between fieldwork, England and Canada.

By David Gibbins

THE
MASK OF
TROY

DAVID
GIBBINS

<u>headline</u>

First published in Great Britain in 2010
by HEADLINE PUBLISHING GROUP

First published in paperback in 2010
by HEADLINE PUBLISHING GROUP

4

Cataloguing in Publication Data is available from the British Library

ISBN 978 0 7553 5397 2 (B-format)
ISBN 978 0 7553 5812 0 (A-format)

Typeset in Aldine 401BT by Avon DataSet Ltd,
Bidford-on-Avon, Warwickshire

Printed and bound by CPI Group (UK) Ltd, Croydon, CR0 4YY

Headline's policy is to use papers that are natural, renewable and
recyclable products and made from wood grown in sustainable forests.
The logging and manufacturing processes are expected to conform to the
environmental regulations of the country of origin.

HEADLINE PUBLISHING GROUP
An Hachette UK Company
338 Euston Road
London NW1 3BH

www.headline.co.uk
www.hachette.co.uk

Acknowledgements

I am most grateful to my editors, Martin Fletcher at Headline and Caitlin Alexander at Bantam Dell; to my agent, Luigi Bonomi of LBA; to Gaia Banks, Alison Bonomi, Darragh Deering, Sarah Douglas, Sam Edenborough, Mary Esdaile, Harriet Evans, Kristin Fassler, Emily Furniss, Tessa Girvan, David Grogan, Jenny Karat, Celine Kelly, Nicki Kennedy, Kerr Macrae, Alison Masciovecchio, Tony McGrath, Jane Morpeth, Peter Newsom, Amanda Preston, Jenny Robson, Jane Selley, Rebecca Shapiro, Jo Stansall, Nita Taublib, Adja Vucicevic, Katherine West, Leah Woodburn and Theresa Zoro; to the Hachette representatives internationally; and to my many other publishers around the world.

I owe special thanks to Oya Alpar and my Turkish publishers, Altin Kitaplar, for inviting me to the excellent Istanbul Book Fair, which led me to return for several inspirational days to Troy while I was writing this novel. I'm grateful to my brother Alan for joining me on that trip and for his photography, as well as for his work on my website www.davidgibbins.com. I first visited Troy and Mycenae in the early 1980s with help from the British Institute of Archaeology at Ankara, the British School of Archaeology in Athens, the Society of Antiquaries of London and the University of Bristol, where I was fortunate to study archaeology under scholars who were at the forefront of research on the Aegean Bronze Age and the world of Homer, and who themselves were only a generation or so removed from the 'Heroic Age' of archaeology that began with Heinrich Schliemann. I have also been fortunate to participate in many ancient shipwreck excavations in the Mediterranean, and my research into the maritime archaeology of the Aegean owes much to a Fellowship awarded by the Winston Churchill Memorial Trust while I was a graduate student at Cambridge University.

I am extremely grateful to Ann Gibbins for all of her help and advice; to my father, who gave me the 1806 edition of Pope's *The Iliad of Homer* as a graduation present; to Angie, for Plato and the Hero and much else; and to our lovely daughter Molly, who had her first proper view of the undersea world through a diving mask while I was writing this book, off the north-west coast of Wales.

Present-day map of the east Mediterranean

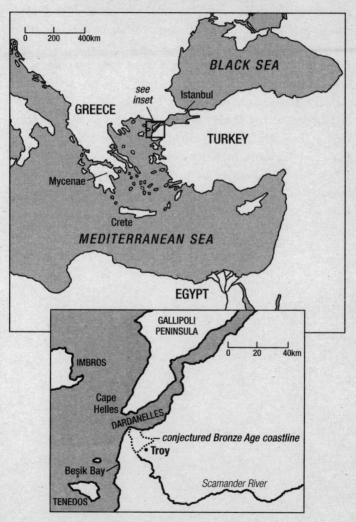

I give you a tablet of war; I give you a tablet of peace.

After a letter from King Tudhaliyas IV of the Hittites
to the Assyrian king, late thirteenth century BC

His sharpen'd spear let every Grecian wield,
And every Grecian fix his brazen shield;
Let all excite the fiery steeds of war,
And all for combat fit the rattling car.
This day, this dreadful day, let each contend;
No rest, no respite, till the shades descend;
Till darkness, or till death, shall cover all:
Let the war bleed, and let the mighty fall.

Homer, *The Iliad*, Book II, lines 382–94,
eighth century BC or earlier,
translated by Alexander Pope, 1715–20

Prologue

Mycenae, Greece, 28 November 1876

The man stepped off the upper rung of the ladder on to the edge of the excavation pit, his shoes crunching on a pile of ancient potsherds the workmen had shovelled aside a few days before. In the moonlight the rough-hewn masonry around him glistened, as if the great citadel of the Bronze Age were new again. He swept his hand over his thinning hair, and pushed his pince-nez spectacles up his nose. He reached into his waistcoat pocket and pulled out his fob watch. Four a.m. He and Sophia had been here almost three hours, and it was now less than an hour before first light. *Before the child of morning, rosy-fingered Dawn.* He closed his eyes, thrilling at the epithet. Homer was never far from his thoughts here, when he was alone among the shadowy ruins with his wife, astonished at what they had found. *Well-built Mycenae, rich in gold*. It had been his dream since discovering Troy five years before, since he and Sophia had secretly made the find that would one day astonish the world, to come here to this other great bastion of the Bronze Age, this citadel of the king of kings, to find the key that would allow him to stand in front of the world and reveal the truth. Only then would people know it was not treasure that had driven him to search for the reality of the Trojan War, but the salvation of humanity. *The key that could save the world from Armageddon*.

He shoved the watch back in his pocket, and saw that he was streaked with mud. He would get Sophia to brush him down thoroughly before they returned, to remove all evidence that they had been up here. He was still wearing his dinner clothes from the evening before. They had planned to resume digging the following day, in a final effort before the excavation was closed down for the season. They had invited the Greek inspector to join them for a lavish celebratory meal, and had plied him with the most expensive wines and brandy until he had collapsed in a stupor. They had stolen up here afterwards, with nothing more than a spluttering oil lamp and a trowel. He had been waiting for this chance. Sophia had seen something in the first royal shaft grave several weeks before, in the final hours before the storm broke and halted the excavation of that tomb. He had made sure one of them had been there always, in the grave circle, personally taking the excavation deep into the bedrock below the citadel, at the place where all his instincts told him they would find what he had come here for, the final ingredient in the revelation that would soon astound humankind.

For now, what they found would be their secret. The world

would know only that he, Heinrich Schliemann, maverick millionaire, genius linguist, myth-lover, had come here after discovering Troy, on his relentless quest for the king who set the war in motion, the war that so many had dismissed as legend. He smiled wryly to himself. He would give them what they wanted. He peered cautiously around. In front of him were the upright slabs that formed the grave circle, enclosed by the massive ruined walls of the citadel that rose behind him in the cleft between the mountains. Walls built not by men but by Cyclopes, one-eyed monsters the men of Mycenae had yoked like slaves to create their rock-girt fortress. He half believed the myth himself, marvelling at the colossal size of the stones that lay where they had been placed more than three thousand years before. Yet it was not gods and giants he sought, but the deeds of men, real men, flesh and blood: what men could do, how high they could rise, how far they could fall. And the men he sought were not the heroes of myth. They were the shapers of history.

'Heinrich! You must come at once!' Sophia's voice came from the darkness below. Schliemann turned and stared into the excavation trench, his heart pounding. Could this be it? They had found treasure already, unimaginable quantities of it, revealed to gasping onlookers over the weeks of the excavation: gold diadems, jewellery, weapons, a golden goblet he had loudly proclaimed to be the cup of Nestor, the very cup Homer said had been brought before the Greeks on the plain of Troy. But it was not treasure they were looking for now. They were looking for the deed of a king; for what a king had hidden. He peered again, and saw only a faint golden glow at the base of the ladder, where Sophia was working at the bottom of the rock-cut shaft. He tried to control his excitement. 'Keep your voice down,' he whispered sharply in German. 'And keep anything you've found concealed. I need to be sure we're alone.'

His eyes swept from right to left. For a second he thought he saw a shadowy form, then it was gone, a trick of the moonlight. He saw the rocky path they had come up three hours before, through the gateway with its triangular capstone carved in the shape of two lions holding a pillar. *The Lion Gate of Mycenae, wall-girt fortress of Agamemnon, lord of men, wide-ruling one, noble son of Atreus*. The lions were decapitated now, but still exerted extraordinary power, and seeing them for the first time had strengthened his resolve that this place was more than just the stage set of myth. He turned away from the gate and gazed out as the great king once had from his mountain fastness over the plain towards the sea, to the place where he had set forth for Troy. *Troy*. Schliemann still shuddered at the name. They had been there, just like this, three years before, he and Sophia. They had found the treasure of King Priam. And they had found more. More than he could possibly have dreamed of. *More than the world yet knew*.

He saw the twinkling lights of their camp on the edge of the plain. He looked for flitting shadows in the gloom, for lights moving on the rocky path, but there was nothing. The Greek inspector would still be sleeping off the drink. The Greek authorities had heard rumours from Troy, and mistrusted Schliemann. There were some who thought he and Sophia were little more than tomb-robbers. Yet the Greeks were covetous enough of their place in history to want a part in the drama, to give him permission to excavate. And he was grateful to them. If the academics of the world had had their way, he would never have been allowed here. They had derided him for being self-taught, for having more money than sense, too used to getting his own way, too used to certainty. They thought he was absurd, a fantasist. But they were wrong.

He had not come in search of myth.

He had come in search of truth.

He had come in search of the real heroes.

He turned back to the trench and took a deep breath. The air had been cleansed by the rain, but the smells were rising again: rosemary, thyme, the sweet ether that seemed to float above these ancient sites, an exhalation from history too powerful to be washed away by a transient act of nature. He smelled the earth, the richness of it, the soil that had buried this place for millennia. He glanced up. The moonlit clouds were moving with speed, and for a second he fancied he saw the ghostly galleys of the Greeks heading east, drawn towards their nemesis at Troy. He swung his leg over the ladder, and moments later was at the bottom of the trench, encased in the smooth square walls where the tomb chamber had been hacked out of the rock. The lamp glowed in one corner. Sophia was there, raven-haired, bedecked in jewellery copied from their finds at Troy, streaked in grime like him. She was his Mycenaean queen, hunched over the grave as if she were preparing to join the dead king in the afterlife. 'Heinrich,' she whispered, pointing. He stared at the ground. He stopped breathing. He felt his knees buckle under him, and fell forward. It was not lamplight he had seen from the surface. It was gold. A mask of gold. He reached out and touched the metal. It was cold, pristine, untarnished. His heart was pounding. The fine, aristocratic features, the beard and moustache, the high cheekbones, the thin, hard lips. And those eyes, almond-shaped with a line across the middle, at once open and closed. A face just like others they had seen below Troy, a discovery he and Sophia had kept secret, a discovery too precious, too momentous, to squander in the game to put facts behind myth. He stared again. They had found it.

The face of a king. The mightiest earth-shaker of them all. *The king of kings.*

'Shall we take it now?' Sophia whispered.

He stared hard at the mask, then shook his head. 'No. We need to give our supporters what they want. What I said I believed in, all my life. Heinrich Schliemann will be vindicated. We will rebury this, and find it again with the workmen tomorrow. This image, this mask, will be etched for ever in the history of archaeology, for ever be associated with my name, with yours.'

'What will you tell them?'

He carefully pushed the tips of his fingers under the edges of the mask. 'I will tell them,' he said slowly, 'that I have gazed upon the face of Agamemnon.'

'But we must see what lies beneath,' she said. '*Now.*'

He gazed at her, his eyes suddenly moist with emotion. 'What we find here will be my gift to you. To the children we will have. To the children of the world.' He dug his fingers in further. He stared at the face on the mask again, those eyes at once open and closed. He held his breath. It was what he told the world he would find. A *Herrscherbild*. The image of a lord of men, a warrior king. He continued staring. For the first time he felt a pang of doubt. Was this truly the face of a hero, a face that could bring back a golden age? Or was it another face, the face of a man who had unleashed a war that destroyed the world's first great civilization? He remembered the myths again. The curse of the House of Atreus. He thought of the wars he had known, wars in his own lifetime, wars that had ravaged Europe, America, the East. Millions killed, whole countries devastated. Wars where there were no longer heroes. Wars fought with weapons forged in the fires of hell itself. He thought of the wars that could come. Total war. He and Sophia, their secret circle of friends, the powerful and good from around the world, had dreamed of a world where war was vanquished, where heroes once again would rule supreme, champions willing to sacrifice themselves for their people, for peace, a creed that he, Heinrich Schliemann, would reawaken by his determination to find the truth of what lay buried in this land of legends.

He stared into the eyes of the mask. He thought of those who had wielded power in his own world. Of those who might come. A kaiser. *A Führer.*

He thought of what he might unleash.

Sophia nudged him. 'You must do it, Heinrich. You must. It's nearly dawn.'

He swallowed hard, then took a deep breath. He smelled the earth again, the deep metallic odour. The exhalation of history. *The smell of blood.*

He lifted the mask.

PART 1

1

Off the island of Tenedos, the Aegean Sea, present day

The diver stared at the sea bed in astonishment. He had never seen treasure like this before in his life. He reached down and touched it, closing his fingers round the hilt, drawing the blade out of the sand to its full length. It was a magnificent sword, a weapon fit for a king, perfectly preserved as if it had been dropped this day, not lost thousands of years ago in the time of legends. He lifted it up, dazzled by the studded jewels of the hilt, by the gleaming bronze blade inlaid with gold and with red niello, images of warriors, spear-girt with figure-of-eight shields, following a great lion lunging at the front. He raised it towards the sunlight that streamed down from the surface, for a moment imagining he was passing it back up to the great king himself, war-bent, eyes locked on Troy, his galley riding the waves above. But as the blade reflected the sunlight it blinded him, and when he looked again it had disintegrated into sand, showering down *through his fingers on to the sea bed below. His breathing quickened, and he began desperately digging for it again, reaching into the hole he had made, pushing hard with his fingers. How could he tell the others? How could he tell them he had found the treasure that had brought them all so far, and then lost it?*

Jack Howard woke with a start as a Turkish air force F-16 shrieked low overhead, the roar dropping to a deep rumble as the jet hurtled over the coastline to the east. He shut his eyes, then rubbed them, trying to calm his breathing. The dream was always the same, and ended the same way. Maybe today reality would take over. He checked his dive watch, shading his eyes against the glare of the sun. In forty-five minutes he was due at the briefing, and twenty minutes after that he would be kitting up to dive on the shipwreck in the depths below them. He took a deep breath, sprang to his feet, then rolled up his sleeping mat and stashed it in its usual place beside the bow railing. It was his favourite spot to take a siesta, where he felt close to the elements – the intense Aegean sky, the noise and smell of the sea – yet within hailing distance of the bridge should he be needed.

He glanced back at the bridge windows, waving at the watch officer, and then looked down the sleek lines of the ship. *Seaquest II* had emerged from a refit only two weeks previously, and the white paint on her superstructure was still gleaming. Beyond the Lynx helicopter at the stern he could see the flag of the International Maritime University, bearing the anchor from his own family coat of arms, and above that a red flag with a white crescent moon and a star, their courtesy flag in Turkish waters. He shaded his eyes and scanned the horizon, picking out the lines of sight he had spotted before lying down, mentally triangulating their position. To the south-west lay the island of Bozcaada, ancient Tenedos, less than two nautical miles off the port bow. To the north-east he could just make out the low cliffs of Gallipoli, the long peninsula that jutted out from the European shore and flanked the Dardanelles, the narrow strait that divided Europe from Asia. He glanced at the GPS receiver he had left propped by the railing, confirming his fix. His pulse quickened. Captain Macalister was returning to the sonar contact they had made just before noon. The sea was rougher now, but the decision had clearly been made. Jack coursed with excitement. He remembered the extraordinary shape he had seen on the sea bed earlier that morning. *The dive was still on.*

He gripped the railing. The dream had left him jumpy, unable to relax. He remembered what he had come up here planning to do, when he had thought he would not sleep. He picked up the makeshift wooden target, three pieces of plank nailed into a crude triangle, and tossed it overboard, feeding out the line and tying it to the railing. He looked back to the bridge and put his hand up, and a moment later heard the triple warning blast on the tannoy indicating that a live firing exercise was about to take place. He put on the ear protectors and unholstered the heavy revolver he had put on the deck beside him. He slipped the lanyard over his neck, then pressed the thumb catch to break open the revolver and load six .455 calibre cartridges from the pouch on the belt. He snapped the gun shut and took aim, his right arm locked straight out, his left hand supporting the grip. He cocked the hammer with his left thumb and curled his right index finger round the trigger.

The target was thirty, maybe thirty-five metres away, a challenge at the best of times, but compounded by the rise of the swell and the heave of the ship's bow. He pulled the trigger and the revolver jumped back, its dull subsonic report almost lost in the noise of the wind. He fired again, and saw a stab of bubbles just short of the target. He pursed his lips. The powder load was right, but the bullets needed to be lighter. He fired off the remaining four chambers double-action, squeezing the trigger each time the revolver returned from the recoil, aiming high. The final bullet hit the target and sent it spinning crazily above the waves. He lowered his arms, pressed the thumb catch and broke the gun open, ejecting the spent cartridges into a bucket at his feet. He pulled off the ear protectors and hung them round his neck, raised his arm again and listened for the tannoy blasts to signal the end of firing. As he waited, he stared at the horizon, at the line of open sea to the south between the island and the Turkish mainland.

He braced his tall frame against the roll and pitch of the ship, and swallowed hard. The sea swell was making him feel uncomfortable, though he hated to acknowledge it. Captain Macalister had deactivated *Seaquest II*'s stabilizer system as he reacquired their position over the site. The sea had been calm that morning, but the wind had picked up as usual in the early afternoon and the waves were now racing over the crests of the swell, sending occasional swirls of spindrift above the whitecaps like horses' manes as the sea drove towards the shore. Jack concentrated on the low coastline where the F-16 had disappeared. For a moment he wished he was over there with the other team, on dry land, excavating the most fabled archaeological site in history, the ruins of an ancient citadel once thought to be no more than a figment in the imagination of a blind poet. Then he remembered what he had seen that morning, almost a hundred metres deep on the sea bed, a shape barely discernible on the edge of the darkness. He still did not know if it was a hallucination, the fulfilment of a dream that had obsessed him, the dream that had drawn so many to this place and left them yearning for more, for one more discovery to transform the legend into rock-solid reality. He thought of Heinrich Schliemann, almost a century and a half before. Schliemann had come here chasing a dream. *And he had found Troy.*

Jack stared at the grey sky that seemed to hang over the shoreline of Troy like a shroud, and then looked down into the darkness below the waves, straining to see deeper. He had excavated many fabulous wrecks in his years as an undersea explorer, but this one could be the most extraordinary ever. This time they could be stepping back into the world of myth, to the time when men had not yet learned to cast off the yoke that tied them to the fickle judgement of the gods. What they found today could reignite the passion that had driven Schliemann, the conviction that the Trojan War was historical reality. Jack whispered the words to himself. *A shipwreck from the Age of Heroes. A shipwreck from the Trojan War.*

'Jack! Don't shoot! I surrender!'

Jack turned, and saw a stocky figure making his way up the foredeck, waving at him. Costas Kazantzakis swayed from side to side as he walked, a gait born of generations of Greek fishermen that seemed to allow him to barrel on in defiance of all the natural laws. Jack had even noticed it in their dives together, as Costas hurtled down to the sea bed regardless of currents or any other obstacle. Jack stared in disbelief as Costas came closer. He was wearing sandals, some kind of pyjama pants, a Hawaiian shirt, aviator sunglasses and an extraordinary hat, a faded leather affair with ear flaps. Jack bit his lip to stop himself from smiling. Costas stopped in front of him, and saw Jack's expression. 'What?' he said defiantly.

'Nothing.'

'It's the pants, isn't it? Mustafa gave them to me.' Costas had a distinctive New York accent, picked up despite every effort of his wealthy parents to shield him from the reality outside his exclusive school. Jack had always loved it, and with Costas he never felt conscious of his own accent, a result of a peripatetic childhood in Canada and New Zealand as well as England. 'They're Ottoman Turkish. Just blending in with the local culture.'

Jack cleared his throat. 'The Ottoman Empire crumbled a little while ago. About a century ago, to be exact. Anyway, no, it wasn't those.'

'The hat? A present from your old digging buddy Maurice Hiebermeyer. You gave him those baggy British Empire shorts he loves wearing, and he gave you your beloved khaki bag. So he gave me the hat when I took the heli out to Troy yesterday and saw him. He said it made me an honorary archaeologist. Only honorary, of course. He found it in the Egyptian desert while he was looking for mummies. It's an Italian tank driver's hat from the Second World War. He said Italian gear had real style. Said it suited me.'

Jack looked at Costas unswervingly. 'He said that.'

'You bet.' Costas wiped his stubble with the back of his

hand, and then thrust a phone at him. 'Text message from your daughter.'

Jack looked at the screen. It was one word. *Paydirt*. He looked up, his eyes gleaming. 'They must have found it,' he exclaimed. 'The passageway under the citadel. Maurice *knew* it was there. I've got to get over there as soon as we finish the dive.'

Costas shook his head. 'Mission creep.'

'What do you mean?'

'Well, first your old professor James Dillen finds some clue on an ancient papyrus, something about a shipwreck from the Trojan War. You get all excited. *Seaquest II* gets booked. A few weeks go by. Then Mustafa pulls all the strings and the authorities grant us a blanket permit to excavate the entire north-west corner of Turkey. Before you know it, Maurice Hiebermeyer arrives with Aysha and their team from Egypt. Rebecca somehow gets off school and flies here even before asking you. Even my buddy Jeremy leaves his beloved Anglo-Saxon manuscripts, and is over there right now at Troy, neck deep in dust. What starts off as a long-shot recce ends up as a campaign to solve the entire mystery of the Trojan War. *That's* what I call mission creep.'

Jack grinned. 'Big questions deserve big resources.'

'Big questions? You mean big treasure.'

Jack laughed, slapping Costas on the back. 'Treasure? Me, an archaeologist? Never.' He snapped shut the revolver, unclipped the lanyard from the metal ring on the butt, eased the cord over his head and opened the holster. Costas gestured at it. 'Having fun? Not your usual Beretta.'

'It's an old Webley service revolver, naval issue. Captain Macalister keeps it in his day cabin. The .455 slug was designed to knock down fanatical tribesmen, and Macalister reckons that'll do for any modern-day pirate. You can see the 1914 date stamp when it was refurbished, at the beginning of the First World War. It could have been used in the Gallipoli campaign the following year. Macalister says holding this makes him feel close to that, to the horror and tragedy out here in 1915.'

'Sounds like you've infected him with your passion for artefacts.'

Jack holstered the revolver and shut the flap. 'It's what I always tell you. Artefacts sing the truth of the past. Have you ever noticed if you put your ear to an old gun barrel and open the breech, you can hear an echo of the past wars it's fought in? It's haunting. You should try it.'

'It's called the wind, Jack. And I'm not in the habit of playing Russian roulette.'

'I thought we did that all the time.'

'You're a father, remember. I have to keep you alive. It's not like the old days.'

'You mean not like five months ago, searching for the celestial jewel in Afghanistan, pinned down on a mountain-side by the world's most lethal sniper?'

'When I saved your life. Again.'

'As I recall, it was my shot that took him out.'

'I mean before that. All those times diving. Stopping you from taking that extra plunge into the abyss.' Costas squinted over the bows, and pointed. 'Anyway, if saving my life's your job, it looks like you got rusty. The target's only wounded, Jack.'

'I had Ben make up some reloads. The bullet weight's a little off.'

'It makes a nice change when our security chief has the time to do that.'

Jack gestured at the vapour trail dispersing above them. 'It helps being in a restricted military zone. I don't think anyone who might be shadowing us is going to mess with the Turkish armed forces.'

'That's what I came up here to talk to you about. Our permit from the Turkish navy only allows us to maintain position on one spot for three hours continuously. We've just come back on site now. Macalister says that gives us time either for a sidescan survey, or for a dive. A scan gave us that beautiful image of the Byzantine wreck yesterday, down to individual pots and blocks of stone. A great find, but we knew it wasn't what we were after even before we got in the water this morning to check it out. The Byzantine wreck's seventh century AD. We're looking for something almost two thousand years older than that. Macalister says a scan might give us all we need this time too. He's worried about the wind picking up this afternoon. It's your call.'

Jack squinted at Costas. 'We'll do it the old-fashioned way. See what's down there with our own eyes. Whatever the sonar might show, I'd want to dive anyway. And that way we don't have preconceptions. If you think you know what you're going to be looking at, your mind sometimes only seeks confirmation. You miss vital clues.'

'You mean it's more exciting, Jack. Plunging into the unknown. It keeps the adrenalin pumping. Which is when Jack Howard does his best thinking. Makes the connections. Joins the threads.'

Jack grinned, and nodded. 'Okay. You know me too well.

But if the sea conditions allow a twenty-minute sonar run during the briefing, we'll do that too. It can work the other way round. The sonar data this morning meant we knew the wreck was Byzantine, so when we did the dive I was able to concentrate elsewhere, beyond the obvious. I might not have seen that shape.'

'If it was a shape.'

'I trust my instinct.'

Costas gestured over the channel towards the entrance to the Dardanelles. 'There's a lot of war debris down there, Jack. I knew about the carnage of the 1915 land campaign at Gallipoli, but not the scale of the naval losses. Macalister showed me the British Admiralty wreck map. The approaches to the Dardanelles are littered with them. Battleships, destroyers, submarines, gunboats; British, French, Turkish. Some of them were salvaged, but there's plenty still down there.'

'And debris from a previous war,' Jack murmured. 'A war more than three thousand years earlier.'

'You wish.'

'I know.' Jack stared hard at Costas, his eyes intense, then his face creased into a smile. 'You remember your first ever archaeological dig, fifteen years ago? Over there, on the plain of Troy?'

'I remember three weeks sweltering in a dust bowl, wondering what on earth I was doing there,' Costas replied. 'Yeah, I remember. Like yesterday. I was a submersibles engineer with the US navy at the Izmir NATO base. You were some English guy fresh from a stint in your navy about to do an archaeology doctorate. You were a diver. A passionate diver.

That's where we clicked. You said there was a fabulous shipwreck waiting to be discovered, just up the coast. What you didn't tell me was that it was on dry land.'

Jack grinned. 'But we *did* find the ancient beach of Troy, *and* the remains of war galleys and an encampment. The first big leap forward since the days of Schliemann. Just the two of us, chasing a dream. It captured the imagination of the world. It got the funding we needed, and launched the International Maritime University. It got us where we are today.'

Costas grinned. 'And if it hadn't been for my guys doing the technology and the hard science, your dreams would never have got anywhere.'

Jack nodded. 'A team effort. I mean it. Not just two of us now, but the entire IMU team.' He stared out at the horizon again. 'You remember that evening at the end of the excavation, when we sat over there above the ancient harbour of Troy, having a few beers? I said I'd make it up to you for all the dust and heat. I said one day we'd be back, with a state-of-the-art research ship, all the submersibles and gadgets you ever wanted, searching the sea bed here for a real shipwreck. An *underwater* shipwreck.'

Costas gripped Jack's shoulder. 'That's why I'm still your dive buddy. Chasing that dream.'

'A pretty awesome dream,' Jack said.

'What are you thinking?' Costas asked.

'I was wondering whether we could do it again,' Jack murmured.

'Sweltering in a dust bowl? No thanks.'

Jack shook his head. 'I mean, whether we could do what Schliemann did. Chase the really *big* dream. He came out here with huge personal wealth, and was able to do pretty well what he wanted. For the first time since then, a team is here again with fantastic resources. We're not bogged down by bureaucracy. We don't have to answer to sceptical academics. We can ask the really big questions. Search for the really big answers.'

'You mean find the really big gold.' Costas grinned.

'The priceless treasure. The truth.'

Costas paused, then nodded sagely and punched Jack on the shoulder, sending him reeling sideways. 'Okay. I'll go with that. To me, you've always been Lucky Jack. Nothing's changed.' He turned to walk back. 'See you in the briefing room in twenty minutes?'

Jack righted himself, feeling his shoulder. 'Thank God you're my friend, not my enemy.'

'See what I mean? I'll look after you. At school in New York City, they called me Achilles.'

'Say that again.'

'Achilles. You know. The Trojan War. This place. Famous Greek hero.'

'I know who Achilles was.'

Costas pulled up his pantaloons and looked up at him defiantly. Jack reached over and gently pushed Costas' aviator sunglasses back up where they had slipped down his nose, and then straightened the absurd hat. 'There we go,' he said soothingly. 'Achilles.'

'Right on.' Costas put his hand gingerly on Jack's shoulder. 'Twenty minutes?'

'Roger that.'

★

Jack watched Costas go and then turned back to reel in his wooden target. He would wait out here on deck until the ship had stabilized. He looked to Gallipoli, and then to the shoreline of Troy, and thought of the two wars. He had visited the Gallipoli beaches a few days before, a bleak, beautiful place where the eroded ravines were still full of bleached bones and the rusted detritus of battle, where life seemed only tentatively to have taken hold again after almost a century. The plain of Troy must once have been like that too, and even after three thousand years it still seemed burdened by its place in history, as if the river Scamander still watered its shores with grief.

Jack had read the diaries and letters of young soldiers at Gallipoli in 1915, men who thrilled at being within sight of Troy, the plain where Hector and Achilles had fought before the fabled walls. Those young men had not been taught the truth of war, a truth that Homer surely knew but could barely bring himself to say, a truth those soldiers only learned in fleeting final moments as they rose above the parapet, bayonets fixed, on those shell-torn escarpments. Jack remembered the first lines he had ever learned of Homer, the ones Professor Dillen had insisted he memorize before all others. He whispered them into the wind now:

> *Heroes sink to rise no more*
> *Tides of blood drench Scamander's shore*
> *No rest, no respite, till the shades descend;*
> *Till darkness, or till death, shall cover all:*
> *Let the war bleed, and let the mighty fall.*

23

He braced himself as the bow of *Seaquest II* swung eastward, towards Troy. The swell heaved under the ship and he felt as if he were riding the upwelling that had once pushed foam-flecked galleys towards those shores, towards fabled Ilion, bristling with spears and shields, rumbling with bellowing rage. For a moment he yearned again for that sword, the one in his dream, to raise it high, to lead war-bent men of Mycenae to their fate, to see what it was like to be their captain, to see what it was that drove the king of kings to trounce the rules of war and lead his warriors to do their worst. Jack thought of the present day, of those he knew and loved below the walls of Troy now, of his daughter Rebecca, and he felt a strange foreboding, as if his imagination were leading him too close to a dark reality, a reality that had frightened even Homer.

He pushed back from the railing and shook the thought from his mind. He was an archaeologist, not a warrior. The ship was stable at last, the lateral thrusters engaged. He remembered Rebecca's text message, that single tantalising word: *Paydirt*. For years he had dreamed of taking up where Schliemann had left off, of revealing the truth of this place once and for all. And Costas had been right. It was a treasure hunt. He took a deep breath. Archaeology was a game of chance, but today, on this day, the odds might just be stacked in their favour. He slung the holster and walked determinedly across the foredeck towards the briefing room. He was coursing with excitement, remembering what Costas had called him, mouthing the words to himself as he always did. *Lucky Jack.*

2

Professor James Dillen shifted on the foam mat and stretched out his right arm, relieving the persistent ache that had been developing in his elbow all morning. He was thrilled to be here, but he was beginning to realize that archaeology came at a price. All those years he had spent in libraries and his study in Cambridge had given him the patience he now needed, but not the particular set of physical attributes required to kneel all day in a trench under the withering Mediterranean sun, working away with a trowel and a brush. He pushed himself upright, feeling a jab of pins and needles in his leg, and peered over the ancient stone revetment in front of him, relishing the afternoon breeze that was now sweeping across from the Dardanelles. The keening of the wind through the trees that flanked the ancient mound sounded like the wailing of mourners, and seemed to eclipse any residue of the clash of arms and the bellowing of heroes that had once resonated from the plain below.

He slipped awkwardly on his elbow, and jerked his head back to avoid scraping it against the solidified black mass on one side of the trench. He came to rest with his nose against the mass. He smelled an acrid odour, and moved his head, sniffing. It was there, definitely. He could hardly believe it. *He could smell the fires of Troy.* He pushed back and stared at the mass, a conglomeration of ash and carbonized material that rose up the ancient wall to where it had been eroded away. When Maurice Hiebermeyer had inspected his work the afternoon before, he had said the mass was not the result of a general conflagration, the destruction debris seen elsewhere on the site. Instead it was an astonishing discovery, a deliberate fire, the remains of a massive signal beacon on top of the citadel. *An astonishing discovery.* Dillen had been thrilled. This morning he had arrived before dawn, and had watched the red glow from the sun rise up the mound as if it were burning again, and imagined flames roaring high, swathed in smoke. He had opened his mind to words, as he always did, imagining how the ancients would have described it. The Greek word ἑλένή kept coming into his head: the word for torch, for flame. It was also a woman's name. Ἑλένή. Helen. An extraordinary thought coursed through his mind. Had he discovered the truth behind the legend of Helen of Troy? Had Helen, Helen of the flaming hair, Helen of myth, been not a woman, the woman of ravishing beauty whose abduction caused the war, but instead a great burning beacon above Troy, a fire that drew the Greek army forward, that signalled the destruction of Troy and the annihilation of the Bronze Age world?

He picked up a potsherd that had fallen from the scorched mound, a thick black sherd, charred, and sniffed it. He could smell it there, too. *He could smell Helen of Troy*. He shook his head in amazement. He pushed the sherd into his shorts pocket. Something to show Jack. He sat up, squinted against the sun and stared west, over the flat plain of the river Scamander towards Beşik Bay, the harbour of ancient Troy. Somewhere beyond lay the island of Tenedos, and *Seaquest II*, with Jack on board. Two nights before, in Jack's cabin, they had drunk whisky together, sharing their greatest dreams about what they might find here. Once, years ago, they had been teacher and pupil, separated by a generation that had seen archaeology advance by leaps and bounds, with dazzling results. When Dillen had been a student, underwater exploration had been in its infancy, and most who wished to study the ancient world had come to it through languages, through ancient Greek and Latin. Language was Dillen's passion, and he had excelled at it, specializing in the early development of Greek. But through Jack he had come to have a vicarious second life, and he had revelled in his former student's discoveries. He had yearned to join Jack in the field, and Jack had known exactly where and when, a project that would fuse their passions. *To excavate at Troy*. It had seemed a pipe dream, and then Dillen had made the extraordinary discovery in an ancient text that had brought them here. That night in Jack's cabin they had been like two treasure-hunters together, copies of Homer's *Iliad* opened out in front of them, poring over well-thumbed passages. For Jack, it was a fabulous treasure he believed had been lost at sea. For Dillen, it was another extraordinary artefact mentioned by Homer, something that had once existed in this huge mound of rubble and earth beneath him. *Something that might still be here.* That night he had felt as if they were a secret society of true believers, like Heinrich Schliemann and his closest supporters, fuelled by a belief that might now be given another dazzling burst of reality, as powerful as the one that Schliemann had released when he came here and first revealed the splendours of Troy to a stunned world.

Dillen looked at his watch. It was nearly three p.m., the official end of the digging day, when Hiebermeyer normally came round for his inspection. Hiebermeyer had been one of Dillen's star students, a close friend of Jack's, and seemed to take a certain pleasure in inspecting his old professor's carefully laid-out tools and notebooks, scrutinizing them like a barracks-room sergeant. Dillen smiled to himself, remembering his first encounter with Hiebermeyer, a generously proportioned youth with sagging shorts, little round glasses, a tousle of unwashed red hair, and an unquenchable enthusiasm for all things Egyptian. Maurice had changed little in the years since, apart from losing his hair and acquiring a wife, the least likely event anyone could have imagined. Jack said that Aysha's insistence that Maurice broaden his horizons was the only reason Hiebermeyer could be dragged away from his mummies and pyramids to work at Troy. But Dillen knew that Maurice secretly loved being back in the field with his friend Jack, and that his grumbles about shipwrecks and treasure-hunting were just part of their banter, something that had begun when they first met at boarding school in England and had mapped out their futures together.

Dillen lay down on his front again, propped up on his

elbows, his face close to the ancient masonry. His trench had begun as something of a sideline, a room in an aristocratic house on top of the citadel that had escaped Schliemann's great gouge through the site a hundred and thirty years before, and Hiebermeyer's attention was focused on the extra-ordinary tunnel he had revealed just inside the south-west corner of the citadel. This morning Hiebermeyer had made some kind of breakthrough, and it would probably be a while before the inspection. Dillen decided to carry on for another half-hour. He stared at the exposed wall. It was separated by a narrow gap from the massive rampart of the late Bronze Age citadel, high up on the mound, some thirty metres above the surrounding plain. His excavation had revealed wall plaster and the remains of a painted fresco, an extremely rare find at Troy. He had finished brushing off the fresco that morning, and it was now shrouded by a plastic sheet.

All that remained to be dug out was a small area of impacted debris against the lower few centimetres of the wall. It had turned out to be an extraordinarily interesting deposit, and Dillen had devoted painstaking hours to it. He had just been photographing his prize finds: three bronze arrowheads, stuck into the ground, angled in the orientation of the arrows as they had come hurtling in from over the outer rampart wall. They were two types, one leaf-shaped with a slight mid-rib and a long tang, the other triangular with a pronounced rib and long barbs. He stared at the arrowheads, then back at the carbonized remains of the beacon fire. Words flowed back into his mind again, a fragment of the Trojan epic cycle: *Earth, being weighted down by the multitude of people, there being no piety among humankind, asked Zeus to be relieved of the burden, and he*

destroyed the race of heroes and fanned the flames of the Trojan War.
Dillen thought hard. This was what archaeology revealed.
This was why it was worthwhile. The poem was wrong.
These arrowheads were not thunderbolts of Zeus, nor the
trident of Poseidon. They were weapons wrought by mortals.
It was not gods who had destroyed Troy; it was men.

'James! Professor! Where are you?' The voice came from
somewhere down in the trench dug by Schliemann, on the
narrow path they had cleared up the side. Dillen sat back up
and peered over the wall. He had recognized the American
accent. 'Jeremy? Is that you?'

'Coming up.' A tall young man with a shock of blond hair
and glasses came into view, wearing a T-shirt, khaki shorts,
and hiking boots. 'Only just arrived,' he said breathlessly.
'Maurice sent me straight up here. Wanted me out of the way,
I think. Said you had something to show me.'

'It's good to see you, Jeremy. I meant to say how much I
enjoyed your paper on the Hereford Mappa Mundi library at
the conference last month. Marvellous stuff. What is it now,
three years since you discovered it?'

'Three and a half.' Jeremy stepped over the wall and sat
down, taking a long swig from a water bottle and shaking
Dillen's outstretched hand. 'And then a year later, the Roman
library at Herculaneum, and the reason we're here. Which
reminds me. I've got some more lines of the ancient text for
you to translate.' He wiped his mouth and put down the bottle.
'And I've got some great news.' He paused to catch his breath.
'Our benefactor. Ephram Jacobovich. He's made another ton
of money, with the transition to wi-fi. Always one step ahead
of the game. So much for the recession. The reason I couldn't

come out here earlier was that Maria and I were having a meeting with him. We didn't even need to make a case. Jack had prepped him completely. We get all the research funding we need for the Herculaneum library, enough to buy in the top specialists from around the world. Which is good, because I've decided I don't want to spend the rest of my life sitting in a manuscripts room staring at ancient texts under a microscope.'

'But you're brilliant at it. And you love it.'

'But there's a problem. Costas taught me to dive.'

'Ah.' Dillen smiled. 'Your excellent friend Costas.' He paused. 'So how is Maria?'

'Once the funding's in place, she's taking a sabbatical in Mexico. She's got family there. Did you know she was about to be married? I probably shouldn't tell you. Some professor she met at a conference. It was a bit of a whirlwind. But then when it came to it, she bailed.'

'It's because she really wants Jack,' Dillen murmured.

'And Jack wants her. But he also wants Katya. And neither of them are women you want to mess with.'

'Bit of a problem for Jack.'

'After the last time they nearly hitched up, Maria said Jack was like one of those famous British sea captains of the Napoleonic period, just like one of his revered Howard ancestors. She said it must be in his blood. Brilliant at sea, commanding ships and leading men, but completely useless on land, at managing his affairs, so to speak. Always doing a runner back to his ship.'

'She told you that?'

'I'm her protégé, remember? I may be fifteen years younger than her, but she tells me everything.'

Dillen smiled. 'So tell me about your flight here. Good view?'

'Fantastic,' Jeremy replied. 'The Lynx helicopter picked me up at Istanbul airport and we flew right over the Sea of Marmara and down the Dardanelles, along the Gallipoli peninsula and then south over the strait towards Troy. You would have heard us, about mid-morning. The pilot's a military history buff and gave me a running commentary on the 1915 Gallipoli campaign. Then as we flew over the plain of Troy it was like we were war-gaming Homer. Brilliant. After that we flew west and dropped down on *Seaquest II* for lunch, before coming here.'

'What's the mood on board?'

'Optimistic. Very optimistic. I didn't see Jack because he was in the chamber decompressing after a dive, but everyone was upbeat. You know they found a Byzantine shipwreck? Not what Jack wanted, but encouraging. The crew thinks he's on to something else, he's seen something more down there he's not letting on about. He thinks he keeps these things secret, but the crew can tell. Those Napoleonic-period captains Maria talked about? *Seaquest II*'s crew have the same kind of faith in Jack that those naval crews had in their captains. They also know him a lot better than he thinks. They even call him Lucky Jack.'

'He's been called that as long as I've known him.' Dillen smiled. 'I was too young to serve in the Second World War, but the schoolmaster who taught me Greek had fought through North Africa and Europe with the SAS. He told me that in a tight unit, a soldier can always tell when their leader's on to something, a kind of sixth sense, like a hunter knowing his dog has sensed prey before the dog has made a move.'

'Jack was in the navy, of course.'

'As a diver, special forces. But it was only a short-service commission, at the end of his undergraduate degree. He always wanted to be an archaeologist, but he had a strong feeling for keeping up his family tradition in the navy. Howards were there all the way, from the Spanish Armada to the Napoleonic Wars and beyond.'

'Military training has stood him in good stead,' Jeremy said.

'He's a scholar and an adventurer, not a warrior. Too much of a maverick for peacetime soldiering, that's what my old teacher Hugh said about Jack. Wouldn't be any good at taking orders from people he doesn't respect. He's his own boss. But he's got a hard edge, and I wouldn't want to put him in a corner. Or threaten anyone dear to him. I've always felt that. And when he makes a decision, he'll stick to it.'

'You might want to hear Maria's views on that.' Jeremy squatted down, picked up a small sherd of blackened pottery and rubbed a finger over the burnished surface, then looked round him. 'So you think this room's late Bronze Age, the time of the Trojan War?'

Dillen nodded enthusiastically, and knelt down beside Jeremy. 'It's very similar to houses built just inside the eastern rampart of Troy VII, Homeric Troy. But I think this one was grander. The view over the plain would have been magnificent. It may even have been part of the palace. That's my pet theory. The only surviving part of the palace that once capped the citadel. What do you think?'

'King Priam's palace,' Jeremy murmured. 'That's a hell of a

shout line. *Distinguished Homeric scholar joins old student's dig and three days later discovers the lost palace of King Priam of Troy.* Maybe this was the very room where his son Paris kept Helen after abducting her from Greece. Maybe we're standing right in the crucible of the whole legend.'

'Maybe we are,' Dillen said quietly. 'In more ways than you might imagine. You'll be amazed. I've got some incredible stuff to show you. A few more radical theories. But first things first.'

'Go on.'

'The house is built in typical Troy fashion, a socle of stone with the upper storey made of flat sun-dried mud brick. A few courses of brick survive, over there, baked red by the fire that left that charred mass. Maurice thinks that's the remains of a beacon fire. Can you believe it? A beacon fire from the Trojan War. Now look over there. You can see the beam slots in the stone below the bricks that once held the cross-timbers for the floor above. We're in a basement room, dug into the mass of compacted mud brick that makes up the citadel mound. The earth beyond the bricks contains detritus from the earlier phases of the city, stretching back to the beginning of the Bronze Age two thousand years before.'

'Phenomenal,' Jeremy murmured. 'So what makes you sure this house is late Bronze Age?' He held up the sherd. 'Pottery?'

Dillen pursed his lips. 'We've found a few Mycenaean sherds, painted fine-ware. And radiocarbon dating of a charred reed mat has come up with the right time frame. But the main evidence is structural. Did you have a chance to look at the outer wall of the house as you came up? It slopes slightly inward, from bottom to top, probably to give stability against earthquakes. And the wall's divided by vertical offsets every five metres or so, made of rectangular hewn masonry, each offset providing a strengthened base for a timber frame in the wall of the house above.' Dillen slapped his hands in excitement. 'It's exactly the same technique as the rampart outside, the city wall of Troy VII, the citadel at the time of the destruction, about 1200 BC. *The time of the Trojan War.*'

Jeremy stared at the unexcavated deposit on the edge of the wall, and took a few steps over. 'This must be what Maurice wanted me to see. Arrowheads. Beautifully excavated, and still *in situ*. Has anything like this ever been found at Troy before?'

'Not *in situ*, embedded like that.' Dillen lay back down on his mat, propped on his elbows. 'Maurice said you were the man for this?'

'It's my hobby. Archery.' Jeremy got down on his knees and elbows and edged close, until his face was only a few inches away, then reached out and gently touched one of the arrowheads. 'Fascinating. There's a small collection like these on display in the British Museum, in the same case as the artefacts they have from Schliemann's excavation at Troy. A few miserable pots, frankly. Most of it went to Germany, of course. But it makes you wonder what Schliemann really *did* find down there.' He jerked his thumb in the direction of Schliemann's trench. 'Anyway, Jack and I met up for lunch in the BM a few days before he came out here, and we had a quick look at the Mycenaean stuff. What you've found here is fantastic, where scientific excavation really comes into play. This is what Schliemann could so easily have missed, hacking down aggressively with picks and shovels, going for the treasure. You see what I mean? You've got two completely different shapes of arrowhead, in exactly the same context. These were shot by archers standing side by side, at the same time on the same day. If you'd seen these individually in a museum collection, or hauled out of the spoil heap from an excavation like Schliemann's, you'd be thinking mainly in terms of typology, a time sequence, evolution, maybe that nastier barbed one being a more effective later type. What you've got here shows you'd be completely wrong.'

Dillen stared hard. 'Here's a thought, then. The Mycenaean Greeks were not like the Egyptians, or the Hittites. They were never a single kingdom, and if we're to believe Homer, they were only ever united for this famous expedition, under a single paramount leader.'

'You mean Homer's king of kings. Agamemnon.'

Dillen nodded. 'Each of the Mycenaean palaces we know about – Mycenae itself, Athens, Pylos, Thebes, the others – was a kingdom unto itself, controlling its own fiefdom like a feudal barony. The clay tablet archives from those places show that the armaments industry, bronze-making, was tightly controlled by each palace, but not centralized across the Mycenaean world. There was no Enfield factory, no Springfield arsenal, but instead lots of smaller arsenals, controlled by individual palaces but under no central armaments directive, all keeping up with each other broadly in technology but with small differences. Some of the differences could even have been deliberate, to give the weapons of a particular kingdom a clear identity.'

'I'm thinking of the ship list in Homer's *Iliad*,' Jeremy

murmured. 'All the different kingdoms sending ships and men, rallying to the cause.'

'And then all of them standing shoulder to shoulder on the beach, men of Mycenae, Pylos, Tiryns, a hundred other kingdoms, showering the walls of Troy with arrows.'

Jeremy bent down again until his face was nearly touching the deposit, staring, murmuring numbers to himself. He then shuffled back and put the thumb and forefinger of his left hand in front of the arrows, measuring them up. He kept his hand exactly where it was, fumbled in his shorts pocket with his other hand and pulled out a compass, holding it flat and squinting along it. He rolled away and jumped up to his feet, then peered over the rampart wall at the plain of Troy before the citadel, a flat alluvial landscape of fruit trees and vegetable plantations extending towards the distant shoreline of the Dardanelles. He sighted the compass, then looked at Dillen, grinning. 'As Jack would say, I'll be damned.'

'What is it?'

'Well, the angle of impact shows that these arrows were shot at pretty well maximum trajectory. When Jack and Costas were here fifteen years ago doing their famous excavation on the ancient beach line, they found a charred fragment of an archer's bow. Well, Costas found it, to be exact. As he'll never cease telling you. He showed it to me, and I made a replica. I've shot it using arrows with bronze heads based on those British Museum examples. The compass bearing on these arrowheads points almost exactly to the place where the heli pilot showed me the remains of their trench, about two hundred and forty degrees from here, almost a kilometre away. It's a long shot, but plausible for a Bronze Age bow with a really strong following wind, the kind the pilot said you sometimes get from the north-west coming off the sea, a real storm wind. Maybe there was one of those on the day of the assault when these arrows were fired.'

'What's the dating evidence for this type of arrowhead?'

Jeremy pursed his lips. 'Late Bronze Age, definitely, but that could mean anywhere between about 1500 BC, when bronze took over from obsidian for arrowheads, and about 1000 BC, when iron took over from bronze. But even that latter date's contentious. Scholars used to think references to iron in the *Iliad* were anachronisms, showing that Homer was writing about his own world in the Iron Age, around the eighth century BC. But iron arrowheads have now been found at Troy too. It's possible that there was corroded iron in Schliemann's excavation that he just didn't see when he hacked his way down. Another black mark against treasure-hunting.'

'It sounds like Troy,' Dillen said. 'Just when you think you're there, that grey shroud of uncertainty settles over the whole thing again.'

'But it's still fantastically exciting,' Jeremy said. 'It's this room that gives those arrows a date. If it's Troy VII, then that's Homeric Troy. The arrows were fired together from the beach line. They're different types, from different places. These aren't just raiders. There's an army out there. A big, besieging army, from many different places. *A Mycenaean army*. It all adds up. You just need a tiny dose of faith.'

Dillen rocked back on his haunches and smiled. 'Sometimes, you know, when I'm up here alone at night, I think I can hear music, very distant, like the backbeat to an epic,' he said. 'It seems to be telling me all I need to know, as if all this scientific detail, the proof, is just confirmation.'

Jeremy grinned, then pointed to a shrouded form in the corner of the trench. 'I was wondering when you were going to bring music up. Looks like you have a hobby of your own.'

Dillen looked over. 'Oh, that.' He got up, stretched, walked over, and picked the object up. 'It's a lyre, a hand-harp, meant to be a replica of a Bronze Age lyre. I made it myself, over the last few months. It's based on all the literary and artistic evidence I could muster, and a few archaeological discoveries.' He carefully removed the cover, revealing a tortoiseshell soundbox with two raised arms curving outward and forward from it, with a crossbar at the top and strings leading down from it to another bar on the shell forming a bridge. 'The different notes come from the thickness of the strings, which are made of animal gut. All the ancient poets, the bards, used a lyre. I realized I could never hope to understand Homer without trying it.'

'Will you play?'

Dillen replaced the cover. 'Maybe when the digging's over. Rebecca's been badgering me to put Homer to music. I'm not sure if she knows quite what I mean. Sometimes I think the music is meant just to be in my head.'

'Oh, I think she knows. When we're together she often refers to things you've said. You and she seem to be on much the same wavelength.' Jeremy cocked an ear. 'Speaking of Rebecca, I forgot to say. I can hear someone approaching. She wanted me to warn you so you'd know she wasn't Hiebermeyer and wouldn't get into a panic about tidying up. I'm sure that's her coming up the path now.'

3

There was a scrambling sound on the path, and Dillen and Jeremy turned to see a tall, slender girl appear, wearing hiking boots, shorts and a T-shirt with the IMU logo, her long dark hair tied back under a baseball cap. She was carrying a suspended silver tray holding little glass cups filled with tea. She stepped into the trench, saying nothing, and solemnly handed one to Dillen, then another to Jeremy.

'*Teshekkur ederin.*' Dillen smiled, holding up the glass and taking a sip, trying not to recoil from the powerful liquid. Rebecca bowed, put down the tray and took off her sunglasses. Dillen looked at her fondly. He had taught her mother as well as Jack, and Rebecca had inherited much from both of them, Jack's long limbs and angular features, her mother's dark beauty. A wave of sadness came over him when he thought of Elizabeth, but he put it from him and focused on the continuity he saw in Rebecca, the familiar eyes and vivacious manner. Rebecca had remarkable determination, but they all knew they had to work with her to overcome the pain of her mother's death, to focus on the future and stave off a past that could engulf her. She squatted down, arms on her knees. 'So, guys. How's the bard?' She spoke with an American accent from her upbringing and schooling before her mother had died, but with English idiom she had picked up from Jack and the IMU crew.

Jeremy looked at her, then glanced quizzically at Dillen. 'Bard? Your lyre? I thought you didn't play.'

Rebecca shook her head. 'No. I don't mean Professor Dillen. I mean *the* bard. Over there. Maurice gave me a lightning tour when I arrived this morning, and it was there.' She pointed at the excavated wall of the room behind them, covered by the plastic sheet.

'Ah, yes.' Dillen got up. 'I haven't shown Jeremy yet. We've been talking about my arrowheads.' He reached over and carefully rolled up the plastic sheet, placing it on top of the masonry. Jeremy gasped. The image below was extraordinary, a life-sized fresco on white plaster, reminiscent of Bronze Age paintings from other sites around the Aegean. It showed a person in a white robe sitting on a rock, holding a lyre, as if in readiness for playing. The background and the skin of the player were dark; the rock was off-white, covered with swirling tendrils of green leaves, and above it was a stylized bank of clouds.

'*Now* I see,' Jeremy exclaimed. 'A lyre-player. It's wonderful.'

'It's astonishing corroboration for my lyre,' Dillen said. 'I've only uncovered this painting in the last two days, but I finished my lyre several months ago. I think I got it right.'

Jeremy peered closely, shading his eyes. 'Is that a man or a woman?'

'Impossible to say,' Dillen replied. 'You might expect it to be a man, but that may just be wrong. There were doubtless men and women.'

'So you think this is a bard, a poet?'

'There's only one other image of a lyre-player like this, from the Mycenaean palace of Pylos in Greece,' Dillen replied. 'I think it's possible.'

'Could there be an inscription?' Jeremy said. 'Still concealed below, where the arrows and earth cover the plinth?'

'If there is, it'd probably be in Luwian or Hittite, the languages of Anatolia, or perhaps in early Greek, the language of Mycenaean Linear B. I know Rebecca's just done an essay on that for school.'

'Linear B was the syllabic script of the Greeks before they adopted the Phoenician alphabet,' Rebecca said. 'The Mycenaeans borrowed it from the Minoans. Trouble was, it was basically designed for palace records: numbers of sheep, bronze-workers, and so on. It would have been an awkward script for recording anything else. And almost all the Linear B finds have been on baked clay tablets. Maybe we just haven't found others yet, but it doesn't seem to have been used for inscriptions on stone or walls.'

Dillen nodded. 'Another problem is, there doesn't seem to be a Linear B word for bard, for poet. Maybe we're missing something, mis-translating another word, but it just doesn't seem to be there. So even if there were an inscription here, it might be unreadable.'

Rebecca took a swig from her water bottle. 'While I'm here, Dad mentioned this fragment of ancient text you found referring to a shipwreck during the Trojan War, a ship of Agamemnon. What he and Costas are searching for now. I really need to be got up to speed. I only came in on the flight before Jeremy. I was in school two days ago and I shouldn't even be here now. We have an art trip in France beginning in a couple of days' time. Bottom line is, apart from Maurice's twenty-minute tour and Dad on the phone, when he was mostly telling me off for getting a flight here without telling him, I have just about no idea what's happening.' She took another swig. 'Well?'

Jeremy glanced at her. 'You haven't heard it yet?'

'Dad said to get Professor Dillen to tell me.'

'You won't believe it. It's just about the greatest clue to treasure ever found,' Jeremy said.

Dillen took a deep breath, his eyes gleaming. 'It's been a truly remarkable find. The most important of my entire career.' He paused. 'As well as the *Iliad* and the *Odyssey*, there's a mass of fragments known as the Trojan epic cycle, poems that purport to fill the gaps in the story of the Trojan War. Most date from the Hellenistic and Roman period and are edited compilations of fragments, some perhaps genuine Homer, some by lesser poets attempting to emulate him. Some of the most famous stories of the Trojan War are known mainly this way, such as the Trojan Horse. One of those poems is called the *Ilioupersis*, "The Destruction of Troy". Before now, only a few fragments of that survived, and only a few scholars thought it was by Homer.'

'And now?' Rebecca said.

'And now we have the genuine *Ilioupersis*, a complete poem of very early date that may have been deliberately concealed, and is now revealed for the first time since the Dark Age that followed the Trojan War.'

'It was found three months ago,' Jeremy said to Rebecca. 'Maria and I were back in Herculaneum to work on the final clearance of the ancient Roman library. The archaeological superintendency are now planning to shore it up and make the tunnel accessible to the general public, who'll be able to look through a glass front right into the Emperor Claudius' secret study itself.'

'That was my mother's job in the superintendency, to oversee the villa,' Rebecca said quietly. 'That's the last time she and Dad spoke, when he saw her in the excavation, the day before the Mafia took her. Her own family. Her brothers and uncles.'

Dillen put a hand on hers. 'You have a new family now.'

Rebecca gave him a fathomless look, and then stared intensely at Jeremy. 'So it was you who actually found the text?'

'Glued into the back of one of Claudius' notebooks, a collection of material we think he'd been planning to use in his huge *History of Rome*, for a volume on the founding of the city. It was with material related to the Trojan hero Aeneas and the exodus of survivors from Troy, really fascinating stuff that seems to prove that Rome really was founded by Trojan warriors fleeing west. These pages, the *Ilioupersis*, were actually part of a very old text of Book 12 of the *Odyssey*. They were recycled, a palimpsest, evidently at a time when papyrus was scarce, before the classical era. Maria spotted the faded ink underneath the *Odyssey* text and we took the pages for an X-ray spectrometry scan, which revealed about three hundred lines. There's little doubt it's the entire poem, as it ends mid-page. The lab is refining the scan line by line, and as each few lines are finished I'm sending them to James for translation. I've got some more for him with me.'

Dillen pulled an iPod from his pocket, clicked it and then passed it to Rebecca. 'That's only a small fragment of it, but you can see the letters. They're separately spaced, careful, a little awkward, as if the scribe is not entirely familiar with the symbols, at pains to get it right. You see the letter A? It's sideways, toppled over. That's what really excited me. It's the Phoenician letter A, the way it looked in the earliest version of the alphabet adopted by the Greeks. Archaeologists have found a few potsherds from the Greek Dark Age scratched with letters like this, but no other actual script of Greek this early.'

'So what's the date of the text?'

'The iambic hexameter is Homeric in form, and that makes it at least eighth century BC. But I've always argued that the hexameter is much older than that, as old as the early Bronze Age, from the time of the first epic bards. The bards continued to use it through to the dawn of the classical era, when people began to write it down. Add to that the Phoenician letters, and we may be looking at something incredibly early.'

'Dad says you've always thought Homer was earlier than the eighth century.'

Dillen nodded. 'I believe there was indeed a Homer who wrote down the *Iliad* and the *Odyssey* as we have them. I say *a* Homer, not *the* Homer. I see Homer not as one genius, but as one in a line of gifted poets – consistently, extraordinarily gifted – who shaped and transmitted the poems, a lineage that may have ended about the eighth century BC with the advent of wider literacy and the demise of the bardic tradition, so that those later poets who emulated Homer had none of that spark. I see the Homeric bards, the earlier ones, almost as shamans or seers, maybe as a family line, possibly both men and women, with an inherited poetic genius nurtured from childhood. There are plenty of parallels in the bardic traditions of other cultures.'

'The Trojan War took place about 1200 BC,' Jeremy said, staring pensively at the arrows. 'Civilization out here pretty well collapses. Invaders sweep down from the north. It's a dark age, a time of destruction and hopelessness unparalleled in history. But then small communities hidden away in mountain refuges begin to rebuild. Iron technology takes over. The survivors pull away from the brink, and the classical age dawns. So where does this poem fit in to all that?'

Dillen replied quietly. 'All of my instinct puts this text no later than 1000 BC. It may even be a century earlier. I can barely believe I'm suggesting it, but this text could have been written by a bard who actually witnessed the fall of Troy, who actually saw those arrows being fired, who felt the heat of that beacon fire burning into the night sky, above these very ramparts where we are now.'

Rebecca whistled, then looked at the bronze arrowheads embedded in the trench, and at the solidified mass of ash. 'That's awesome. Seriously awesome.'

'And that,' Jeremy announced, 'is also a triumph of textual scholarship, because our radiocarbon result for the papyrus has just come through.' He had been quickly checking his BlackBerry, and passed it to Dillen, who read the screen and broke into a smile. Jeremy turned to Rebecca. 'The problem was getting a sample of the papyrus that wasn't impregnated with later ink and glue from when it was reused, but the IMU dating lab seem to have done it.'

Dillen handed back the BlackBerry. His voice was quavering. 'Eleven fifty BC, plus or minus seventy-five years. *I knew it.* I just knew I was reading poetry written in the Bronze Age.'

'That's so cool,' Rebecca said, putting her hand on his shoulder. 'Remember when you were my age, dreaming of finding something like that.'

Dillen looked at her, his eyes welling up. 'I'm always that age. It's what I told your dad. Never give up on those dreams.'

'And one day they may come true,' Rebecca said, leaning over and kissing him gently on the forehead.

'One question,' Jeremy said, putting away his BlackBerry. 'The *Ilioupersis*. The destruction of Troy. That's the biggest event in the whole Trojan epic cycle. Why do we only now have this text? Why is the destruction only hinted at in the *Iliad* and the *Odyssey*?'

Dillen took off his glasses and wiped his eyes, then put them back on again, swallowed hard and looked at Jeremy. 'The Trojan cycle represents the end of the bardic tradition,' he said. 'It's art mirroring history, myth mirroring reality. Before the Trojan War, the Bronze Age was a world of heroes and demigods, a world ruled by the gods, always fickle, often cruel, where contests between men were the contests of heroes, not the wholesale carnage of war. Epic poetry grew up around those contests: violent, bloody for sure, but noble and thrilling, part of everyday life. They existed in a world of peace and stability that allowed civilization to flourish, that didn't eclipse it. But then something happened. Something calamitous, which overturned that world. The ambition of one man, perhaps, one king. The age of heroes and gods gave way to the age of men. Duels between heroes gave way to total war.'

'And nobody wanted to hear about that,' Rebecca murmured. 'Not a good fireside story.'

Dillen stared at the fresco. 'People seated at the feet of a bard want to hear an uplifting story. They want to hear about noble deeds, about chivalry, about violence and cruelty to be sure, but not about apocalypse. So the *Iliad* is about the time before darkness swept over the plain of Ilion, when the war was still a contest of heroes: Achilles and Hector, Ajax and Telemachus. But Homer knew of coming darkness. He knew what men could do. He hints at it, in the *Iliad*. And the audience knew. They had been part of it, the survivors, their parents, their grandparents. It was an unspoken truth, a common experience of all humanity, like the Holocaust.'

'Maybe the truth was just too awful to contemplate,' Rebecca said. 'Maybe Homer was a seer, just as you said. Maybe he gazed over the Dardanelles and somehow saw the future horrors of war, that mankind would go to the brink again.'

Jeremy looked hard at Dillen. 'So maybe when the *Ilioupersis* was written down, it was a private expression by a poet who knew he had to tell himself the truth. He puts it away, but then – almost by accident – it survives.'

'How much more do you have to translate?' Rebecca asked.

'I've translated twenty-five out of three hundred and twelve lines. Another couple of weeks. Depending on the distractions of archaeology.'

'Maybe then you'll play that lyre,' Jeremy said.

'Speaking of archaeology,' Rebecca said, looking at Dillen quizzically. 'We know Dad wants to find something fabulous underwater. Some treasure from the Trojan War. What do *you* want to find?'

Dillen narrowed his eyes. 'Well . . .' He sat back, took out his pipe and tobacco, then saw Rebecca's disapproving look and thought better of it. Instead he pointed the stem of the pipe at the painting. 'Something more than images. I want to find words. Inscriptions. I want to find something in Greek, in Linear B. Something from the conquerors of this place.'

'*Agamemnon was here,*' Jeremy murmured.

'Mmm.' Dillen put the pipe in the corner of his mouth and dry-sucked it, folding his arms over his chest and staring at the painting.

'No,' Rebecca said, shaking her head. 'I mean, what do you *really* want to find? Dad said you had a session the other night in his cabin on *Seaquest II*. Drank whisky like a pair of old pirates. He said you both came up with your dream find. He's going to tell me his after he comes up from the dive today. He said I could probably cajole yours out of you, because you'll do anything for me.'

'He said that?' Dillen murmured, his eyes twinkling.

'Go on,' Jeremy said.

Dillen sucked for a moment, then took out the pipe and gave them a penetrating look. 'All right. Just between us.

There is one object, an artefact that's beguiled me since I first read Homer as a schoolboy. It was the most sacred object of ancient Troy, held in a temple to the god Pallas, who the Greeks identified with their goddess Athene. Homer called it the palladion.'

'The palladion!' Jeremy exclaimed. 'I remember that. Didn't Odysseus and Diomedes steal it, after they snuck into the city through an underground passageway and Helen told them where to find it?'

Dillen nodded. 'That's the story. As long as the palladion remained within the walls, Troy wouldn't fall. After stealing it, they took the wooden horse filled with warriors into Troy, and the rest is history.'

'Or myth,' Rebecca said.

'So what happened to the palladion?' Jeremy asked.

'A thousand years after the fall of Troy, the Roman poet Virgil imagined the Trojan prince Aeneas bringing the palladion to Rome. For the Romans, that became a central part of their foundation myth. For them the palladion was a small wooden statue of Pallas, and was hidden away some-where in Rome. Then, in the late Roman period, rumour was that it was secretly taken to the new capital city, Constantinople, along with so many of the old treasures of Rome, and buried under the column of Constantine in the forum.'

'So isn't that where we should be looking for it?' Jeremy said.

'A wooden statue doesn't sound, um, very exciting,' Rebecca said. 'I mean, you know, treasure-wise.'

'Do you believe any of this?' Jeremy asked.

Dillen clasped his pipe bowl in one hand, and leaned forward. 'Well, we do know that statues of gods in the Aegean Bronze Age could be wooden, quite crude. People still venerated inanimate objects, and had only just begun to anthropomorphize their gods. The Romans are unlikely to have known that. If they were making up the story of the palladion, they're far more likely to have imagined an impressive statue of stone, of marble. That would have been an instant giveaway. So I can believe the story.'

'But?' Jeremy said.

'*But*,' Dillen replied. 'Even if there were a wooden statue, I don't believe that it *was* the palladion. Rebecca's right. A wooden statue's hardly treasure. Odysseus and Diomedes may have snatched a statue from the temple, but the true palladion is most likely to have been concealed by the Trojans. And there's a tantalizing snippet of evidence. One of those epic fragments says the palladion had "fallen from heaven", a gift to Dardanos, founder of Troy. That could be meta-phorical, meaning an extraordinary treasure, a gift of the gods. Or it could be literal.'

'I've got it.' Rebecca clapped her hands. '*Fallen from heaven*. A meteorite.'

Dillen looked at her. 'It wouldn't be the first time a meteorite has been venerated.'

'So this is what you think we might find here?' Rebecca said quietly. 'That's so cool.'

'Just guesswork. But the idea that the most sacred object from ancient Troy, the richest city in the Bronze Age world, should have been a little wooden statue doesn't ring true. If a thousand years later the Romans had the true palladion, it would have been an extraordinary object, something people came to gawp at, an object that would resonate through history, like the golden menorah they took from the Jewish temple.'

'So Odysseus and Diomedes made their way into Troy by a secret passage,' Jeremy mused. 'Maybe the palladion's what Maurice is really after, at the end of the tunnel he's found.'

Rebecca shook her head. 'He wants to find a hieroglyphic inscription. Not *Agamemnon was here*, but *Rameses was here*. He says he wants to prove that Egypt truly was the superpower of the ancient world. He says that's the only reason he ever leaves Egypt to come on these digs with Dad.'

Dillen cast a glance at Jeremy, and they both grinned. 'Your dad and Maurice go back a long way,' Dillen said. 'And don't discount the lure of treasure. I can remember interviewing Maurice when he was applying for a place at the university. He'd brought along the catalogue from the Tutankhamun exhibition, the one that travelled the world in the 1970s. It had the famous golden mask of King Tut on the cover, and Maurice was almost weeping with excitement when he showed it to me. I knew then I had to offer him a place.'

'Dad says every archaeologist worthy of the name secretly wants to find treasure,' Rebecca said. 'He told me they may spend their careers specializing in something as dry as bones, but unless they have that fire within them, they'll never have the vision, the passion, to take their exploration that one step further, to make the big leap of imagination.'

'Mmm.' Dillen smiled. 'Where have I heard that before? I seem to remember telling that to Jack and Maurice in their first tutorial with me. And who was it who told it to me? Sir

Leonard Woolley, or was it Sir Mortimer Wheeler? And they'd been told it by Sir Arthur Evans. And he'd been told it by Heinrich Schliemann. It's the thread that ties all the great archaeologists together. Not science, not techniques, but the passion, the drive. The yearning for discovery.'

'And the willingness to take risks,' Rebecca said.

Jeremy gestured at the jumble of overgrown ruins behind them. 'The palladion. It could have been anywhere here?'

Dillen nodded. 'The temple to Pallas would have been close to where we are now, though I fear it may have been where Schliemann put in his great trench. But temples often had repositories, underground strongrooms. That's where something as sacred as the palladion might have been kept.'

'Maybe the palladion is what Agamemnon was really after when he came here,' Rebecca said. 'Maybe that's what the Trojan War was actually about. Not about women, about Helen of Troy, but about treasure.'

'Maybe that's what Schliemann was after too,' Jeremy added. 'And maybe he didn't find it here, so he went in search of it at Mycenae, where Agamemnon might have taken it after looting and burning Troy.'

'There's nothing about the palladion in Schliemann's notes,' Dillen said. 'Jack asked me to look at them before coming out here. But Schliemann was a man of powerful imagination, and capable of great secrecy when his ego would allow it. And he truly believed in the myths. Let's imagine the palladion was what he was really after. He may never have confided his thoughts to paper. He may only have told his wife, Sophia, and maybe a few close friends. Schliemann was perfectly prepared to gamble his reputation with big announcements, but he was also shrewd, and this would have been an extraordinary treasure.'

An excited shout came up from below, a man's voice with a German accent. 'James. Rebecca. Jeremy. Come on down. James, bring your camera gear. We've found something wonderful.'

'They're nowhere near the end of the tunnel yet,' Rebecca said. 'I was just there. They were only finding rubble. What on earth could it be?'

'Maybe Maurice has got his Egyptian inscription,' Jeremy said, getting up quickly. 'And I haven't even seen this tunnel yet.' He paused, looking at the wall painting of the bard with the musical instrument, and then at Dillen's lyre in the corner of the trench. 'You really did get your lyre right, you know. Exactly right. It's uncanny. What you were saying earlier, about the bardic tradition? You said you felt as if you'd heard music up here. Maybe I shouldn't have been so flippant about it. Maybe there really is a bit of Homer in you.'

Dillen looked at him, started to say something, and was suddenly speechless, overwhelmed. He stared down, blinking hard. In all his years of academic achievement, he had never had an accolade like that. He swallowed hard and spoke, his voice gruff. 'I should tidy up. Herr Professor Doctor Hiebermeyer's inspection, you know.'

'Leave it,' Jeremy said. 'We won't tell.' Rebecca touched Jeremy's hand and smiled at him, nodding her head towards Dillen, saying nothing. Jeremy went over and rolled the plastic cover back over the wall painting, while Rebecca helped Dillen to his feet. As he reached down to pick up his camera bag, a jolt of pain shot through his knee, and he winced. He leaned against Rebecca for a moment, feeling her warmth, her youth, letting the pain go, and remembered what he had been thinking before she and Jeremy had arrived. Archaeology did come at a price. But he was loving every minute of it.

4

London, England

The man in the greatcoat turned left off the busy street and strode into the forecourt of the British Museum, swiftly negotiating the milling groups of tourists and the puddles that had spread over the pavement like quicksilver. The drizzle that had enveloped London all morning was now a persistent rain, and he clicked open his umbrella. His phone buzzed and he stopped, holding the phone to his ear with one hand and his umbrella with the other, peering out under the brim at the imposing columns of the museum façade. He replied quickly, snapped the phone shut, checked his watch and remained still for a moment, glancing up at the pediment sculptures above the columns, at Sir Richard Westmacott's allegorical figures depicting the rise of civilization, culminating in the central female holding a golden orb and sceptre.

He curled his lip, and snorted. Even the gilding seemed dull in this weather. He was contemptuous of it, of the entire museum, a neoclassical folly of the first order. As a student he had been to the temple at Priene in Turkey that had inspired Sir John Soane's design for the museum, and had seen with his own eyes the power of ancient architecture in its setting, the mastery of man over the elements. And at Linz in Austria he had traced the plan of the greatest museum ever devised, walked the streets with the blueprint in his head, populated the phantom galleries with all the works of art that had once been collected for the highest cause ever conceived. It was a museum to harness the power of the past, to radiate it, not to trap it like this one. A museum from the greatest architect of them all. A museum for the thousand-year Reich. *The Führermuseum.*

He ran up the steps under the pediment, closed the umbrella and shook it, and then walked through the front door into the museum vestibule. He nodded at several familiar faces coming out of the museum, students and colleagues, faces he recognized from his lecture at the academy the evening before. It had been an exhilarating event, the culmination of a career that had seen him rise from star student to professor in less than a dozen years, and now recipient of the most prestigious medal of his profession. He had been recognized for his study of architecture in the cause of fascism. *A warning from history*, he had called it. He revelled in the irony. He had never made any secret of his own family's past, his father a member of the Hitler Youth, his grandfather an SS officer. He had used it to explain his fascination with Nazi architecture, almost as if his research were an atonement, part of the upwelling of guilt in modern Germany he so despised. He had argued that the genius of Linz lay not with Hitler but with the architects commissioned to draw up the blueprint, to build the great scale model in the bunker in Berlin that had so captivated the Führer in his final days.

But this was a lie. He knew where the true genius lay. It lay with the Führer himself, in the dream that had elevated Hitler above those who had betrayed him, those who had lost the war. The museum was his platform for apotheosis, for his ascent beyond earthly existence. Nothing had concerned the Führer more in his final hours, not even the Jewish question. The man knew the words of Hitler's final will and testament by heart. *It is my most sincere wish that this bequest be duly executed.* He felt a thrill course through him. The time had come. And he would be the one to do it. *The will of the Führer would be done.*

He entered the museum and veered left, past the cloakroom and into the ancient world galleries. He looked down the hall into the heart of the museum with its colossal Egyptian and Assyrian sculptures, pharaohs and god-kings and human-headed lions, and felt an upwelling of anger at this dislocated mass of fragments, at those who had ripped these pieces from the monuments and palaces that had given them meaning. He stopped before the doorway of the Bronze Age Greece gallery and gazed at the green limestone half-columns on either side, taken from the entrance to the Treasury of Atreus, the great circular tomb outside the citadel of Mycenae in Greece. He reached out and put the flat of his hand against the left-hand column, pressing against the carved zigzag motifs on the shaft. Here, at least, he felt a frisson from the past, as if the columns still retained an echo of their original purpose, guarding the treasure vault within.

He let his hand drop and walked into the gallery, stopping for a moment in front of a case containing a dazzling collection of beaten gold jewellery and precious stones, amethyst from Egypt, lapis lazuli from Afghanistan, a beautiful one-handled golden goblet. In the case beside it was a nondescript row of pots from Troy, one with a crude face in relief, another still retaining a label in Heinrich Schliemann's own hand. *Schliemann*. The pots were the only artefacts in the exhibit from the fabled site. The man reflected on the fickle nature of discovery, on how so many of the great works in the museum had come to light not through scientific excavation but through chance finds, often shrouded in mystery. Schliemann had dug a great trench through the centre of the mound at Troy, and for years the whereabouts of his richest finds had been unknown. It was as if human nature – greed and deceit and ego – had added another layer to archaeology, a layer that needed to be excavated through the archives and museums and vaults of Europe, through understanding the psychology and motivations of men like Schliemann, before the truth could be revealed. That had been his task, for today. And now it was near completion. The greatest treasures would be uncovered, greater than any in this woefully sparse gallery.

He glanced at his watch again, and walked to the case at the rear. He leaned over and stared at a large painted pottery bowl. The painting showed an ancient warship with a double row of oars; beside it were two crude figures with triangular bodies, a man grasping a woman as if leading her into the ship. He glanced at the label. It was from Thebes, in Greece, from the eighth century BC, about the time when Homer might have lived, four centuries after the fall of Troy. He looked at the pot again. He saw a reflection in the case, a presence behind him. *So it begins*. It was a man's voice, quiet, a mellifluous tone with a hint of a French accent. 'When I was an undergraduate at Cambridge, I went to a lecture by an eminent linguist, a Professor Dillen, about fact and myth in Homer. He used the image of this painting as a centrepiece for his argument. The pot dates from the time of Homer. But does it? Homer could have been earlier. And those figures. Are they Theseus and Ariadne, or Paris and Helen? And is that any old warship, or is it a galley of the Trojan War? Where is the truth? Can we ever find it?'

The man replied quietly, still staring ahead. 'The double layer of oars is an anachronism. Bronze Age galleys were probably paddled longboats. I have some interest from my own student days, as a rower in Heidelberg. And by chance, it was one of Dillen's students, Howard, who found fragments of late Bronze Age ships on the beach at Troy that seemed to confirm it. But the question still needs to be laid to rest. We need a well-preserved shipwreck.'

'Perhaps they will find one. Howard and his team are at Troy again.'

'Indeed. This morning's papers.'

'Good. You have been keeping abreast of events. We will walk, Professor Raitz?'

Raitz turned, and saw a trim man, bearded, about thirty-five, with striking brown eyes and dark features, expensively dressed in a suit and a gaberdine raincoat. 'Your Excellency.'

'Don't call me that. We don't want to excite attention. Saumerre will do.' He gestured with one hand, and they slowly made their way around the exhibits, pretending to study the artefacts. Raitz turned towards him, speaking quietly. 'Howard's daughter was in my office at the institute a few weeks ago. The Howard Gallery had a Dürer, given to Jack Howard's father after the war by a friend of his who'd bought it at auction in Switzerland in 1945. The gallery had discovered it was a painting stolen – or should I say borrowed – by Reichsmarschall Göring, from a museum in Mainz. I have a reputation for facilitating the return of stolen works of art to the former Reich, and Miss Howard had come to me representing the gallery for that reason. Naturally, those wishing to return works to Jewish owners are politely told to go elsewhere. I do not deal with private ownership claims, only public museums and galleries.'

'Of course. We know your reputation. That's why I am here. You have open-door access to the back rooms of museums and galleries across Europe. And we know about Rebecca Howard.' He took out an iPod and a photograph appeared, showing a vivacious-looking girl with long dark hair, wearing jeans and a T-shirt with the letters USMC on the front. 'Seventeen years old, born in Naples to Elizabeth d'Agostino, an archaeologist with the Italian superintendency. She and Jack Howard ended their affair nine months previously, when d'Agostino returned from her studies at Cambridge to Naples at the insistence of her family, who are Mafia. She told Howard nothing of their daughter and arranged for her to be brought up by friends in New York State, where Rebecca is still at school. Howard first met his daughter less than two years ago, shortly after her mother had been murdered. Since then he's involved Rebecca in an archaeological project in India and central Asia, where she acquired that shirt from a US Marine dive team in Kyrgyzstan. She and her father are very close. In fact, she's become close to the whole team.'

'Impressive surveillance.'

The man checked his watch. 'Right now she's at Troy. But she's due back for a school trip to Paris in two days. She touches down at Heathrow from Istanbul at five thirty-five tomorrow morning.'

'But what about now?' Raitz said urgently. 'You have brought what you promised?'

Saumerre opened the flap of his coat to reveal a document bag. He unzipped the top, and raised the contents enough for the other man to see the slightly foxed cover and the faded red capital letters along the top, in Gothic script.

Raitz stared at it. He was shaking with excitement, his voice hoarse. 'You are certain this is genuine?'

Saumerre paused for a moment, then stared at Raitz. He spoke urgently, barely audible against the background noise of the museum. 'I will let you in on a secret. A deadly secret. What you are about to embark on would destroy your career if it came out. What I am about to tell you would do more than destroy mine. It would put a bullet in the back of my neck.'

'I understand,' Raitz murmured, looking around, seeing that the gallery was empty. 'You have my absolute word.'

'You know my background from the media. Our embassy is in the news every day now. Officially I'm of North African descent, Algerian. But what you didn't know is that one of my grandfathers was French, from Marseille. He was a small-time gangster, ran a petty crime ring, drugs, prostitution, protection rackets. He was arrested by the Vichy police in late 1940 and ended up in a concentration camp in Germany. His lifeline was that he'd trained originally as a chef, and they put him to work in a small labour camp near Belsen. In the final weeks of the war the camp was flooded with Jews force-marched there from Auschwitz, and in the chaos he escaped. But he knew what had been going on in the camp. What it had been built for. What was stored there.'

'Is that it?' Raitz whispered, his heart pounding with excitement. 'What we're after? Stolen works of art?'

'There's more.' Saumerre paused, and steered Raitz over to the case containing the Troy artefacts, staring studiously at them as a class of schoolchildren streamed by. He waited until they had disappeared into the Egyptian gallery, then spoke again. 'There is another secret. *Our secret.*' He paused again, checking carefully around, then moved close to Raitz. 'When my grandfather returned to Marseille, he picked up where he'd left off. There were rich opportunities in the years after the war. He already had an Algerian wife, and he extended his interests to French North Africa. It was the time of the French–Algerian war, and he profiteered. It became a multi-million-dollar business. When my father came of age, he inherited it.'

Raitz stared at him. 'And now you?'

'Keep your voice down. Please.' Saumerre took out a handkerchief, and dabbed his forehead. 'Perhaps I have said enough.'

'I swear never to tell.'

Saumerre took a deep breath, then nodded. 'You're right. There's no going back now. But you must understand. I have always kept my political career and my business interests strictly separate.'

'What was your grandfather's secret? What had he seen? *What did he know?*'

'He told my father, and my father told me. As a boy, I was fascinated by the stories of lost Nazi loot, hidden away in lakes and bunkers and mines. I became determined to chase up any leads, to find what was left. We all know there's more to be discovered. There's a long list of works of art that have never been found. A huge fortune to be made.'

'Stop there.' Raitz stood back, suddenly wary. 'We may be at cross-purposes. I thought you were behind my dream. I am not doing this for money.'

Saumerre put up his hand. 'Relax. All of the paintings are yours. But this is a business arrangement. You have the paintings, we have the rest.'

'What do you mean, the rest?'

Saumerre gestured at the cabinet. 'What do you know about Schliemann's lost treasure?'

Raitz stared at the pots. 'You asked me to research it when we first made contact two weeks ago. Some of the gold from Troy went missing for years, then showed up in Moscow. That's common knowledge. But there's always been a question over whether Schliemann found more at Mycenae. Nothing's ever been proven.'

'We know,' Saumerre said. '*We know*. And that's our cut. We want gold, antiquities, unique items that have huge cachet as collateral in arms deals, pipeline deals, multi-million-dollar enterprises that can rest on a single handshake, a single gesture of goodwill. Yet you and I have much in common. I am an educated man too, a lover of the arts. One day we should come here and talk more about these marvels.' He swept his hand about the room. 'We may regret that some of the great cultural treasures might never end up in museums. But some have been lost for so long, stolen so long ago and never found, that their very loss has become part of our culture. Schliemann's treasure, for example. And look around us here. Already there are too many wonders to comprehend. And for you, my friend, it is our price. There is no compromise.'

Raitz looked at him, and then remembered the huge step he had taken to come here, the risk, his mounting excitement. His heart was pounding. He nodded. 'Agreed.'

'We will provide you with security. They call themselves *Totenköpfe*, after the Nazi death's-head units. But they are mainly Russians. Ex-military. Mercenaries. Thugs for hire.'

'They will do any dirty work.'

'You need have no worry. That is out of your hands.'

'There will be no killing?' Raitz asked anxiously.

Saumerre peered at him, his eyebrows raised. 'My friend. You forget your heritage. Your legacy. Why you are here.' He paused, then put a hand on his arm. 'As I said. You need have no worry.'

'These *Totenköpfe*. They can be controlled?'

'The ones you will see will be mere employees. Their leaders are united by their common allegiance to your cause. They swear to uphold the Nero Decree, Hitler's order to destroy Germany, to have the thousand-year Reich or nothing. But this of course is fantasy. We have used them before in our business dealings in eastern Europe, and have found them more than willing to forgo ideology if the stack of gold bars is high enough. And this time it will be higher than any they have ever seen.'

'And what if we don't find it? Who do they blame?'

'Business is about risks. You modify your plans. But that will not be necessary.'

'Will there be anyone else?'

'I believe you will be assisted by a colleague. By several colleagues.'

'What do you mean?'

'The place you will be going may require technical expertise. Skills that few have to the level required.'

'These are your people too?'

Saumerre looked at his watch. 'Exactly twenty-four hours from now, you will know.' He paused, looked round, listened, then opened his coat and withdrew the document case. 'And now for what you want. On the twenty-ninth of April 1945, Adolf Hitler issued his final will and testament from his bunker in Berlin. We know you have often spoken of it, to sympathizers, to the secret network of friends you have developed over the years, others who share the same legacy, the same passion. That's how we came to know of you. We were seeking just such a man.'

'Go on.'

'When my contact told you to meet me here, the message said that I would pass on all that you needed to realize the dream, to create the museum the Führer so craved, to fulfil his legacy.'

'Yes. *Yes.*' Raitz gripped Saumerre's arm tight, his eyes

blazing. 'A secret museum in Bavaria, in the mountains he so loved. A shrine, a rallying point for all those who carry on the dream. A Führermuseum, reborn.'

'This document is genuine. You can subject it to all the tests you want. You have all the laboratories of London at your disposal, a scholar of your influence. But you have my word. It was typed in duplicate in the Führerbunker by Adolf Hitler himself, then handed over to Martin Bormann for dispersal. It's dated the fourth of April 1945, less than four weeks before the Führer took his own life. One copy went by motorcycle courier towards Holland. It has never been found. Another went to somewhere near the labour camp where my grandfather worked. He found it on the body of a German Luftwaffe officer, and kept it secret all this time, finally revealing it to me only this year, just before his death.' Saumerre pulled the envelope out, hesitated, then passed it to Raitz, who took it and quickly concealed it under his coat. 'It has what you want, for your dream. But now. When we contacted you, we asked about anything you might have seen with that swastika on it, the counterclockwise swastika. You said you had something for us?'

Raitz pulled out a scrap of paper from his pocket. 'A former Dutch antiquities dealer. Became a police informant. Rebecca Howard contacted him too, because he had an interest in Dürer. When Interpol used me as a consultant I insisted that they send me all of his papers, for my eyes only. I already knew of him for his interest in Schliemann's treasures. My instinct was right. He had hundreds of Nazi documents. And one, one only, had the reverse swastika on it.'

'I must know. Where is this document?'

'In a safe in my house.'

'Is it a map?'

'It's some kind of plan, a route. Perhaps underground. The Dutchman may know more. He has gone into hiding.'

'Then that is it,' Saumerre whispered. 'I was right, when my grandfather told me the story. He said he had spoken to Jewish inmates who had worked underground. *I knew it was in a mine.* Our preparations have not been in vain. Guard the document with your life. We will be in touch.' Saumerre turned to go, but Raitz kept hold of his arm, stopping him.

'One question.'

'What is it?'

'The Nazis always gave top-secret directives names. What did they call this one?'

'Look at the top.' Saumerre shook away the hand, straightened his coat and walked away, out of sight towards the museum entrance. Raitz glanced around, then quickly unzipped the bag and pulled out the document inside, reading the Gothic letters in red he had glimpsed earlier. Further down, he saw the reverse swastika, a platinum colour. And the words under it. He gasped.

Der Agamemnon-Code.

The Agamemnon Code.

He stood motionless for a moment, staring at the case in front of him, in a daze, looking beyond the pottery, the jewellery, the broken swords and arrowheads, seeing only in his mind's eye what had once mesmerized him in another museum, years before in Athens, the great golden mask that had been raised from a royal tomb more than a hundred and thirty years ago. He was thinking again what he had thought then. *What did Heinrich Schliemann really see when he raised the Mask of Agamemnon?*

Back then, standing in front of that mask, it had been idle speculation, the dream of a student. Now it was part of a deadly path he was on. A path that would burn his name in history. *A path that would raise again the glory of the Reich.*

He closed the bag and held it under his coat, as if it were the greatest treasure ever found. He hardly dared think of the signature he knew must lie at the bottom of the document. Soon, he would touch it. *That name.*

The signature of a man whose will would be done.

Heil, mein Führer.

5

Off the island of Tenedos, the Aegean Sea

Fifteen minutes after Costas had left him on the foredeck of *Seaquest II*, Jack walked into the conference room below the bridge and pulled the door shut behind him. About thirty of the ship's crew and scientific personnel were seated on plastic chairs facing a table with a laptop computer and an old-fashioned overhead transparency projector. On the wall behind it was a screen showing the British Admiralty chart of the north-east Aegean, with their position highlighted. Jack reached the front and turned round. Costas was seated at the far left of the front row, talking with two of his submersibles technicians, but he stopped when he saw Jack and leaned forward intently. Seated directly in front of Jack was Dr Jacob Lanowski, their CGI simulations expert and all-round genius, the main reason for the briefing. Lanowski was staring expectantly at Jack through thick round glasses, nervously sweeping his long lank hair from his face, clutching a sheaf of notes and transparency sheets. Jack smiled at him, glanced at his watch and held up his hand. 'Captain Macalister tells me we have twenty minutes before the ship is fully stabilized over the site and the docking bay is ready. Costas and I will be doing the dive, but this is a team effort and every one of you is a part of it.'

He turned and aimed a light-pointer at Troy on the map. 'I called this briefing mainly to let Dr Lanowski give us a run-down on the bathymetry and sedimentology. But some of you are recent arrivals and still don't know the reason we're here, so I want to spend a few minutes talking about that. And there's a connection with what Dr Lanowski's going to tell you, an incredible connection. Even I haven't had the full picture yet.' He beamed at Lanowski, who looked around, smiling awkwardly at the others, before dropping his sheaf of papers and scrabbling to pick them up. Jack glanced at Costas, who had raised his eyes to the ceiling. Not for the first time Jack wondered if their resident genius would last the course.

Jack tapped a key on the laptop, bringing up an aerial photograph on the screen. It showed an archaeological excavation under way, an open area of perhaps ten by twenty metres surrounded by dense rows of tomato plants. He pointed to the sole person visible, a desultory figure wearing a huge sombrero sitting on one side of the trench, clutching a water bottle and staring at a dark patch on the otherwise featureless sand in front of him. 'Some of you may recognize our esteemed colleague Dr Kazantzakis. His first ever experience of archaeology.'

'And so nearly my last,' Costas piped up. There was a ripple of laughter.

'We're about a kilometre north-west of Troy, fifteen years ago,' Jack continued. 'Our first excavation together, on a shoestring budget. Before IMU. Before *Seaquest*. But what we found there kick-started it all.' He clicked again, and the screen transformed to a 3-D CGI rendition of the Dardanelles and the plain of Troy. 'A farmer had found some charred timbers while he was ploughing. We knew the river Scamander had silted up the plain, and our excavation proved that this spot had been the beach in the late Bronze Age. Amazingly, the timbers were from ships, war galleys that had burned on the seashore. We found only a few fragments, but enough for radiocarbon analysis, which gave a date of about 1200 BC, exactly the time of the destruction of Troy. And there was more. In the picture, Costas thinks he's looking at nothing. But he's wrong. That dark stain proved to be an open fire pit. It was filled with butchered bones, huge joints. The entire carcass of a bull. It was a feast fit for heroes. Where Costas was sitting, Achilles had once sat. Achilles was sulking too, but over a woman.'

'If only,' Costas said.

Everyone laughed again. Jack held up his hand. 'I thought that discovery, that incredible connection with the past, was about as good as it gets. It was fantastically exciting. I felt like Heinrich Schliemann, on the trail of Agamemnon. And now we're back there again. This time it's not just charred fragments we're after. This time it's a full-on shipwreck. But the clue to that didn't come from the beach excavation. It came from somewhere completely unexpected, from one of the most amazing places we've ever discovered, about a thousand miles due west from here.'

Everyone in the room was silent, riveted. Jack clicked again, and the image changed to a page of ancient manuscript, showing lines of precise writing, many of the letters recognizably Greek. 'This was found three months ago in the lost library of the Roman emperor Claudius at Herculaneum, in Italy. Jeremy Haverstock's been in charge of the restoration work. As each new text is unrolled and put through X-ray fluorescence, he's sending the digital images to Professor Dillen at Cambridge for translation. This one had Dillen speechless. In his view it's the most important new discovery of an ancient text ever, full stop. He thinks it's a previously unknown verse by Homer, possibly containing eyewitness details of the end of Troy. That makes it a truly fantastic find for anyone interested in the Trojan War. He thinks it's a lost part of the Trojan epic cycle called the *Ilioupersis*, meaning the destruction of Troy. And this particular image shows the lines of verse that really excited me.' He pulled out a folded sheet of paper from his pocket and opened it. 'Here's Dillen's translation.'

Look closely now: far out to sea
From the isle of Tenedos
The lion-prowed ship of the King of Mycenae
Mast raised, sail spread, wind-filled,
Dark wave singing loudly about the stern
Brings tidings of home-strife
To Agamemnon, unheeding, sole of purpose, back-turned, war-bent.
Too late. Already I feel it. The west wind sharpens.

Jack looked up. Everyone was staring at him, stunned. Costas raised his hand. 'If that's the ship we're after, I thought galleys didn't sink. No cargo, limited ballast. Wrecked galleys disperse as flotsam. That's why we hardly ever find them.'

Jack nodded. 'But this time it's different. Wait for the next two lines, the lines that put the fire under me.' He recited from memory:

> *The ship, booty-laden, weighed down with gold,*
> *Drives too hard down falling waves, and is no more.*

There was a collective gasp. ' "*Weighed down with gold*",' one of the crewmen repeated, astonished. 'What exactly does that mean? What are we looking for?'

Jack glanced at his watch. 'First, Dr Lanowski.'

The crewman kept his hand up. 'But what are our chances?'

Jack looked at the man, a new member of the submersibles team. He paused, then replied. 'If you let your imagination lead you, then everything can lock together. You have to take a gamble, and believe in yourself. And this place, the Trojan War, a shipwreck of Agamemnon? Believing all that's a big leap of faith, but it's one I've taken. And I know that if I'm on the wrong track, one of you will let me know. Our chances? I think this is as good as it gets.'

'With a small dose of luck,' Costas murmured.

Jack tapped his watch. 'And now for some hard science.' He gestured to Lanowski, and then quickly walked over and sat beside Costas. 'Here goes,' Costas whispered to him.

Lanowski got up, dumped his overhead sheets on the table and turned round, his eyes feverish with excitement. He cleared his throat. 'Detailed analysis of air-gun lithoseismic profiles in the north Aegean basin shows fault structures trending north-east to south-west, with the dominant structure apparently an extension of the North Anatolian fault. That's the one across northern Turkey that causes all the earthquakes.' He peered over his glasses at the audience, then wiped the sweat off his forehead. He gave a lopsided grin. 'Y'all with me?'

'So far so good,' Costas whispered to Jack. 'Didn't understand a word of it.'

'Wait for it,' Jack whispered back.

'*Y'all with me?* What's with that?' Costas whispered.

'My fault, I think,' Jack whispered. 'Told him to be jokey.'

Lanowski cleared his throat again, and aimed a laser pointer at the screen. 'This is the tectonic map superimposed on the bathymetric map. As you can see, we're over the continental platform, here.' He aimed the pointer down. 'The platform shows no significant internal deformation, but the slopes on the edge are shaped by marginal faults. As you can see, within the basin, higher vertical throws occur on marginal faults bordering the intermediate horst structure, with pronounced shear zones.'

Costas nudged Jack. 'Oh-oh.'

Lanowski peered over his glasses again. He glared at Costas, then spoke deliberately slowly. 'An angular unconformity occurs within the Plio–Pleistocene sequence linked to uplifted and tilted neotectonic blocks and anticlinal hinges.'

'Here we go,' Costas whispered.

Jack shot his hand up. 'Jacob, that puts us in the picture brilliantly. What you're saying is that we're not above fault structures here, but just north-west of us is an active zone that might produce localized instability.'

Lanowski looked pleased. 'You got it. You understood. The structural architecture shows a complex strike-slip zone, on a dextral north-east to south-west line.'

'Exactly,' Jack said, getting up quickly when he saw Lanowski picking up and shuffling his overhead transparency sheets. 'Earthquakes. That's what you mean. Earthquakes. And what we really want to know is, could that have happened here in 1200 BC? Enough to sink a ship?'

Lanowski held up a transparency sheet. 'I've got a whole sequence here modelling the subduction and strike-slip zones. I had to draw them by hand. It was too complex for the computer.'

'*Too complex for the computer,*' Costas whispered, putting his head in his hands.

Jack looked around. 'Anyone wants to go down to Dr Lanowski's lab afterwards for a full exposition, queue up at the end of the briefing. I won't be far behind.' He turned to Lanowski. 'Right now, we've only got five minutes. I know you're bursting to tell us. Your main discovery. What you were so excited about earlier.'

Lanowski looked defiant for a moment, holding his sheet covered with a mass of red scribbles, then he sighed, nodded and put it down. He clicked the laptop, changing the screen to a new map. 'Okay. This is a bathymetric and topographical map showing the Troad, the peninsula of Troy. You can see the Dardanelles to the north bounded by the southern edge of the Gallipoli peninsula, and to the west the little island of Tenedos and our location. What I want you to focus on is the plain in front of Troy, to the north-west, what Homer called the plain of Ilion. It's an alluvial plain, watered by the river the ancients called the Scamander. Here's what we think it looked like three thousand years ago.' He clicked again, and the image changed dramatically, showing the shoreline much closer to Troy, in the shape of a basin.

Jack aimed his own laser pointer at the shoreline close to the citadel. 'The site of our excavation fifteen years ago.'

'Right,' Lanowski said. 'You may think it looks like the ideal harbour, protected and close to the walls of the citadel, but you'd be wrong. The actual harbour of Troy was several kilometres to the west, on the Aegean coast south of the entrance to the Dardanelles, here.' He pointed to it. 'There were two reasons for this. One, the alluvial plain of the Scamander opens out on to the Dardanelles, not on to the Aegean Sea. Sailing ships coming up from Greece or Egypt would have had a hell of a time beating up against the current coming out of the Dardanelles. Two, the floodplain would have been shallow, only a couple of metres deep. Too shallow for a fully laden merchant ship.'

'But deep enough for a rowed galley,' Jack said.

'And rowed galleys could easily have made their way around the headland into the Dardanelles,' Lanowski added, stumbling over the words in his excitement.

'You're talking about the ships of the Greeks, the ships of Agamemnon?' Costas asked.

'Bingo,' Lanowski said awkwardly, looking at Jack and then at Costas, letting out a nervous laugh. He was flushed with excitement, and his hands were shaking slightly as he shuffled his notes. 'You asked me to give a rundown of the sedimentology. Here goes.' He clicked the computer again, and the same map outline remained on the screen but with different colours and textures. He cleared his throat. 'The sedimentary strata begin at the bottom with Eocene turbidites and limestones, continue upward with Oligocene–Lower Miocene detrital rocks and andesitic volcanoclastics, and end with loosely consolidated sandstones of the Upper Miocene–Pliocene. Each depositional sequence consists of a lower mainly parallel-stratified sub-unit, and an upper oblique to sigmoid-oblique pro-graded sub-unit. Needless to say.'

Costas slumped back and shut his eyes, and the others looked on in various attitudes of stunned silence. Jack nodded sagely, glancing around. 'The questions I asked of Dr Lanowski were, first, the sedimentary characteristics of a possible shipwreck site beneath us, and, second, any abnormalities in the plain of Troy that might be pinned to the late Bronze Age.' He nodded towards Lanowski. 'Jacob? In layman's terms? Please?'

Lanowski took a deep breath. 'Okay. The first one's easy. There are thick silt deposits below us from the Dardanelles outflow. The downside is, any ancient shipwreck's likely to be deeply buried. The plus is, buried wrecks can be spectacularly well-preserved. There's all the usual scope for localized current variation, scouring channels in the sea bed, exposing strata that have been buried for millennia. That seems to account for the exceptional preservation of our Byzantine shipwreck yesterday. There's lots of modern debris down there, especially from the 1915 Gallipoli campaign. Modern wrecks can create an obstruction in the current causing scour channels, revealing older deposits. That *could* be the case here.'

'Okay. Excellent. And the plain of Troy?'

'I'm basing it on your work fifteen years ago. Most of the sediment samples show exactly what you'd expect, typical alluvial outflow from the surrounding land and mountains, increasing as you get into the classical Greek period as a result of deforestation. But the really fascinating thing is the sample you took from the Bronze Age beach deposit. One of the strangest discoveries you made was realizing that those fragments of ship timbers were *inland* from their stone anchors. That's what really piqued my interest. You may not believe this, but at Princeton and then Oxford I was on the college rowing team, and when a reconstructed Greek trireme was first trialled in Athens in the eighties I went along as a volunteer. It was a long time ago and I'm a little out of shape now, but I do know a bit about galleys and how you beach them. You do *not* beach them like that.'

Costas whistled. Jack had not known, but he nodded. 'You mean you row hard into the beach, and then take out the anchor and carry it forward.'

'You didn't find enough timber to be certain of the orientation, but I'll wager those ships you found were back to front, with their sterns facing the shoreline. As if they'd been picked up and blown inland, and swung round on their anchor chains.'

'And the sedimentology?' Jack said. 'What does that say?'

'It's brilliant. Absolutely brilliant.' The atmosphere in the room was suddenly electric, with all eyes on Lanowski. He seemed about to burst with excitement. 'Thank God for your careful excavation, Jack. In fact, it was Costas who took the samples. They've got his handwriting on them. I found them in the excavation archive, unopened.'

'I remember,' Costas said, leaning forward, staring at Lanowski intently. 'I saw it one morning, after there'd been rain. We'd exposed what we thought was the level of the Bronze Age beach. It looked as if it was streaked, with lines of sediment coming up the beach that were denser than the underlying alluvial sediment, retaining the rainwater longer.'

'Bingo,' Lanowski said, more confidently. 'That's because it was different. It was *offshore* sediment. Sediment that had been swept up from the north Aegean basin. Swept up the very day the ships were thrown violently forward.' He leaned back triumphantly with one elbow against the wall, swept his hair back over his forehead and beamed at Jack, nodding.

One of the oceanographers in the front row put up her hand, a Turkish woman who had worked closely with Lanowski in the CGI lab. 'What about this?' she said. 'You get an earthquake out in the north Aegean basin, the kind of thing that must have caused those fault lines. The quake sinks the ship, as described in the poem. Then the *same* event, maybe an aftershock or a secondary quake, causes a water surge that rises up the slope into the Dardanelles, travels over the continental shelf and hits the lagoon where the plain of Troy now lies. It's so shallow that the surge rises up and travels far inland, as far as the walls of Troy, with enough force to lift some of the beached ships up and drive them forward.'

'You're talking about a tsunami,' Costas murmured.

There was a murmur from the audience. Captain Scott Macalister, the Canadian ship's master, a genial bearded man wearing tropical whites, put up his hand and spoke. 'A point of interest. Tsunamis and quakes are often accompanied by weather disturbance. There's an effect on atmospheric pressure, especially when there are frequent aftershocks. I've been in the western Pacific when this has happened. So I'm imagining a terrifying storm accompanying the tsunami, black clouds, thunder and lightning, the waves being whipped up to whitecaps.'

'Horses,' Lanowski said, chuckling to himself. 'Horses.'

'What?' Jack asked hesitantly. Costas gave him an alarmed look.

'Horses.' Lanowski had a mad glint in his eyes. He shook his head, laughed out loud, then murmured to himself, '*Horses*.'

'Okay.' Jack took him firmly by the shoulders and steered him back to his seat, sitting him down. He looked at everyone else. 'I think that about does it. I'd like to thank you all very much. That's been fantastically interesting. It's time to get cracking.' He kept his hands firmly on Lanowski's shoulders. 'And I'd especially like to thank Dr Lanowski. He's killed two birds with one stone. He's explained how there could be an ancient galley wreck out here, how the weather could have caused a ship to drive into the sea bed, as in the poem. And he's explained how the Greeks may have reached the walls of Troy. Ours is a joint project, at sea and on land, and we've just seen how hard science can knit it all beautifully together. Brilliant. Thank you.'

'Hear hear,' Macalister said. Everyone rose from their chairs and filed out. Jack looked down at Lanowski. 'You all right?'

'I'm not mad, you know.' Lanowski spoke quietly, his face now pale. 'I studied ancient Greek at school. That's what I was on about. Horses. *Ippoi*. That's what the Greeks called waves, whitecaps. And it's what they called ships. Horses.'

'Horses,' Jack repeated quietly, nodding slowly. *Horses*.

'Horses, being driven towards the walls of Troy.' Lanowski began muttering to himself again. Costas passed over the pile of overhead sheets and placed them firmly in Lanowski's hands, raising him up and steering him towards the door. They watched him shuffle out, still muttering and chuckling to himself.

Costas shook his head. 'A genius, but crazy. You handled that well.'

'Maybe not so crazy,' Jack replied quietly. *Horses*. There was something there, but he couldn't quite pin it down. Something about Homer. Something probably glaringly obvious. He put it away in his mind and looked at Costas, shaking his head. 'And imagine him rowing.'

Costas put a hand on Jack's shoulder. 'Never second-guess anyone around here. I'll just barge my way through the queue waiting to hear his detailed lecture. I'll be back in a moment. We've got twenty minutes before kitting up. There're a few things you need to explain to me.'

6

Jack watched Costas go, then took a deep breath, exhaling slowly. That had been a hell of a prep talk. He hoped to God he was right. Every time he led his crew on a chase like this it was a gamble. He was glad Professor Dillen had not been in the audience. Dillen might have taken him down a notch or two. But then he remembered the thrill in the professor's voice when he had spoken over the phone of the *Ilioupersis* discovery, as if his entire career had found its culmination. And he remembered Dillen taking him aside at the end of his first year as an undergraduate, telling him that he had seen a few others with the same passion as Jack, but none with the ability to seek out and empathize with individuals in the past, to understand what motivated them, to ally his own quest with theirs. Jack had seen something in Dillen too, in the countless hours he had spent watching him translate and analyse Homer, something more than just declaiming words from the past. It was as if Dillen inhabited the imagination of the poet, and knew Homer emotionally, not just intellectually. Jack had promised Dillen that one day they would combine to investigate a moment in history that drew on both of their talents, somewhere at a critical juncture where myth and history met. He was sure of one thing. Flying Dillen from retirement to join the excavation team at Troy had been one of the best things he had ever done.

He stared through the open doorway at the salt-streaked window and the Turkish shoreline beyond, a hazy outline of low sandy cliffs flecked with spray. They were over there, Dillen, Hiebermeyer, the others, at fabled Troy, where the tendrils of fact and legend seemed forever to dance around each other, sometimes drawn close by a new discovery, by a fresh wave of belief, but then as quickly blown apart by doubt and uncertainty. Jack knew that history was sometimes best left that way, where the reality of events was unclear even to those who witnessed them. But Troy seemed to demand more than that. There had been a darkness here, a truth about the human condition that had lured people for generations, since archaeology was in its infancy. Jack remembered one of the first things Dillen had taught him. History was about individuals, about individual people making decisions. The cold facts of history, the artefacts that Jack cherished, were his key to getting into their minds. And he knew it was not gods who had set the Trojan War in motion, it was men. *One man above all others*.

For weeks now Jack had been putting himself in the mind of Heinrich Schliemann, poring over his publications, visiting his home in Athens, exploring the ruins of Mycenae, the site of Schliemann's other great triumph. But always he had felt the presence of another, a towering, shadowy figure whose steps Schliemann had tried to follow, a giant among men from the age of heroes. It was at Mycenae that Jack had first tried to go there, standing alone in the ruins of the Bronze Age palace, on the edge of the grave circle where Schliemann had found the famous mask, staring out towards the sea where the king of kings had set off at the head of a thousand ships. *Broad-shouldered Agamemnon, cattle-stealer, earth-smiter, sacker of cities, who knows war in all its bloody ways.* What had Agamemnon seen? What had he done? What had made him come here, to Troy, to set in motion the war to end all wars, the war that would obliterate civilization, that would reduce men to their most base condition?

Sunlight streamed through the door as the ship changed position, obscuring his view of the shoreline. If Dillen had been there and not taken him down a notch, Rebecca would have done. She was out there too, learning the tricks of the trade from Hiebermeyer. Jack had missed seeing her at the briefing. It was now nearly two years since her mother had died, since he had taken over responsibility for her, but already those years when she had been brought up apart from him were receding into the background. He tried to keep her mother close in their memory, and there was much that reminded him of Elizabeth too, the dark eyes, the vivacity, the determination. But there was a Howard in Rebecca as well. Dillen said he had seen the same light in her eyes, the same drive. Jack hoped she had a dose of the Howard luck. Maybe together they could crack this place.

'Okay, Jack.' Costas reappeared at the door, and shut it

behind him. 'We've got fifteen minutes before the dive-master wants us in the equipment bay.' He walked back to the front row of seats and sat down, a glint in his eye, then jerked his thumb towards the picture on the screen. 'So what's this really all about? You can tell me. Your old buddy Costas. Everyone else has gone. What's the scoop, man? What's the treasure?'

Jack pretended to look affronted. 'The treasure's in the ideas. In the revelations about the past. The lessons for the future.'

'As if.'

'Where did you learn to say that?'

'Your cool daughter. It's what she says when I tell her that one day you're going to put up your fins, and pass all this on to her.'

'She's only seventeen, you know. And our greatest discoveries lie ahead of us.'

'Let's talk about the here and now, Jack. Come on. The treasure.'

'Okay.' Jack paused. 'You remember those lumps of charcoal – as you called them – we found all those years ago on the beach near Troy? The ancient ship's timbers? Well, I've always wanted to find more, to prove that Bronze Age galleys were built using the same edge-joined mortise-and-tenon technique as the galleys of the Greeks and Romans. That would help prove the reliability of Homer, too. If we can push the technology of Homer's age, about the eighth century BC, back four centuries or so to the likely date of the Trojan War, then that makes it all the more likely that the history of the war was real too, that it wasn't being made up by the bard.

The more threads we have like that, the more the truth is locked down. So that's what I want. A wreck with enough hull to prove it's a galley, not a merchantman, and a nice big section of joined planking. And some keel, too. Icing on the cake.'

'Jack.'

'What?'

'You can't kid me. Jack Howard doesn't get a five-million-dollar special grant from IMU, talk about nothing else for months on end, book *Seaquest II* for an entire summer and assemble the biggest team of experts we've ever fielded, just to find a lump of soggy timbers. It just doesn't happen.'

Jack sighed dramatically. 'You *really* want to know.'

'You bet.'

Jack jerked his thumb at the screen. 'It's the next image. I would have told the team, but I didn't want someone talking and the press getting hold of it. This project's already front-page news. We'd have every treasure-hunter and pirate in the world descending on this place.'

'Go on.'

Jack took a deep breath. 'Okay. In the *Iliad*, Achilles lends Patroclus his armour, but then Hector kills Patroclus and strips it off him as a trophy. So Achilles' mother, the sea-nymph Thetis, goes to Hephaestos, god of the forge, and has him fashion new armour for Achilles. The centrepiece was a magnificent shield, covered with images. Homer devotes almost two hundred lines to it. It's the first time in literature that an object is described in that way, as a work of art. The shield beguiled later classical authors, from Hesiod to Virgil, as well as modern writers. W.H. Auden wrote a poem about it.'

Costas cleared his throat. 'You mean this? Auden's talking about the images Hephaestos is creating on the shield, watched by Thetis. Instead of beautiful cities and flourishing fields, he creates "an artificial wilderness, and a sky like lead".'

Jack stared at him, stunned. 'You never cease to amaze me.'

'My English teacher at school in New York. Dead Poets Society, and all that. It must have sunk in while I was doodling submarines. I liked the "ships on untamed seas" bit.'

'You were a member of the poetry society at school? *You?*'

Costas fidgeted. 'Never underestimate an engineer.'

'Does your inseparable buddy Jeremy know this?' Jack flipped open his phone. 'He's over there at Troy now. This is breaking news.'

Costas clamped a hand over Jack's. 'Does the world know that the famous marine archaeologist Jack Howard gets seasick?'

Jack stared at the phone, sighed and snapped it shut. 'Touché. Just no more secrets.'

'It wasn't a secret. It was a hidden depth.'

Jack grinned, looked at his watch, and carried on. 'You'd be surprised by Jeremy's reaction. But back to Auden. He'd gone as an observer to the Sino-Japanese war in 1938, and worked for the US Strategic Bombing Survey in Germany in 1945. He'd seen the reality of war. For him, it was an all-encompassing horror that obliterated everything around it, that neutered images of life, of light and colour. A painting of Auden's poem would be monotone, grey, with none of the gold and silver in Homer's description. Imagine those black and white photographs of bombed-out cities of

Germany, or images of the death camps, all colour sucked out of them.'

'So what do you think the shield might have looked like?' Costas asked.

Jack tapped the laptop keyboard. Lanowski's bathymetric map on the screen transformed into the image of a magnificent circular shield, gold and silver, its surface divided into concentric circles densely populated with figural scenes. Costas whistled. 'Now *that's* more like it. *That's* what I call treasure.'

'Here it is according to the Italian artist Angelo Monticelli,' Jack said. 'He followed Homer's description by showing a figure of divinity in the centre, then five concentric circles – zoomorphic representations of the constellations, then those two registers showing vignettes of people in city and pastoral scenes, some playing music. The figures look classical, too late for the Bronze Age. But Monticelli finished this about 1820, before anyone knew what Mycenaean art looked like. Many people still thought Homer's world was entirely mythical. It was more than half a century before Schliemann was to discover Troy and Mycenae.'

'Do you think Schliemann knew of this image?'

'As a boy in Germany he'd been fascinated by a picture in Georg Ludwig Jerrer's *Universal History for Children*, showing Aeneas rescuing his father Anchises from burning Troy. Schliemann knew the lure of treasure. He'd made his fortune in America on the back of the California gold rush, in the early 1850s. But it wasn't greed that propelled him to Troy and Mycenae, it was a fascination with the power and meaning of artefacts, the people behind them. That's why the image of the shield would have fascinated him. It's why I've always felt I understood Schliemann. God knows, he had his faults. He mythologized his own past. He dug Troy like a bulldozer. And who knows what happened to his greatest discoveries, what he and his wife Sophia really found when they disappeared at night to dig alone. But look at his achievements. He opened the world to the glories of the Aegean Bronze Age. He changed our perception of myth and history. You can't knock that. I don't know any archaeologists today who would have the courage or imagination to make the leaps he did.'

'I can think of one,' Costas murmured.

Jack tapped the keyboard again. Two images came up, one a beautiful golden cup with scenes in relief, the other a group of swords. 'When Monticelli made that painting, the only available images from antiquity came from the art of Greece and Rome, so that's what he used. His figures look as if they've been lifted from sculptures in Rome. But these two images here are the real thing, actual Mycenaean art. The one on the left is the Vapheio Cup from Greece, with wonderful relief work in gold, showing scenes of a hunt. And those are swords found by Schliemann at Mycenae, inlaid with gold and niello. These images suggest what we might expect to find on a shield, bronze decorated with inlays and gold relief. But they tell us more than that. Look at the bull on the cup. It's stretched, powerful, a scene of intense action. The classical figures on Monticelli's shield are indolent, posed, idealistic. Mycenaean art had an edge to it. The shield may have contained pastoral scenes, images of peaceful life, but there would have been a vibrancy to them, a dynamism, as if everything were tightly wound. In the world of the late

Bronze Age, violence may have been ritualized, channelled through the contest of heroes, but it was still violence, a visible part of day-to-day life. It was a world where men at leisure didn't lounge around in gymnasia or bathhouses as in the classical period, but went outdoors to hunt and play, to engage in bloody combat with boars and bulls and each other.'

'So what about images of real men?' Costas said. 'Are there any Bronze Age portraits? Heroes and kings?'

Jack nodded slowly. 'One stormy night in 1876 in the royal grave circle at Mycenae, Schliemann found this.' He tapped, and the image changed to one of the most fabulous archaeological discoveries of all time, a golden mask in the shape of an angular, bearded face, the eyes hooded, elusive. It was the ultimate image of kingly power, aloof, unknowable, but unmistakably human, not the idealized image of a god.

'The Mask of Agamemnon,' Costas murmured. 'When I was home in Greece as a boy, my grandfather took me to see it. It's virtually a national symbol. It's the pride of the National Archaeological Museum in Athens.'

Jack stared hard at the image, trying as he had done a thousand times before to see beyond those hooded lids, to reach into the soul of the man who lay behind the mask. 'According to the *Iliad*, the shield of Achilles was made during the siege of Troy, in the ninth year, close to the end. An expeditionary army in the field for so long would have had its own smiths and forges, its own armourers, probably at their base on the island of Tenedos. When Achilles needs new armour, he sends word back there. Forget about mythical Thetis and the forge on Olympus, but imagine some down-to-earth Hephaestos whose job is to keep the heroes supplied with all their finery, whose workshop does more than fix helmets and churn out spearheads. Our guy's an artist, used to creating pieces of armour for swagger and display. And look at that mask. Mycenaean artists could do portraits.'

'So you're suggesting that the images on the shield, the people, could be *real* people, actual portraits?'

'After nine years, everyone knew the faces. The images of generals are etched on the minds of soldiers. Think of Alexander the Great, King Henry V of England, Napoleon, General Ulysses S. Grant. We all know what they looked like. To the soldiers at Troy, the faces of their captains and heroes would have been as familiar as Hollywood actors are to us. These were not distant figures in some headquarters tent, but were there every day in front of the soldiers on the beach, shouting, feuding, drinking, whoring, sulking, just as Homer describes them. So yes, the people on the shield could be real people, real heroes. And a real image of a real king.'

'*A real king*,' Costas repeated, pointing at the image of the golden mask. 'And that one. Do you think that's really Agamemnon?'

Jack paused, then spoke quietly. 'I think he existed. I think we're on his trail, here and now. Agamemnon, what he did, is where the truth of the Trojan War lies.'

'And for Jack Howard, the fact that this shield would be one of the most priceless treasures ever discovered is neither here nor there?'

Jack grinned. 'It would make a pretty good centrepiece in a new archaeological museum at Troy, don't you think? Along with everything that Hiebermeyer and Dillen and Rebecca and Jeremy are discovering. Finding the shield would repay the Turks for giving us a permit to dig here.'

'And you think the shield's somewhere on the sea bed, in a wreck.'

'In the funeral games of Achilles, Homer has the armour going to the champion who won the contest for it, the outstanding hero. But by the final chapters of the war, all of the heroes were dead, and their treasure had reverted to Agamemnon. The age of heroes was over, the age that saw chivalric contests to claim the armour of a slain warrior. Agamemnon was no longer merely coalition leader, the first among many; he was now mighty ruler of them all, king of kings. Achilles' armour would have become part of his prestige display. All the treasures of the heroes would have been stashed away in his personal war galley. Remember Dillen's translation? *The ship, booty-laden, weighed down with gold.*'

'Holy cow,' Costas said quietly. 'Now I've got you.'

'Treasure. Big time.'

'Bring back the age of pirates,' Costas sighed, shaking his head. 'Treasure like that could set me up for life.'

'That's exactly why I want this kept under wraps,' Jack said. 'If word slipped out, every treasure-hunter in the world would be hovering around us, the good, the bad and the ugly.'

'The whereabouts of Schliemann's stolen treasure has attracted some pretty rough customers. The Nazis were after it.'

'What do you know about that?'

'Dillen told me. It was when Rebecca was involved with returning that painting in the Howard Gallery, the one Göring had pilfered. Dillen was at the IMU campus at the time and we got to talking. A great-uncle of mine was a Monuments Man, with the US army, responsible for recovering art stolen from Jewish families in Greece. Dillen mentioned a schoolteacher of his who had some connection with the search for the lost treasures from Troy.'

'That'd be Hugh Frazer,' Jack murmured. 'I knew Frazer had been in special forces during the war, but I didn't know anything about that. Intriguing. I'll have to plug Dillen on it.'

'It was something he had just remembered. Something this guy, Frazer, knew about some other guy, a British officer friend of his, who went missing. Something to do with one of the death camps.'

'It was a more hazardous job than you'd think. And there was a lethal subtext, that the places where treasures were hidden could also conceal other secrets, weapons ready for use to execute the so-called Nero Decree.'

'I know about that. Hitler's order to destroy the Reich.'

'And take the world with it, if at all possible.'

Costas checked his watch. 'So, the shield of Achilles. Mum's the word on your dream find?'

'Radio silence until we find out what's actually down there.'

Costas nodded. 'Okay. For now, soggy timbers it is. But between you and me?'

'What?'

'This really is a treasure hunt, isn't it? I mean, you owe me. It's why you convinced me to get into this game in the first place. You promised, fifteen years ago at Troy.'

'I thought that was submersibles. Getting your own shed full of gadgets.'

'Means to an end. It was seeing those pictures just now, the shield, the golden mask. I think I've finally got the fever.'

Jack sighed. 'Okay. Just to keep my old dive buddy happy. Treasure it is.'

'Right on.'

'I want to give Dillen and Hiebermeyer a call. See how they're getting on. I'm due to be choppered over there after the dive. And see Rebecca.'

'Tell her Uncle Costas expects her to be able to strip a dive regulator the next time we meet.'

'Uncle Costas,' Jack muttered. '*Uncle* Costas.' He put his hand on his friend's shoulder. 'Speaking of regulators, time you went below to prep our gear.'

Costas broke into a huge smile. 'Now you're talking.' He got up, collected his things and walked towards the door, rolling from side to side. Jack stood up to follow, glanced at the image of the shield of Achilles on the screen, then clicked it off and picked up the laptop. He remembered waking up on the deck little more than an hour ago, those images from his dream still fresh in his mind, the light shining dazzlingly through the depths, the greatest treasure always just beyond his grasp. He remembered the other treasure Dillen had dreamed of finding, the most sacred artefact of Troy, the palladion. Had Agamemnon, the king behind the golden mask, the bearer of the shield of Achilles, once held that aloft too, borne it away from burning Troy to his mountain fastness at Mycenae, snatched a prize won at the cost of darkness and death, of civilization torn asunder? *Had that prize been what Schliemann had sought?* He watched Costas disappear down the stairs towards the equipment bay, then took a deep breath. His heart was suddenly pounding with excitement, the huge adrenalin rush he always felt before diving on a new site, the possibility of making a discovery that might change history. And this time it was not a dream. *This time it was real.*

7

Jack floated motionless ten metres below the surface of the Aegean Sea, just outside the huge shadow created by the hull of *Seaquest II*. He and Costas had exited from the ship's internal docking bay, so had avoided struggling in the choppy afternoon swell that Jack could see above him pulsing in the direction of the shoreline to the east, towards Troy. He looked up at the hull, and saw the wavering faces of the support team peering down through the calm water inside the docking bay. He raised his arm to Costas and held his thumb and forefinger together in the 'okay' sign, then watched Costas repeat the signal. He glanced again at Costas' gear. They were wearing e-suits, Kevlar-reinforced dry suits with a computerized temperature and buoyancy control system, and full-face helmets that incorporated an intercom. They had toyed with using the Aquapods, the one-man submersibles that were Costas' pride and joy, but had opted instead for SCUBA with oxygen rebreathers mounted on their backs in streamlined yellow cases. The rebreathers would give them twenty minutes at ninety metres' depth, ample time for the job in hand, and diving would allow them close-up exploration impossible from the Aquapods. Jack disliked the constraints of a submersible and was always more happy diving. He felt supremely relaxed, perfectly in his element, but coursing with excitement at the prospect of what they might find in the inky depths below.

He finned over to Costas and gave his equipment a closer check, reading the tank pressure. Costas had grumbled at the decision not to use Aquapods, but then had brought out his tattered old boiler suit and was as happy as a child with a toy box. The suit was barely recognizable after years of use, a torn and faded grey layer that Costas wore over his e-suit, but the multiple pockets contained his precious collection of tools and gadgets ready for any eventuality. Jack glanced at his dive computer, and then up at the line on the surface that extended from the ship to a buoy, nearly above him now. It marked the spot where they had to descend to avoid the current from the Dardanelles sweeping them beyond the wreck. He made the 'okay' sign to Costas, then extended his arm with his thumb down. 'Good to go?'

'Good to go. Twenty minutes no-stop time, starting now.'

Costas flipped upside down and barrelled into the depths. Jack expelled air from his suit and dropped behind him, spreadeagled like a sky-diver. The water was sparklingly clear for the first thirty metres or so, but on the landward side it had a haze to it, red-tinged, an algae bloom perhaps, as if the Trojan shore were still seeping blood. Somewhere below them lay the ugly residue of conflict, the raw, unsanitized legacy of the sea bed, a legacy that always brought home more vividly to Jack the reality of war than immaculate cemeteries and carefully tended battlefields.

He remembered what they had seen in the operations room when *Seaquest II* had first pulled the sidescan sonar 'fish' over the site an hour before. The wind had been less severe than anticipated and Captain Macalister had decided there was time for a sonar sweep before the dive. As the fish moved beyond the Byzantine wreck, the screen had shown a featureless sea bed, the sand ruffled like waves where the current had swept over it. Then the room had erupted in excitement as they saw the unmistakable lines of another shipwreck, exactly where Jack had thought he had seen something during their earlier dive. The scour channels in the sand on either side of the new wreck accentuated the lines of the hull: thirty-five, maybe forty metres long, narrow of beam – perhaps seven metres wide – with parallel lines running athwartships that looked like frames. There were none of the telltale signs of an ancient wreck, the rows of amphoras and stone blocks they had seen on the Byzantine wreck, a much wider-beamed hull as befitted an ancient merchantman. But Jack had seen a shadowy globular shape in the centre of the hull and had become excited. Could it have been an ancient *pithos*, a huge pottery vat? The citadel of Troy was littered with fragments of *pithoi*; they were what Jack had always imagined ancient galleys must have held, to carry the large quantities of water needed for a crew of rowers. Could this be an ancient galley? Could it be a galley of the Bronze Age, the ship of the Trojan War mentioned in the poem? *Could it be the ship of Agamemnon?*

Jack had hoped against hope, but despite the initial euphoria, his final instinct was against it. He had stared at the image for fifteen minutes while the ship turned round for a high-resolution scan. The first lines of the more detailed sonar image clinched it. They showed the decayed remains of a metal vessel, a hundred years old, no more. The lines athwartships that had looked like wooden beams were the skeletal remains of a metal hull, left after the wooden deck planking had decayed. The globular form was still partly concealed, covered by a collapsed mass of metalwork, but seemed to be in the right position for a boiler, part of the engine machinery.

Jack had realized why his instinct told against it. The scour channels had clearly formed as the vessel had settled into the sea bed. This was not a wreck that had been buried, and then revealed by some shift in the current. An ancient wooden hull would never have survived as this wreck had, exposed to the current. The only remains of an ancient wreck might have been the lower part of a hull driven into the sea bed, and that would have been buried and invisible to the sonar. It was what worried Jack most about the search for a Trojan War wreck. The pottery and stone of the Byzantine wreck were visible because they were durable, materials that would survive exposed on the sea bed. But there was no certainty that any materials like that would have existed on board an ancient galley; pottery *pithoi* were just Jack's conjecture. Nobody had ever found an intact war galley from the Bronze Age before.

And he had another fear: that the sediment might prove too mobile, too aerated, for the survival of even buried timbers.

Lanowski's appraisal of the sedimentology showed how easily wrecks could be buried, but also suggested a lot of instability and sediment movement. The undisturbed anaerobic layers might prove too deeply buried and too ancient for any chance of a Bronze Age discovery. Now that they knew the wreck below them was of limited interest, those scour channels were the main objective of the dive. They gave a chance to examine an exposed section of sediment to a depth of two metres or more into the sea bed. What they found could be the linchpin of the expedition. If it was grey anaerobic sediment, there was a chance that somewhere they might yet find a Bronze Age wreck. If not, then the cold logic of science told against it, seemed to stack the odds a mile high.

The cold logic of science. Jack thought about that as he descended, scanning the deep azure below for the first signs of the sea bed. The cold logic of science had counted against so many of the greatest discoveries in archaeology. It had counted against Howard Carter discovering the tomb of Tutankhamun. It had counted against Heinrich Schliemann discovering Troy and then the Mycenae of Agamemnon. Schliemann had been driven by a dream, and by powerful instinct. It was what drove Jack too. There was something about this site. Something he had felt the day before when he had looked across the sea bed and seen that shape. In truth, he was not undertaking this dive to collect sediment. Any one of the team could have done that. He was diving because of what he had felt the day before, when he stared out from the edge of the Byzantine wreck and saw something in the gloom. The sonar scan had shown what it was, the rusting hull somewhere beneath him now, a hull that could not conceivably be ancient. Yet there was something more, something that seemed to defy that cold logic of science. It might be no more than a ghostly presence, an imprint. But he had to go there, to see it for himself, to know whether his instinct had just been a fantasy, a yearning to see a truth that seemed forever beyond their grasp, like so much else about the Trojan War.

Costas' voice crackled on the intercom. 'Depth forty metres. Cross-check. Over.'

Jack looked at the LED screen inside his helmet, then down at Costas descending about ten metres below him. 'Cross-checked. Over.'

'So what do you think? A First World War minesweeper?' Costas asked.

Jack touched the audio control on the side of his helmet to compensate for the high pitch in Costas' voice, caused by the increased helium now streaming into their breathing mixture as they descended beyond safe air-diving depth. 'That's Scott Macalister's best guess. The state of metal decay in this environment suggests we're looking at a wreck maybe ninety, a hundred years old. That puts it bang on time for the 1915 Gallipoli campaign, the biggest single cause of shipwrecks in the Dardanelles in recent times.'

'Macalister's got a database, hasn't he? I told you I saw his Admiralty wreck chart.'

'He's plotted all known wrecks from the campaign. But he says the records are sketchy for smaller vessels, especially from the Turkish side. There were gunboats, torpedo boats, balloon ships used for gunnery spotting, lighters, mini submarines, some of them used in covert missions to land men for sabotage. For all these vessels the approaches to the Dardanelles were suicide alley, running the gauntlet big-time. The Turks had no aircraft and the British only used theirs for reconnaissance, but there were big guns on either side, British battleships off the island of Tenedos, Turkish shore batteries on the mainland. The Turks had batteries at Beşik Bay, the harbour of ancient Troy. They would have had the range of this spot where we are now.'

'And there must have been mines.'

'Mostly within the Dardanelles, where the Turkish mine-layers could operate more safely, but some daring captain may have tried to lay mines this far out. The minelayer captains were heroes to the Turks, like U-boat commanders or fighter aces. Always pushing the boundary. That's why Macalister thinks we may have a minelayer, or more probably a mine-sweeper. The British used converted trawlers as minesweepers, about this size. The civilian crews made the transition from trawling to sweeping easily enough, but the fishing boats had draughts that were deeper than was ideal for minesweeping, and there were plenty of accidents when they hit mines anchored just below the surface.'

'Seventy metres. We're nearly there.' The water around them was now a dark indigo, becoming almost black below. Jack rolled over and looked up. He could just make out the hull of *Seaquest II*, but no longer the sparkle of sunlight on the surface. He rolled back, and suddenly could see the mottled sand of the sea bed some fifteen metres below. He switched on his headlamp, startling a school of bream that darted off out of sight ahead of him. 'That's a good sign,' he said. 'A school like that over a featureless sea bed usually means a reef or a wreck nearby.'

'Bingo,' Costas said. They were now less than ten metres above the sea bed, and Jack could see the ripples in the sand. He angled his beam up slightly, and there it was, a mass of decaying metal rising five or six metres above the sea bed, sitting in a deep scour channel that extended out of sight ahead of them. As their headlamps converged on the wreck, the dark blue transformed into vivid reds and yellows, a mass of encrusted anemones and other sea life that clung to the corroding metal; some of the rust lay exposed where the structure had recently collapsed. Jack was always amazed at the speed of decay of metal-hulled ships underwater; most of them would vanish long before the wooden hulls of antiquity that were preserved in anoxic sediments below the sea bed.

He paused to orientate. It was one thing seeing an entire wreck in one image on the sonar screen in the operations room, another trying to make sense of it underwater, from a different angle and in confusing light conditions. The view ahead was a tangle of structure and marine life, but he could see that they had come down behind the stern of the vessel; they were looking forward to where the deckhouse had collapsed, leaving only a few girders intact. The ship had evidently sunk upright but then heeled over to port, with the deepest scour channel running along the starboard side just ahead of Jack, where it angled into the current. As he panned his beam over the stern, he could see that the damage was more than just natural decay. 'That's a hell of a hole,' he murmured. Costas followed the direction of his beam and swam forward, peering under the jagged metal of the deck, pointing up at the parallel struts running athwartships that they had seen on the sonar image. 'Looks like her entire stern was blown off,' he said. 'That's consistent with a mine-sweeper, snagging a mine and accidentally detonating it. On a vessel of this size, the shockwave from two or three hundred pounds of high explosive would probably have killed everyone on board instantly.'

Jack panned his beam to the right, along the exposed starboard side of the hull. The deepest part of the scour channel was in shadow, under the corroded remains of the keel. 'I think I've found what we're looking for. I'm dropping down into that scour channel to collect sediment.' He glanced at the LED readout inside his helmet. 'We've got twelve minutes, otherwise we spend the afternoon in the recompression chamber. Not my favourite place.'

'Roger that. I'm going to take a quick recce inside the hull.'

'Be careful. God knows how stable this is. Some of those girders are probably completely corroded, only held together by marine accretion. And remember, this has to count as a war grave. Go easy.'

'Roger that. Eleven minutes.'

Jack swam up and over the surviving framework of the stern deck towards the scour channel, trying to decipher the jumble of structural elements that had fallen from the deckhouse and starboard railing. The vivid reds and yellows of marine life added further confusion, and he switched off his headlamp, reducing everything to a uniform dark blue. He was conscious of Costas swimming under the deck frames below him, towards the hull amidships where the remains of the engine room should lie. The beam from Costas' headlamp flashed through jagged holes and fissures where the metalwork had corroded away. Jack sank down until he was inches above a thick metal girder that ran longitudinally along the deck for at least ten metres, from somewhere in the gloom below the deckhouse to a point behind him where it had been buckled upwards by the force of the explosion that had destroyed the stern. The girder was well-preserved, clearly a high-grade steel. He stopped, and stared. It seemed oddly out of place. It was a flat-bottomed rail from a train track, evidently used to support something on the deck. He reached out to it. Even a slight touch released a cloud of red oxide, and he withdrew his hand. *He had seen this before*.

He remembered where. Two days earlier, Macalister had taken him on a tour of the 1915 Gallipoli battlefields, and they had finished in Çanakkale at the Turkish naval museum. The highlight was a replica of the celebrated Turkish minelayer *Nusret*, which had laid the mines that sank three Allied battleships in the Dardanelles. That was where he had seen it. *Two reused train rails, laid parallel on the stern deck*. He finned two metres to the left, peering through the red oxide haze he had stirred up in the water, and then carefully felt the mass of rusted metal. Bingo. It was another rail, exactly the right distance apart. He pushed back, and then finned above the plume of rust where he had touched the metal. He looked along the line of the two rails, towards the collapsed mass of the deckhouse, and saw a dark form, oval-shaped, directly above the place where Costas' headlamp beam was flickering. He stared at it, swimming closer. Then he froze. That shape, the shape on the sonar readout he had thought might be an ancient *pithos*, was not a boiler. *It was something else*.

'Costas.'

'Jack.'

'You need to get out of there.'

'Just a few moments longer.'

'Costas, listen to me. This isn't a minesweeper. I've just found the rails on the deck. It's a *minelayer*. And there's a mine still in the rack. That shape from the sonar I got all excited about. Directly above you.'

'Relax.'

'What do you mean, *relax*?'

'I mean, I know. German Mark VI contact mine. Never seen one of those before. Underwater *and* live, that is. Macalister told me most of the mines laid by the Turks were supplied by the Germans, so that makes sense. Big question is, which type of detonator? I wish I could see it more clearly. So much stuff in the way.'

There was a dull clang, then another. Jack's heart sank. 'Costas, I hope to God you're not doing what I think you're doing.'

'We're in luck.' Costas' voice sounded slightly strangulated. 'I'm upside down, but I've got my face right against one of the horns. You know, the protuberances that stick out of a contact mine?'

'I know what they are,' Jack said weakly. 'That's why they call it a contact mine. You hit the horn, and the mine blows up. Exactly how close are you?'

'Oh, about four, six inches.' There was another clang, and Jack's heart seemed to stop. Costas made a straining noise, then spoke again. 'Phew. You can really relax now.'

'Relax?'

'Yeah. Relax. Kind of. I've worked out which type. The early horn contained a glass phial filled with hydrogen peroxide, surrounded by potassium perchlorate and sugar. When the phial was broken, the acid ignited the sugar and the mine exploded. The advanced type leaked the acid into a lead-acid battery, energizing the battery and detonating the mine. I'm pretty sure that's what we've got here. Lucky, because there's not much you can do with the early type. But with the later type, if you can locate the position of the battery inside the mine, you can drill a hole through from the outside and flood it, neutralizing it.'

'Or you can miss it and drill into high explosive. Good idea.'

A voice crackled through on the intercom. 'This is Macalister. I've just dropped in on your little chat. Kazantzakis, get out of there. I'm pulling *Seaquest II* off position immediately. I repeat, get out of there. Do *not* touch that mine.'

The sea filled with the churning sound of the ship's twin screws. Jack injected a small blast of air into his buoyancy compensator and rose a few metres above the wreck, until he could clearly see the jagged hole in the stern and the tangle of collapsed central superstructure where the deck housing and funnel had been.

'Problem,' Costas said.

Jack's heart sank again. 'What now?'

'I've just off-gassed.'

'Christ.' Jack shut his eyes. A rush of exhaust bubble through corroded metal. That was the last thing they needed. Their rebreathers were semi-closed-circuit, meaning that every few minutes they automatically expelled accumulated carbon dioxide. An override allowed the waste gas to accumulate to a higher pressure before being expelled, but that had not been activated; the dive plan had not involved defusing a mine. Jack kept his headlamp trained on the superstructure, and watched the first bubbles percolate upwards. There was a sudden explosion of bubbles, wreathing the corroded metal. *The worst was happening.* The silvery shimmer gave way to red, as the bubbles blew through the corroded metal and released a cloud of rust. He braced himself. There was a lurch, and he watched in horror as the mine sank slightly into the metal that had been cradling it. He counted the seconds. How long before that battery energized? Five seconds? Ten? Any longer and the contact, the enemy vessel, might have moved off. That was how it was supposed to be. In 1915. When there was a war on. Not now. He shut his eyes. *Twenty seconds. Twenty-five. Thirty.*

The intercom crackled. 'Make that one inch away,' Costas said. 'Nearly knocked my helmet off.'

'For God's sake get out of there,' Jack said hoarsely.

'We're in luck, again,' Costas replied. 'The mine's come to rest on two steel girders. It's wedged hard into the metal. I can see the shiny surface below the corrosion. It's not going anywhere. And none of the horns made contact. We're safe.'

'*Safe,*' Jack exclaimed. 'Right.'

The ship-to-diver feed crackled again. 'Macalister here. It sounds as if the buoyancy chambers in the mine are flooded. We'll need to attach lifting bags and float it off, then remotely detonate it. I say again, *detonate* it, Kazantzakis. That's a job for the Turkish navy underwater demolition team. They've done it often enough in the Dardanelles. And it's just the kind of liaison we want. Might help to extend our permit. Not, I repeat, *not* a job for us. Do you read that loud and clear? Copy.'

'Copy that,' Jack said. 'You hear, Costas? Not defuse. *Detonate*.'

'Copy that.' Jack saw movement, and Costas' fins appeared through the ragged hole in the stern of the wreck, followed by his body. He came upright beside Jack, his boiler suit barely recognizable beneath the grime and rust. 'Never defused a First World War German mine before. I was looking forward to putting one of those horns on my mantelpiece, beside my other relics.'

'You wouldn't have done it, would you?'

Costas reached into the thigh pocket of his suit, and pulled out a rubber-encased gadget the size of a Dremel tool. He tossed it upwards and it circled in slow motion in the water, coming back to his hand with a long titanium drill bit extended from the front. 'Multiple function. Six different bit sizes.'

'But then you would have thought of how nice it is to be alive. About how much I might want to stay alive. About Rebecca.'

Costas spun the tool again, retracted the bit and shoved it back in his boiler suit pocket. 'Copy that.' He tapped the side of his visor. 'Six minutes to go. You got that sediment sample?'

'Just going for it. Now that your little diversion is finished.'

'Fun's over.' Costas rose a few metres, and hovered above Jack. 'I'm watching your six. Nothing else.'

'Roger that.'

Jack dropped below the starboard side of the hull. The sand was coarse-grained, the type Lanowski said had been swept down by the currents from the Dardanelles, perhaps even from the river Scamander and the plain of Troy itself. He aimed his headlamp at the base of the scour channel. A wooden beam was sticking out from under the metal hull. Jack suddenly forgot the mine. This was not right. *He was looking at timber*. It was blackened with pitch, forming a solid glossy surface where it had oozed out. He lay on his front in the sand, his visor inches from the wood. It showed minimal erosion, only a few pockmarks from wormholes near the top. It had clearly been buried until recently, until the scour channel had revealed it. He looked at the edge of the channel, at the surrounding sea bed. The top of the timber was at the same level. Whatever had protruded above that level must have eroded away, but there was a chance that more was buried, undisturbed. Buried some time before the minelayer had sunk. He stared at the timber. Buried a *long* time before. Jack realized he was already working on a fantastic assumption. *He had found another wreck. A much older wreck.*

He remembered the charred fragments of Bronze Age timbers he and Costas had discovered on the beach near Troy fifteen years before, a small section of planking with pieces of three frames still attached. He remembered the distance between the frames, about twenty centimetres. He put his left hand against the timber where it protruded from the sea floor, and put his right hand about that distance away. Where it touched the sediment he wafted, and seconds later the blackened end of another timber appeared. His pulse quickened. *Two frames, the same distance apart as those he and Costas had found*. He wafted between the frames, using both hands, kicking up a small storm of sediment that took a few moments to settle. He pushed his face into the suspended silt. Bingo. *Not just frames, but planking*. He reached over the upper edge of the nearest plank, then felt the join with the next plank. He moved his fingers along until he felt two bumps, one on each plank, an equal distance apart from the join. There was no doubt about it. They were treenails, hardwood tenons hammered through each plank. His heart was pounding with excitement. He had to control his breathing. *He had found an ancient hull.* The planks were edge-joined with mortise and tenon, a technique used by shipwrights from the Bronze Age. But how could he be sure these timbers were that old? *Could he even think that they dated to the time of the Trojan War?*

He looked up, and saw Costas ten metres or so above him, silhouetted against the smudge of light from the surface of the sea far above. He glanced at his computer. Only three minutes left. He rose a metre or so, and looked down again. His wafting had revealed something resting on the planking where the timbers protruded from under the rusting hull of the warship. He dropped down and wafted again, strong, quick strokes. This was no time for finesse. What he discovered in these moments could determine the future course of the excavation. He stopped to let the sediment clear, and there it was, intact, lying half embedded in the sea bed in front of him.

His heart pounded. It was unbelievable. It was an ancient pottery cup, beautifully preserved, a *kylix*, a distinctive Greek form, raised on a stem with a broad, wide bowl that tapered down, like a large champagne glass but with small vertical handles on either side of the bowl. Jack stared at it, his mind racing back to Troy, to the finds he had seen in the Çanakkale archaeological museum that day with Macalister. *This was Mycenaean.* The shape, the details of the stem and the handles were absolutely distinctive. The part of the bowl he could see exposed above the sand was decorated with a marine pattern, a beautifully painted octopus that wrapped round the cup, the red paint still radiant. He knew the Mycenaean *kylix* dated to the late Bronze Age, between the fifteenth and the twelfth century BC. The style of decoration tightened the date even further, to the thirteenth, perhaps early twelfth century BC. He hardly dared believe it. *The time of the Trojan War.*

He needed to think fast. Mycenaean pottery had been found at Troy, but it was rare, probably highly prized. This cup could have been cargo, brought by a trader some time in the lead-up to the war, when Troy was a hub of commerce. But that must be wrong. These timbers were not those of a merchantman, but a galley. *A war galley.* The cup must have been the possession of someone on board. A crew member seemed unlikely, even the captain. They would have used bowls, ladles, to dip into the water vats, drinking their wine crudely, as sailors did. A cup like this would have been far too delicate for shipboard use. So it must have been a passenger. A Mycenaean noble, taking a galley to Troy? The *Iliad* showed that nobles, princes bent on war, took their prized possessions with them, the accoutrements for lavish feasting and wealth display. *Princes bent on war.* Jack knew where his thoughts were leading him, but he hardly dared go there. He wafted his hand over the bowl to reveal the rim, to see whether he could raise it in one piece. He waited for the sediment to settle.

Then he saw it.

First one letter, then another. A word, painted below the rim of the cup. A word in ancient Greek. He stared, transfixed, at the letter A toppled over on its side, the early Phoenician form of the letter, just as Dillen had shown him in the *Ilioupersis*. He could barely believe it. *Letters in ancient Greek, on a Mycenaean cup from the thirteenth century* BC. This proved it, beyond a shadow of a doubt. This showed that the Greeks of the late Bronze Age, of the age of heroes, had started to use the alphabet several centuries before anyone had previously thought, just as Dillen had argued. Jack's mind was reeling. Dillen had been right about the *Ilioupersis*. It could have been written by a bard who actually witnessed the events of Troy. Jack was suddenly bursting to tell him. But there was more. As he deciphered the word, he gasped into his mouthpiece in astonishment. His mind raced back to all those hours spent with Dillen as a student. The Linear B syllabary – the script used by the Mycenaeans, the *other* script – had several words for leader, for king. One, *basileus*, the term used by Greeks of the classical period, was rarely encountered. Another, *lawagetas*, the most common term, meant chieftain, prince of one citadel, one city-state. In Homer's *Iliad*, the men who led the contingent from their home territory, men like Achilles, Ajax, Nestor, would have been called that. But there was another word, a rarer one, the one staring Jack in the face now: *wanax*. That meant the ruler of many city-states, a paramount ruler, one elected in times of peril. The *wanax* was the biggest of them all, bigger than the greatest hero, a man whose power might rival that of the gods. *A mighty wielder of the sceptre. A king of kings.*

Jack reached down with his left hand and gently pushed his fingers into the sand around the stem of the cup, touching the pottery for the first time, feeling that wave of excitement that always coursed through him when he touched an artefact undisturbed by human hands for millennia. He remembered the sanctity of this place, the probability that the site was a war grave. *A grave from two wars*. But this cup deserved to be raised into the sunlight once again, to complete the voyage that was thwarted by catastrophe over three thousand years before, to be held aloft over the walls of Troy just as the great king would have done. Jack wanted to take it to where Dillen was excavating, to the highest bastion of the citadel overlooking the Plain of Ilion, so that they could share in the triumph of archaeology, revel in a find that not only gave Dillen proof that the Greek of the *Ilioupersis* was the Greek of Agamemnon, but also put them one huge step closer to the reality of the great king and his war to end all wars.

'Jack.' Costas' voice crackled on the intercom. 'Zero hour. Time to go home. Now.'

'Roger that.' Jack eased the ancient cup out of the sand and held it up, watching the sediment fall away in a silvery shower. It was intact, one of the most beautiful finds he had ever made. He blasted air into his buoyancy compensator and rose slowly above the sea bed, wreathed in a sheen of bubbles. His e-suit automatically bled air as the external pressure decreased, the computerized sensor maintaining his buoyancy just above neutral. He knew that the same was happening to the gas bubbles in his bloodstream, and he glanced at his wrist computer to double-check his ascent rate. He looked up at Costas, then back down at the wreck. The beam from his headlamp reflected off the particles stirred up where he had left the sea bed, and he switched it off, closing his eyes to help them adjust to the gloom. When he opened them a few moments later, he saw the clear outline of the minelayer, but now he imagined another wreck, the ancient ship underneath, twenty, maybe twenty-five metres in length, lying diagonally below the minelayer's hull, its stern protruding through the smaller scour trench along the port side of the minelayer, its fore a few metres beyond where he had found the cup.

He stared at where he had been, straining his eyes. *There was something else down there*. Something was visible ahead of the spot where he had seen the planking, where he imagined the timbers tapering towards the galley's bow. It would have been out of his line of vision from the scour trench, and on the sonar readout it would have looked like some broken-off structure from the minelayer. He pressed the buoyancy button on his suit to override the computer and manually expel air, and stopped dead in the water, staring downwards. There was no doubt about it. It was on exactly the right alignment, in exactly the right place, rising from the sand just beyond the outside edge of the scour trench. *The prow of the ancient ship*. It was a curved timber, but there was more shape to it than that. Was he seeing things? He was more than twenty metres above the sea bed now, and everything was receding. Suddenly he had a flashback to the famous stone gate of Mycenae, Agamemnon's capital. Two lions, paws raised, facing a column. He stared again. Was that the shape? Was it the shape of a lion? A lion-prowed ship of Agamemnon? Or was his mind imprinting desire on to reality, playing the trick that had led so many before him up a blind alley in their search for the Trojan War?

'Jack. You're still at seventy metres. We'll need to do a safety stop at thirty.'

Jack shut his eyes tightly, then opened them and reactivated the ascent program. 'Roger that. Just taking one last look.'

'*Seaquest II*'s standing off, but Macalister's sending a Zodiac. I can hear the outboard engines. I'm popping a buoy.'

'Roger that.' Jack watched the sea bed recede into dark blue, the jagged mass of the shipwreck disappearing into the gloom. He looked up, holding the cup now in both hands as a king might once have done, a great king toasting his heroes, Achilles and Ajax and Patroclus and the others. The shape of the cup was framed by a halo of light on the surface of the sea, just as Jack imagined it once being backlit by the sunshine of a brooding sky, etched in the eye of a king who was to lead a thousand ships to Troy. *Could it really be?* He felt a tremble go through him, and the cup suddenly seemed impossibly delicate, a phantasm from history, like a floating leaf that would disintegrate on touch. He remembered his dream, on the deck of *Seaquest II* that morning. Then, it had been a sword. But that was just a dream. Now he was no longer the archaeologist, but holding the cup as Agamemnon might have done. *This was real.* He saw Costas a few metres above him, staring, and pressed his intercom. 'You're not going to believe what I've found.'

'Jack goes silent at the end of the first dive on a new wreck, and disappears into a hole in the sea bed? I guessed something was up. I can see what you've got. Looks pretty incredible.'

'What if I told you we're on the trail of the greatest treasure ever found underwater?'

'You found gold?'

Jack came level with Costas and held the cup in front of him. 'Not gold. Something more precious. A word. A word in an ancient language. *One word*. One word that opens the door on the reality of the Trojan War. On the reality of the wreck below us. Not one wreck, but two.'

'The ship of Agamemnon? The wreck in Dillen's text?'

Jack's heart pounded with excitement. *The lion-prowed ship of Agamemnon.* 'I saw timbers, Costas. Not just shapes in the darkness. Real timbers. I touched them. And this cup is Mycenaean.'

'So we're going back down there? To defuse mines? I mean, to hunt for the *greatest* treasure? For the Shield of Achilles?'

'You bet.'

Costas punched the water. '*Yes.*'

8

'What the hell is *that*?'

Jeremy Haverstock stood in the middle of the ancient passageway leading beneath Troy, staring in wide-eyed astonishment at the crumbling wall of rubble and earth he had been excavating. He could barely believe it. Hiebermeyer had led him and Rebecca straight from Dillen's excavation to this passageway – a deep trench open to the sky – and set them to work. He had been at Troy less than three hours, and now *this*. He was literally reeling. The trowel slipped from his hand and hit the ground, but he remained standing, swaying slightly, staring. Rebecca stopped brushing and stood up beside him, then gasped. The shadows created by the late-afternoon sun made strange illusions of shapes along the walls, but there was no doubt about this one. Jeremy reached out and put the flat of his hand on it. 'Incredible,' he whispered. 'That shape. It looks Egyptian.'

'It's fantastic,' Rebecca murmured, putting her hand out but not quite touching it. She shivered, in spite of the heat. 'A little spooky.'

A bobbing light from a headlamp appeared and Dillen came up from the unexcavated end of the passageway, some ten metres ahead of them, where the sloping walls narrowed as it led into the side of the ancient mound of the citadel.

'Where's Maurice?' Jeremy said hoarsely, still staring at the wall.

'Having his Schliemann moment,' Dillen replied, oblivious to their discovery, stopping to glance at a pair of crows flying overhead. 'Digging all by himself at the end of the passageway. Jack went straight from the helicopter to find him. Did you see when he passed you, Jack's got his trusty old khaki bag with him, and it's got a big bulge in it? He says he's got something incredible to show me. All he said is that an hour ago it was on the sea bed. He says it has to be the right place, the right time. I told him two can play at that game. I've got something to show *him*. We've got a rendezvous at my excavation up on the walls after supper. Showdown time.'

'Maurice needs to come and see this. And Jack. Like right now.'

'See what?'

'Be careful, James,' Rebecca said. 'You're being watched.'

Dillen gave her a startled glance. 'What do you mean?'

'In front of Jeremy.'

Dillen followed their gaze towards the wall of rubble, perplexed. He stood back, then caught his breath. 'Good Lord.'

A huge sculpted eye was staring out at them. It was almond-shaped, like the eye of an eagle. Jeremy snapped out of his trance and reached up to pull away a lump of compacted earth beside the eye, and suddenly the entire remaining conglomerate fell away, revealing a massive stone face. They stared in astonishment. The face was about two metres high and a metre across, and was topped by a conical helmet, cracked and broken off at the top. 'This has got to be the image of a king,' Jeremy exclaimed.

'Which one?' Rebecca said with bated breath.

'Not a Greek one,' Dillen murmured, staring. 'This is an eastern king, with that conical helmet, those eyes. The Mycenaean Greek kings, kings like Agamemnon, were mortals, first among men. We don't even have any statues of them. But this one is different. He's a god-king, larger than life, in the eastern fashion.' He stared more closely. 'All-powerful, perhaps once a warrior, but this is the image of a benign king, I'd say. Not someone who flayed his enemies alive. Someone who was confident in peace, at least when this statue was made.'

'What about Agamemnon's adversary?' Jeremy exclaimed. 'Priam, King of Troy?'

Dillen's voice was tense with excitement. 'It's possible. *Just possible*. Priam is one of the few characters in the *Iliad* who might be known from other contemporary records. The clay tablets of the Hittites – the powerful empire to the east of Troy – mention a Piyamaradu operating in this area. That name could easily be rendered as Priam. The Hittites saw Piyamaradu as a renegade, establishing his own independent kingdom, aligning himself more with the Ahhiyawa, the Achaeans, the Hittite term for the Mycenaeans. To me, this all fits very convincingly. Homer's Priam is powerful, an old warrior, but he's a king of peace, not a king of war. He'd enjoyed good relations with the Mycenaeans before Agamemnon came along. He'd found a way of breaking away from the warlike tradition of the Hittites and becoming part of the great civilization of the Aegean; his sons had even become heroes, champions, in the Greek tradition. Somehow I can see all that in this face.' Dillen stared pensively at the statue. 'But we'd need an inscription to be sure. And some way of dating this sculpture with certainty to about the later thirteenth century BC.'

Rebecca gently brushed the huge stone nose, waited a moment for the dust to settle, and then peered closely. 'I can tell you one thing. In my lightning tour this morning, Maurice gave me a five-minute tutorial about building materials. Said it was the first thing you have to know about when you look at a new site. This isn't the local limestone, the stuff used in the city walls. Look at the surface. It's granite. I've seen that in the British Museum. All those statues of the pharaohs. That *has* to be Egyptian granite.'

Dillen peered closely. 'Good Lord. You're absolutely right. Egyptian red granite, *at Troy*.'

'So how on earth does *that* get here?' Jeremy asked.

'We know the Egyptians shipped obelisks and huge stone blocks down the Nile,' Dillen replied, thinking hard. 'So why not overseas too? The Egyptians traded with Troy. For a people who had built the pyramids, offloading a few blocks of granite at Beşik Bay and dragging them a couple of kilometres over the plain of Troy would not have been a big problem.'

'But this isn't the image of a pharaoh,' Jeremy said.

Dillen shook his head. 'No. It's Egyptian stone, and very probably an Egyptian sculptor. The Trojans didn't do this kind of thing. There was no tradition of monumental sculpture here. So they import the stone, and they import the sculptor too. The details, the style of those eyes, look Egyptian. But this is a local king. I'll stake my career on it. A king of Troy.'

'And I think we may just be one step closer to who he was,' Jeremy said, squatting down. 'Check this out. The sculpture's integral to the wall, not earlier or later. The limestone blocks of the wall have been shaped around it. And look at the cut of the blocks, the slope of the wall, those vertical offsets. It's what excited Maurice so much about this passageway. It's the same as your excavation on the citadel, James. It's all contemporaneous. Exactly the same construction techniques as the ramparts of Troy VII. If ever there was a Troy of the Trojan War, then this is it. And if there ever was a King Priam, then that's him. I just *know* it.'

'*Whoa*,' Rebecca said slowly. 'We need to tell Maurice about this. Big time.'

'James!' The shout came from down the passageway ahead, where the side walls were still largely concealed beneath earth and rubble. Rebecca and Jeremy glanced at each other, then followed Dillen back down the way he had come. Jack was squatting down panning a torch over the unexcavated face of rubble at the end of the passageway. He glanced up at Jeremy and Rebecca. 'You two finished for the day?'

Jeremy cleared his throat. 'You need to come and see what we've found. You and Maurice, together. Something sticking out of the wall.'

Jack shone his torch. 'You mean like that?'

Rebecca and Jeremy knelt beside him and peered ahead. Where the sides of the passageway disappeared into the unexcavated mound, there was a freshly exposed face of earth and rubble, shored up with timber planks put in place by the excavation team. Jack aimed his torch at the base of the rubble. They could see a hole about a metre high, dug back into the jagged edges of the rubble. In the centre, virtually filling the hole, was a large, shiny protrusion, as if a boulder were wedged in. Jack kept his torch resolutely aimed below it. 'You may not want to look too closely,' he said.

The boulder had legs with scuffed desert books sticking out of the bottom. The boulder was in fact a familiar pair of khaki shorts streaked brown and stretched taut, flying somewhere well below half-mast.

'Oh my God,' Rebecca said, grinning. 'I see what you mean.'

There was a rumbling noise from somewhere inside the tunnel, and then a pause. '*Scheisse,*' a distant voice exclaimed.

'What is he *doing*?' Rebecca demanded.

'He thinks we're only about five metres from the end of the passageway,' Jack replied. 'The ground-penetrating radar revealed a pocket of space against the left wall of the passageway, close to the end. It's deeply buried, but the compacted rubble may have prevented soil from filling the gaps. He's burrowed in to take a look.'

'That sounds safe,' Rebecca said, looking dubious.

'Maurice has had pyramids fall on him and has crawled out unscathed.' Jack cracked a smile, then aimed his beam at the top of the hole. 'There's a stone wedged above him that acts like a lintel. I told him to go no further than that.'

'You mean you told him to keep his butt in view?' Rebecca peered mischievously at Jack.

'Not exactly the words I used, but yes.'

There was a sound of intense digging and scrabbling, intermingled with grunts and curses. Hiebermeyer's rear end shifted several inches further into the hole, plugging it completely, accompanied by a discharge of dust that completely shrouded his legs. He suddenly went still. 'My God.' The words were muffled, but excited. '*Mein Gott.*'

Jack knelt down and peered in, waving away the dust. 'Maurice! What is it?'

'Unbelievable.' Hiebermeyer coughed violently, a rumble that sounded like a small earthquake. 'I can see the wall. Only a few square centimetres. But there's an inscription on it. I'm sure of it, Jack.' He coughed loudly. 'An inscription at Troy. *The first one ever.*'

The ground shook and there was a violent discharge of dust from the hole. Hiebermeyer's body dropped down, apparently flattened. Jack gestured quickly to Jeremy. 'I knew this would happen. *I knew it.* Quick. Take the other leg.' He passed the torch to Rebecca and grabbed Hiebermeyer's left leg, pulling hard. 'Maurice! Are you all right?' he shouted. 'Can you hear me?'

A sound of coughing and cursing came from the hole. 'I'm fine. Let me have another go. I was nearly there.'

'Not a chance.' They heaved, and Jack grimaced. 'Now, where have I done this before? At Stonehenge, on a school trip. Maurice got stuck head-first down a hole, just like this. He thought he'd seen an Egyptian mummified cat. Actually it was a very old dead rabbit. Everything,' Jack heaved again, panting, '*everything* was Egyptian with Maurice.' They heaved one last time and Hiebermeyer's head appeared, covered in dust. They dragged him clear, and he rolled over and coughed hard, then got up on his knees, shaking and patting himself. He took off his glasses and peered at Jack, his eyes burning with fervour. 'In there.' He coughed again, pointing. '*In there.*'

'What?'

'A carved stone inscription. I only saw a few centimetres of it, but I'm absolutely sure of it. *Sure of it.*'

'You've already said,' Jack replied. 'Sure of it. An inscription.' He stared at Hiebermeyer. 'What do you mean? Sure of what?'

'Hieroglyphics. *Hieroglyphics*, Jack. An *ankh* symbol. *Egyptian.*'

'No way,' Rebecca exclaimed. '*Egyptian*. You should hear what we found.'

Jack put his hand up, staring at Hiebermeyer. 'In a moment.' Hiebermeyer staggered to his feet, patted the dust off his shorts and hitched them up, then gave Jack a triumphant look. He coughed violently again, and the stone over the hole he had been in suddenly collapsed. He turned and looked at it, swore under his breath, then raised his hands as if appealing to the gods. He let them fall again. 'This is going to take days to excavate. *Days.* We've only got a week until the end of the permit.'

Jack patted him on the back, releasing another cloud of dust. 'You'd better get cracking, then.' He paused. '*Hieroglyphs?* You sure? This isn't, you know, another mummified rabbit?'

Hiebermeyer glared at him, his nostrils flared. Jack put up a hand. 'Okay. *Okay.*' He stared back at the rubble. His mind was racing. Hieroglyphics? Maurice had given him a quick rundown of the excavation after he and Costas had arrived by helicopter half an hour before, straight from a mercifully brief stint in the recompression chamber after their dive. Jack had been astonished to see the walls of the passageway now revealed for some fifteen metres of their length, increasing in height as the passageway cut into the centre of the citadel mound. The walls were of typical late Bronze Age Trojan form, slanting inwards towards the top. That was exciting enough. But it was the design of the passageway that was so extraordinary. It was remarkably similar to the entranceway to the great tomb outside the citadel of Mycenae, the so-called Treasury of Atreus. Was that what Maurice had found? Would there be a cavernous domed burial chamber at the end? A great royal burial chamber beneath Troy? But it didn't make sense. If this was a tomb, how could a Trojan king, a Trojan dynasty, be buried with Egyptian inscriptions?

Hiebermeyer peered at him. 'I know what you're thinking,' he said.

'I'm thinking,' Jack replied, 'that I've got a shipwreck to excavate, and you've got something fantastic here as well.'

'Paydirt,' Jeremy said. 'That's what Costas calls it. We've hit paydirt.'

'I know what you're *really* thinking,' Hiebermeyer persisted.

'I just wonder whether Schliemann got here first. How he could have missed something like this.'

Hiebermeyer nodded pensively. He stared at the rubble, wiping the grime from his face. 'With all this collapsed earth and masonry, it's very difficult to tell. It seems to be one massive destruction layer. Late Bronze Age, no doubt about that. Very soon after the fall of Troy. As if somebody had this deliberately done, perhaps to create a platform for a building above.'

'Or to hide whatever lies at the end of this passageway,' Rebecca said.

Hiebermeyer narrowed his eyes, then sneezed. 'There *could* have been a nineteenth-century excavation. If this were a layer cake of stratigraphy, we could easily tell. But because of the single destruction deposit, it's hard to see evidence of disturbance. It's odd, though. If it was disturbed, it was deliberately concealed again.'

'Maybe it was,' Rebecca added. 'Maybe to conceal what Schliemann had found.'

'I did find this.' Hiebermeyer turned away and blew his nose noisily between his fingers, flicking off the drip from the end of his nose, then reached into his shirt pocket and pulled out a handful of dust. Nestled in the middle was a ring. He extracted a half-crumpled water bottle from his pocket, screwed off the top with his teeth and trickled water on the ring, rubbing it, then passed it over to Jack. Rebecca and Jeremy moved over to look, and Rebecca gasped as she saw it.

'It's gold!'

'I found it close to the wall with the inscription.'

'It's modern, of course,' Jack murmured, staring at it.

Hiebermeyer nodded. 'A signet ring, maybe late nineteenth century. My grandfather used to wear one. My American grandfather, my mother's father. It was the fashion then, for men of means.'

'How on earth does a Victorian signet ring get down here?' Rebecca murmured.

Hiebermeyer stared at the rubble. 'Wealthy people came to Troy after Schliemann discovered it, his supporters, invited by him. Maybe one of them lost the ring on the mound. You've seen how that rubble and earth can shift. The ring could have worked its way underground through the spaces between the stones, reaching the base of the passageway.'

Rebecca looked at him doubtfully. 'Or someone has been in this passageway before.'

Hiebermeyer pursed his lips. 'Someone could have dug their way in, then carefully refilled the passageway to make it look as if it was undisturbed. Only an archaeologist could do that. Someone intimately familiar with this site, who would know how to make it look convincing. I wouldn't put it past Schliemann and Sophia. But how? How could Schliemann, showman par excellence, find something like this passageway and not tell the world? He'd have been telegramming his friends, the British Prime Minister Gladstone, or Bismarck in Germany, the other great and the good he courted. Schliemann could never keep his discoveries secret.'

'Maybe the showmanship was an act, carefully calculated,' Jack murmured. 'You know my feelings about Schliemann. A lot more there than meets the eye.'

'You mean to persuade people that he'd told them everything he'd found, when really he hadn't?' Rebecca said slowly.

'We know for sure he hid away some of that gold he and Sophia found at Troy, the so-called Treasure of Priam,' Jeremy said. 'Sent it secretly back to Germany. That gives a lot of weight to what Jack says.'

Jack peered at the ring. 'There's a design on it, a family crest.

It's a double-headed griffin, in a shield. Very German-looking.' He paused, thinking hard. 'I'm sure I've seen this somewhere before.'

'Schliemann's crest?' Jeremy suggested.

'No.' Jack shook his head. 'Not Schliemann. It was when I was a student. A long time ago. Something I saw in a library. I'll have to think.'

Hiebermeyer turned and stared defiantly at the rubble face, his hands on his hips. 'We need to dig, dig, dig. That's the only way to solve this. It's about time Troy gave us some answers.'

'And you're the man for the job.' Jack slapped Hiebermeyer's shoulder, and a shroud of dust erupted over them. They both sneezed explosively, then caught each other's eye and suddenly convulsed with laughter, shaking uncontrollably, holding on to each other. Jack knew it had to happen. The pent-up excitement needed a release. Rebecca and Jeremy and Dillen watched, smiling broadly. Jack looked at Hiebermeyer, the shrouded form of his schoolboy friend, glasses askew and all steamed up. *It couldn't get much better than this*. He pushed away, composing himself, wiping his eyes. 'And now,' he said, clearing his throat, glancing at his watch. '*Now* it's time for supper. Costas is waiting for us at the excavation house. Having a well-earned gin and tonic, I hope. Our excellent Turkish foreman and his wife have laid on a feast fit for King Priam.'

Jeremy coughed quietly. 'Speaking of which. Priam, I mean.'

'Yes?'

'It might be,' Rebecca cautioned Jeremy. 'Only *might* be.'

'Yes?' Jack said.

'Something we found.'

'Yes, of course,' Jack said, looking at them intently. '*Of course*. I hadn't forgotten. Not a chance. Maurice, they've found something. Where you set them digging. On our way out.' He carefully lifted his khaki bag with the shape in it and slung it over his shoulder, eyeing Dillen as he did so. 'It looks as if today is the day for revelations. Jeremy, lead the way.'

Two hours later, Jack walked out on to the veranda of the bungalow that served as Hiebermeyer's excavation head-quarters, the very place where Schliemann had stayed almost a century and a half before. Costas and Jeremy followed, and they went over to where Rebecca and Dillen were sitting together on a long bench swinging from a frame in the garden, with the mound of the ancient citadel looming beyond the trees in front of them. Rebecca was rocking gently to and fro, humming to herself, and Dillen was cradling his pipe, an unopened packet of tobacco on his lap. Jack and the other two sat down on garden chairs facing the swing. It had been a long day, and Jack suddenly felt dead tired, drained by the dive that afternoon and the decompression, which always sapped his energy. He and Maurice had rushed off before the main course to have another quick look at the sculpture in the passageway wall, and that had been the subject of intensive conversation for the rest of the meal. It had been a day of extraordinary discoveries, a portent of what might come. And Jack still had not told Dillen about the ancient cup from the wreck. The time for that would be later, in the right place, a special moment alone with his old mentor.

He stared off into the sunset beyond the mound of Troy,

then turned to Rebecca and smiled. She was holding an old book, about five by two inches across, with faded gold lettering on the spine. Jack peered at it, and then at Dillen. 'I recognize that, James. It's your old edition of Pope, isn't it?'

Dillen put the pipe between his teeth, clenched it and nodded. '*The Iliad of Homer*, translated by Alexander Pope in the early eighteenth century, this edition published in 1806.'

'I recognize that tear on the spine. It was always on your desk in Cambridge.'

'It's so cool,' Rebecca murmured, carefully opening and closing the cover, then tracing her fingers over the worn leather boards. 'Professor Dillen has just given it to me. I feel like a real collector now.' She looked at Dillen. 'Dad gave me John Wood's *Source of the River Oxus* for my birthday. We're planning to go back there again, you know, to Afghanistan, to search for it.'

'When the war's over,' Jack murmured.

'You're a rare breed, Rebecca,' Costas said. 'The only seventeen year old I know who collects antiquarian books.'

Jack grinned at Costas. 'And you're the only submersibles engineer I know who can quote Auden.'

'Jack!' Costas looked aghast. 'You promised not to tell!'

Jeremy looked in astonishment at Costas. 'You? Poetry? I don't believe it.'

Costas gave a theatrical groan. 'See? My credibility shattered.'

'No. Not at all.' Jeremy shook his head emphatically. 'Auden was the subject of my undergraduate dissertation at Stanford. Before I switched to palaeolinguistics, I wrote about Homeric imagery in Auden.'

'You're kidding me.' Costas had been playing with a spanner, and spun it between his fingers. He looked at Jeremy quizzically. 'I was thinking of Auden again when we arrived here this afternoon, seeing James photographing the excavation. You know?'

'Sure,' Jeremy replied, nodding enthusiastically. 'About the eye of the crow and the eye of the camera, looking on Homer's world, not ours.'

'And earth being more powerful than both gods and men, yet being impassive, uncaring,' Costas said.

Jeremy nodded. 'That was published in 1952, but it was written in memory of a friend who died in April 1945, in the final weeks of the Second World War. It's the poem I studied most intensively, along with *The Shield of Achilles*.'

'Funny. Jack and I were just talking about that one,' Costas said. 'On board *Seaquest II*, before our dive.'

Jeremy cocked an eye at Jack. 'Really? He and I talked about it in Oxford several months ago, when he and James came to talk about the *Ilioupersis*, just after Maria and I had found it.'

'Jack.' Costas narrowed his eyes at him. 'You knew about Jeremy and Auden all along.'

'I said you'd be surprised.'

Rebecca opened the old book, and examined the frontispiece. 'This is what I really love,' she murmured. 'Where people have annotated books, written in them. It really makes them come alive.'

Dillen shifted in his seat, and raised the unlit pipe again to his mouth. 'I was going to point that out to you,' he said between clenched teeth. 'Read the inscription out to us, would you?'

Rebecca angled the page, finding the best light. Jack got up to glance at it, to remind himself. The ink was faded, but the handwriting was bold, elegant. '*To Hugh, with love and affection from Peter. Remembering our summer at Mycenae, 1938.*'

Jack glanced at Dillen. 'That's Hugh Frazer, your old school-master?'

Dillen nodded. 'And Peter Mayne, a fellow undergraduate of Hugh's at Oxford. They both studied classics, and dug together on the British excavation at Mycenae just before the war. They were close friends.'

'Must have been *very* close,' Rebecca said, looking at the inscription again.

Dillen sat back, rocking slightly. 'They were steeped in Homer, in a world of heroes and gods, of Arcadian groves and lovers. I think it was pretty innocent, though. The war changed all that.'

'Of course,' Rebecca murmured. 'Young men in 1939. Just like the young men of 1915, over there at Gallipoli.'

'They both became soldiers, army officers,' Dillen said, putting his pipe in his mouth, thinking for a moment, then taking it out. 'I know little about it, actually. They both ended up in special commando units, but I don't know what happened to Peter in the end. Hugh never spoke about it, and I never pressed him. Hugh had been one of the first into the concentration camp at Belsen, so he'd seen the worst. When I was a schoolboy in the fifties, you didn't speak to veterans about that. Chaps like Hugh who'd found some way of surviving mentally just wanted to get on with life. Maybe he'd talk now, though. The defences fall away in old age, all that suppression of trauma. They say talk can help.'

'Where is he now?' Costas said.

'Lives in a flat in Bristol, the same place as when I was a schoolboy there. My parents had been killed by German bombing in the Blitz, and he put me up. He's frail, but perfectly alert. I visit him a couple of times a year. I owe him a visit about now.'

'Maybe his friend Peter was killed,' Rebecca murmured, staring at the inscription.

Dillen put his pipe in his mouth, dry-sucked it, then took it out again. 'The only time he ever said anything was when he gave me that little book as a graduation present, almost fifty years ago now. He said Mayne had been badly wounded, at Cassino. I think the wounds were more than physical. Afterwards he went into a special unit involved in the reparation of works of art, antiquities stolen by the Nazis. Funnily enough, it was Costas who jolted my memory, a few weeks ago when I was at the IMU campus, when you were arranging for the return of that painting from the Howard Gallery to Germany.'

'We talked about my great-uncle,' Costas said. 'The US army Monuments Man.'

Dillen nodded. He looked at his pipe, then cleared his throat. 'There *is* something else. Something that's been especially on my mind here, at Troy. I've always kept it to myself, but this is the right time and place to tell it.'

'Please do,' Jack said.

Dillen tapped his pipe on the arm of his chair, then put it down and spoke. 'Something Hugh said to us at school, in a Greek lesson. It was my first year there, when I was twelve. He told us the story of Heinrich Schliemann and the discovery of Troy. I remember it as if it were yesterday. He was sitting on the edge of his desk, passionate. Gesticulating. We were utterly entranced. The fifties was a pretty grim decade, with post-war deprivation and the threat of nuclear annihilation, and the distant past seemed a far more interesting place than the future. Hugh said he believed in the Trojan War, *absolutely* believed in it. And he said he knew something top secret. During the war, he'd heard about the most incredible treasure, something Schliemann had found and hidden away and then the Nazis stole. He didn't say anything more. He swore us all to secrecy. It became a kind of myth. There were half a dozen of us, but I was the only one who carried on with Greek. I never knew for sure whether he was telling a real story, or just trying to inspire us with a dream. I didn't want to burst that bubble, to discover it was only fiction. That's why I never brought it up with him again. I still want to believe in it. He was an inspirational teacher.'

'Not the only one,' Jack murmured.

Rebecca carefully closed the book, and held it in both hands. 'I'd love to meet him.'

'He was always very fond of your dad,' Dillen said, picking up his pipe again. 'I first took Jack to see Hugh when he wasn't very much older than you are now.'

'Well, then,' Rebecca said, suddenly businesslike, looking at Jack. 'Professor Dillen and I both have to fly back to London tomorrow, right? He's got a conference at the end of the week, and I've got my school trip to France. We've both got tomorrow afternoon free. Why don't we take a trip to Bristol? I've been there, to the university open day. I might even study there, actually. You don't know that yet. Now you do. It's only an hour and a half on the train from London.'

Dillen sucked thoughtfully on his pipe, smiled to himself, looked at Jack and raised an eyebrow. Jack glanced at Rebecca, then nodded. 'It seems that when my daughter sets her mind on something, she does it.'

Dillen pointed his pipe. 'What was it you just said about Hugh? "Not the only one"?'

Jack smiled, looking serious. 'If there's a chance this story's true, then it's part of the archaeology of this place. We should try to chase it up. But only if Hugh wants us to.'

'I think he will. And we don't need to pussyfoot around him. For all the trauma, chaps like Hugh are also tough as nails. Remember what they've seen and done and had to live with. He'll tell us exactly what he wants to tell us.'

'Mission creep, yet again,' Costas sighed. 'We need to keep focused. On the archaeology. On the diving.'

'We need to keep all possible avenues open,' Jack said.

'I just want to talk to him,' Rebecca said quietly. 'Maybe about Peter, if he wants.'

'I'll have a word with Ben, who's personally taken charge of security for this project,' Jack said. 'He and Macalister have just liaised with the Turkish navy to get a demolitions team in tomorrow morning to clear that mine from the wreck. Once they're done, we're good to go with another dive, Costas. I want to shore up the minelayer wreck and begin doing airlift excavation on the ancient hull straight away. If you can get the Aquapods up to scratch, we'll be in the water tomorrow afternoon. With the Turkish navy around, I don't think we've got anything to worry about with the security of *Seaquest II*. I think we can spare Ben or one of his guys to accompany you, Rebecca.'

'Dad.' Rebecca looked at Jack defiantly. 'It's not like I'm a little girl any more. I'm seventeen. I don't need a chaperone.'

Jack paused. 'Remember Ben's reaction when you marched off alone to organize the repatriation of a work of art stolen by the Nazis? There are a *lot* of shady characters out there. Art and antiquities are big business on the black market.'

'Dad. I'm going to see a lonely old man in a flat in Bristol. And James will be with me.'

Jack looked at her, shaking his head, then at Dillen. 'We'll talk about it.'

'Good. That's a yes, then. We're going. Thanks, Dad. And I'll look after Professor Dillen, don't worry.'

Hiebermeyer came out of the excavation room carrying a large perspex board with a plan of Troy taped to it. He was still streaked with dirt, and his eyes were gleaming with excitement.

'You got a result?' Jack asked.

'Better than you could have imagined. *Wundervoll.*' He turned to the others. 'When Jack and I nipped back to that sculpture during dinner, it was because I wanted to take photographs. I e-mailed them through to the institute in Alexandria. I've got a brilliant student there who specializes in Egyptian New Kingdom portrait sculpture. She can spot an individual sculptor's hand. She knew this one immediately. She calls him Seth IV. She knows him from Thebes. It's incredibly exciting, because three of his four other known sculptures show officials of the Nineteenth Dynasty, the later thirteenth century BC. And the fourth is even better. It's a recently revealed statue of Usermaatre-setpenre, otherwise known as Rameses the Great, died 1213 BC.'

'*Perfect*,' Jeremy exclaimed. 'Priam would have been about contemporary with Rameses, wouldn't he? So this sculptor, Seth IV, takes a commission to sculpt the greatest king of Troy, and comes up here with his stone. That clinches it for me.'

'We'll do a laser scan and compare the data from the other statues. It's like fingerprint analysis. But she can tell by eye. You can completely trust it.'

'Another small step closer to the Trojan War,' Dillen murmured, shaking his head. 'I never thought I'd see anything like this in my lifetime.'

Jack pointed at the board. 'What have you got there?'

Hiebermeyer put it on the ground between them and knelt in front. 'Look at this. We've dug out enough of the passageway walls to project the walls inward to their apex. I'm convinced it'll be a circular chamber or a tomb.' He stabbed a finger at the centre of the plan. 'I'm putting the ground-penetrating radar over that spot first thing tomorrow morning. And I've worked out what we need to get through the remaining rubble. I've got a crack team coming up from the institute in Egypt. Experienced at digging out pyramids, monumental tombs. *Real* archaeologists. And Aysha's coming. She's my top hieroglyphics expert.'

'You mean she's your *wife*,' Rebecca said.

'This is science, Rebecca. *Science*. I'm talking about assembling the best possible archaeological team. Period.'

'Dad says archaeology isn't a science. He says it's all about emotional understanding of the past. About passion. About your *own* passion, Maurice. Aysha tells me she really wants children. This would be the perfect place to get serious, don't you think? Professor Dillen and I will be away. You've got the excavation house to yourselves. Jeremy can go and camp with his sleeping bag up on the ruins, can't you, Jeremy? What about it, Hiemy?'

Hiebermeyer was silent for a moment, apparently absorbed in the plan. Then he looked up, narrowing his eyes at Rebecca. 'Here's what Hiemy thinks. You remember how Hiemy offered Rebecca the job of site assistant at the mummy necropolis next summer? Hiemy thinks that if Rebecca's excellent plan comes to fruition, that job brief might just change. It might change to *nanny*.'

Rebecca looked aghast. '*Not*,' she said vehemently.

Jack bit his lip to stop himself from smiling. He cleared his throat, and turned to Hiebermeyer. 'Hieroglyphics,' he murmured, shaking his head doubtfully. 'Is that *really* what you saw down there in that tunnel, Maurice?'

Hiebermeyer gave him a defiant look. 'Did you *really* see the lion-shaped prow of a Mycenaean galley on the sea bed this afternoon?'

Rebecca looked at Dillen. 'Dad has a bet with Maurice that he's going to find the Shield of Achilles before Maurice finds the palladion.'

'An extra team from Egypt,' Jack murmured, scratching his stubble. 'That sounds like an unfair advantage. That raises the stakes. It's a crate of whisky, not a bottle. And James chooses the malt. It's for him, after all.'

'Done,' Hiebermeyer said.

Costas stood up, spun his spanner, checked his watch and

looked at Jeremy. 'That reminds me. I've got an Aquapod to fix. The chopper's waiting. Want to come and help?'

'Thought you'd never ask.'

Dillen stood up as well. 'And I need to go back to my trench. To clean up.'

Hiebermeyer wiped his face, leaving a streak like war paint across his forehead. He looked at Dillen seriously. 'Of course you do, Professor.' He grinned. 'Inspection in half an hour.'

9

James Dillen walked down from the excavation house to the dirt lane that encircled the site of Troy, on the edge of the rich humic plain that seemed to lap the ancient citadel like a sea. There were tomatoes everywhere, rows of lush plants in the fields, ripe red fruit dropped from carts and squashed on the trackway, oozing into the stagnant pools that lined the fields. He remembered what a French soldier had called the plain of Troy: *marais sanglant*, bloody marsh, after the French had fought the Turks to a standstill beside the Dardanelles in 1915. The dark waters of the past always seemed close to the surface here, as if to step off the track would be to risk being swallowed up in it; to navigate this place meant knowing the latticework of dykes and causeways used by the farm workers who dotted the fields, visible here and there like distant scavengers picking their way through the aftermath of battle.

Dillen stopped for a moment, and looked out. The sun was nearly set far out over the Aegean, leaving a fiery orange glow that deepened to dark red from west to east. The ancient stage-set of war was all visible here: the plain of Ilion, the river Scamander behind the low line of trees to the east, in front of the place where the ancient shoreline had been, an arrow-shot away from where he stood now. He could see across the distant waters of the Dardanelles to Cape Helles, the westernmost point of the Gallipoli peninsula, capped by the stark white tower of the memorial to the British dead of 1915. Two nights before, with Jack on *Seaquest II*, they had gone on deck and seen the far-off speckle of phosphorescence in the surf, on the beaches where so many had died. It was as if the ghosts still lingered there, dancing as their corpses had once danced in the lapping waves. Now he saw the same coast rimmed red, where the setting sun reflected off the phosphorescence; above it the ravines and gullies shimmered white, where the shattered bones of men lay too thick to nurture new life, as if the storm of death still reeked and echoed across the years. Behind him the crumbled citadel of Troy was verdant, overgrown, but it too seemed gutted by history, a place that never again would pulse to the sounds of running feet and laughter and children, gone for ever in the whirling vortex of war three thousand years before.

He closed his eyes for a moment, savouring the silence, the preternatural stillness that followed the afternoon wind. Then a diesel tractor coughed to life somewhere away in the fields, and a donkey brayed. He slapped his arm, leaving a bloody smear. Mosquitoes did not seem to live on the citadel, and it was a good enough reason for getting off the plain. He stepped off the path into Schliemann's trench and made his way towards his excavation, high above the trench on a grassy knoll that marked the northern edge of the ancient city. He scrambled over the makeshift wooden revetment and into the Bronze Age house, pausing, as he always did, to remember where he was, standing on a floor that had been buried for three millennia: a house whose last inhabitants had seen the great beacon burning high above the wall, and had watched the men of Mycenae storm across the plain towards them on a wave of destruction, harbingers of rape and fire and death.

What he had said to Jeremy earlier was too easy, too glib. The Trojan War was not a clash of civilizations, of east and west. Troy was a crucible for all mankind, for men to do their worst. He looked out from his new vantage point high above the plain, to the north-east. Darkness was enveloping the Gallipoli peninsula, blotting out the afterglow of dusk; it was the darkness of an impending storm that had been building up all afternoon. Distant lightning flashed on the horizon, revealing cavernous folds in the clouds. There was a far-off rumble, whether of thunder or the fighter jets that had streaked overhead all day he was not sure. War was never far from this place. He remembered what he had smelled that afternoon, the smell of ancient burning in that pyre against the wall.

He looked up and saw the shadowy shapes of a pair of birds flying west, fleeing the storm, their wings beating the still air. It was going to rain, but he would stay here until it began, wait for Jack. He took off his camera, stowed it in its bag, sat down and nursed his aching knees for a moment, then reached over and rolled up the plastic cover on the wall, revealing the extraordinary fresco of the lyre-player. He stared at it, still astonished at what he had found. The lyre-player seemed to be an observer, looking over the dark plain just as he had been doing, standing apart from history: Auden's mother earth, remaining immutable as gods and men came and went.

The music of the lyre. Dillen remembered Jack's passion for the Shield of Achilles, that evening over whisky on *Seaquest II*. Before they had gone up on deck, Dillen had read out Homer's description of the pastoral scenes on the shield: *And in their midst a boy made pleasant music with a clear-toned lyre, and to it sang sweetly the Lindos song.* The scene was a tipping point in the *Iliad*: the old order was about to go, the age of heroes about to end. The music of the lyre, the music of the child, changed from pleasant melody to lament, from joy to despair. The shield itself was a metaphor for the book: an ornament, yet concealing within it a reality known to the poet, the grim reality of war, the *pity* of war.

Dillen thought about the *Ilioupersis*, the extraordinary ancient text they had found, the lines that still remained for him to translate. For the first time in three thousand years people would know what had really happened here: a reality the poet had recorded for poetry's sake but then put away, its message perhaps unbearable, too bleak and pitiless. Dillen looked out over the darkness, over the plain of Ilion towards Gallipoli. *But had the poet been right?* What if his poem *had* been read, a warning from history, a warning of what men might do, unrestrained by gods and honour and nobility?

Would the young men of 1914, of 1939, have looked to battle not excited by images of heroic contest, images of Achilles and Hector, but overwhelmed by horror, fearful of impending apocalypse? Would they have looked to battle at all? Would war, total war, war without honour or glory, have been extinguished millennia before, here below the shadow-girt walls of Troy?

Dillen went over to the corner of the excavation and took the cover off his own lyre, then carried it back to where he had been sitting. He balanced it on his right knee, just as the player was doing in the painting, holding it with his right hand and reaching over with his other hand for his flashlight, twisting it on and aiming it at the painting. He wanted to study the angles, the hand positions of the player, to emulate them exactly. He shifted slightly, and in so doing panned the torch down to the plinth where the bronze arrows remained embedded in the floor. Something caught his eye. Earlier he had noticed that the soil remaining against the wall was cracking in the sun, and now he saw that some of it had fallen away. It was his mistake for not covering it over. He peered closer, leaning his lyre aside. For the first time he could see the lower edge of the painting, a plinth for the lyre-player to sit on. He stared at it. There was something else, just below. His heart began to pound. *It was an inscription*. He could see symbols, in red paint on the dark background. He twisted his torch for a more intensive beam, and aimed again.

There was no doubt about it. It was incredible. It was Mycenaean Linear B, the script used to write Greek in the Bronze Age, the language of the Greeks who came to Troy. The language of Achilles. *The language of Agamemnon.*

He could make out four symbols, simple linear signs. He knew the Linear B syllabary by heart. He had been studying it all his life. The first symbol was a simple vertical slash, with a serif above. That meant the sound O. The second, number 13 in his syllabary, was like a V with serifs, meaning ME. The third looked like a lower-case letter t, meaning RO. The fourth, number 49, was untranslated. He knew it was not a syllable, but an ideogram: a stick figure that looked like a horse, but was not, with four long legs, a stubby tail and a high curving neck. He pursed his lips, annoyed. *Why did it have to be that one?* Number 49 had frustrated him for years. He knew it did *not* mean horse, as that was represented by another ideogram. He stared at it, and then his eyes wandered up to the shadowy form of the lyre in the painting above. Something caught his eye, and he quickly raised the torch and panned it over the painting and the inscription, comparing. The painted lyre had four strings, and a small protrusion at the top of the bridge close to the player's face, perhaps for tuning. At the front was a curved extension, like the prow of a Bronze Age ship. Dillen shut his eyes tight, then opened them again. *Of course.* How could he have been so blind? *Number 49 was the ideogram for lyre.*

He looked at the whole inscription again: O + ME + RO + lyre. He could barely breathe. He thought hard. It was probably an aspirated O, so HO. *Homeros.* He whispered the word. It had been the most perplexing absence from the Mycenaean Greek lexicon, the one word scholars had sought in vain, not seeing the ideogram for what it was. *The word for bard.* Images came flooding into Dillen's mind, images from the *Iliad* and the *Odyssey*: Tieresias, blind sage; Thetis, mocker of kings; Calchis, son of Thestor, far-seeing snake-prophet. Dillen suddenly felt a certainty, an intense proximity, sitting up here alone, so close to what he had been seeking all his life. That was who Homer was. That was what Homer meant. *The immortal bard*. Homer was all of them. All of them were Homer. *Homer meant bard*. Dillen remembered Jack. 'Well I'll be damned,' he whispered. '*I'll be damned*.'

After a lifetime, he had finally done it.

He had found Homer.

He took a deep, shuddering breath, then picked up the lyre again and leaned it back against his shoulder, the flat of each hand against the strings, sensing the noiseless vibrations, unsure whether it was the movement of his hands or some fugitive wind, perhaps the passing of those birds. He thought of the conversation they had just had, about his old teacher Hugh. Looking at the image of the lyre-player, seeing the shape of the symbol, he had suddenly remembered something else from his school days, from Hugh: he had come across a half-finished drawing in one of Hugh's notebooks, with the inscription *The girl with the harp*. It was a notebook with other sketches from the war, and he just knew that it had something to do with the concentration camp, from the hints of the setting, the clothes the girl was wearing, her shaven head. Dillen would ask Hugh about that too, when he went with Rebecca. He pushed the lyre up on his knee, and stared back at the extraordinary inscription on the wall. He felt as if he should stay here as long as he could, utterly still, not taking his eye off it, as if to leave would be to risk the inscription disappearing, those faded symbols vanishing back into the uncertainty of Troy. He looked at his camera, then thought better of it, fearful that the flash itself might extinguish the image. He remembered Auden's imagery, of the camera in battle and the crow on the crematorium chimney; the bard too was seeing timeless war, recording it like the camera, like the eye of the crow.

He heard a crunch of footsteps on the path below, the sound of Jack and Hiebermeyer talking, and Rebecca singing quietly to herself. It was inspection time. He put down the lyre and pulled the cover over it, then quickly arranged his tools and laid the torch on the wall beside him, aimed directly at the inscription. He glanced up. The sky was dark now, an ominous storm-darkness from the east. The first drops of rain were falling against the wall, deepening the colour of the inscription, the contrast of the red lines with the dark paint of the background.

Jack appeared over the revetment, carrying his old khaki bag with the bulge in it. 'Rebecca and Maurice stopped on the way up. Maurice wanted to show Rebecca how close Schliemann got in his trench to the passageway, where Maurice thinks the chamber at the end should be. It'll give us a few moments alone.' He stepped into the excavation, cleared his throat, and put his hand on his bag. 'James. About the oldest inscription ever found in the Greek alphabet. I've got something I want to show you. But first, in readiness.' He pulled out a bottle of Turkish red wine, uncorked it with his penknife and produced two plastic cups, putting them on the stone revetment and filling them close to the brim. 'We can't use what I've found. It's a bit too precious. But it calls for some wine. You'll see why.'

Dillen looked at the bag. He had known hours ago that Jack

had found something in the wreck and had been itching to tell him, waiting for the right place. He looked intensely at him. 'Jack. About never finding a Linear B inscription at Troy. I've got something to show *you*.' He nodded his head in the direction of the lyre-player. Jack gazed at it, put down the wine bottle, and then took a step forward, kneeling, clutching his bag, staring along the beam of the torchlight. 'Well I'll be damned,' he whispered.

'You remember my tutorials all those years ago? The Linear B syllabary?'

'I remember that one, the stick figure that looked like a horse,' Jack murmured, pointing. 'Number 49. I wrote an essay on it in an exam. An ideogram, but not meaning horse. Had everyone stumped.'

Dillen said nothing, but picked up the torch and angled it to the painting of the lyre-player, then back down again. Jack was silent for a moment, staring. 'Well I'll be damned,' he whispered again. 'Of course. *It's a lyre.*' He stared at the other three symbols, and Dillen could see him remembering, putting them together. Jack suddenly gasped, then turned to him, his eyes wide with astonishment. He looked like an eighteen year old again. Dillen nodded, and Jack looked back at the wall. '*Incredible*,' he whispered. 'It says Homer. *Homer.*' He grinned broadly. 'Homer, the Bronze Age bard.'

'Homer, who sat here like this lyre-player, who witnessed the fall of Troy,' Dillen said.

Jack extended his right hand, still staring at the wall, and shook Dillen's free hand. 'Congratulations. *Many* congratulations. To see you find this is just about the biggest thrill I can imagine. *Finding Homer.*'

Dillen followed Jack's gaze. This was real. And the bard's secret poem, his greatest work, would not be lost to history. He felt a huge rush of adrenalin, like nothing he had ever felt before. Now he knew what drew Jack back to the quest again and again, the lure of lost treasures, of fantastic discovery. This had been the most exciting day of his life. They both continued staring at the wall, stock still, and then Jack began to undo the straps on his bag. 'And now this.'

Dillen put his hand on Jack's shoulder. He could hear Rebecca singing again, coming up the path. 'I think I know what Costas would say to you now,' he said, smiling. 'I think he'd say, "Game on."'

Jack took a deep breath, then exhaled forcefully. He looked up at the dark clouds overhead, now spattering the site with big raindrops. 'I wonder what price there is to pay.'

'What do you mean?'

'I mean what it was that kept Homer from telling the world the truth about what really happened here. What made him write the *Ilioupersis*, but then hide it away. A truth maybe better left concealed.'

Dillen shook his head. 'It's too late to turn back now. I'm already well into translating the *Ilioupersis*. Jeremy brought me the final batch of lines today. And we're doing the same to this site. Peeling away the layers, revealing more and more. We can't undo it, wherever it's taking us. And I keep looking across to Gallipoli, thinking of all those young men in 1915. The truth is *never* best left concealed. And if this is all about the truth of war, so be it. Maybe if Homer had revealed it three thousand years before, then those young men might never have gone to die with dreams of glory in their hearts, or the next generation twenty-five years later on the killing fields of Europe and Asia. I feel we owe it to them.'

Jack took a deep breath again, and nodded. 'Of course you're right. And maybe the price we pay is just more sweat and toil. Maurice has already got that sorted out. Dig a bigger hole. Just like Schliemann did.' He grinned. They turned to see Maurice and Rebecca appear on the other side of the revetment, and watched them follow the line of the beam of torchlight through the rain to the inscription on the wall. Jack took out two more plastic cups and filled them. The rain spattered into the wine. He passed a cup to Dillen, then reached down and unbuckled his bag, taking out the bubble-wrapped package inside. He carefully unravelled the packaging until one of the beautiful pottery handles of the cup appeared, still wet with seawater. He paused, staring at Dillen, his eyes alight with excitement. 'I wouldn't dream of turning my back on Troy. You said it. *Game on*. And now for what I was going to show you. Maurice? Rebecca?'

Dillen looked up at the black sky, feeling the rain on his face, relishing it. Jack stood up and stared out over the darkness of the plain, just as Dillen imagined Priam had once done: Priam, peace-lover, guardian of bounteous prosperity, warmth and love in his heart. *Just as Agamemnon, blood-soaked victor, had done*. Jack turned round, revealing the pottery cup. Dillen looked at it with astonishment. He saw the inscription on it, the one word, *wanax*, king. It was incredible. *But which king? Was it a cup of peace, or a cup of war?* With two hands Jack raised the cup high into the night sky, holding it there, then bringing it down and carefully placing it on the floor of the Bronze Age room, in front of the painting of the lyre-player. He went back to the wine, and passed brimming cups to Maurice and Rebecca, then picked up the last one himself. He held the plastic to his lips, then smiled broadly at them. 'A plastic cup is not quite the cup of a king. But I think this calls for a toast.'

PART 2

10

16 April 1945, Lower Saxony, Germany

The jeep bumped and bounced along the shell-scarred road towards the line of dense pine forest visible a few kilometres ahead. Major Peter Mayne shifted in the front passenger seat and braced his left hand against the windscreen strut, wincing as a pothole sent a jolt of pain through the old wound in his shoulder. It had been a long war, and he was dead tired. *Nine years before the walls of Troy*. Homer had been on his mind for the first time in months, lines of ancient Greek he had loved to read before the war, lounging by the river Isis in Oxford with Hugh, then on the mountainside that glorious final summer in Greece overlooking the ruins of Mycenae, citadel of Agamemnon.

Today, on this bleak spring morning, he had felt for a moment as if he were a warrior in a chariot racing over the plain of Ilion, the vast unseen bulk of the army somewhere behind, and ahead the battlements of lofty-gated Troy itself. Yet he was no hero, and this desolation of fields and ditches was a no-man's-land where the gods held no sway, and where the power of one man was nothing. By rights this should be the end of the war he was seeing, surely so close now, and he should be shuddering with relief. But there was a baleful presence out there, a horror they had yet to confront, as if flaming Troy might yet consume them all. Homer had come back to him because he believed in it, not just in the reality behind the myth but in the truth those words concealed. *The truth of war.* He had seen it with his own eyes. He was steeped in blood. He peered ahead, suddenly uneasy, remembering what he had been told about this place before they had set out that morning. The truth of war. He thought he knew.

He peered past his driver, Corporal Lewes, taking in every ditch, every undulation in the fields around them, every place a sniper might be concealed, looking at the landscape as five years of war had taught him. He glanced at the American M1 carbine slung over the dashboard, and felt the Webley in the holster at his hip. He had reason to feel uneasy. They were almost eight kilometres behind enemy lines. *Eight kilometres.* The German area commander had arranged a truce, and had assured them of the safety of the road. Behind them the invisible bulk of British 2nd Army was rumbling inexorably forward, village by bloody village, fighting on German soil against men defending their homeland. Soon organized resistance would crumble. That was where the danger lay. Orders from area commanders would become meaningless. The enemy could be out there in the ditches now: old men with *Panzerfaust* rockets still fighting the First World War, boys of the Hitlerjugend in outsized uniforms who thought they were immortal, a few battle-hardened remnants of the Wehrmacht and the SS who had somehow survived all the carnage since Normandy. Soldiers who would react reflexively, just as he would, who were beyond orders, whose only thought would be to kill their enemy.

A hand nudged his shoulder. He twisted back, hearing the American accent but not making out the words. 'You'll have to speak up,' he shouted over the roar of the jeep. 'I'm deaf in my right ear. Shell concussion.'

'I said out here it looks like the war's over already.'

'Don't count on it,' Mayne shouted. He turned back, peering ahead. They had come up behind a lumbering lorry with Red Cross markings, and were now travelling at an excruciating ten miles an hour. He rapped his fingers impatiently against the door. They were more vulnerable to sniping at low speed. Lewes glanced at him. 'I'll overtake in a moment, sir. The road widens a few hundred yards ahead.'

Mayne grunted, took a deep breath and twisted back again to look at the occupant of the rear seat. They had picked him up at the checkpoint twenty minutes earlier, and he had immediately asked to see the drawing Mayne was carrying, the reason they were here. He had scrutinized it for a few seconds and handed it back without a word. Mayne knew better than to ask questions at this stage. He had done intel ops for long enough to know how to play the game, and he had his own agenda too. Colonel Woolley back at HQ was always drumming it into them. They were all on the same side, all with the same objectives, but all operating in different patches of light and darkness, and sometimes it was best to feel your own way forward before asking others to shine a spotlight for you. He would feel the ground first. The American was an older man, middle-aged, wearing the uniform of a US army lieutenant colonel. Apart from his sidearm he looked as if he had walked straight out of a London tailor's. 'You seen much action?' Mayne asked sceptically.

The man had shrewd eyes. 'I'm just an honorary officer. Flew in from England yesterday. Before the war I was at the Courtauld Institute teaching art history, on sabbatical from Yale. But my family background is German and I volunteered to work for the BBC German Service Workers' Programme, the Psychological Warfare Department. After the Americans joined the war I transferred to the Monuments, Fine Arts and Archives section, the MFAA. They decided we should be commissioned into the army to give us clout. We've been preparing for this since before D-Day. The name's Stein, by the way. David Stein.' He extended a hand over the front seat, but Howard only nodded. It was too painful to twist his right arm around. And his eyes were fixed on a pair of RAF Typhoon fighter-bombers that had appeared at tree level down the road behind them. For a terrible moment it looked as if they were about to be strafed. The white star on the bonnet of the jeep would be invisible, but he hoped to God the pilots would see the red cross painted on the back door of the lorry. Their operations behind enemy lines were top secret, and Tactical Air Command was never given any information. It was one of the risks. Then the two aircraft roared overhead, the huge air intakes under their engine cowlings gaping like hungry lions, and banked sharply east, their rocket racks still full. Mayne shut his eyes for a moment, and clenched his hands to stop them shaking. It was getting worse each time. He had managed to keep it from Hugh, when he had seen him at HQ. But how much longer could he control it? Stein withdrew his arm and shaded his eyes, following the aircraft as they disappeared towards a distant pall of smoke where the battle was raging. 'Good to have air cover,' he shouted. He turned back and leaned forward, pointing at the ribbons on Mayne's battledress tunic. 'And you? Don't often see a boffin with a Military Cross.'

'I'm not a boffin. I'm a soldier.' Mayne braced himself again as the jeep lurched forward and sped around the lorry, just squeezing past as the road widened. Lewes floored the accelerator and they hurtled down the open road, by now free of bomb damage. 'I was at Oxford before the war, reading classics,' he shouted. 'Joined the infantry, went to France in time for Dunkirk. Then North Africa with 8th Army, El Alamein to Tunis, then Italy. By the time a shell got me at Cassino I was the last surviving officer of my original battalion. Lewes here was my batman. After I was passed fit, we both volunteered for attachment to the Intelligence Corps, Field Security Operations. They needed experienced soldiers, not boffins.'

'Thirty Commando.' Stein read out Mayne's shoulder flashes. 'Sounds like a combat outfit.'

'Thirty Commando Assault Unit. We're a multi-force unit, army, navy, marines. We operate ahead of the advancing army in search of technical intelligence. It used to be anything of tactical value – codes, ciphers, order books, that kind of thing. Now with the battlefield mostly in Allied hands it's more

general, scientific and technical intelligence. Basically anything we can get our hands on. Anything the Germans might
try to destroy, or which might fall into the wrong hands.'

'What's your brief for this operation?'

'We're looking for the girl in the camp who made that
drawing. The op's top secret, as usual. All I know about it
comes from a chance encounter with an old friend at VIII
Corps HQ this morning, an officer in the British Special Air
Service. The SAS have been doing forward recon ops as well,
and we bump into them. My friend was leaving Intelligence
HQ in a hurry just as I was going in, and we only had a
minute. He knew I was about to be briefed for the follow-up.
He was the one who took the drawing from the girl. He
wasn't supposed to say anything, but he told me there was
something in it that might interest me.' Mayne paused. It was
more than that. It was something they had both recognized.
Something that set their hearts pounding with excitement.
But he was not going to tell this unknown American officer,
yet. 'We'd both been involved in archaeology before the war,
and I could only imagine it was something to do with that,
maybe stolen antiquities. Once I knew we were going to be
joined by an officer from the MFAA, namely yourself, that
seemed to clinch it. That's all I know.'

'I was told we've only got a small window. Today, this
morning.'

'I was briefed about it at Corps HQ, just before we picked
you up. Once the local ceasefire's over, HQ thinks the
remnant German 2nd Marine Division will form up behind
the forest and make a last stand. They're only remustered
Kriegsmarine sailors, but they've given 11th Armoured

Division a few knocks south of Bremen. Shows how good basic infantry training was, even in the navy. They'll be overrun, but they could give us hell if they get into cover. We don't want any repeat of what we went through in February in the Reichswald, and what the Americans went through in the Hürtgen Forest. So the plan calls for an RAF heavy bomber raid to smash the whole western sector of the forest. Unless we have very good reason to stall them, Bomber Command have it scheduled for thirty-six hours from now. The camp will be safe, but not the forest. But any new intelligence about German troop movements could alter that. The SAS are keeping an eye out. If German troops have already infiltrated the forest, then everything gets evacuated pronto, the camp included. The RAF will destroy the entire place. We have to be ready for that possibility.'

'You been on operations like this one before? I mean, to one of these places?'

'A week ago Corporal Lewes and I were the first Allied personnel into a Nazi prison near Sell. Torture chambers, guillotines. Political prisoners, mainly. Pretty bad, eh, Jock?'

'Makes you realize what we're fighting for, sir,' Lewes replied.

Mayne glanced back at Stein. 'I take it you know what's been going on out here? I don't mean the prisons. That's grim, but predictable. I mean the camps.'

'When I was with the BBC, we broadcast the Soviet reports from Majdanek, the camp the Red Army liberated last July in Poland. The whole Nazi state was based on slave labour. Most of the factories, the munitions works, you name it. There were big area camps for labourers, and satellite camps at particular factories and installations. The aerial photos for the one we're heading towards show an opening in the forest the size of a football field with a row of barracks and huts. You can't see anything in the surrounding woods, but they could conceal a bunker or underground storage facility. The Nazis looted huge amounts of art and antiquities and hid them away. This might be one of those places. That's why I'm here.'

'Something a lot worse than slave labour has been going on,' Mayne said, shouting again as Lewes geared down and then revved up around a pothole. 'My SAS friend said he'd been into a camp near Bergen a couple of days ago, a place called Belsen. Just up the road from here. Frightful scenes, corpses everywhere. He said survivors had been force-marched from those places in Poland, brought here to work on clearing bomb damage in the cities. But after the Allies crossed the Rhine and broke through into Germany, the prisoners got dumped in these camps. Mass starvation, disease. Just so you know. We might see some of that today.'

'We've just been following a whole truckload of medical supplies,' Stein replied. 'The DP organizations, for managing displaced persons, have been preparing for the refugee problem for several years now. They can deal with it.'

'Let's hope so.' Mayne turned and looked at the road ahead. The rumble of artillery from the front line had receded, no longer audible above the roar of the jeep. The line of trees was only a couple of kilometres away now, but still seemed like a distant mirage. It was as if they were crossing some kind of empty quarter, a bleak, monotonous landscape that seemed to go on for ever. He suddenly wished it would stay that way. He wanted monotony. He wanted oblivion. He desperately needed sleep. He felt a yawning emptiness in the pit of his stomach. He had been feeling that a lot lately. He knew it was his frayed nerves, a fear of what every moment ahead might hold, a fear that for him the war might never end. It was as if he knew there was something still to come in the unravelling horror, in his own role in it, something his instinct told him. And as a soldier who had survived five years of war when almost all his friends had not, he had learned to trust his instinct, to rely on it. *That was the rub*.

He reached up and put his hand on his upper tunic pocket, which held the notebook, the passages of Homer he had carefully transcribed that afternoon with Hugh, on the mountainside above Mycenae. It had been the summer of 1938, the end of his second year as an undergraduate. They had scrambled down the slope to the ancient grave circle, and had sat reading Heinrich Schliemann's account of uncovering the mask of Agamemnon. He remembered the fire it had kindled inside him. Then there had been the conversation with the old foreman who had known Schliemann, who had seen what happened that night when Schliemann and Sophia had stolen up to the citadel, when they had raised that mask. *It had been his secret with Hugh, their pact*. After graduating, they had been going to find it, to uncover what Schliemann had hidden. They were going to be a team. He was going to be the archaeologist and explorer, with Hugh in the library delving and researching and sending him on ever more quests, above all to solve the mystery they had heard about that extraordinary evening on the slopes of Mycenae.

All that had seemed a lifetime ago. And then this morning at HQ, those fleeting few minutes with Hugh. That drawing,

made by the girl in the camp. Hugh had described it to him,
then before the briefing he had unfolded the drawing and
glanced at it while Lewes was fuelling the jeep. It could be
coincidence. That symbol was hardly unusual out here. *But
not that way round. And not in those colours. Exactly as the foreman
on the excavation had described it.* He remembered Hugh's face.
It had been flushed, feverish. He wondered whether the
malaria had caught up with him again. He wondered what his
own face looked like. It made him wish he could cry. But they
had stared at each other, suddenly excited, forgetting the war
for a few seconds. *It was just possible.* And now Stein was
suggesting that this camp might contain a secret bunker.
Mayne twisted around, wincing as he jarred his shoulder. 'Just
out of curiosity. Have you MFAA chaps had any luck with
stolen antiquities? What about the Trojan treasure of Heinrich
Schliemann? It was a bit of a passion of mine before the war.
What might have happened to it.'

'What did you say?' Stein stared back at Mayne.

'Schliemann's treasure. King Priam's treasure, from Troy.
And whatever Schliemann and his wife might have secreted
away from the royal graves at Mycenae.'

'What do you know about that?' Stein spoke sharply.

'I worked on an excavation at Mycenae just before the war.
With the British School of Archaeology at Athens. After
Oxford I was going to become an archaeologist. We all heard
the rumours that Schliemann had spirited stuff back to
Germany.'

'I know the story, but I don't know anything more about it.'

Mayne grunted, and turned to face forward again as the jeep
sped on. *King Priam's treasure.* He had last thought about those

passages from Homer on leave in Naples, almost a year ago, recuperating from his wound, sitting by the steaming fumaroles of Aornos, the fabled entrance to the underworld. He had wanted to see where the Trojan hero Aeneas had descended, where he had gone to hell and come back. But he had not read the passages then, and had returned to the crucible of war after that. Perhaps now those lines would help to assuage the emptiness he felt. The fall of Troy seemed to be happening all around him, had been happening for as long as he could remember. He had witnessed awful scenes of destruction, of indiscriminate death, men, women, children. *He had been part of it.* Maybe Homer would show him what he needed to see, help him make sense of the horror that had engulfed the world. Or maybe Homer would seem vapid, no longer meaningful, all talk of heroes and honour and pride. He felt the notebook in his pocket again. He would find somewhere to read it, later today perhaps. He took a deep breath. Lewes glanced at him, then nodded down the road. Lewes knew how close to the edge he was. 'Up ahead, sir. I can see the roadblock.'

'Right.' Mayne steeled himself. They were coming to a junction with another road that ran parallel to the line of the woods, about a kilometre out from it. The road they were on continued beyond the junction towards the treeline. He noticed a kind of grey pall above the forest, like a rising mist, that kept the morning sunlight from streaming in. That was why the place looked so dark, forbidding. There must be a fire somewhere inside. They drew up to the junction. Four jeeps blocked the access routes, and Bren guns on bipods had been set up covering each road. A large sheet of canvas painted with the Allied white star recognition symbol had been laid on the adjacent field. Tactical Air Force might not have been told about covert intelligence missions, but they would have been told about the surrender of the camp. A couple of dozen soldiers had taken cover in the surrounding ditches, rifles at the ready. Mayne saw the shoulder flashes of the 66th Anti-Aircraft Regiment, an artillery unit that had been used as reserve infantry since the destruction of the Luftwaffe over the past weeks.

Lewes came to a halt and switched off the engine. Mayne jumped out and strode briskly towards a group of officers. A man saw him and detached himself from the group. He was wearing rubber boots and off-white dungarees over his battledress. He was of average height, and had pasty skin and a shock of blond hair. 'Are you Major Mayne?' He had a Scottish accent, and seemed terribly young. Mayne nodded. The man looked relieved. 'Good. I'm in medical charge. I'm supposed to take you in.' He turned and watched the medical lorry draw up behind them, then pursed his lips and called back to the group of officers. 'Captain Hamilton. You'll have to block out the red cross on that lorry before it goes any further.' He turned to Mayne. 'I'm ready. We have to go *now*. The lorry can follow us.'

Mayne gestured at Lewes, who had lit up a cigarette beside the jeep. Lewes nodded, carefully stubbed his cigarette butt and pocketed it, then climbed back inside again and fired up the ignition. Mayne turned to the man before getting in. 'How big's your team?'

'Three nurses from an army casualty clearance unit, and six civilians from the UN Relief and Rehabilitation

Administration. We arrived yesterday afternoon. Have you heard of the other camp, up the road? A place called Belsen. That was liberated yesterday too. We're all they could spare. At Belsen there are tens of thousands. Here, there are maybe two and a half thousand, about four hundred still alive. It'll be half that by tomorrow morning. My name's Cameron, by the way.'

'*Two and a half thousand?* You mean people?'

'Ever been into one of these places before?'

'Not like this.'

'Two days ago I was a final-year medical student at Guy's Hospital in London. The call came for volunteers and we were flown out immediately. I've discovered that two days can be a long time in war.'

Mayne said nothing, but sat back in the jeep. For the first time he allowed himself to think properly about where they were going. The empty feeling came back in the pit of his stomach. Cameron swung into the rear seat beside Stein, who nodded at him. Lewes gasped, his nose crinkled up. 'Blimey. What's that stink?'

Cameron looked up. 'That'll be me, I'm afraid. On my clothes. In my hair. I can't smell it any more.'

'Lord above.' Stein turned away, a hand on his face. 'What *is* it?'

'Faeces, rotting flesh, burning rags, unwashed bodies. Sweat, old sweat. That's the warm, sour, acrid smell.'

Mayne glanced at Lewes. 'Time we got some air flow.'

'Sir.' Lewes released the clutch and the jeep jumped forward down the narrow paved lane towards the trees. The smell coming off Cameron disappeared briefly, but soon the air was full of it, a terrible stench billowing out of the place ahead of them. Mayne peered at the greyness above the trees again, and could see wisps of smoke. He had been right. There was a fire, and they were getting closer to it. He swallowed hard and twisted back to Cameron. 'Why blot out the Red Cross symbol on the truck?'

'It terrifies them. The people here. The SS doctors and nurses wore it when they carried out medical experiments. And they used it to delude the new arrivals that they were going for medical check-ups when they got off the train at the camps. In reality they were being sent to the gas chambers.'

'Gas chambers?'

'Do you remember the Soviet accounts of Majdanek, the camp in Poland they liberated last year?'

'Colonel Stein and I were just talking about it.'

Cameron paused. 'Most of the Jews here came from a place called Auschwitz. They've got a number tattooed on their wrists. They were force-marched west as the Russians advanced through Poland. What seems to have saved them from the gas chambers was the Allied bombing of Dresden. They were going to be used as work parties to clear the ruins. But as the Nazi machinery crumbled they were pushed into existing slave labour camps out here and abandoned. Some of the camps were *Konzentrazionslager*, like Belsen. Others were satellite camps, *Arbeitslager*. That's what this one seems to be, some kind of forestry labour camp, originally using Soviet prisoners of war. What you're about to see amounts to mass murder, nothing less, a horrible crime against humanity. But this place was not an extermination camp. Unless, that is, you count the daily summary executions, the medical experiments and all forms of bestiality meted out by the SS guards on these people.'

'How on earth did they survive the other place, Auschwitz?'

'They all talk about the end of the train track, the railhead. Some kind of selection took place. It's as if everything after that is expunged from their memory. But the people who survived it had been selected as slave labour, living in a camp next to the gas chambers. Armaments, munitions, you name it. Some of them worked underground, in a salt mine converted to an aero engine assembly plant. It sounds like Dante's inferno. A pit of hell. But not as bad as the hell above ground. It must have been a huge camp. And the gas chambers. We're talking hundreds of thousands murdered, more. Men, women, children. And not just at Auschwitz. There were more of those places. They called them *Todesmühlen.*'

'Death mills,' Stein murmured. 'My God.'

'What you're about to see . . .' Cameron looked down. 'It's like . . .' He paused, struggling for words. 'It's as if Europe has been struck by a gigantic meteorite. I mean the Jews. What we see here, what we'll only ever see, is like the residue round the edges of an impact crater, the detritus blown out of the middle. Everything else is pulverized, destroyed without trace.'

Mayne tried to keep focused. 'In the camp. This one. Where we're going. What's the drill?'

'Our priority is to treat them with DDT, to kill lice. The lice carry typhus. We spray and scrub them, in a kind of human laundry. The next stage is a makeshift hospital. The huts are too filthy, indescribable. We're going to burn them. The Red Cross lorry should contain army tents and folding beds.'

'You'll set them up out here, away from the camp?'

Cameron shook his head. 'Unless we're ordered to evacuate, everyone stays inside. The horrible truth is that we can't release these people. The risk of spreading typhus is too great. Already some of the healthier ones have escaped and are living rough in the forest. We need to get them all back and disinfect them.'

'What about food?'

'The first troops in here yesterday gave them everything they had. Standard British army compo rations, greasy pork in tins. Virtually inedible at the best of times. The soldiers watered it down into a kind of soup. It was well-meaning, but for some of the inmates it just brought on diarrhoea that killed them within hours. One thing that did work was tea. We're brewing it by the gallon. The lorry's also bringing sacks of Bengal famine mixture – sugar, dried milk, flour, salt, water. But for many it'll be too late. Even the healthier ones, the small number who can take solids, are a problem. They keep half their food and hide it. It'll just rot, and cause another health hazard. They simply can't believe they're being fed. They're hoarding it for when the guards return and the nightmare resumes. I shouldn't say it, but they're like animals, hiding food and squabbling over it. There's no morality here. It's far beyond that. This is war, my friend. Not on the battlefield, but here. This is what war does.' He covered his eyes with one hand. 'I'm sorry,' he said hoarsely. 'This is the first time I've actually tried to describe it.'

Howard gestured back at the Red Cross lorry, now trundling along the lane behind them. 'And medicine?'

Cameron cleared his throat. 'Nicotinic acid and

sulphaguanidine for diarrhoea. Mild cases, anyway. For those with beds in our makeshift hospital, we'll try protein hydrolysates by nasal drip. But there's a problem with injections. The sight of a needle terrifies them. They saw Nazi doctors inject dying people with petrol to make their corpses burn more easily. Just a few beats of the heart before it killed them, enough to circulate the petrol. But an excruciating death. The other inmates would have heard the screams, day in and day out.'

'Jesus,' Mayne whispered.

Stein turned to Cameron. 'We're not medical personnel. You know that. We need to find out why they were here. I don't mean the arrivals from Auschwitz, I mean the original slave labourers. What was going on here, in the forest. Why the Nazis needed them. Can we talk to them?'

'Of course. Many of them were educated people. *Are* educated people. We have to remember that. *Are*, not *were*. These are still human beings. What am I saying. *My God*.' Cameron shut his eyes and put his hand to his face again. Mayne noticed that it was shaking, just like his own. The lorry edged up behind them, and Lewes slowly accelerated. Mayne could make out individual trees now. Cameron opened his eyes. 'You see it in the children, the teenagers, those who were eight, nine, ten when they were taken, old enough suddenly to shine, as linguists, artists, poets, musicians. Children wrenched from that, but who still live the long days of childhood, where a day can seem like for ever. Endless days of anguish and fear, yet some of them preserve fragments of their past, before the horror. It's like a lifeline for them. Trauma patients we were shown at medical school, shell-shocked soldiers, often focus on one event, one shocking experience. With these children, it's as if the shocking event is too much, but they are able to bury it under one vivid memory of happiness, a memory powerful enough to anchor them against the horror. It can be the words of a song they repeat over and over again, or one image they draw repeatedly, or one phrase of a foreign language they'd been learning. I'm only talking about a few. Most have been too traumatized. Most are beyond our help.'

'We're looking for a girl,' Stein said. 'A teenage girl.'

'A girl who made a drawing,' Mayne said.

'Something unusual in it,' Stein added. 'Something drawn very precisely.'

'We gave the children crayons,' Cameron said. 'A drawing? It could have been anything. Not necessarily something she saw here, but maybe a fixation from her past, before the horror. What I was just saying. But I'll do what I can. There's a nurse who might help.'

The jeep trundled on. The edge of the forest loomed larger now, forbidding, like the circuit walls of a dark citadel. *Like the shadow-girt wall of Troy.* Mayne glanced back at Cameron, who was staring into space. It was a look he had seen in young officers who had survived their first experience of battle, a look of shock, exhaustion, dulled fear and impossible responsibility, of being thrust into making snap decisions about who was to live and who was to die. Only here it was something far removed from the age-old rite of passage for the soldier. Here it was something utterly without precedent in their experience, in the literature of war they had grown up with, even the stories of their fathers, who thought they had experienced the worst that humanity could offer on the battlefields of the First World War, on the Western Front, at Gallipoli. It was as if that war, the war to end all wars, had been just the first act.

Mayne remembered a painting he had seen in a ruined chateau in Normandy of the Franco-Prussian War in 1870, of the victorious German leader Otto von Bismarck and the defeated Napoleon III sitting outside a tent, agreeing to cede Alsace-Lorraine to Germany. In a stroke they had destroyed the balance that had kept Europe peaceful since Waterloo. Was the horror that lay ahead of them now foredoomed that evening seventy-five years before, on the battlefield of Sedan? Or was it set in place millennia earlier, when men dispensed with heroes and champions and first learned to make untamed war? *How could humanity have let this happen?*

'Stop here.' Cameron tapped Lewes on the shoulder, and they came to a halt outside a cut in the treeline. Ahead of them the lane continued into the forest. Tangles of barbed wire extended off among the trees on either side. In front of them was a wrought-iron gateway, interwoven with cut branches and camouflage netting, and a partly concealed sentry box, empty. Attached to the gate was a white-painted sign with faded red letters: ACHTUNG!! SEUCHENGEFAHR. ZUTRITT VERBOTEN!!

'Warning! Danger of epidemic. Entrance forbidden!' Stein translated.

'Those signs are all round the perimeter,' Cameron said. 'They're permanent metal signs, dating a long time before the last few weeks when the typhus took hold. The Nazis really didn't want anyone getting near this place. Seems odd for a labour camp, but maybe the SS just didn't want the local population knowing how they were treating these people.'

'Or what they were using them for,' Stein muttered.

Mayne looked around. There was nobody else to be seen. It was eerily quiet, but the smell was atrocious. Then he saw it. A bundle of rags against the barbed wire, about ten yards into the woods from the road, pressed up against the fence. A bundle that looked like tumbleweed, as if it had been blown there by a hurricane. Rags, with bony hands protruding through the wire, leathery feet hanging below. He stared in horrified fascination. His heart began to pound. How could this be shocking, after all he had seen, all he had done? He was a hardened killer. He could see this through. He held his hands against the seat, held them hard to stop the shaking, and turned away, facing the forest ahead.

Cameron reached into a pocket and pulled out a little black book, a Bible. He stared at it, but kept it shut between his hands. 'Jeremiah two, verse six,' he said slowly. '*A land of deserts and of pits, through a land of drought, and of the shadow of death, through a land that no man passed through, and where no man dwelt.*' He looked up at the gate, squinting. 'The padre with the soldiers at the crossroads gave this to me, just before you arrived. He saw the state I was in. Thought it might help.' He shook his head, then reached over the door of the jeep and gently dropped the book on the ground.

He handed Lewes a set of keys. Lewes got out, marched over to the gate and unlocked it, swinging out both doors so that it would be wide enough for the lorry to get through as well. Then he marched back and sat down again, switching the ignition back on, waiting for the lorry to pull up behind them. Mayne steeled himself and looked back at the corpse on the wire. A flash of sunlight lit it up, and for a second it seemed as if it were burning, a human torch. *A torch on the battlements of Troy*. Then the light went, and he stared ahead through the gate, down the dark tunnel beneath the trees. For a split second he was back beside the Bay of Naples, at Aornos, those unread passages from Homer in hand, searching in his mind's eye for the sulphurous passage where the Trojan hero Aeneas had descended into the underworld, a passage from which there might be no return.

That place had just been fantasy, myth.

Now he was truly entering the gates of hell.

11

The jeep accelerated past the gate and down the lane through the pine forest, the Red Cross lorry following close behind. Mayne braced himself for what lay ahead. The stench was indescribable. After about two hundred yards the trees ended abruptly at a clearing about the size of a football pitch. About eighty yards ahead of them was a row of single-storey wooden buildings like army barracks, and at right angles to that another line of huts extended along the far right side of the clearing, obscured in smoke and haze. The lane went across the clearing through the line of huts and disappeared to the right, towards the far buildings. Two British soldiers with rifles and white kerchiefs over their faces stood guard where the lane passed between the huts. Mayne saw other forms milling about, as if in slow motion. Smoke was rising from several points on the open ground beyond the buildings, the smoke he had seen outside forming a pall over the forest. In the still morning air it lingered like a miasma over the camp, cloaking it, blotting out the sky. There seemed to be no noise, as if that too had been stifled. They drove forward at walking pace through a bare landscape, denatured, all vibrancy gone, only pastel shades of green and blue and brown remaining: the colours of decay, colours that matched the smell. It was a landscape of death.

They passed a man sitting with his back to a tree stump, one arm extended, rested on his knee, as if begging. He was wearing the tattered remnants of a blue striped uniform, like a patient's hospital garb, smeared brown. His hair was cut to stubble and his face was emaciated: his skin taut, yellowish-grey, his eyes sunk deep in hollow sockets. Mayne stared at him. There were no eyes in the sockets. The man was long dead. He realized what the other piles of rags lying all around were, little clumps of decay all over the clearing. He stared ahead. They drove past the guards between the huts and veered right, then drew to a halt behind a line of soldiers with their backs to them, holding rifles at the ready with fixed bayonets.

Lewes switched off the ignition. Mayne could hear no talking, only a dull thumping sound. Through the line of soldiers he saw other people, around an open-backed truck. To the left a large pit had been dug in the ground, the size of a swimming pool. The pit was half filled with a grotesque entanglement of bodies, most of them naked, some with rags still clinging to them, a mass of skeletal limbs and wizened heads, hundreds of them. Two men in jackets with SS insignia were flinging in the bodies, one holding the fleshless ankles and the other the wrists, with the shaven heads lolling in between. Another SS man was in the pit, and another was on the back of the lorry, pushing the bodies to the rear to be taken off. Beyond the truck was a group of well-dressed men, women and children, evidently local civilians brought in to watch. The adults stood with arms folded, impassive, or too shocked to respond. One little girl was crying. Mayne and Cameron got out of the jeep. Lewes took out his unfinished cigarette, lit it and inhaled deeply. He caught the eye of the nearest soldier, jerked a thumb at the bayonet on his rifle, then gestured at the SS men. 'Why don't you fuckin' pig-stick 'em, mate?'

The soldier turned. His eyes were dull, and his skin seemed to have taken on the hue of the place. 'Later, mate. Don't you worry about that. *Later.*'

Mayne cleared his throat, trying to control his nausea. He turned to Cameron. His voice sounded muffled, distant. 'These SS men, the guards. How on earth have they survived?'

'We were amazed they were still here to surrender. But they're arrogant and defiant. They seem to have no idea of the crimes they've committed. Utterly indoctrinated. For them, the Jews, the Slavs are all animals, and they don't understand how we don't see that too. They're even rather proud of some they've kept alive, rich Jews that Hitler wanted kept as ransom to their families in the West. Like all gangsters, the Nazis were perfectly able to put profit before ideology. We've even got the commandant, an *SS-Untersturmführer*. He'll stand trial. It's important we don't kill them all. But there are others hiding in the forest, being hunted by the more able-bodied of the inmates, those who only arrived here in the last days. It's a kind of ghastly no-man's-land out there, as if the hell of this place is seeping out like an infectious disease. They especially loathe the *SS-Helferin*, the female auxiliaries. One of the women still at large is the *Lagerführerin*, the camp leader. She seems to have been a particularly vile bully. They think she's hiding in the woods. They want to rip her to pieces.'

'Can't say I blame them,' Mayne muttered, looking around.

'I just want them to get it over and done with. My main job now is dealing with the typhus. We need to get the inmates all back in the camp for scrubbing and delousing. If typhus spreads among the local population and then gets into the advancing Allied troops, it could seriously impede the war effort.' He gestured at the SS men. 'And there's another factor. Doing this job, helping us, is also their survival strategy. The more enthusiastically they help, the less likely we are to take revenge. That's what they think. And they're probably right. With each hour that passes, the horror will become part of our landscape, will become almost mundane. It's a ghastly thing to say, but true. It's our own survival strategy, mentally. The emotions switch off. We get numbed to it, just as they did. And they know it's a relief for us to have them do this appalling job.'

Mayne stared at the scene, mesmerized, watching the SS men repeat the same odious task over and over again. It was like a medieval image of hell, like one of the punishments set in Hades to those condemned forever to repeat the same task, like Tantalus or Sisyphus. Only here the SS were not tormented by what they were doing. They almost seemed to be relishing it. He swallowed hard, and felt a cloying sensation at the back of his throat. He knew it must be the reek of this place, but he seemed no longer able to smell it, as if it had overwhelmed his senses. He suddenly felt tremulous all over, barely able to stand. He forced himself to concentrate on the scene, abstractly. He had tried his hand at painting before the war. He thought how he might frame the image, how he might capture his emotional response, refracted through his own experience. He watched a naked body sail through the air, a woman, her arms flung out before her, like a diver plunging into a swimming pool. But she was dead, and the swimming pool was a pit of rotting bodies. Mayne shook his head. Here, art as metaphor, art as suggestion, had no place. Here it could only be reality. Stark, unadorned reality. He turned to Cameron. 'Is anyone photographing this?'

Cameron shook his head. 'This place is top secret until you chaps give it the all-clear. Only essential army and medical personnel are allowed in. Bringing in those civilians to watch was understandable, but burdens us even more. I warned the CO but he'd made his mind up. With the typhus risk, they'll have to be interned, probably until the war is over. But the horror's on record, if that's what you're asking. The Army Film and Photographic Unit is at Belsen. Come on. I haven't got much time. I need to supervise setting up those hospital tents.'

Mayne and Lewes followed him. Stein was still in the jeep, ashen-faced, wiping his mouth. Mayne could see that he had been sick. He climbed unsteadily out of the vehicle and followed them around the far side of the pit, towards the other line of barracks. On the open ground in front lay smouldering piles of rags, so impregnated with human grease that they burned like funeral pyres. They passed the entrance to the first of the barrack buildings, and Mayne stopped to peer in. It took him a moment to adjust to the gloom. All he could hear was the droning of flies. The air was fetid, humid. He had completely lost his sense of smell. He tried to look through the squalor, to remember what Cameron had said. *They are human beings.* The body nearest to him was naked, a man, the skin like parchment, discoloured with filth. He was lying on his back, his abdomen grotesquely hollow, as if he had been disembowelled, as if the life had been sucked out of him by the hurricane force that had blown the other man against the barbed-wire fence, the first body Mayne had seen in this place. His arms were outstretched, touching two other bodies that were curled up, facing away in opposite directions. Mayne saw no backdrop, only darkness, and as he stood aside to let the light in, the bodies seemed almost luminous, like a painting of Christ on the Cross and the two thieves. He swayed slightly, nearly retching. These were not images of atonement. These people did not die for the sins of mankind. They died horribly because the world had let it happen. He clenched his hands. This was reality. Stark reality.

He pushed away from the barrack entrance and went to where the others were waiting for him, further along the building. Lewes offered him a cigarette, but he shook his head. Stein turned to Cameron. 'Before we go on. We know you've got to get back to your job. Is there anything more you can tell us? About what was going on in this place?'

Cameron stared hard at the ground, then looked up. Mayne noticed how pale he was, his eyes bloodshot. Cameron pointed to a long, low mound on the other side of the clearing, against the line of the pine forest. 'Just a few things.

Over there, that's where they buried the Soviet prisoners back in '41. Hundreds of them, used as labour to build this place, then shot.'

'That's four years ago,' Mayne murmured. 'Yet you say most of the Jews here arrived from Auschwitz only in the last few months. What was going on here before then?'

Cameron took a deep breath. 'All right. It may as well be me who briefs you. This should have come from the intelligence officer with the AA regiment, but I couldn't see him anywhere when we came through and I haven't got time to hunt for him. At any rate, he probably wouldn't be able to tell you any more than I can. When we arrived, he interrogated the camp commandant, the *SS-Untersturmführer*. I was there, as a witness. The IO was a newly commissioned replacement, been out here about as long as I have, with a smattering of Italian and fluent French. Wrong theatre, wrong war. Typical army foresight. I was the only German-speaker. I said I could spare ten minutes, no more. People were dying as we spoke. I'm supposed to be a doctor. *A doctor*.' Cameron rubbed his forehead, suddenly distressed.

'All right. Go on,' Mayne said.

'The commandant said it had been an *Arbeitslager*, a labour camp, for forestry workers. There are tracks leading off from the compound into the forest, and he said they were used by work parties. He said the wood-cutting operations wound down last year and after that the camp was used to house rich Jews, the ones Hitler intended to use as bargaining chips with the Allies. According to this man, they seriously believed they could use Jews in this way as recently as a few months ago, only shelving the idea when the Allies crossed the Rhine. God knows what other desperate schemes the Nazis had prepared.'

'That's what we're interested in,' Mayne said. 'Anything you say might help.'

'All right.' Cameron nodded, more collected now. 'The *SS-Untersturmführer* said that for this reason the camp had only ever housed a relatively small number of healthy inmates: first the fit young men selected for forestry work, and then the members of wealthy Jewish families, who were well fed and looked after. He claimed he only arrived as a replacement commandant six weeks ago. His job was to remove the remaining inmates and shut the camp down.'

'Remove?' Mayne said.

'Remove. You can guess what that means. But we didn't have time to pursue that. We wanted him to talk, not clam up. That'll doubtless come up at his trial.'

'So then what?'

'He said they were totally unprepared for the influx of Jews marched here from Poland, and had no way of dealing with them. But take that with a pinch of salt. He seems to have had a full team of seasoned SS guards, including the female camp leader. It wasn't chaos in here until the final week or so. Before then, they seemed perfectly able to inflict a systematic regime of brutality and sadism.'

'The story seems plausible,' Mayne said slowly. 'But it doesn't account for the extreme secrecy of the place, those signs outside warning of epidemics.'

Cameron nodded. 'There's something else. I spoke to one inmate who claimed to be the only survivor from the earlier phase of the camp, a man the SS used as a cook. Evidently quite a good one, a trained chef. He'd been here since at least

'42. He was some kind of common criminal, a Frenchman from Marseille, not a Jew. I didn't think he was a particularly savoury character. He said that when the new commandant arrived, the SS shot everyone still in the camp, stripping them naked and throwing them into a ditch over where the Russians are buried. He said that with the new commandant and guards, none of them would have known of his cooking skills and given him special status, so he survived by hiding in the barracks and then commingling with the new influx from Auschwitz when they arrived, disguising himself as a Jew. They were all supposed to be kept alive for the work gangs in the cities, but that never happened. He was one of the healthier inmates when we arrived, and he went straight to me, evidently trusting the idea of a doctor more than a soldier to talk to.'

'Why was he keen to talk?' Stein asked.

'The other inmates knew he wasn't Jewish,' Cameron replied. 'They were suspicious of him. He knew they'd finger him. He wanted to assure us that he wasn't a former SS guard disguising himself. He also thought that by showing us he wasn't Jewish, we'd give him preferential treatment. A bit of an anti-Semite. He had short shrift from me there, I'm afraid.'

'Where is he now?'

'After I put him at the back of the queue for treatment, he disappeared. Gone into the forest and then headed south, I imagine. He claimed he was from Marseille, arrested by the Vichy police and then handed over to the Gestapo. Probably some kind of small-time gangster. A pretty wily character. I doubt whether you'll find him again.'

'So did he tell you? About this place?'

'Before I went cold on him and he clammed up, he was eager to please. He said the Soviet prisoners in '41 hadn't just been used to make this clearing and build the camp. They'd also built something deep in the forest, involving a lot of concrete. It became a feared place. By the time our French- man arrived, rumour was that nobody who went there came out alive. He said that every few weeks a truck with a Gestapo motorcycle escort would appear at night at the camp entrance and disappear down a track into the forest. Once he watched the truck become enmired in mud and saw the people inside taken out. He said they were fit, healthy-looking young men and women, some with the Star of David on their sleeves, but of all different races and types – Slavs and Mongolians who were probably Soviet prisoners, fair-haired Nordic types, maybe from occupied Norway and Denmark, darker Mediterranean people, and North Africans like he grew up with in Marseille, perhaps French colonial prisoners of war.'

'Almost as if they'd been chosen to represent every race the Nazis came across,' Mayne murmured.

Cameron nodded. 'The trucks would disappear into the forest, and a few days later there'd be activity at a deep pit beyond the mound where the Soviets had been shot. Our Frenchman said he knew there were fresh burials because of the lime, which was trucked into the camp in large quantities and taken over there. Huge amounts of lime, apparently, far more than you'd need unless the bodies were really contaminated, I thought.'

'Contaminated with *what*?' Mayne asked.

Cameron stared at him. 'I don't know. I dread to think. I'll come to that. Our man also said an SS servant he'd befriended in the kitchen told him a story, about an SS guard who'd lost his temper with the Jews who were used to carry the lime. The guard had said that unless they worked harder, he'd send them to the *Geherer* in the forest and they'd suffer the fate of all the others who had gone in there. The Gestapo who were apparently always lurking around this camp got wind of his threat and took the guard away the next day, never to be seen again. Whatever was going on was clearly very top secret.'

'*Geherer*,' Stein murmured. 'That means bunker, storage room.'

Mayne started to take a deep breath, then stopped abruptly. His sense of smell had returned. The stench suddenly seemed to fill his stomach, and he nearly threw up. He swallowed hard. '*Geherer*. A bunker. That sounds like a place for storing stolen art. What you suspected, Stein? That's what we're after. But it's hard to tally with this man's story, if it's true. Perhaps the people he saw going in were just more construction labour, fit young men.'

'And women,' Cameron said.

Stein turned to them. 'Two weeks ago, the US 8th Infantry Division stumbled on a sealed-up copper mine at Siegen, near Aachen. Inside they found a huge cache of art treasures, old masters by Rembrandt, Rubens, Van Dyck, as well as priceless artefacts, including the crown of Charlemagne. Some were local cathedral treasures there for safekeeping during the war, but there was also art looted by the Nazis. It was just what the Monuments, Fine Arts and Archives section had been looking for. It was our breakthrough. That's why I was rushed here. We believe there will be many more such places, dozens, hundreds, some of them in mines and other makeshift hiding places, others in purpose-built bunkers.'

'What could hiding art conceivably have to do with this place? With all this horror?' Cameron asked, gesturing around them, then letting his hand drop.

'The all-encompassing ideology,' Stein said grimly. 'The looting of art, the destruction of art, is all part of the same ideology, the Nazi programme of hate. In 1907, Hitler was rejected by the Vienna Academy of Fine Art. He was a competent artist, but lacked imagination. Two of the academicians were Jewish. Hitler never forgot that, nor the modernist art he never had the flair to create. When he came to power, he ridiculed it, destroyed it or had it sold out of Germany. Art was to be cleansed, just as race was to be cleansed. This – what we see around us, the horror this represents – was Hitler's ultimate canvas. Absolute ideology. Absolute realism.'

Mayne looked at Stein. 'And stolen antiquities?'

'On the way in, you asked about Schliemann's treasure,' Stein replied, eyeing him shrewdly. 'I said nothing. But now I think I owe you an explanation. Heinrich Himmler ran a department known as the Ahnenerbe, the Department of Cultural Heritage. Before the war they went all round the world searching for evidence of Aryan roots, for the origins of the master race. In Europe they excavated sites they thought would reveal Germany's heroic past. They became fixated on kings, on rulers who seemed to display the characteristics the Nazis most admired, absolute power, absolute ruthlessness. The emperors of Rome were a huge inspiration. But they also looked further back, to the semi-mythical kings of prehistory.

Any artefacts associated with those kings had huge lustre in the eyes of the Nazis, and they would do anything to get hold of them, to glorify their heroes.'

'So you're saying that anything of that treasure from Schliemann would have huge cachet.'

Stein nodded. 'Huge.'

'It's time we showed Cameron that drawing.' Mayne took out a sheet of notepaper from his tunic pocket, unfolded it and held it for the others to see. The sheet had been torn from a German order book, with Gothic typeface at the top, and was thin, almost diaphanous, so the grey sky seemed to suffuse the drawing with depth, with dimensionality. The lines were precise, in crayon. In the centre were simple sketches of a man in a dark suit and a woman, gaily coloured. Between them was a little girl, holding hands with them. Below the adults were two words, *Mama* and *Papa*. But it was the object drawn above the child's head that was so extraordinary. It was golden, luminous, with a silvery interior, and the child was looking up at it.

'*Good God,*' Cameron whispered. 'It's a swastika. But a *reverse* swastika. And those colours.' He looked up. 'Why would a Jewish child draw that?'

Mayne looked at Stein, then at Cameron. 'We assume it's something she's seen. What you were saying earlier. Somehow associated with trauma. But we're putting two and two together and thinking it's here, somehow associated with that bunker.'

Cameron looked at them. 'Have you seen this before? This symbol?'

Stein spoke quickly. 'We don't know what it means. Not yet.

But we've had it described to us, very exactly. The interrogation of a top Nazi official. The details are top secret. That official is no longer alive. That's how deadly serious this is.'

Mayne stared at Stein, his mind in a whirl. *It had been seen somewhere before.* When should he tell Stein? About the treasure the old foreman had seen under the Mask of Agamemnon? A treasure that had become a dread symbol in Nazi Germany? Stein had spoken of the Nazi fervour for ancient mythical kings, for Aryan roots, and everyone knew their fetish for symbols and secrecy, for codes and decrees. Was that what had happened? Somehow, someone had found this treasure, symbol of Agamemnon, symbol of Troy, secreted away in Germany by Schliemann, and made it instead into a symbol of hate, of some hidden horror that Stein could not bring himself to tell, *or did not even yet know*. It was suddenly imperative that they find out more. Mayne turned to Cameron. 'Where is the girl who drew this likely to be found, if she's still alive?'

Cameron pointed. 'That hut ahead. That's where the children are, the *Kinderbaracke*. A Red Cross nurse is looking after them. Come on.' He led them around the hut to a line of stretchers in the shade, facing away from the camp, away from the bodies and the horror. Each stretcher held a small form, beneath a blanket. Two British soldiers with Sten guns slung over their backs crouched among the children, offering cups of water. A woman got up from beside one stretcher, gently raised the blanket to cover the head of the still form beneath, then bowed her own head for a moment. She was wearing dungarees, gaiters and rubber boots like Cameron's, with her hair tied in a scarf. She looked up as they approached.

'Helen,' Cameron said quietly, gesturing back at the two officers and Lewes. 'Just a few questions. We won't take up any of your time.'

Mayne saw that the nurse's eyes were tired and grey like Cameron's. She nodded, but remained where she was, turning away from the dead child to the one on the stretcher on the other side, holding the emaciated head in one hand and a cup in the other, dripping water into the open mouth. She put down the cup and gently raised the child's left arm, showing a black smudge below the elbow. 'That's the Auschwitz tattoo,' she said. 'They all have it. Their parents are gone, murdered by the Nazis, in the Polish ghettos, in Krakow, Warsaw, in the death camps. According to the adult inmates we've spoken to, almost all of the children who arrived at Auschwitz were gassed immediately. These are the ones who survived selection. Some are Dutch children of Jewish families in the diamond trade, kept alive by the Nazis for ransom. Others are children who had arrived in Auschwitz before the gas chambers were built, and had made themselves useful in the camp. They somehow survived the march from Auschwitz a few months ago. We brought them here, away from the barracks, to get them away from the typhus.'

Mayne showed her the drawing. 'Do you know who did this?'

She glanced at it. 'Several of them have done drawings like that. It's the first thing they draw when we give them crayons. Images of their parents. Sometimes on the railhead at Auschwitz, where the Nazi doctors separated parents and children. It's as if . . .' She paused, just as Cameron had done, at a loss for words. 'It's as if that moment lives with them for ever, frozen in time, as if all that's happened afterwards is a nightmare. They want to wake up and go back. So they draw it, the last image of their parents. It's as if liberation has allowed them to see an image of happiness that the survival instinct has denied them for so long, and they become fixated on it, see nothing else. It's heartbreaking.' She glanced at the picture. 'Yes. That was the girl with the harp. She's over there.'

They followed her gaze. About fifty yards away they saw a figure seated on a chair, with her back to them, in the middle of open ground. Mayne could see her shorn head and thin neck, but not her face. She was wearing an outsized army shirt and trousers, evidently given to her by the soldiers, but she was barefoot. Her hands lay on her knees, and she seemed motionless, staring ahead. 'She's about seventeen,' the nurse said. 'According to the others, she survived Auschwitz because she worked in a place called Block Twelve. She was a sex slave, used by the SS guards and privileged inmates. Shortly before we arrived here, the female camp leader, the *Lagerführerin*, found out what the girl had been at Auschwitz, and took her into the forest one night along with several of the guards. I can't bear to tell you what they did to her. After the camp's surrender, several inmates who went after the guards found her in the forest and brought her here. She hasn't spoken a word, but she did do that drawing. She's done many like it, almost identical, but that's the only one I've seen with the swastika above her parents. Odd. It's reversed. But they have seen that hated thing so much, it must be burned into their minds. Who knows why she drew it there.'

'The drawing was taken from her by an SAS patrol who

were in here yesterday,' Mayne said. 'Their officer took it to VIII Corps HQ.'

'I know,' she said. 'I gave it to him. A Captain Frazer, Hugh Frazer. They'd shot some of the guards, and a German officer who fired at them. Captain Frazer stayed with me for a while afterwards, and tried to help with the children. He was pretty frayed. Spent a long time here, on the edge of this bed, just sitting and looking at the girl with the harp. It was strange. It was almost as if . . . as if he'd found peace, just sitting here, looking at her. Funny how it takes men like that, killers one moment, and then just sitting there, broken by it all. I only wish you chaps could cry a bit more easily. God knows, I'm close to it myself after having been here for twenty-four hours.'

Mayne swallowed hard. Hugh. 'Frazer's a friend of mine, actually. Saw him back at HQ. Thought he needed a rest.'

She nodded. 'I thought it was malaria. I was in India before this. So many of them coming out of Burma had it. You get pretty good at spotting the signs.'

'We both picked it up in Egypt. Long time ago now.'

'What's she doing now, sitting out there all alone?' Stein asked.

'The others said that before she was used as a prostitute, she survived selection at Auschwitz because her parents told the SS she could play the harp. Her parents were taken away to be gassed. The Nazis ran a camp orchestra, the *Lagerkapelle*. Many of the Jews were accomplished musicians, and the Nazis had them play the music the Jews had loved, the classics, folk songs, especially modern jazz, songs like "I Can't Give You Anything But Love", you know? Used to be one of my favourites too. It was meant to calm the arrivals during selection. Some of the people here hum snatches of it, or words from the Shabbat, in Yiddish. But so much of what they sing is anguished, despairing. I wish there was music here. There aren't even any birds any more, with those awful fires we lit to get rid of the clothes. It's all death, like the entrance to hell.' She paused, swallowing hard, then nodded towards the girl. 'You saw the local German people the soldiers brought in to see all this? I asked if anyone had a harp, and a schoolteacher brought one, a child's harp. She's sitting in front of it now.'

Mayne stared again at the girl, and saw the harp. He felt dizzy and swayed slightly, the ringing he had heard since Cassino going from one side of his head to the other. Lewes came silently up. 'Sir,' he said quietly, holding his arm. Mayne shut his eyes, opened them again, then nodded. 'I'm all right, Jock,' he said quietly, squeezing Lewes' arm. 'Good man.' Lewes moved back, still watching. Mayne tried to focus on the girl, as if he were at sea and she was a fixed point on the horizon. He blinked hard, then remembered what he had done at the death pit. He made himself think as a painter again, framing the scene, trying to imagine how he would distil it. There was no need. Absolute realism. *Girl with a harp*.

Stein stepped forward. 'We need to question her.'

'Not if she won't talk,' Mayne said.

'What is it you want from her?' the nurse asked.

Mayne pointed at the drawing. 'That object: the reverse swastika.'

'I tried talking to her about her drawings. There are some-times other objects in that place, flowers. She kept pointing at the forest. I think it could be something she saw there, where she was taken. Or maybe it's something she imagined, while she was in the hands of those SS monsters. I don't know.'

'She won't talk?' Mayne said.

'Not a word. None of them have heard her speak, even at Auschwitz. She probably has no family left in the world, nobody who knew her before. We don't even know her name.'

'All right.' Mayne looked at Stein. 'We leave her alone.'

Stein nodded. 'Time for a little recce in those woods.'

Mayne turned to Lewes, who had lit up and was smoking a few feet behind them. He folded up the drawing and handed it to the corporal. 'Take this back to VIII Corps HQ. Tell Colonel Woolley in Intelligence that I want the back-up team here as soon as possible. We want a tracker dog, Sergeant Parker and his demolition chaps for blowing open doors, the usual. And some MPs.' He glanced at his watch. 'See you back at that first sentry post outside the barracks in, say, four hours, at seventeen thirty. Got that?'

'Sir.' Lewes dropped his cigarette butt, ground it into the earth, took the drawing and buttoned it into his tunic breast pocket. Then he stood to attention and saluted. Mayne returned the salute, but Lewes remained in place, ramrod straight. Mayne gave him a tired smile, and put his hand on the other man's shoulder.

'I'll be all right, Jock. No need to worry. I've got Stein here to look after me. You get on, and look after yourself, all right? Dismissed.'

'Sir.' Lewes swivelled round and walked swiftly off in the direction they had come. Mayne nodded to the nurse.

'Thanks, Helen. And . . . thanks for letting Hugh, Captain Frazer . . . help you.' He was suddenly at a loss for words. She gave him a tired smile.

'I know,' she said quietly, touching his arm. 'I know how you chaps who've been through so much look out for each other.' She turned back to the stretchers.

Mayne looked at Cameron. 'We'd better let you get on too.'

'I'll show you the track into the forest.' Cameron led them towards the treeline, and stopped on a dirt road that led to a cut in the trees, evidently an old bridleway. They could see the barbed-wire compound fence, with an open gate. 'Anyone who's going to try to leave the camp will have done so already. We leave that gate open to let in the former inmates who want to return, who've got exhausted and realize the SS really have gone.' Cameron shook his head. 'But it's a wild place. SS still out there, I'm sure. Rather you than me.'

Mayne knelt down. The track was well-trodden, but there were no wheel ruts. 'If there's some sort of installation out there, this can't have been the main route in.'

'They wouldn't have put the main route through the camp,' Stein said. 'There'll be another way in, probably on the other side of the forest, for trucking in building materials and whatever they might have been storing there. The aerial photographs don't show anything clearly, but tracks in forests are easy to conceal. It's all consistent with something top secret.'

Cameron turned to them. 'Good luck. I won't shake hands.' He checked his watch. 'I may not see you again. I'm sure you know that the plan is to bomb the forest, to deny it to the Germans as a defensive position once the ceasefire is over.

That's what I was talking about to those officers outside on the roadblock when I met you.'

Mayne nodded. 'Thirty-six hours, a little less.'

'It shouldn't affect your activities, but what you don't know is that we may be moving the camp after all. The CO of the AA unit has been into Bremen and seen what a night raid by a thousand Lancaster bombers does. Obliterates everything, not necessarily very high-precision. The weather report's changed too, could be nasty for a few days, so the bomber pathfinders will have their job cut out to pinpoint the western edge of the forest. It's just too risky for us to stay here. In a way it's a relief. The sooner this place is blotted out, the better. By tomorrow, typhus will have killed half the inmates still alive here now anyway. It seems callous, but we're waiting before moving them, until those who are going to die do so, to free up the transport for those with some hope. They'll be trucked to the field hospital being built at Belsen. The bodies left here will all be buried and the trench bulldozed by this evening, then we'll torch the buildings. After that, the RAF can rain ten thousand bombs on the place for my money. It'd be as if this place never existed.'

'What about these people?' Stein said, gesturing back. 'I mean those who recover, physically?'

Cameron started to say something, then stopped. He took a deep breath. His voice was quavering. 'Yesterday, just after we arrived, one of the British officers gave his revolver to an inmate, to shoot one of the guards. The man immediately shot himself. He'd been talking about his little son, asking for him, a child taken from him at the Auschwitz railhead to be gassed. The man knew what had happened, he had seen it with his own eyes, but had been unable to comprehend it. That's the true horror. The horror of what happens when they start to remember. It's as if they wake up from a ghastly nightmare, but then realize it was real. I don't know what good I'm doing here. If we nurse them back to physical health and they can't live with it, how can that be right?'

They watched as Cameron hurried away, his form framed by the pastel wasteland behind him, the sun's rays diffused by the opaque miasma above. Then they turned towards the forest. They passed the bloated body of a German officer, his uniform torn open, his boots gone. He was Luftwaffe, air force, not SS. He must have been the officer who had shot at Hugh's men. Mayne remembered what Cameron had said about SS guards having escaped into the woods, about marauding inmates searching for them, living wild. He undid the flap of his holster. Stein saw him do it, and removed his own Colt automatic pistol. He clicked out the magazine, checked that it was full, slammed it back in again and pulled back the slide, seeing that a round was chambered. Mayne watched him, saying nothing, and they both moved forward cautiously along the dirt track under the trees. The pines along the edge gave way to old-growth deciduous forest, with huge oaks forming a canopy that would have concealed the track from aerial reconnaissance. 'The RAF photos show about three kilometres of dense wood in this direction,' Stein murmured. 'If the bunker's concealed in the middle, we're looking for something twenty minutes' walk, maybe half an hour ahead.'

'Are you comfortable with this?' Mayne said. 'We could wait for reinforcements.'

'No. Now or never. I have a gut feeling about this. There could be more at stake here than lost treasures. Much more.'

'And you should know we're both here on the same ticket. My unit, 30 AU, are more than just a tactical recon outfit. I hadn't heard about the interrogation of the Nazi official you mentioned, but my colonel at Corps HQ took me straight off our planned op and put me on this one as soon as that drawing appeared. That's why we were rushed out here without the usual back-up. And our job isn't just to prevent material falling into the hands of the wrong people. It's to prevent this war ending the way Hitler wants it to. '

'Okay. We do this as a team. Clean slate from now on?'

'Agreed.' Mayne raised his revolver and edged forward. 'Let's do it.'

12

Mayne and Stein walked forward in an uneasy silence, one on either side of the bridleway, occasionally raising their arms high to avoid patches of stinging nettles. Mayne kept his revolver cocked and at the ready. Suddenly there was a commotion and a woman lurched out of the undergrowth in front of them. He aimed his revolver and kept it trained on her. She staggered about, and then stood a few yards away from them, swaying. Her hair had been tied back in a bun, but was dishevelled, and her face was scratched and bruised. She wore an overcoat, muddied but decent, and she was stout, well-fed. She was clearly not one of the inmates.

She lurched closer, staring around as if she were being hunted, then peered hard at Mayne, looking at the unit flashes on his battledress, at the crown of his rank on his shoulder lapels. She had little piggy eyes. She smiled to herself, muttering feverishly. 'You are Englisher, *ja?*' She spoke with a heavy accent. Mayne nodded, keeping the pistol trained on her. She clapped her hands, her face beaming, and came closer, grabbing his arm. Her breath smelled like food, like meat, a foul smell in this place, obscene. He shook her off and pushed her roughly back. She came at him again. 'English officer? Thank *Gott* you have come. You will rescue me from this filth, these *Juden*. I know what you English really think. You don't believe me? Look. I am not one of them.' She peered furtively around and then shrugged off the overcoat. Underneath she was wearing the tunic of the SS-Totenkopfverbände. She had been a camp guard. Mayne suddenly remembered. The *Lagerführerin*, the hated camp leader. The one who had escaped into the forest. The one who had taken the girl. She thrust her lapels towards him, showing the death's-head insignia, then stood back and held her hands out, as if to rest her case. She grinned insanely, gesturing at Stein as well. '*Ja? Ja?*'

Mayne raised the Webley, aimed at her stomach and fired. She lurched backwards and then fell forward on her knees, a look of shock on her face. A gob of blood spurted out of her mouth and she made a terrible gurgling sound. He raised the revolver again and shot her in the head. She snapped back, her knees contorted. The bullet had blown the top of her head off, and fragments of bone and brain spattered the ground. Blood pumped out of the wound in a gush, and then stopped. She lay still, with one eye open and the other half shut. The sound of the shots had been a dull thud, not a crack, as if the trees and the weight of this place had dampened the report. Mayne broke open the revolver, extracted the two spent cartridges and replaced them with new ones he took from his webbing pouch. He snapped the revolver shut, then glanced at the body. 'Funny. That's the first blood I've seen in this place.'

Stein stared hard at the corpse, then looked at Mayne. 'I'm Jewish, you know.'

'I guessed it. Your name.'

They continued walking up the track. The trees were now bigger and the canopy denser, obscuring the sunlight. The thick scrub on either side of the track near the forest entrance gave way to large trees, their lower branches dead and leafless, allowing them to see into the gloom on either side. Regular rows of pines from an old plantation were bisected by the path. As they passed each row it was as if they were parting veil after veil, compressing the view ahead, making them look sideways down the tunnels between the trees where the perspective seemed clearer. It was a curious trick of the mind, disconcerting. There was no sign of any more people, but Mayne knew there were others out there. He wished he could hear better, wished his body was less damaged. In past wars he would have been dead by now, a warrior who had done his deeds on the battlefield and could die with honour. He felt as if he were on borrowed time, and those words, glory, honour, had a hollow ring to them, only meaningful in brief snatches of daydream when he remembered an innocent version of himself before the war, before he knew what Homer had really meant, what heroes really did.

The image of the woman he had just shot flashed before him, grotesque, gushing blood. It meant nothing to him. He wondered whether like Homer he would be able to turn away from the fall of Troy, leave unsaid what no poet could describe. Perhaps this place, this horror, was beyond description, and would be blotted out in a paralysis of imagination that would follow this war, a war whose end seemed to recede the closer he thought he had got to it.

'This must be it.' Stein paused as the track came out on another roadway, with tyre tread marks clearly visible in the dried-up mud on either side. He took a compass out of his pocket and held it level. 'This runs east–west, exactly where I thought a road might run into the forest from the far side.' He pocketed the compass, and looked up at the trees. 'Completely invisible from the air.'

They turned right and followed the track as it curved round and headed west again. After about a hundred metres it began to drop in a slight gradient, cutting down into the forest floor. They carried on down until they came to an overhang created by giant tree trunks that had been deliberately laid across the track like roof beams, with enough space beneath them for a large lorry to back down. Mayne scanned the gloom ahead. 'This must lead to an underground bunker, cleverly concealed. They had to remove some big trees to dig it out, but then they covered it again by transplanting trees over an area about two hundred yards square, beyond those beams. That's what must have kept those Soviet prisoners busy. They've even cabled together the tops of some of the big trees surrounding the clearing to bend them inwards, to make it look like continuous forest from the air.'

He held his revolver at the ready and they advanced cautiously under the beams. About ten metres ahead he could see the dull grey of a concrete wall, just as he had guessed. In the middle of the wall was the black face of a metal door, with two massive metal latches padlocked over it. Mayne reached the door and tried the padlocks, to no avail. He stood back, took a deep breath, then squatted down. 'We can't do anything here by ourselves. We need to wait for my sappers to come and blow these latches off.'

Stein tried the locks. 'What time is Lewes due back?'

Mayne checked his watch. 'Seventeen thirty hours in the camp. That's almost three hours from now. We can either go back to the camp now, or leave going back for an hour so we don't have to spend any more time than we need to in that place.' He looked at Stein, and they both slumped back wordlessly against the metal door. Mayne took out his cigarettes, but then thought better of it. He craved the nicotine, but the smell was too close to the smell of burning in the camp. He wondered if he'd ever smoke again. He shoved the pack back into his battledress tunic, cracked open his revolver to check the chambers again, then stared at Stein. 'This monuments and fine arts stuff. It's really a front, isn't it? You've pretty well implied as much. I never bought the idea that art was such a priority. I was there when we bombed the monastery at Cassino, remember? And look what we did to Dresden. This is total war. And anyway, I saw the way you handled that pistol. You're not just an honorary soldier.'

Stein was silent for a moment, then spoke quietly. 'The MFAA is genuine. And we're all experts, passionate about art. But you're right. I did the full Special Operations Executive training course. We're the kind of people they wanted. Academics, art historians, archaeologists, people with a keen eye, able to spot details, to find clues, accustomed to working in the field. But not laboratory scientists. They come later.'

'Scientists?'

Stein stared at him. 'The war may nearly be over. This war. But this may only be the beginning. We know the Nazis were developing super-bombs, using nuclear fission. We're pretty confident that most of the research was still on the drawing board, and the Allied bombing campaign has wiped out most of that. But there's another threat, even more terrifying. Have you ever wondered why Hitler never used chemical or biological weapons on the battlefield? It wasn't for any ethical reason. Look at what we've just seen, the camp. There were no ethics.' Stein shook his head. 'It's because the Nazi research efforts were not going towards *tactical* weapons, but towards *strategic* ones. Not battlefield weapons, but weapons of mass destruction. Towards something even worse than that. Towards a doomsday weapon.'

'*A doomsday weapon?* What the hell do you mean?'

'With the end so near, there might be a final fanatical edict. Remember what Hitler said at the Nuremberg rally in 1938? He said that either there would be a thousand-year Reich, or there would be no Germany. No Germany means no world. Hitler made a suicide pact with his own people. And if the time came, if his armies were truly close to annihilation, there had to be a way of unleashing Armageddon. We know from our interrogated Nazi official that the signal was the Allied crossing of the Rhine. That was when Hitler knew he could never win on the battlefield. A small number of men were activated to be ready to unleash hell, to wait for the time of Hitler's choosing. We fear that time is nearly upon us.'

Mayne tapped the steel door. 'And you think this is it?'

'We believe that stolen art caches, maybe in bunkers like this one, might have been a cover for research facilities. They would have been the most top-secret facilities of all, concealed with all the ingenuity the Nazis could muster, even from their own people. Nuclear weapons research needs a lot of space. For biological research, the kind of thing I'm talking about, you only need a small room and a school chemistry set.'

Mayne suddenly had a cold feeling in his gut. 'Good God. *And a supply of human test subjects*. Those people the Frenchman told Cameron about, trucked in here by the Nazis.'

'That's why the camp was also a plausible cover. Nobody was going to bat an eyelid if they saw truckloads of people go into camps like this but never come out again.'

'So what do we do?' Mayne murmured. 'Get the RAF raid cancelled? Corps HQ could get a reserve brigade up to this forest by nightfall. Mop up any SS still out here.'

Stein shook his head. 'This has to stay top secret. It's not only Nazi fanatics we're worried about. There are others, too.'

Mayne paused. 'The Soviets?'

'Allied intelligence is riddled with spies, Communist sympathizers from before the war. A lot of them came out of Oxford and Cambridge. I took a chance with you. For all I know, you might be one of them.'

Mayne snorted. 'I was an idealist, but my fantasy world was three thousand years old, the world of Homer. You're right, though. There were plenty of Communists among my school and university friends. And while we're pointing fingers, several art historians I knew, even at the Courtauld.'

'That's what I mean. I could reel off some big names from the art world, really big names, now working in intelligence. Keeping these people in place, using them, has been part of the complex planning for the world after the war. Some of our discoveries of Nazi research have deliberately been leaked. And that's where the background of the MFAA comes into play. We're scholars, not generals or politicians. We want to do all we can to end this war, but our aim is not to find weapons that can be used against the Nazis. Our aim is preventing such weapons from ever being used. Here's the take. Either everyone has them, or nobody does. If both sides in the new world have horror weapons, then nobody will use them, right? That's the gamble. Our intelligence planners call it mutually assured destruction. If everything works according to plan, that'll become the catchphrase of the new war ahead of us, a war of standoff. It'll be the nearest we can get to recreating the détente in Europe during the decades after the defeat of Napoleon, before the Franco-Prussian War tipped the balance and set all this in train.'

'So both the Allies and the Soviets will have nuclear technology,' Mayne murmured, keeping his eyes on the woods.

Stein nodded, waving his pistol. 'But a biological weapon is another matter. All you need is a test tube. There may be many bit-players who could become terrifyingly dangerous in a fragmented world: resurgent fascist groups, or religious extremists like the Wahabists of the Middle East. A flashpoint may be a new Jewish homeland in Palestine. Our arrival may have saved those people in the camp today, but the fate of their children is what I'm talking about. The fate of *all* children.'

Mayne checked his watch. He looked around, scanning the trees, cocking his good left ear up, listening. He turned to Stein. 'All right. So what exactly are we talking about?'

'Tell me about 1918.'

'What do you mean?'

'What happened.'

'Well, the end of the Great War. The year I was born.'

'And the year of the influenza epidemic.'

'That too.' Mayne paused. 'That killed my mother, a few months after I was born.' He stared at Stein, feeling an icy grip in his stomach. He stared again, then looked at the metal door. *'You're not serious.'* His voice was hoarse. 'They couldn't have done that. It'd be suicidal.'

Stein spoke urgently, under his breath. 'I'm deadly serious. The Nazis could contemplate anything. Spanish influenza was the worst epidemic in human history. Allied scientists have been desperate to understand it. Here's why it's so terrifying. Normally, most flu deaths are among people with weaker immune systems: the elderly, children, those already ill. In 1918 it was different. Most of the victims were healthy young adults. I'm old enough to remember it. The scientists have made a breakthrough, and it's terrifying. It looks as if the virus caused the body's immune system to auto-destruct. The stronger the immune system, the more deadly the result. At the time, so many young adults were being killed in the war that the epidemic just seemed like an extension of that. But the Spanish flu infected at least a third of the world's population. It probably killed fifty million people. *Fifty million.* That's more than *five times* the number killed in action in the Great War.'

Mayne swallowed hard. 'And you think the Nazis have been experimenting with it?'

'The alarm bell rang after we liberated Paris. By then, most of the French Jews had been deported to the camps, but there were still a few slave labourers left. One of them told US interrogators a bizarre story. In 1941, a small group of Jews had been detailed to join two SS doctors in a night visit to the Père Lachaise cemetery, the largest in Paris. They dug up half a dozen graves. The doctors knew what they were looking for. The graves all contained people who had died in 1918. They were well-off people, all buried in lead-lined coffins.'

'Meaning the possibility of intact bodies? Where the virus might still be found?'

Stein pursed his lips. 'The coffins were dug up but left unopened and quickly trucked away. The Jewish labourers were shot over the open graves. One man escaped among the tombs. The entire Gestapo in Paris were detailed to hunt for him. He remained on the run. He's in quarantine in an isolation facility in England now.'

Mayne was beginning to feel physically sick. 'Do you think this place, where we are now, was where they brought the bodies?'

'Something was going on here. Remember what I said. You don't need much space. Cold storage for bodies, incubators, a basic microbiology lab. The kind of weapon we're talking about is invisible to the human eye.'

'And what Cameron told us. A place with a supply of healthy young people for experimentation.'

Stein stared at Mayne. 'All I can tell you for certain is this. Hitler had it planned from before the war. Either a thousand-year Reich, or nothing. Here we are, probably days from the end of the Reich. If Nazi scientists did manage to isolate the Spanish flu virus, to nurture it – maybe, Lord help us, to mutate it to a more virulent form – then someone will have been detailed to use it. *Someone who might be here now, waiting.* You've seen how fanatical the SS can be. There would be no morality to hold them back. Only the order of their Führer, and that would be absolute. I saw the flu epidemic of 1918 with my own eyes. Whole wards full of young people drowning in pneumonia, screaming as their immune systems ate into their brains. It seemed like a world gone mad. Even H.G. Wells couldn't have thought it up. And now, in this war, in this place, at Belsen, at Auschwitz, we've seen what war can do. There are no boundaries. With a virus like Spanish influenza deliberately infecting the world, with all the cold efficiency of Nazi planning, there will be no miracle this time, no recovery from horror and death.'

Mayne shut his eyes for a moment. *A world gone mad.* He looked at Stein, started to speak, then stopped. He had had a terrible thought. The war in north-west Europe, the war since Normandy, had gone on far longer than anyone had thought it would. The Allies had mustered overwhelming forces. Yet there had been long periods of stalemate, of slow progress, of seeming vacillation as the armies lumbered forward. He could barely think it. *Had it been deliberate?* Had the generals been forced to stall by Allied intelligence, to allow intelligence agents to find this horror, this doomsday weapon, before the armies entered the homeland and Hitler issued the order? He stared at Stein. 'You think the reverse swastika is the secret symbol?'

'We think it's an activation code. We captured a high-ranking Wehrmacht officer who was one of the few who knew of the plan, and he eventually talked. He only knew a little about it, but it was enough. We think the orders were sent out from the Führerbunker at the British and American crossing of the Rhine, Operation Plunder, on the twenty-third of March. That was three weeks ago. There will probably be a redundancy, maybe two, three, four individuals converging on the place where the weapon is kept, if we're right. Enough to ensure that one gets through.'

'And then some kind of final code. A trigger.'

'The word that Hitler is dead. Has committed suicide.'

'What was the code called?'

'The officer eventually told us. It was Der Agamemnon-Code.'

'The Agamemnon Code,' Mayne repeated. 'My God. I knew it.'

'What is it?'

'It's that name. Agamemnon. I know where that symbol came from. It was a device, an ancient artefact. One of the most astonishing artefacts ever unearthed.'

Stein paused. 'From Mycenae. We know. We don't know the details of how it was discovered. That's irrelevant to us. But the man we interrogated told us it was from Mycenae, and secretly stored for decades in Schliemann's home town of Neubukow in Mecklenburg-Schwerin. The Ahnenerbe officers found it when they went there under the express orders of Heinrich Himmler to look for Schliemann's treasures. They loved everything to do with Troy because of the swastika imagery. Himmler had done his research. He thought the golden swastika was the palladion, the lost symbol of Troy. It was made of gold and meteoritic material, from an ancient meteorite that fell on Troy far back in prehistory. They took it in secret triumph to the SS fantasy-castle at Wewelsburg, where it stayed reverently locked away. It was going to be the centrepiece of the Führermuseum at Linz, another Nazi fantasy. Where it is now is anybody's guess. But somewhere on the way it got hijacked as the symbol of the final apocalyptic decree. The Agamemnon Code.'

Mayne was silent for a moment. He spoke quietly. 'Just one question. *When* was that Nazi interrogated? *When* did you know that the crossing of the Rhine would be the signal?'

'Soon after the liberation of Paris. August 1944.'

'*Christ*. August 1944. So you've been searching for more than six months.'

'As you have been. You didn't know it, but you were too. You said it yourself in the jeep on the way in. Strategic intelligence. Look how many outfits there are operating ahead of our lines. Your unit, 30 AU. Mine, the MFAA. After Normandy, the whole of British Special Operations Executive redirected their efforts towards uncovering secrets. But hardly anyone knows the real reason. If all goes to plan, *hardly anyone will ever know*. It will go to their graves with them. *With us*. I happen to be one of those few. And I'm telling you because we're so close to it here, closer than we've ever been. And the clock is ticking. Hitler can't last much longer. What frightens me is that whoever it is might be frightened themselves into taking action now, in case they're discovered. If I'm right about this place.'

'Still a big if.' Mayne leaned back. He had meant to ask, but could not. It would do no good to know. It was almost beyond contemplation. He thought of the terrible grind of the war since Normandy, all the friends he had lost, the killing he himself had done, then the dreadful camp, all of those deaths, the girl with the harp, what had happened to her in this forest. Was all of that a price that had been paid to get them, the two of them, by chance, to where they were now, this day? He shut the thought from his mind. He took a deep breath and knelt up, checking his watch. 'Right. I think I need a breather from this place. From everything you've just been saying. Let's get back. Lewes should be setting out from Corps HQ by now. Knowing him, he'll be early. Doesn't like to leave me alone. We can meet him at the camp gate.'

There was a rustle in the foliage behind them. Mayne spun round, revolver at the ready. A man lurched out, dressed in the tattered blue-striped uniform of a camp inmate. His arms were up, hands open towards them. His head was roughly shaven and he was gaunt-faced, his eyes sunken. *'Jude. Jude,'* he said in a cracked voice, pointing at himself with one hand, gesturing desperately with the other at Mayne's revolver. He pulled back his left sleeve and revealed a tattoo like the one the nurse had shown them on the child from Auschwitz, but raw, inflamed. Stein put his hand on Mayne's arm and he slowly lowered the pistol. Stein waved at the man to calm down.

'Shalom aleichem,' he said.

'Aleichem shalom,' the man replied, looking pathetically grateful. Stein spoke urgently with him in Yiddish, asking short questions and the man answering rapidly, several times pointing to the structure behind them and then down the side of the building, where all Mayne could see was the buried concrete wall. Stein put his hand up to silence the man and turned to Mayne.

'I think he's genuine. He says he's Hungarian Jewish.'

'There were Hungarian fascists among the Waffen-SS we captured at Cassino,' Mayne murmured, his finger still on the trigger. 'Not Jews, of course, but some of them knew Yiddish and could pass muster.'

'He speaks the Hungarian dialect of Yiddish flawlessly. I know it, because my mother's family were originally from the German borderland near Hungary.'

Mayne pursed his lips. 'So what's his story?'

'He says he was one of the final batch who were deported by the Nazis from Budapest to Auschwitz, late last year. He was selected for something called the Zondercommando, Jewish assistants who cleared the bodies from the gas chambers and then burned them.'

'He told you that?'

'That's what I mean. Why tell something like that if you're spinning a tale?'

'Because it makes the story more convincing. Go on.'

Stein saw Mayne's concern, and paused. 'He said he was singled out with several others and brought here about three months ago. He said the Nazis were always bringing small batches of healthy young people to the camp. That's exactly what Cameron told us. They were kept separate from the others, well fed, then brought into this building. None of them came out alive. The bodies were never sent to the camp crematorium but were buried in a deep lime-filled pit on the edge of the forest, by men in protective overalls and gas masks.'

'He must have overheard us talking about the virus. That sounds like confirmation of experimentation on humans. Exactly what we might want to hear.'

Stein looked uncertain. 'He says he doesn't speak English. Look at him. He doesn't understand a word we're saying. He says he and several others escaped into the forest five days ago. They've been hunting down and killing any of the former SS guards they've found hiding out here. That's also what we heard was going on.'

'Strange they didn't get that woman, the *Lagerführerin*. Her disguise wasn't going to fool anyone.'

'I mentioned that to him. Apparently she only fled into the forest yesterday, when the troops arrived. But this man and his comrades didn't want to put themselves at any more risk. Once the camp was liberated, they just wanted to survive. They knew she'd be caught eventually, precisely because she made so little effort to disguise herself. He said that he and the others just wanted to wait for Allied soldiers like us to arrive so they could show the world this place. I told him the forest was due to be bombed, that it was time to leave. He got agitated. You saw that. Went very pale. He said we had to see what was inside the bunker then, immediately. They've got the keys. They took them off a dead SS man. He knows another way in.'

'You mean where he was gesturing?'

'Around the corner. Behind those fallen logs. Apparently, it's where they used to take the bodies out.'

Mayne took a deep breath. He felt a sudden jolt of pain in the old wound in his shoulder, cutting into him like a knife, but he kept steady and gestured with his revolver. 'All right. We haven't got time for more of this. We need to get back to Lewes. Tell him to show us the way. Quickly.'

Stein spoke in Yiddish to the man, who put his hands

down, nodded enthusiastically and scurried towards the corner of the concrete wall about five metres beyond the barred door. Mayne and Stein followed him around the corner, ducking beneath a jumble of logs and cut boughs that partly concealed a ramp leading down at a low angle along the side of the building, ending about three metres below the level of the surrounding forest. It was a loading bay, wide enough for a small lorry to back down. On the side of the building was a jumble of cut logs that Mayne guessed had been dropped there within the past few weeks to hide the entrance.

The man began to shift the logs aside, working with ease. Mayne remembered his story. His strength seemed plausible. In the death camps, only the most proficient workers would have been kept alive, and this man's job at Auschwitz had been to haul and stack bodies. Even so, his wiry frame concealed remarkable strength for one who had eaten little for weeks. Perhaps the adrenalin of the moment was what kept him going, if liberation was what he and his comrades had been waiting for. Mayne kept his revolver unholstered, but lowered it. The man pushed aside the final log to reveal a metal door, smaller than the other entrance. He straightened up, wiping his brow, then produced a key from the chain around his neck and inserted it in the padlock that hung from a massive metal latch across the door. The lock sprang open and he removed it, dropping it to the ground. He swung open the latch, pushing the door inwards, then reached inside and switched on a light, before turning and speaking quickly to Stein in Yiddish. Stein followed and gestured back to Mayne. 'He says the place has its own generator, but after the Allied bombing of the hydroelectric power stations last year, they installed a couple of charged-up U-boat batteries for back-up. There's enough electricity to keep the basic amenities going for years, decades. They needed it for dehumidifiers, apparently, and other equipment.'

Mayne peered in. 'I wonder what that equipment might have been,' he murmured. 'Dehumidifiers I can understand, though. It must get damp down here. A problem for storage.' He followed Stein into a dimly lit corridor about ten metres long. At either end were glass-fronted booths, evidently security posts. He peered into the booth at the entrance. Everything still seemed in place, as if it had been hastily abandoned, the phone still on its receiver, and stationery and other paraphernalia neatly arranged.

The man spoke in Yiddish again, and Stein looked back at Mayne. 'Apparently it was only abandoned by the SS a few days ago, when they knew the camp was about to be surrendered. Our man says he and his comrades were waiting in the woods and ambushed the guards. This place was stocked up for a siege, and this is where he and his friend have been getting their food.'

They reached the far end of the corridor. The booth contained an MG-42 machine gun on a tripod, its receiver still glistening with oil and a bullet belt slinking down to a cartridge box on the floor, like a coiled serpent. There was a clang and Mayne turned back in alarm, his revolver raised. The metal door had swung shut. The man spoke quickly to Stein, who put a hand on Mayne's arm. 'Don't worry. He says the door's on an angled pivot, and closed itself. The Nazis didn't want anyone stumbling in here.'

Mayne felt uneasy, confined. It was as if they had entered the underworld, and passed beyond a portal where return might be impossible. 'All right. Let's get this over and done with.'

A locked door barred their way. The man produced another key and opened the padlock, and the door swung open. The interior was already lit, with bare bulbs hanging from wires strung high above. It was a cavernous chamber, with curved walls like a Nissen hut. The lattice of steel reinforcement rods in the concrete was clearly visible, evidently designed to withstand bomb blast. The shape reminded Mayne of the London underground station where he had sheltered during a German bombing raid early in the war. He looked around. It was packed with wooden shipping crates, pushed together like old coffins in a crypt, leaving a narrow passage ahead to another door at the far end. The man was already halfway down the passage, gesturing for them to follow. Mayne and Stein stood transfixed, staring at the crates.

'Is this what I think it is?' Mayne murmured.

'Only one way to find out.'

Mayne holstered his revolver and unsheathed the commando knife he kept at the back of his webbing belt. He approached the nearest crate, then quickly prised up the lid and toppled it off. He sheathed the knife, and they both peered in at a mass of crumpled paper and straw packing material. He reached in and pulled out handfuls of the material, and they both gasped. 'These are canvases, old paintings,' he exclaimed.

'*I knew it*. Let me have a look at one,' Stein said, reaching in and pulling out more of the packing material. 'I just need to identify one painting. Just one old master. Then we can keep going.'

Mayne carefully pulled out a framed painting, propped it on the crate and ripped open the protective paper that had been wrapped crudely around it, revealing the canvas beneath. Stein caught his breath again. 'This is wonderful.' He whipped on a pair of spectacles and took out a torch, shining it at the painting, the deep colours and imagery of the canvas reflected at them. '*Portrait of a Young Man*, by Raphael,' he murmured. 'Stolen in 1941 from the Czartoryski Museum in Krakow, Poland, on the personal orders of Göring.' He took off his glasses and looked around. 'That makes this place very important indeed. It could be an absolute treasure trove.'

Mayne looked at the canvas, and shook his head in disbelief. He knew this painting well. He had given a print of it to Hugh before the war, had hung it over the fireplace of his college sitting room in Oxford. They had shared a bottle of wine in front of it, then gone for a walk along the river Isis. It had been one of those perfect days. He looked down for a moment. He wondered how Hugh was now. He hadn't looked at all well. He hoped he wasn't with his SAS unit somewhere on the edge of this forest, looking for the Germans, waiting. He hoped they had taken him out of the line. The end of the war was so close now. Hugh must survive. Mayne found himself suddenly crying, weeping, here of all places, in this awful bunker. He wiped his eyes, and shuddered. *Please God, let Hugh survive.*

The man shouted to them in Yiddish, his voice harsher now, agitated. Stein listened, then turned to Mayne. 'He says this is only the beginning. He says there's more, much more. He says we need to follow him to the end, to the door at the other side.'

Stein stared hard for a moment into the eyes of the young man in the painting, shook his head, smiled broadly and then turned away. Mayne pulled the protective paper back over the painting, then followed him. A few steps on he saw another open crate, close to the wall. He squeezed quickly between the boxes to have a look. This crate had also been packed with straw. It was lit by a bare light bulb directly overhead. He leaned awkwardly over and put his fingers on the edge of the crate, pulling himself forward by the strength of his arms, careful not to twist his bad shoulder. He peered inside.

He had found it.

It was there, nestled in straw at the bottom of the crate, partially wrapped in a piece of old burlap, as if it had been brought here recently and hastily unpackaged, not part of the carefully packed collection around him. It was resting the way the old foreman of Schliemann's had described it, in reverse. A swastika, symbol of unimaginable horror, but somehow different, speaking of a different world, one Mayne had stepped out of six long years ago. He heard the ringing again in his ears, but this time it was like a distant clash of arms, like the mighty contest that had once transported him to the age of heroes. For a moment he was back on the hillside overlooking Mycenae, wondering what had driven the king of kings to set it all in motion, to lead his army to Troy. Now he saw what Schliemann had seen. *The most fantastic treasure ever found.* And he remembered what the girl had drawn, the girl with the harp, sitting out there in that wasteland. *So this was what she had seen too.* They must have taken it out, paraded it around when they brought her here.

'Mayne.' Stein's voice broke in, a dull, resounding echo. 'He's going to open the door for us.'

Mayne pushed back from the crate, twisted round and searched for the voice. His mind was in a tumult. He saw Stein and the man standing by the door at the far end of the room. He felt the dread lurch in the pit of his stomach again. Another door, another room. Something else had been going on here. Perhaps the art, the treasure, had all been a front. *Perhaps Stein had been right.*

He made his way through the crates quickly and reached Stein. 'You've got your Raphael. Now listen to what I've found.'

Stein jerked his head to the door. 'It can wait. This is more important.'

The door was metal. Halfway down was a swastika, saucer-sized, impressed into the metal within a roundel. It was tilted sideways in an X shape. Mayne realized that it was some kind of keyhole, and had been opened. It was magnetic, pulling his wrist with his watch towards it. *It was exactly the same shape and size as the swastika he had just seen in the crate.* Mayne looked higher. There was a small clouded window, like a porthole. It was dark inside, but he could see green growth around the inside edges of the window, like algae. Maybe the dehumidifiers in this room had failed. Stein stood to his right, the man to his left. The man raised his right arm to pull out the upper latch of the door. As he did so, the sleeve of his tunic fell back, revealing the raw red tattoo on his wrist and then another tattoo, an older one, further up under his bicep.

Mayne stared. He remembered the soldiers they had captured in Italy, with their blood group tattooed in that way.

He froze. *Only the SS did that.*

In that split second the man realized what Mayne had seen. He pulled Mayne's right arm back and twisted it up, shoving him violently against the door, pressing his cheek hard against the window. Mayne heard a click under his right ear and felt cold steel against the nape of his neck. He cursed himself for letting his guard down. The man had come at him on his right side, where he was deaf. He should never have holstered his pistol. It was what he always told his soldiers. *It only takes one mistake.* The cold steel was removed and there was a deafening crack. He felt a warm wetness splatter the side of his head, and Stein's body slumped to the floor. The man let go of his arm, and Mayne's hand dropped, instinctively searching for the hilt of the knife in his belt. Then the barrel was pressed into his neck again, burning hot now. 'Your Jewish friend is dead,' the man hissed, close to his ear, speaking in English, barely audible through the ringing in Mayne's ears. 'You see? They will never escape us. And now I will unleash hell. This war has only just begun. *Heil Hitler.*' Mayne felt the muzzle thrust into his neck, and saw the man's other hand push up the second latch on the door. He unsheathed the knife, then flipped it so the blade faced upwards, holding it flat against his back. The man kicked the door and Mayne could feel it give, edging inwards. '*Raus,*' the man snarled, pushing his body hard against Mayne. '*Schnell.* You wanted to find out what was going on in here. Now you will have your wish.'

A light flashed on inside the room. Mayne looked through the window.

He saw something too horrible for words.

The door swung open, and he lurched forward, bringing the knife up, deep into the heart of his assailant. The pistol cracked. They fell together.

Then blackness.

Part 3

CONSTANTER

13

Bristol, England, present day

Rebecca Howard stood on the gloomy landing of the flat in front of the chipped white door and straightened her fleece, then eased off her backpack and waited hesitantly, glancing back at Dillen. He reached the top of the creaky wooden stairs and smiled at her. They had arrived in Bristol half an hour before, on the train from Paddington in London, having landed at Heathrow airport from Istanbul soon after dawn that morning. In the taxi from the station Dillen had called Jack on *Seaquest II* to confirm their arrival and his plan to escort Rebecca back to the hotel in London, where she would meet her school party that evening for her trip to Paris. He shivered slightly, pushing his hands into his coat pockets. The old house was one of a row of villas off Royal York Crescent, a magnificent location overlooking the city and the

Avon Gorge but exposed to the westerly winds coming off the Atlantic. For once, at least, it had not been raining, and it promised to be a beautiful June day.

He felt the cold because he was tired, and he looked forward to the warmth he always found here, sitting back on the dilapidated sofa and cradling a cup of hot chocolate in front of the gas fire, relishing the familiar smells of old books and coffee and drying clothes. It felt as if he were returning home. His parents had been killed by German bombing in London when he was only five years old, and Hugh had taken him under his wing at boarding school and offered this place as a home. There had been other young people like Dillen, and they had grown up together as an extended family. Every time Dillen mounted these stairs he felt as if he were on vacation from university, bursting to tell Hugh what he had seen and done, to introduce him to new friends. He glanced at Rebecca, and remembered with a jolt that more than fifty years separated them. He had made this same pilgrimage with her father when Jack was her age, almost thirty years before.

Rebecca gestured back down the stairs. 'Does he always leave the front door unlocked?' she whispered.

'He usually has young people staying here,' Dillen said. 'Always has done, since I was a boy. They used to be pupils like me from Clifton College and Bath School for Girls, orphans from the war with no other family to stay with out of termtime. We had the other rooms off this landing, the doors behind you. Nowadays the net's wider, I think. Street kids. Come on, knock on the door. He'll be waiting for us.'

Rebecca raised her hand and rapped on the door. A muffled voice shouted, 'Come in!' She turned the knob, pushed the door and stepped inside. Dillen slipped in behind her and shut the door. Hugh was crouched with his back to them over the electric ring in front of the gas fire. The warmth was lovely, just as Dillen remembered it. The room was large, the bedroom of a spacious Victorian townhouse, with a shuttered window that overlooked an untidy garden with large trees, the rear windows of the adjacent row of houses just visible beyond. In the centre of the room was the old sofa-bed, folded back with the bedding stowed beneath, and beside it the battered oak table that was the only gift Hugh had wanted from the school on his retirement, scarred with the graffiti of generations of boys he had taught Greek and Latin. The walls were buried under books, thousands of them, in cases and tottering piles, the spaces in between filled with old prints and drawings.

Everything was as Dillen remembered it. On the mantelpiece was Edward Dodwell's 1821 print *The Gate of the Lions at Mycenae*, the image that had so fired his imagination when he had first sat here as a boy. Beside it was the black-and-white photo from the Second World War. It showed a tanned, good-looking young man leaning languidly against the bonnet of a jeep, desert sand in the background, goggles hanging around his neck and a holster slung low over his shorts, cracking a smile at the camera. He was wearing the ersatz uniform of an irregular soldier, a tattered old jumper that made him look like a schoolboy, yet he exuded the confidence of a seasoned veteran. It was the picture of a man who had been forced to grow up fast, been toughened before his time. At the bottom was a faded signature, the words *Peter, Egypt 1941* clearly visible, in the same handwriting as the dedication to Hugh in the volume of Pope's Homer that Dillen had given Rebecca at Troy the day before.

Hugh took the pot off the electric ring and poured the contents into three mugs, then picked up a spoon and stirred them. He watched the steaming liquid for a moment, then picked up two of the mugs and turned towards them. 'Perfect timing,' he said, looking intensely at Rebecca, a twinkle in his eye. 'It's a fine art, you know. If you'd arrived a moment later, this would have been ruined.' He had an educated accent of the 1930s, with clipped vowels but a softness that came from his West Country childhood. He was wearing corduroy trousers, threadbare in places, an oatmeal-coloured jumper with holes in the elbows and a frayed silk scarf tucked in around his neck. He had thick white hair, swept back and neatly cut, and he was clean-shaven. Dillen thought he was a strikingly handsome man, and he had seemingly lost none of his vigour, despite having passed his ninety-second birthday a few months before.

Rebecca nodded politely. 'My dad told me about your hot chocolate. He said it was the best ever.'

Hugh smiled back at her. 'I do apologize. I've been rude. But I couldn't take my eye off the pot.' He held out the two mugs. 'Hello, Rebecca. Your dad has told me all about you. And hello, James. I can't believe what you told me on the phone. Marvellous discoveries. *Marvellous*. That cup from the shipwreck, with the word for king. You really think it could be Agamemnon? And the painting of the lyre-player with that word *Homeros*. Quite astonishing. It really puts the fire under our translation project.'

Rebecca took the mug and shook Hugh's hand, and Dillen

did the same. 'Hello to you too, Hugh,' he replied warmly. He nodded at the papers and manuscripts piled on the table. 'How goes the war?'

Hugh followed his gaze, then exhaled forcefully, stooped down and picked up the third mug. He stood with his back to the fire, legs apart, his free hand behind his back, and took a sip from his mug. 'The war,' he replied, 'goes slowly. Too damned slowly for my liking. It's those wretched fragments of the *Cypria* in the Trojan epic cycle. I just can't make up my mind whether they're genuine Homer or not. There's Homer in them, no doubt about it. But I just can't say whether it's the poet himself, or some later pastiche of bits and pieces that survived down to the Hellenistic period, thrown together to look plausible. I'm completely stumped. I can say that to you, but not to my editor at the university press. My siege, James, is in need of a Trojan Horse.'

'Then I can be your Odysseus.' Dillen took a large envelope out of the laptop case he had been carrying, stepped over to the table and dropped it on the pile of manuscripts. 'As I promised.'

'You're certain you want me to do this?'

'Never more so.' Dillen turned to Rebecca. 'I've asked Hugh to help me translate the *Ilioupersis*. After spending time with your dad and Maurice over the past week, it became clear to me that the translation is about more than a clue to an ancient shipwreck. The fall of Troy, this text, is the backdrop to everything we're doing out there. What with my work on the excavation, it was going to take me a month or more to get the text done. Jeremy's too busy, and he doesn't have the expertise in early Greek. With Hugh's help, it might get done in a week, maybe ten days.'

'That's about how long Dad sees the fieldwork running,' Rebecca said.

'As tight as that?' Hugh murmured.

Dillen nodded. 'Very tight, I think, with the shipwreck as well as Hiebermeyer's excavation. The Turks are planning a major naval exercise in the region and everything has to shut down by the beginning of August. The IMU operation is going to have to run with military precision. They need you there really, Hugh, an old soldier, but HQ have assigned you to intelligence, I'm afraid.'

'*Plus ça change*. They were always doing that. I was too damned cocky for my own good. Always being treated like a boffin, but I preferred being at the sharp end. Still, I'm sure Jack can handle it. Wars need young men, not old ones.' He rocked on his feet in front of the fire. 'And the *Ilioupersis*. It'll be marvellous to get my teeth into some real Homer. Some Homer I can truly believe in.'

'You're convinced I'm right?'

'Those lines you sent me? Absolutely.'

'Excellent. *Excellent*.' Dillen put down his mug and rubbed his hands. 'After I've taken Rebecca back to London and got her settled in her hotel, I'll come straight back and we can get cracking.'

'You *really* don't have to take me,' Rebecca said. 'I *can* manage.' She looked at Hugh, and sighed. 'Sometimes they treat me like I'm some kind of innocent little girl from a finishing school. I'm not.'

'I promised Jack,' Dillen said. 'And there'll be an IMU security man waiting for us at the hotel. That's a done deal.'

Rebecca rolled her eyes. 'IMU security? *Please*.'

'Problems?' Hugh said to Dillen.

'Precautions,' he replied. 'Rebecca was involved in the repatriation of that Dürer from the Howard Gallery earlier this year, you remember? Art stolen by the Nazis. She overstepped the mark rather by going off on her own and doing a shady deal with some character in Amsterdam. Jack went ballistic when he heard.'

Rebecca stared defiantly into the air. 'It was *not* a shady deal. His name was Marcus Brandeis. Not really a bad man, exactly. He said he'd had a change of heart about the antiquities black market, but I knew perfectly well he was turning informant because he needed protection. I was just the right person for him to talk to. *And* it helped make one of Europe's most notorious black-market art dealers into a police asset.'

'*And* stirred up something of a hornets' nest,' Dillen said. 'All of the bad guys who wanted his neck, and their armies of neo-Nazi and Russian thugs.'

Hugh grinned at Rebecca. 'You're a chip off the old block. That's the real problem. Jack sees too much of himself in you.'

'He also remembers what happened to my mother in Naples,' Rebecca replied, more quietly.

Hugh reached out and touched her arm. 'Of course.' He steered her to the sofa. 'Sit, please.' She put down her mug, then shrugged off her fleece and sat down. Dillen took off his coat and sat beside her. Hugh turned back and adjusted the dial on the gas fire. 'I hope you can bear the heat. It's my one indulgence. From the war, you know. Winter of '44, in the Ardennes. Too many nights in the open. Once you've known the true meaning of cold, heat becomes the most precious thing.'

'It's perfect,' Rebecca said. 'It feels very homely.'

'That's what James said the first night he spent here, in my old army sleeping bag in the room across the landing, with the other children I put up.'

Dillen sipped his drink, fingering the pipe in his pocket. He turned to Hugh. 'About Rebecca's security. Jack thinks the IMU operation at Troy is bound to set the underworld buzzing, antiquities smugglers and dealers like Rebecca's friend in Amsterdam. Everyone knows Jack's projects are rarely piecemeal, but go for the big questions, leave few stones unturned. The advantage of having virtually unlimited resources.'

'Ephram hasn't been hit by the recession, I take it?'

'Ephram? Far from it. He keeps pumping more and more into the endowment for IMU. And he's just agreed to fund the Herculaneum ancient library project.'

Hugh turned to Rebecca. 'Ephram Jacobovich was one of my last pupils before I retired. I sent him on to James at Cambridge. I knew he was going to make a fortune. You can tell, with some boys. I was determined to stoke his fascination with ancient history and archaeology, to push him to study that at university, rather than computers. He knew all that anyway. And look what's happened.'

'That must be very satisfying,' Rebecca said.

'I was going to be a kind of archaeologist once,' Hugh said quietly, glancing back at the mantelpiece. 'With a friend of mine. Long time ago. That couldn't happen, but all of this, everything with IMU and your dad, means I'm living a little bit of that dream.' He turned to Dillen. 'Speaking of Jack. You were saying. Carry on.'

Dillen nodded. 'Jack's never made any secret of his belief that part of Schliemann's treasure is still hidden away, somewhere in Europe. It's one occasion where he felt that going public was the best way to spirit up the clues. You remember the TV documentary he did last year? He thinks the gold that showed up in Moscow in 1993 was only part of it, that Schliemann secretly sent other finds back to Germany, and that some of those may have ended up in Nazi hands.'

'So you're saying that these underworld characters just have to watch and wait.'

'Jack's worried about kidnapping and extortion,' Dillen said. 'It's becoming a bigger problem now in Europe. And of course Rebecca is vulnerable.'

Rebecca gave an impatient shrug. 'I *can* look after myself, right? Every time I've been on *Seaquest II*, Ben's given me self-defence training, and taken me through another weapon. He says I'm a natural with Dad's Beretta nine-millimetre.'

'I don't doubt it,' Hugh said. 'I don't doubt it at all.' He gave Rebecca a steely look, then turned back to Dillen. 'Now, let's get to the other reason you're here. You said on the phone that you'd been researching Schliemann's papers.'

'Only skimmed the surface. Schliemann was a prodigious correspondent. Do you remember Jeremy Haverstock, Maria's American assistant in the Institute of Palaeography? I mentioned him a moment ago. He and I worked together through Schliemann's papers from the time of his first dig at Troy in 1871 to his final visit there in 1890. It was fascinating, and Jack was right. He says treasure-hunters worth their salt always leave clues for future explorers, in case they don't make it. To find the clues, you have to get into the mind of the treasure-hunter, something Jack was sure Schliemann knew too. But it's what we *didn't* find that was so revealing. Schliemann had a virtually uncontrollable urge to tell the world everything he discovered. At Troy he found the treasure of Priam; at Mycenae, the Mask of Agamemnon. He trumpeted them both to the world. His name was splashed over the newspapers, and he loved it. But then there's something not quite right. He abruptly departed each place, Troy, Mycenae, at the moment of his greatest breakthrough, when he should have stayed and dug for more. After finding the mask at Mycenae he embarked on fifteen years of restless exploration, in Greece, in Italy, in Egypt, chasing dreams that seem half-baked, almost unhinged. It was as if he'd lost the plot, let his ego get the better of him.'

Hugh nodded. 'I was at Mycenae the summer before the war, you remember, digging with the British School. I recall sitting on the hillside staring at that magnificent place, wondering how on earth an archaeologist like Schliemann could have left it unfinished. I always thought there was something else driving him, something that allowed him to turn his back on the gold and other treasures he knew must still lie there, as if he'd found what he needed and had to move on, some kind of obsessive quest that we can only guess at now.'

Dillen pursed his lips. 'It's there in his papers, only it isn't. It's like a void. It's everything he should have said, but didn't. All the odd reasons he gave for going to those other places. To Egypt, to search for Alexander the Great's tomb? Not likely.

Why does someone on the cusp of revealing the truth about the Trojan War, the greatest discovery ever in archaeology, suddenly veer off and search for something completely different? I believe he was on a trail of clues that only he and Sophia knew about, one that began and ended at Troy.'

Hugh moved from the fireplace and sat down in the battered leather armchair opposite them, putting his mug on the floor and leaning forward on his elbows. 'So,' he said quietly. 'Why have you *really* come to see me, James? You could have e-mailed me those scans of the ancient text.' He looked at Rebecca. 'And a Howard doesn't pay a social visit in the middle of an excavation campaign. Not one producing finds like you've had in the past few days.'

Dillen gestured at the table. 'Your other project. The one I encouraged you to start. Those pages I can see with the National Archives symbol at the top. Scans of hand-written British army unit diaries from the war.'

'So that *is* it.' Hugh sat back. 'I'd guessed it when you started talking about Schliemann. All those years ago, that story I told you boys in your first Latin lesson. That's it, isn't it? About something I found during the war, a clue to the greatest treasure ever concealed?'

'And then you clammed up on us.'

'I thought you might have forgotten, or thought it was just a story to get unruly boys interested in translating Latin. I should have known better. For a long time I wished I'd never told you. I wanted to forget the war, you know. I've tried to, for more than sixty years. But as you get older I suppose the defences drop, and it's all there again as if it were yesterday.'

Rebecca undid her backpack and took out a bundle wrapped

in a sweater. She carefully extracted the copy of Alexander Pope's *The Iliad of Homer* that Dillen had given her the day before and handed it to Hugh, who took it and stared at it for a moment, then put one palm gently on the cover. 'How nice to hold this again. When did I give this to you, James? Your graduation, wasn't it?'

Dillen nodded. 'And now I've passed it on to Rebecca. I thought you'd approve.'

Hugh smiled. 'Of course.'

'I've seen the dedication,' Rebecca said cautiously.

'Ah.' Hugh swallowed hard. 'And you want to know about Peter.'

'He's tied in with this story, isn't he? James told me something on the plane, about a sketch he'd found. The girl with the harp.'

'*The girl with the harp*,' Hugh whispered. 'How do you know about that?'

'My guesswork,' Dillen said. 'Once when I was a boy you let me use one of your old sketchbooks, and there was a page with those words written in pencil at the bottom. You'd tried to rub it out. *The girl with the harp*. You'd pencilled in some outlines above, a drawing, a sketch of her perhaps, but you'd abandoned it. I guessed it was something to do with the war. I'd seen your face whenever you heard harp music. I knew you were one of the first troops into Belsen, and I just guessed.'

'She was in a camp, a small camp near there,' Hugh said quietly. He paused, picked up his mug, then put it down again. Dillen saw that his hand was trembling. He wondered whether this was right, whether they should have asked him after all, but then Hugh continued. 'The guards had gone. We'd seen to that. My chaps and I. We were in there before the liberating troops arrived, but there was already a Red Cross contingent. A nurse with the children, named Helen. Always remember her. She'd got a German living nearby to bring a harp. And there she was, the girl, sitting with the harp amidst all that death and squalor. I tried drawing it years later. It should have been Peter doing that. He was the artist, not me. I just couldn't finish it. It was a mistake even trying. I thought it might help, but it didn't.'

'You mentioned the Ardennes,' Rebecca said gently. 'That was the Battle of the Bulge, wasn't it? We did that at school. James told me you were in the SAS.'

Hugh stared at the fire, picked up and cradled his mug, then looked back at Rebecca, his eyes steely again. 'There was no glamour in it then, you know. No mystique. Nobody knew about the SAS. That was the whole point of it. I always thought the acronym was a bit silly, actually. *Special Air Service*. The only time I ever jumped was from a practice tower in the desert. Our job was to go behind enemy lines and kill. In North Africa, we crept into airfields at night and bombed and shot up sleeping men. In France before D-Day, we knifed and strangled. In Germany, after the Rhine crossings, we ambushed remnant SS and Wehrmacht, and old men of the Volkssturm, and Hitler Youth, boys as young as twelve. We didn't take prisoners, unless we were ordered to. We gave as good as we got.'

'Hitler's commando decree,' Dillen murmured.

Hugh nodded. 'All captured commandos were to be executed. I lost most of my stick – my patrol – that way, in

France. They should never have surrendered. Didn't drum that into them well enough. New chaps mostly, hadn't been with us long. Always felt guilty about surviving. But sometimes they were handed over to the Gestapo first. That's why we went to Belsen, to this other camp. We were looking for one of our chaps. We didn't find him, but we did find some SS who tried to surrender to us. Those guards I mentioned. Gave them pretty short shrift. That was when I saw the girl with the harp. She'd made a drawing, and I saw it, saw something extraordinary in it, and asked Helen if I could take it. The girl had done others, but not that image. Intelligence at Corps HQ were pretty interested too. And that was the last day I ever saw Peter.'

'Was he in the SAS too?' Rebecca asked.

Hugh shook his head. 'We'd served together early in the war in North Africa, in the Long Range Desert Group.' He gestured at the photo on the mantelpiece. 'That's when I took that picture. After the LRDG wound down, he went back to his infantry battalion, and I volunteered for the SAS. But Peter went into another outfit after he was wounded in Italy. Another silly acronym for a tough unit, 30 AU.'

'I know about that,' Rebecca said. 'It kept coming up when I was researching that painting, the art stolen by the Nazis. They operated behind enemy lines too, didn't they? Not ambushing, but searching for intelligence. Sometimes they linked up with the Monuments and Fine Arts men, the MFAA, whenever they came across stolen art and antiquities.'

Hugh nodded. 'That's exactly what happened that day. I was the one who fed the intelligence back. The place where I was given the drawing was a kind of satellite of Belsen, a small labour camp in a forest clearing. We had our suspicions that there was something in the forest and I passed them on to VIII Corps HQ, who had arranged a ceasefire to clear out the camp. Peter's unit happened to be the one operating in the area, and he was sent to the camp with his driver and an American officer, one of the Monuments Men. And of course these covert ops were never just about stolen art. Those places could conceal more sinister secrets. It was the possibility of chemical and biological weapons that was so terrifying. By then we knew what the Nazis were capable of doing. We'd heard about the death camps in the east, Auschwitz, Treblinka, Sobibor, about Zyklon B gas. *A pesticide*, for God's sake. My biggest fear was disease, epidemic. What they might have bottled up, what they could unleash.'

'And what might still be out there, still hidden away,' Dillen said.

'Unquestionably,' Hugh replied. 'That's the horror of it. Europe in 1945 was like a huge Aladdin's cave. How could we possibly have found it all? Buried bunkers, lake beds, disused mines. And it ties in with missing works of art. What you were saying about Schliemann's diaries, James. It's the same thing. It's as if there's a void. With the art, we know what's missing. We know the names of the canvases.' He pointed to a faded print above the fireplace. 'Raphael's *Portrait of a Young Man*, from Krakow. That's a pre-war print I had on my wall at Oxford. Peter gave it to me, actually. It's one of dozens known by name, vanished. And if that's *known* to be missing, what else is there we don't know about? I'm not talking about art and antiquities. It could be the biggest legacy of the Second World War, and the most terrifying. Where it might be, and who might get hold of it. For some of us, for me, that war still rumbles on, not just because I can't get it out of my head, but because it's unfinished, as if there's a gigantic concealed bomb under Europe with the clock still ticking.'

'Tell us what happened to Peter,' Dillen said. 'That final day.'

Hugh paused. 'I wasn't terribly well that morning. A recurrence of malaria, something we'd both picked up in Egypt. Only a few hours of shivers and hot flushes, but enough to make me a liability in the field. I knew that the nurse in the camp, Helen, saw there was something wrong, but I didn't want to ask her, not in that place with all those poor children dying, needing her every second. But when I returned to Corps HQ after leaving the camp, the MO checked me over and I was temporarily grounded, reassigned to Corps Intelligence. Bloody nuisance, you know. There's nothing worse than being pulled from your chaps. But there was nothing else for it. At least they kept me in touch with our ops by putting me in charge of recovering effects from anyone killed behind enemy lines. It was pretty important, in case there was anything the Germans might use, or any intelligence being brought back. A few hours after Peter had left to go to the camp, an army spotter plane reported an overturned jeep beside the road leading back from the camp. An accident, a pothole in the road. It was Peter's jeep, but it only held the body of his driver, a Corporal Lewes. I was puzzled to find that he had that drawing made by the girl in his pocket. I knew the colonel in charge of 30 AU had given it to Peter when I'd handed it in to Corps Intelligence earlier that morning, before he and Lewes set off for the camp. I'd already shown it to Peter.'

'Was that the last time you saw him?' Rebecca said.

'We only had a few moments, in the middle of a busy HQ tent, with a howitzer battery blatting away behind us. Not much time to say anything, let alone hear what we were saying. Not that it mattered, perhaps. There was a flash of exhilaration in his face, and that's what I remember. He was in a pretty bad way, too. But enough of that. You want to hear about the drawing. Peter would have been very careful with it, I'm sure. But then Lewes was his batman, so he would have trusted him with it. That was often the closest relationship, you know, officer and batman. Unspoken bond, all that.'

'Were you ever close to anyone? Like that?' Rebecca asked.

'Me?' Hugh paused, taken aback. 'Good Lord. No. Not by then. Not like before the war. We . . . were romantic then. Naïve. We even looked forward to war, to that bond amongst men we'd heard so much about. It was extraordinary, so soon after the Great War, yet it only seems to take a generation for men to forget. It's as if war has become part of our nature, as if our biology has found a way to make us forget, to allow us to do it over and over again. It was General Lee, in the American Civil War, who reputedly said, it is well war is so terrible, else we should grow too fond of it. The difference was, the civilians in the Civil War saw the horror around them. We all knew terrible loss, our fathers, our uncles, killed in the Great War, but few of us in 1939 had seen carnage close up, seen death and dying. That might have done it.'

'When you say we, you mean you and Peter,' Rebecca said.

Hugh paused, looking down. 'We were a small group. Close friends, at university. But yes. Peter was the closest.'

Dillen leaned forward. 'Corporal Lewes. Why was he driving back to Corps Headquarters?'

Hugh took a deep breath. 'I assumed they'd found something in the camp, perhaps in the forest. Peter had probably sent Lewes back for the usual follow-up team: extra riflemen, an interrogator, sappers for breaking into buildings, a bomb disposal expert, that kind of thing. The unit were a pretty impressive outfit and knew their stuff.'

'Did anyone try to send word back to Peter? Did you? About what had happened to Lewes?'

'I wanted to,' Hugh replied. 'I *desperately* wanted to. It's all such a haze. I've been over it so often in my mind. I think by then the malaria was really clouding my thinking. I had a jeep and was going to do it myself. We didn't have radio communication, of course. But events quickly overtook us. Corps HQ was concerned that the Germans might use the ceasefire to infiltrate the forest, to set up defensive positions and booby traps. We all knew what had happened to the Americans in the Hürtgen Forest, one of the nightmare battles of the war. There was not going to be a repeat of that. We already knew that the remnants of the German 2nd Marine Infantry Division were regrouping beyond the forest, along with a few survivors from an SS panzer training battalion and the 1st Panzer Grenadiers. All of them tough troops who fought to the death. There were probably only seven or eight hundred of them, but that would have been enough.'

'The Teutoburg Forest, Varus' legions in AD 9,' Dillen murmured. 'Three crack Roman legions totally annihilated by the Germans. Same neck of the woods, I think, in Saxony.

You were pretty obsessed with it at school, always seemed to bring it up in class.'

'Now you know why,' Hugh said. 'The problem was, the main road of our planned advance ran through the western edge of the forest. We couldn't bypass it without big delays. We *had* to take that road. The ceasefire would only last long enough for essential consolidation, to strengthen our line for a massive push. That was the priority for Corps HQ, regardless of what Intelligence wanted. Sometimes we felt Intelligence actually would have preferred us to halt, so they could find as much as possible before the Nazis destroyed it. We knew there was a whole secret war going on that we knew very little about. But we were soldiers, and we just wanted the war won. And keeping the momentum going wasn't just a matter of reaching Berlin before the Russians. We were all terribly apprehensive about what the Germans might have up their sleeves. We remembered Hitler's "all or nothing" speech about the Reich at Nuremberg before the war. He'd already unleashed the V-2 rocket against London. You've no idea how terrifying those weapons were. We didn't know about Nazi research into nuclear weapons then, but V-2 rockets with deadly gas or biological payloads would have been enough. And we knew that as long as there was a single fanatical Nazi at large, then all hell could be unleashed. That's why we fought the war to the bitter end. That's why our bombers flattened the cities. That's why we killed the enemy until there was no one left to kill. We felt we were fighting a desperate battle for humankind, a battle against impending doomsday.'

'So you never did try to find Peter,' Dillen said.

Hugh paused, swallowing hard. He shook his head. 'The schedule when Peter and Lewes left HQ for the camp only allowed a thirty-six-hour ceasefire. A five-hundred bomber raid by the RAF was planned on the forest the following night. But as we were recovering Lewes' body, an SAS patrol came down the road, my own chaps. They'd bivvied that night on the far edge of the forest and had watched small groups of German troops moving in, with *Panzerfaust* anti-tank rockets and what looked like demolition charges, probably for taking down trees over the road. They confirmed what Corps feared would happen. So the whole schedule was brought forward. The decision had already been made to clear out the camp anyway, and that was done in a matter of hours. The RAF raid was advanced to that night. One and a half thousand tons of airburst high explosive, as well as incendiaries and four-thousand-pound impact HE. The camp was obliterated. The forest as far as the nearest firebreaks burned for weeks, a total firestorm. The German army units that had infiltrated the forest ceased to exist. But the road through was clear for our advance. Corps HQ had got the result they wanted. Probably hundreds, even thousands of Allied troops spared.'

'But no sign of Peter and the American,' Rebecca said quietly.

'It was all down to me. I was the one who took the intelligence about the German troop build-up from the SAS patrol to Corps HQ,' Hugh replied. 'It was my responsibility. I could have decided to process Lewes' effects first. An hour's delay in passing on the intelligence and it would have been too late to reschedule the bomber raid. It might have given Peter a chance to get out, if he was still alive. But I went straight to HQ. That's the worst thing. *I was responsible for Peter's death.* Five years cheating death on the battlefield, and it was something I did that killed him. I've tried so hard to block it off, all my life, but I just can't.' He put his head in his hands, and took a shuddering breath. Rebecca leaned over and put her hand on his. He let his hands slip off his head and looked at her, his eyes red-rimmed. He took another deep breath, straightened up and wiped his eyes with his handkerchief. 'I'm sorry,' he said hoarsely, clearing his throat. 'Stupid of me. Embarrassing. Not like me at all. Anyway, all that's history now, isn't it?'

'Peter might well have been dead already,' Dillen said. 'If there were enemy troops in that forest, and renegade SS camp guards. That might have been why Lewes was driving back alone.'

'And he would never have forgiven you if you hadn't taken that intelligence straight back,' Rebecca said. 'From what you've said, he was the kind of guy who would have put the lives of all those men way ahead of his own, the soldiers who would have died fighting in the forest if the Germans had been allowed another day to get established.'

'What happened to the drawing?' Dillen asked.

Hugh blinked hard, wiped his eyes again and cleared his throat. 'I put it in my battledress tunic pocket. After I passed on the SAS intel to HQ, everything was a whirlwind. HQ was packed up immediately and moved out. I knew Peter's fate was sealed, but I hadn't yet connected myself with it. I'd passed on the intel without thinking. It was my absolute duty. And I was in a poor way, really. Then the malaria really whacked me, dropped me stone cold. Next thing I remember was coming to in a hospital in France three weeks later, hearing the church bells ringing. The war was over.'

'And you still had the drawing?' Rebecca whispered.

'Carefully folded with my belongings,' Hugh said. 'And I still have it. Over there, on my desk.'

'Can we see it?' Dillen asked.

Hugh gestured at the table. Rebecca got up and went over, scanning the papers. She pointed at a yellowed sheet of notepaper beside the computer screen, and Hugh nodded. She carefully picked it up, and stared at it, then looked at Dillen, her eyes wet with tears. 'These two people, holding the girl's hands. I know they're her parents, because . . .' Dillen stood up and put his hand on her shoulder. She sniffed and wiped her eyes, looking apologetically at Hugh. 'Stupid of me, now. Sorry.' She swallowed, and blinked hard. 'It's just that when I was a little girl, her age, I grew up without my dad, and my mum had sent me away to my foster parents in America to keep me from the Mafia world she'd grown up in. I often used to daydream, and I drew pictures like this. We were always together, holding hands, we three.'

Hugh stared out of the window. 'She would have been about seventeen when I saw her, but this is like a drawing made by a child, a little girl. After the war, I found out that most of the children I saw in those camps had survived Auschwitz, where they had seen their parents selected at the railhead for immediate gassing. Those children had been kept alive for some reason. I was told that this girl was in the orchestra. And worse. There was a brothel. But drawings like these preserved the last memory they had of their parents, as if they were still little children. *As if their whole world had ended at that moment on the railhead.*'

Dillen leaned over, and stared at the drawing. 'How strange,' he said. 'A reverse swastika. She's drawn it above her, and coloured it gold and silver.'

Rebecca took a deep breath, and blinked hard. 'A swastika,' she said, swallowing. 'So, what's the big deal about that? Isn't that what you'd expect? The hated symbol?'

Hugh spoke quietly. 'The last time I saw Peter, the last time I ever spoke to him, was those few moments we had in Corps HQ when I handed over this drawing. He and I both saw that reverse swastika at the same moment. We were both suddenly overcome with excitement. That's how I try to remember him. To understand why we were excited, I have to tell you about an extraordinary discovery at Mycenae.'

'*Mycenae*,' Rebecca exclaimed, sniffing. 'Huh?'

'Before the war. When Peter and I were digging there.'

'You mean when he made the dedication in the book.'

'A lifetime before everything I've been telling you. But what I'm about to say may be the key to the whole mystery. The key that may unlock Troy, but also open up a terrifying discovery. Are you with me?'

Dillen nodded, looked at his watch, then got up. 'Before that. Quick breather to call Jack for an update.'

'Are you all right?' Rebecca said to Hugh, putting her hand on his arm. 'This must be so difficult for you. Are you tired?'

'After all these years bottling it up, I feel I've been waiting a lifetime to tell this,' Hugh said. 'I'm not going anywhere. And a breather gives me time to do another brew-up.'

'Give Dad my love,' Rebecca said to Dillen. 'And everyone else.'

'Will do.' Dillen opened the door and turned back. 'Fifteen minutes.'

Hugh checked his watch, and leaned over the fire. 'No more, no less. Your drink will be ready.'

14

Dillen pushed open the door into Hugh's flat and pocketed his phone. He had caught Jack on *Seaquest II* just before diving, uncertain about the state of the Aquapods. The schedule off Tenedos had been delayed a few hours to allow a Turkish navy minesweeper with an underwater demolition team to remove the mine from the shipwreck. Mustafa, the IMU Turkish liaison, had also arrived, and there had been delicate negotiations with the Turkish commander to convince him that it was feasible to float and tow off the mine, rather than detonate it where it was. The commander had refused to have his divers in the water while the mine was being shifted, and Jack had completely understood. He had taken the man into the lecture room and shown him a picture of Monticelli's *Shield of Achilles*. That had done the trick, in combination with Costas taking the navy team on a tour of *Seaquest II*'s equipment to show them the other available options. Eventually two Turkish divers had gone down to attach lifting bags to the mine, but the actual job of raising it was being done using IMU's remote-operated vehicle.

It had been going on at that very moment, while they were on the phone; Jack was on *Seaquest II*'s foredeck describing it to Dillen. The minesweeper had blast protection so had remained on site, but *Seaquest II* had stood off two miles to the south of Tenedos on Captain Macalister's insistence. Meanwhile there was an issue with the electronics on one of the Aquapods. Dillen could sense the tension in Jack's voice. He was glad he was not there. The good news was that Hiebermeyer had made some kind of breakthrough in the underground passageway at Troy. Jack was going to fill Dillen in at the end of the day, when Dillen would also be able to run through anything new that Hugh might have told them. Dillen had held off mentioning the mysterious swastika until Hugh had explained the connection with Mycenae. And by then Jack and Costas should have completed their dive. If the equipment glitch was sorted out, this could be another day of huge excitement.

Dillen stood for a moment, trying to think ahead. His mind was in a turmoil. He did not know what the next few days might hold for him. Much would rest on what Hugh told them now. He would return here as planned after taking Rebecca to London, to spend time with Hugh on the translation, but only to get it started and to map a course of action. The pressure was already on at Troy to get results, with the deadline of the military exercise looming, and now he felt another line of investigation was going to cascade before them and require his involvement, with Jack and the rest of the team fully committed in the field. And they needed to keep ahead of the game before word leaked out that they were on any kind of new trail, not at Troy this time but in the shadowy underworld of present-day Europe.

He closed the door behind him, and sat down. Hugh handed him another steaming mug. 'Call get through?'

'Perfectly.'

'Good show. Are they diving?'

Dillen looked at his watch. 'Scheduled for fourteen thirty local time. They're planning to use the one-man submersibles, the Aquapods.'

'Blast it all. If only I were younger. Jack got me into a drysuit and tank in the IMU pool a few years ago, and it was wonderful. At least he keeps me up to date, with that gizmo.' He pointed at the computer half submerged under the stacks of papers on his table. 'Real-time video. Not for this project, though, it seems.'

'Media blackout,' Rebecca said. 'Too many bad guys watching. But I'm sure Dad will link you up as soon as it's safe.'

'Do you want to have a proper rest before talking more?' Dillen asked.

'Good Lord, no. Let's carry on.'

'To Mycenae, then.'

Hugh leaned forward. 'All right. The summer of 1938. One of the foremen on the excavation had actually known Schliemann. *Had actually known him.* The foreman was frail and crippled, too arthritic to dig any more, a kind of camp elder. But as a boy, he'd been the one who first showed Schliemann the mound at Hissarlik when Schliemann went there in 1868. It was astonishing to hear his account. It wasn't Schliemann who discovered Troy. It wasn't even Frank Calvert, the British consul who led him to the site. The local people had always known about it. A clan in the village of Hissarlik claimed they were descended from Hector, the Trojan prince. Schliemann knew the power of local legend, and of course he believed that real history lay behind myth. And he knew the power of dreams in childhood. That had been where his own quest had begun, as a little boy in a town in Germany, dreaming of Troy. So when he went to Hissarlik, the first thing he did was to go to the children. He offered them riches beyond their imagination, to open up the world to them as the world had once been opened up to him. And the boy who became the crippled old man had taken the bait.'

'And afterwards he followed Schliemann to Mycenae?' Rebecca asked.

Hugh nodded. 'The boy's father was a Greek sailor his mother had met in nearby Çanakkale, and the boy could pass himself off as a Greek or a Turk. Schliemann was as good as his word and took the boy on as a kind of protégé, teaching him to read, teaching him English and German, showing him the tricks that had led Schliemann himself to wealth and fame. But the boy was unambitious and content to remain by Schliemann's side. After the great man's death, he never rose above excavation foreman, working for the German and British archaeologists who followed in Schliemann's wake. But what he did tell us was fascinating. He knew perfectly well that Schliemann and Sophia had dug secretly at Troy. And he told us the Ottoman authorities knew too.'

'So the Ottomans turned a blind eye?' Dillen said.

'It was more than that. At Hissarlik, the local Ottoman vizier threatened to expose the boy's Greek paternity if he didn't inform on Schliemann. That was why the man opened up to us, all those years later, when he knew he was close to death. All his life he'd felt as if he'd betrayed Schliemann's trust, and he wanted to ease his burden and tell those he felt might forgive him. But Schliemann like many showmen was too absorbed in his own self-image to realize that others were playing him as well. He was a huge international celebrity, a powerful tool for regimes aspiring to improve their status in the world. The Ottoman court in Constantinople was a decaying beast by the 1870s, but was still a byword for intrigue. It suited the Ottomans to know that Schliemann had dug secretly at Troy and found treasure he had spirited away. One day they might use that knowledge as leverage to make him play their game, to enlist him to help blow their trumpet abroad. The Ottomans were well aware of their bad reputation. Schliemann's friend Prime Minister Gladstone of Britain was particularly antagonistic towards them. Schliemann unwittingly became a pawn in the world of international power politics. The Greeks allowed him to dig at Mycenae so they could keep up with the Turks, to allow Greece to lay claim to her own share of the Trojan War myth and the Schliemann celebrity juggernaut. Everyone knew that. But that was only what the world was allowed to see. Behind the scenes, the Greeks were playing the same game as the Turks.'

'You mean Schliemann dug secretly at Mycenae too?' Rebecca said.

Hugh leaned towards them, his voice low. 'One night in

1876, just before the excavation closed for the season, Schliemann and Sophia got the Greek inspector of antiquities – the *ephor* – blind drunk, and secretly made their way up to the citadel. Or so they thought. The *ephor* wasn't really drunk. And the boy, by then a teenager and spying for the Greeks as well, was sent to follow them. He said Schliemann was always visible at night at Mycenae because he loved to stand like Agamemnon at the highest point of the ruins, staring out towards the sea. The boy watched Schliemann and Sophia descend with their tools into the royal shaft grave, the place where a few days later the world would watch as Schliemann raised the golden mask of Agamemnon.'

'The boy saw *that*?' Rebecca whispered.

Hugh nodded. 'Then, almost fourteen years later, he watched Schliemann and Sophia do the same at Troy, secretly digging again, night after night. Schliemann should have known he would be watched. Maybe he did. Maybe that was part of *his* game. Once, when the boy was small and watched the great trench being dug through Troy, Schliemann joked that he was not the descendant of Hector but of Homer himself, always watching, perched above like an ancient bard, playing his toy pipes. The Greeks at Mycenae said that about Schliemann, too. The *ephor* told the boy that Schliemann was a poet, and Sophia was his muse. He said the Greeks had a soft spot for foreign poets coming to their shores, like Byron. He said that was really why they tolerated Schliemann. Do you remember, James, when you were a small boy and I first told you the stories of Homer, I said that we were poets too, and that one day you would sit on the walls of Troy and see the ghosts of heroes, and hear the bellow of Agamemnon?'

Dillen stared at Hugh. 'I *do* remember. You should have seen me at Troy, yesterday. But tell us what the boy saw.'

'This is where it really gets extraordinary. At Mycenae that night, he watched Schliemann and Sophia emerge from the shaft grave and then disappear down the hillside. When he thought they'd gone, he crept down to have a look himself. He saw the Mask of Agamemnon freshly revealed, and he lifted it. *Imagine it*. A small boy alone, seeing that. Just then he heard low voices above, and he quickly replaced the mask and hid himself in the back of the shaft, inside another grave. Schliemann and Sophia came back down the ladder carrying a bundle. There was much digging and exertion, and half an hour later they left, this time for good. The boy waited a long time, then came out and looked again. The earth had been tamped down as if it had never been disturbed, and even had water poured on it to look as if it had been rained on. He dug down where he'd seen the mask, and uncovered it again, and that was when he saw what he hadn't seen before, a human skeleton underneath. He hadn't seen it because it hadn't been *there* before. He realized what Schliemann and Sophia had brought with them, in the bundle. They'd brought a skeleton and buried it under the mask.'

'Ah,' Dillen murmured. 'That explains it. The mysterious deformed skeleton. It's in Schliemann's book.'

'It was apparently in very poor condition,' Hugh said. 'But the boy recognized the misshapen skull. It was from a Bronze Age cemetery the team had been excavating outside the city walls just below the Lion Gate, and then abandoned once Schliemann realized they were just humble graves, not royal tombs.'

'Why on earth would they do that?' Rebecca said. 'Put a skeleton into Agamemnon's grave?'

Hugh held up his hand. 'Before that. To Troy, almost fourteen years later. Night after night the man watched Schliemann and Sophia disappear off into the ancient citadel mound to dig alone, just as they had done in 1873 when they uncovered Priam's treasure beside the great trench. Only this time the dig was *much* more secretive, in a part of the citadel to the west that remains unexcavated today. The last time he saw them digging was the evening after the end of the second Troy Congress, held at the site in March 1890. Schliemann had sat down with the boy, the man, for a few minutes before the congress, and seemed to want to confide in him. He said he'd known all along that Priam's treasure dated a thousand years before Homeric Troy, but only at this congress would he finally acknowledge it.'

'Which he did,' Dillen murmured. 'It's on record.'

Hugh nodded. 'But it wasn't an act of humility. Not Schliemann. No, he told the man that he'd misdated the treasure deliberately, to make it seem as if the greatest treasure of Homeric Troy had been found. He had wanted to deflect attention from the *real* revelation he and Sophia believed they had begun to unearth in 1873. Only now, in 1890, had Schliemann reached the point in his discoveries at Mycenae and around the ancient world when the time was right to return to Troy, to finish the excavation, to make that revelation. The man knew it must have something to do with the secret digging. That very night, Sophia laid a trail of little candles from the site entrance to the tunnel in the western perimeter. It was typical Schliemann, very theatrical. And the man soon realized why. All of the delegates to the conference had gone, but three new men arrived. They were clearly important men, travelling incognito. The man never saw the faces of two of them, and afterwards they left before he could get close enough to see. He was too far away to hear their conversation. But the third man he recognized.'

'Who was it?' Dillen asked.

'Schliemann frequently returned to America to manage his business empire, and on one occasion he took the boy with him. They'd gone to Washington and stayed with one of Schliemann's benefactors from his early days as an entrepreneur at the time of the California gold rush. They'd maintained a close but secret friendship ever since. The man's name was George Frisbie Hoar.'

'*George Hoar,*' Dillen exclaimed, thinking hard. 'Good God. Yes, that makes sense. Hoar was a prominent antiquarian, a patron of the Smithsonian Institution and the Peabody Museum at Harvard. But he was more than that. *Far more.* He was one of the most prominent American politicians of the second half of the nineteenth century. That's why Schliemann would have courted him. Hoar's was a voice of moderation and humanity, famously warning against American imperialism and foreign wars. By 1890 he'd been a senator for years, one of the most respected in the House. If you were going to choose the most important American politician of the time, you might have put Hoar above any incumbent president.'

Hugh reached back and picked up a heavy hardbound volume from his desk, handing it to Rebecca. It had lavish embossing on the cover, a golden bull's head, the horns curving upwards. 'That's Schliemann's account of his excavations at Mycenae, where he describes the Mask of Agamemnon,' he said. 'I had that actual volume with me on the dig in 1938, and I've been reading it again for the first time in years. I remember your dad poring over it when he first came to visit me. His eyes just lit up when he saw the account of the mask. Now, take a look at the inside cover.'

Rebecca carefully opened the book. Dillen leaned over, and saw a pasted coat of arms with the word HOAR in Gothic script beneath. 'It's a complete coincidence, pretty amazing, but these things happen,' Hugh said. 'I bought this book on a visit to New York City the year before Peter and I were in Greece, in 1937. Some of the contents of Hoar's library were for sale and I was expanding my archaeology collection. I'd inherited some money and spent it on books.'

'That's it!' Rebecca exclaimed excitedly.

'What?' Dillen said.

'That coat of arms! The double-headed griffin! You remember the golden ring, the one Hiebermeyer found yesterday in the excavation? Dad said he'd seen the emblem somewhere before, but couldn't remember. This was where!'

'Good God,' Dillen murmured. 'I do believe you're right.' He stared at the arms, then turned to Hugh. 'Yesterday afternoon, Maurice was digging in a tunnel under Troy and found a Victorian signet ring, with exactly that motif on it. We assumed it was somehow lost by one of Schliemann's well-to-do guests.'

'And now we know who it was,' Rebecca exclaimed.

'A tunnel, you say,' Hugh murmured, staring hard at Dillen. '*A tunnel*. I've kept up with the excavations of the last few years. You mean the watercourse tunnel they found on the south-west part of the site, leading to the spring?'

Dillen shook his head. 'Something I was going to tell you, and it may as well be now. It's extraordinary. In the last few days Maurice has found a passage under the Homeric citadel, a deep trench with inward-sloping sides in the same masonry as the city walls, clearly late Bronze Age. That watercourse may perhaps lead to it, to whatever lies at the end. We don't know. Maurice hasn't got there yet. What we do suspect is that it was some kind of monumental entranceway, not to the citadel but to something underneath. The walls were lined with stone *stelae*, some with inscriptions. Maurice thinks he's even seen hieroglyphics. And there's a colossal sculpted head of a king, like a gate guardian. Rebecca and Jeremy found it.'

Hugh continued staring hard at him, then reached over to his desk and took a scuffed old sketchpad from the pile. He held it closed for a moment, deep in thought, then opened it and leafed through to a double-page pencil drawing in pastel colours. He carefully turned the open book around, and handed it to Dillen. 'You mean like this?'

Dillen took it, and gasped. The sketch showed an entranceway as he had just described, but with two gate guardians, one on either side. 'That's incredible. Where on earth is this?'

'The old man described it to us, when we spoke to him at Mycenae in 1938. This is what he saw that night under Troy.'

'Good God. This is it. *This is what Maurice has found.*' Dillen looked across. 'You've kept this a closely guarded secret.'

Hugh paused. 'It's been hard for me to look at that again. It's been locked away, since the war. That's Peter's drawing. Based on the old man's description. Peter was quite a good watercolourist. He was always trying to frame what he saw. He told me once when we met up before Cassino that he did that after battle, to try to take one step back from what he was really seeing, from the carnage and the horror. '

'It looks so much like the entranceway to a tomb,' Rebecca murmured. 'Like the Treasury of Atreus at Mycenae.'

'That's *exactly* what the old man said,' Hugh replied enthusiastically. 'We were there, at Mycenae, and he showed us. And he was convinced that it's what Schliemann thought, too. That somewhere at the end of the passageway was a tomb, a treasury, right under the palace of Troy. But this passageway, as much as you see in this drawing, was as far as Schliemann and Sophia got.'

'What happened?' Rebecca asked. 'Why didn't they finish excavating it?'

'That night in 1890, it was as if Schliemann had invited the three guests to view a work in progress, but at a time when he knew there'd be a great revelation. Perhaps he was prepping them, stoking their enthusiasm, for another visit several months, maybe a year ahead, when all would be revealed. But later that summer Schliemann drove himself to a physical breakdown.'

Dillen nodded. 'It's all there, in his papers. Gladstone was concerned about his health, writing to him about it. And there's one letter Schliemann himself wrote that summer to another of his friends, Prince Otto von Bismarck of Germany. It sticks in my mind. He said, "My workers and I are utterly exhausted. I shall be forced to suspend operations on 1 August. But if heaven grants me life I intend to resume work with all the energy at my disposal on 1 March 1891."'

'But that wasn't to be,' Rebecca murmured.

Dillen shook his head. 'The ear infection that had plagued him for months became acute, and deafened him. It was pretty ghastly. He sought treatment around Europe, but he died in Athens in December.'

'So what happened to the excavation?' Rebecca asked.

Hugh leaned forward again. 'According to the old man, Sophia backfilled what they'd discovered, the *stelae* with the inscriptions, those two statues, all by herself. Then she had the man and his brother come in and bury the trench, turfing it over so that pretty soon it looked as if it hadn't been disturbed.'

'So Maurice was right to be suspicious,' Dillen murmured. 'He thought he was digging through stratigraphy that didn't look entirely plausible, as if it had been deliberately backfilled.'

'But *why*?' Rebecca demanded. 'Why bury it if the moment of revelation was so close?'

'Sophia and Schliemann were truly in love, and were a team,' Hugh replied thoughtfully. 'Perhaps with Heinrich gone, she simply couldn't bear to carry on. But I think there was more to it than that. They were always conspiratorial, digging secretly, spiriting treasures away. Peter and I wondered whether Sophia could have been carrying out Schliemann's last wishes in the event of his sudden death. Perhaps she was to backfill the trench, and look to the future when some distant archaeologist might take up the baton. Someone of similar stature, someone with the personality and drive to make his discoveries come alive, to sell them to the world in the same way he had. If so, I can't help thinking he was right. Troy without Schliemann is inconceivable. Another archaeologist might have dug the mound with greater precision, published a more sober monograph, but the site at Hissarlik would never have caught the popular imagination in the way it did.'

Dillen nodded. 'His papers show that Schliemann was always afraid of his mortality, afraid that his death might extinguish his myth. Maybe he gained solace from thinking that what had already been revealed might inspire another with the same spark, the same imagination, to take up where he had left off. Schliemann was always leaving little clues. The decoration of his house in Athens, the swastikas.'

'Swastikas?' Rebecca said.

'Not a Nazi invention,' Dillen said. 'It's found in prehistory from India through Asia, including Troy. It's actually quite common. The Nazis associated it with their supposed Aryan precursors and hijacked it.'

'That's why the swastika on the drawing might not be all that it seems,' Hugh said.

Rebecca peered again. 'Because it's counterclockwise?'

'Not the usual Nazi swastika, which goes clockwise,' Dillen murmured.

'Those ancient swastikas, the decoration at Troy?' Rebecca asked. 'Which way do they go?'

'Counterclockwise too. Not always, but commonly.'

'So how on earth does the girl with the harp come to draw a Trojan swastika?' Rebecca demanded.

Dillen tapped his fingers on his mug, staring at the Mycenae book still resting on Rebecca's lap. 'That final night at Troy, with those three guests,' he murmured. 'What on earth was Schliemann playing at? Hoar was a pretty important figure. *Who were those other two?* This was about more than just treasure. Schliemann was an ideas man. He wanted to fire up people's imagination. He wanted people to do more than just gape in wonder.'

'I still don't understand how the swastika's a clue,' Rebecca said. 'A clue to what?'

'And you haven't told us what the boy saw in the grave at Mycenae, before Schliemann and Sophia put in the skeleton,' Dillen said.

'He saw the golden mask, where they'd left it, but underneath, when he lifted it, *he did not gaze on the face of Agamemnon*. Instead, there was a void in the clay. A shape, where something had been. He could see fresh marks around the sides, where it had been prised out. He remembered Schliemann had brought a bag with him, a satchel. An object that had been concealed there three thousand years before, and was to disappear again that night until the Second World War, when it was seen by a Jewish girl in the midst of the worst horror imaginable.'

Rebecca gasped. 'The shape. You mean a swastika.'

Hugh nodded. 'A Trojan swastika. With the arms going counterclockwise. Just as the girl with the harp drew it.'

Dillen could barely believe what he was saying. 'So Agamemnon himself could have buried it.'

Rebecca stared at the picture. 'Why? Why in a grave? In *his own* grave?'

Hugh looked at her. 'Where better for a king to conceal

something he may never have wanted found? What better way to stamp your authority over it, to lay claim to it, than to bury it in your own grave under your own mask?'

'What did it mean?' Rebecca said. 'Why did he have it? How? What did the swastika symbolize?'

Hugh looked at them intently. 'The final ingredient of the story. What the old man said he saw that final night at Troy after Schliemann and the three men had left.'

'*He saw more,*' Dillen whispered. 'Go on, Hugh.'

'He'd been spying on them from the rampart above. After they'd gone, he slid down into the unexcavated end of the trench, where the sloping walls disappeared into the soil, converging towards some spot under the citadel. There was a tunnel inside, just wide enough for him to crawl along. It was pitch black, so he took a candle. At the furthest point, a crack in the fallen masonry ahead allowed him to glimpse what lay at the end. He saw what Schliemann must have seen. He realized why Schliemann had summoned Hoar and the others to come to Troy that night. He knew why Schliemann had been supremely confident that a great revelation was to hand.'

'What was it?' Rebecca whispered.

'He saw bronze, the face of a great bronze door. In the centre was a saucer-sized roundel. And within that was a shape.'

Rebecca stared at him. '*A swastika.*'

'A Trojan swastika,' Dillen exclaimed.

Hugh nodded. 'It was impressed, exactly the same shape and size as the void under Agamemnon's mask.'

'Good God,' Dillen exclaimed. 'Of course. In a door. It's

blindingly obvious. That's what Schliemann knew. The swastika wasn't just a symbol of Troy. *It was a key.*'

'No wonder Schliemann wanted it kept secret,' Rebecca said. 'The key to a secret chamber under Troy. How many treasure-hunters would die for that.'

'And it's the key to something else,' Hugh said quietly, sitting up, glancing back at the photo on the mantelpiece. 'Something awful, something I wish I could deny, like a bad dream. It's to do with the girl with the harp, and that drawing she made in 1945. I think she may have seen the Trojan swastika in a bunker in the forest. When she was taken there and raped. One of the SS men who tried to surrender to us was raving about something in the forest, kept jabbing his finger, saying there were hidden treasures, underground. He was trying to bargain for his life. We didn't believe him. We thought the camp was for forest labourers and then was used as an overflow camp for Belsen. We knew there were other SS who had escaped into the forest, so we thought it was just a way of leading us into an ambush. That's what may have happened to Peter. But now I think that the guard might have been telling us the truth.'

'Do you think that's what Peter and the American found?'

'I don't know. We may never know. But there is something else. A few days before we went into the camp, my SAS patrol ambushed a motorcycle courier. We'd been told to kill any we came across. At that stage in the war they might have carried personal orders from Hitler, the kind of thing that might have spurred wavering German soldiers to fight to the death. Stopping messages like that might have saved countless Allied lives, our own chaps. He rode right into a wire we'd strung across a junction. The man was still alive, but his motorcycle burst into flames that destroyed the dispatch box.'

'Did he say anything?' Rebecca said.

Hugh paused. 'Perhaps I could have got something out of him. But we were behind enemy lines, and in a hurry. We didn't take prisoners.'

Dillen leaned forward. 'But you found something.'

'I saw a charred fragment blow away from the flames. I picked it up, and there was writing still visible on it, a few inches square. It was part of Hitler's so-called Nero Decree, the order telling his commanders to destroy the remaining infrastructure of the Reich. I'd been briefed on it at HQ, who had a complete copy, so I recognized it. Only this one was slightly different. At the top of the page was a stamped swastika, but not the usual Nazi one. This one was counter-clockwise. *Exactly the same as the one in the girl's drawing, and the shape described by the man at Mycenae and Troy*. Of course I knew nothing about the girl's drawing then. But when I saw it and remembered the burned fragment, that swastika, it sent a chill down my spine. And I realized the link with Schliemann because of the words beneath it.'

'Those were?' Rebecca whispered.

'Three words, visible above the standard text of the decree, part of the stamp with the reverse swastika, the counter-clockwise one. I reported them, but never heard anything more. Some intelligence chaps came to talk to me about it, swore me to secrecy and that was it. The words appeared directly under the swastika. They were *Der Agamemnon-Code*.'

'*The Agamemnon Code*,' Dillen whispered.

'*Agamemnon*. Why Agamemnon?' Rebecca asked, incredulous.

Dillen turned to her. 'The Nazis loved harking back to the imperial past, to those they regarded as Aryan precursors, great warrior leaders. Agamemnon was always high on the list. Discovering this object among Schliemann's treasure, the Trojan swastika, somehow spirited away to Germany after Schliemann's death, perhaps sent there by Sophia, would have been the greatest of all their plundered treasures. The symbolism, the association with what they may have regarded as Agamemnon's triumphant destruction of Troy, the obliteration of an inferior Eastern race, all that would have fed their twisted imagination. So when it came to contemplating Armageddon, some fearful doomsday weapon, how better to encode it than to use the symbol of that reverse swastika, and name it after the king of kings himself?'

'So that's why you're so fearful of that bunker in the forest,' Rebecca said to Hugh. 'You think there was some terrible weapon there?'

'Not *was*,' Hugh said quietly. 'Not was, but *is*.'

'What do you mean?'

'After the war, the burnt forest, the site of the camp, the bunker, was bulldozed over and turned into a NATO airbase. The bunker will still be there, though. Even the RAF's eight-thousand-pound bombs couldn't destroy the U-boat pens, and bunkers were built of the same reinforced concrete. At least it might have sealed off what could still be inside. And I'm not just talking about stolen art. You know that now. As soon as I began to piece this all together in my head after the war ended, I had a terrible sense of foreboding about that place, about what was inside, the place where the girl had seen that reverse swastika. The horror of that forest isn't just about what happened to the girl with the harp. Or what happened to Peter. It's about what is still there, what could still be unleashed.'

Dillen took a deep breath. 'It looks as if we've got our work cut out.'

'What are you going to do?' Hugh said.

Dillen paused and collected his thoughts. 'We hope to God that nobody else has begun to piece together what we have been talking about this afternoon. We're still only guessing, but there's something terrible at the end of this road. Some Nazi weapon stored in that bunker. A weapon associated with this code, Der Agamemnon-Code. Something which, by all those chances of war, you and Peter may have been responsible for preventing fanatical Nazis from activating in the final days of the war. You, by finding that drawing. And by killing that motorcycle courier, perhaps. Peter, by going into the camp, into that forest. Perhaps he and the American died preventing someone from following Hitler's final order. We can be sure that some in Allied intelligence knew what this was all about, and were afraid enough to obliterate all evidence, to let that bunker be buried under the bombed forest and then, after the war, for all time. There was something in there that not even they could trust themselves to reveal.'

'So we carry on where Peter left off,' Rebecca murmured.

'We keep fighting the war,' Dillen said. 'Hugh?'

'I've never stopped. That's why I've kept this to myself for so very long.'

'Our job is to obliterate any leads. To find any loose ends, and to cut them off. Just as Allied intelligence must have desperately been trying to do in 1945.'

'We've already opened it up by going back to Troy,' Rebecca said. 'We've begun what we don't want, which is to reawaken the search for Schliemann's treasures in Europe.'

'There's no turning back now,' Dillen said grimly. 'It's ironic. That's exactly what I said to Jack last night on the battlements of Troy, looking at what we'd found that afternoon. He'd had a sense of foreboding, about Homer, about whether we wanted to uncover the dark side of the story of Troy. But then we were euphoric. No turning back, because we were on the cusp of the greatest revelations. Just like Schliemann that night at Troy in 1890.'

'That art dealer,' Rebecca murmured. 'The guy in Amsterdam. The one I met. He'd be a good place to start. He seemed to know everything, had had his ear to the ground for decades. If anything's shown up, anything to do with Schliemann's treasure, he'll know. He told me he had a whole cache of Nazi documents he'd collected, and he used those as a bargaining chip with Interpol. We want to comb through everything, everywhere, that might have that reverse swastika, that code on it, and delete it. If it's ever shown up on the black market, he'd know about it.'

Dillen looked at his watch. 'Jack and Costas are diving on the Bronze Age wreck right now. I'll leave a message with Captain Macalister and Ben on *Seaquest II*. I remember you talking to your dad about those documents, Rebecca. After he'd gently told you never to do what you did again. I think they went to somebody high up in the Courtauld, Professor Hans Raitz, wasn't it?'

Rebecca nodded, and curled her lip. 'I met him, too. He took me out to lunch at the British Museum. I know he's a big art historian, but I didn't like him. I asked him whether he was Jewish, with that name, and he nearly spat at me. Then he apologized, said my generation were ignorant and it wasn't our fault, and started touching me under the table. He said I was a good Aryan girl. Can you believe it? I suddenly had a phone call and had to leave. I never told Dad.'

'Probably a good thing you didn't,' Dillen said. 'And Raitz doesn't make any secret of his family's Nazi past. Trumpets it, says it's driven his academic career, to see how architecture and art served fascism. But I wonder.'

'As you say,' Hugh said. 'The war still goes on. The enemy is still out there.'

'This dealer,' Dillen said. 'Where is he?'

'He lives incognito in London,' Rebecca said. 'But I know where.'

'Right.' Dillen looked at her. 'But we aren't going there without IMU security this time.'

'Okay,' Rebecca said quietly. 'This does frighten me.' She got up and walked over to the table, looking again at the drawing of the two people holding hands, with the little girl between them and the swastika above. She brought the back of one hand to her mouth, and Dillen could see she was swallowing hard. Hugh saw too, and put his hand on her arm.

'I've always wanted to find her again, you know,' he said quietly. 'To find out what happened to her.'

'The girl with the harp,' Rebecca whispered, sniffing and wiping her eyes. 'I wish I could hear her play.'

'It was her,' he said, his voice faltering, reaching for Rebecca's hand. 'Not really Peter, or me, but her. If she hadn't made that drawing, perhaps some awful horror would have been unleashed.' He withdrew his hand, and got up, lurching slightly, steadying himself. Dillen looked at him with concern. Hugh suddenly looked terribly tired, and for the first time Dillen saw him as an old man. Perhaps they should not have put him through the inquisition like this. But Hugh had wanted it. Hugh looked at his watch, and cleared his throat. 'Fifteen hundred hours, on the dot. If you go right now, you might just make the fifteen forty to Paddington. Otherwise you wait another forty-three minutes.'

Dillen gave him a tired smile. 'Ever the old soldier, Hugh.'

'And the old schoolmaster. When I retired, I swore I'd never be enslaved to the clock again. But at my age, you also realize that time is of the essence. When you've still got work to do.'

Rebecca turned, and hugged him. 'You loved Peter, didn't you?'

Hugh stood stiffly for a second, then relaxed and put his arms round her. 'I'm still there, you know. Sometimes it's as if the war is like the moment before death, a moment one is forever living. And it's the old cliché. *Age shall not weary them, nor the years condemn.* Peter's forever young. I apologize for being so emotional earlier. Shameful, really. I'm tougher than that, you know. It's just that recently, in the past few years, there have been a few moments. The armour's coming off. Old age, I suppose. I do wonder what Peter would have thought of me now. He the eternal youth, me the shuffling old man.'

'You might have to be tough again, Hugh,' Dillen said. 'We're all being drawn back to that place. Maybe to confront the gates of hell once more.'

Hugh let go of Rebecca, then held out his hands, palms

upward. 'Sometimes, when it's cold and I close my hands, I feel the crackle of frozen blood on my palm. I felt that once in the Ardennes. Other men's blood, not mine. When it's warm, I smell it. The blood of the men I've killed. You don't need to worry about me when I stand there, in front of those gates. I've been there for years.'

Dillen got up. Rebecca put on her fleece, and slung her pack over her shoulder. Dillen zipped up his Gore-tex jacket and picked up his laptop bag. Hugh went over to the door. 'You'll get a taxi to Temple Meads station?'

'We'll walk.' Dillen slung his bag on his shoulder. 'I was telling Rebecca on the way up about my time here as a schoolboy. I haven't seen the place for years. And we might just have time to pop into the Llandoger Trow for a quick drink before catching the train. I want Rebecca to see where Robert Louis Stevenson set the opening scene of *Treasure Island*. The docks are still a place where you can step into the past. And I'm sure a few Howards have set off on high-seas adventures from there before now.'

Hugh put his hand on Dillen's shoulder. 'It's been good to see you here again, James. Always good. Let's hope that what we've been talking about is all ancient history. A closed book, for you two, if not for me.' He turned to Rebecca, and put his other hand on her shoulder. 'And you, Rebecca Howard, daughter of my friends Jack and Elizabeth. I was very fond of your mother too, you know. She came here with Jack once, sat just where you did. Seeing you, it was as if I were seeing her again. She'll be with you for ever, you know. It's not just your dad who will look after you. My home is your home. Any time.'

Rebecca's eyes welled up, and she embraced him again. 'I'll come back. You can count on it. For the hot chocolate.'

Hugh stepped over and opened the door for them, then paused. 'When I was a schoolboy, a famous general named Sir Ian Hamilton came to unveil our war memorial. He'd been commander during the Gallipoli campaign in 1915. He'd known the terrible beauty of war, its seduction, from soldiering in the heyday of the British Empire. When heroes still seemed possible, when wars were not yet world wars. He was steeped in the classics, in Homer, and when he sat in his ship off Gallipoli, he wrote of his troops in Homeric terms, as if when they went over the top into a storm of lead they were men of Mycenae before the walls of Troy. History has reviled him for it, but he was only using the words he knew, the metaphors, the similes drummed into him as a boy studying Homer. And maybe, sitting there with Gallipoli and Troy in his sights, he saw the truth. More than three hundred old boys from my school died in that war. Hamilton stood before us and told us they had hoped to kill war. I'll always remember that. *They had hoped to kill war*. That's what we were doing too, you know, Peter and I and all the countless others. But since then, I've come to realize a truth, perhaps the truth that Hamilton saw. The flames of war were ignited in Troy three thousand years before, not in burning ships and pyres of dead heroes, but in the flaming citadel, in women and children lit like torches. I've seen it with my own eyes. We can never kill war. All we can do is contain it, know it's there but keep the horror boxed away, like that bunker in the forest, like the monster within us that is so easily unleashed, the monster I feel inside me every time I open and close my hands. And fighting that war is no longer a job just for soldiers. It's for all of us.'

'Roger that,' Rebecca murmured.

Hugh grinned, and put his hand on her shoulder. 'Now where have I heard that before? You *are* a chip off the old block. And now enough of this. It's time for you to go. And time for me to get cracking with that translation.' He looked at Dillen, a twinkle in his eye. 'Onwards and upwards, James.'

Dillen looked at him. What would the future now hold, for Hugh, for Rebecca, for all of them? He put his hand on Hugh's shoulder, feeling the sinewy toughness, but the frailty too. It was their old parting expression. He could not imagine coming here and not hearing it. He smiled broadly. 'Onwards and upwards, Hugh.'

15

London, England

The man stood in the corner of the room, fidgeting with his fingers, watching the scene unfolding in front of him. Another man, heavy-set and middle-aged, was sitting on a wooden chair in the centre of the room, sweating profusely, his few strands of hair plastered to his forehead. He was wearing faded army surplus trousers and an artist's smock, smeared with coloured chalk. His legs were strapped to the chair legs and his chest and upper arms to the chair back, leaving his forearms hanging loose. A piece of duct tape had been slapped over his mouth, and his eyes were darting about, terrified, imploring, at the man in the corner and the other man standing in front of the chair, then out of the window, over the river Thames towards the Houses of Parliament and the grey sky.

The man in front of the chair, expensively dressed in a dark coat, stroked his neatly trimmed beard and looked pensively at the bound man, then clicked his fingers at the three other men standing in the room, against the wall behind the chair. One of them came forward, an ugly, heavy-jowled man of Slavic appearance, the sleeves of his leather jacket rolled up to reveal a smudged tattoo with the word *Spetsnaz* above his left wrist. He stood behind the chair, reached down and lifted the man's left forearm, bending the hand back and holding it there. The man struggled, bouncing the chair legs on the floor, and then went wide-eyed and breathed hard through his nose as the thug put pressure on. The man in front nodded, and in one movement the thug pressed his hands together like a vice, snapping the man's fingers. The man made a terrible noise and slumped forward, sobbing, jerking the chair again, mucus dripping from his nose.

The man in the corner shut his eyes, feeling faint. *It was not supposed to be like this*. He opened them again, and saw the man in front of the chair gesturing for him. He walked over and spoke urgently. 'Saumerre. We need to talk.'

'Not now, Raitz.'

He could smell the sweat, the stench of fear. Saumerre looked thoughtfully at the man in the chair, and then clicked his fingers at the thug again, gesturing at the man's mouth. The thug reached over and ripped the tape from the man's face. The man gasped, breathing loud and fast, wheezing and groaning, then looked up, sniffing away the mucus that was dripping off his face, trying to rub it on his shoulders. His cheeks were streaked with sweat. 'What do you want with me?' he said hoarsely, his accent slightly European. 'Who are you? Why did you do this?' He lifted his left forearm, looking at it, the fingers hideously splayed, hanging like the hand of a rag doll. 'I'm an artist. *An artist.* What have you done to me? *My God.*'

'It will be right hand next,' the thug growled, his English heavily accented. Saumerre signalled him, and the thug stepped back against the wall between the other two, men evidently from the same mould. Saumerre sank down on one knee in front of the chair. 'You are Marcus Brandeis, yes? Jewish, I think. Yes, I think you are Jewish, Sephardic with that name, in Amsterdam. My ancestors were in Spain too, you know, Moors, of course, but we have something of a common heritage, you and I. We have common interests.' He shook his head, as if sadly. 'If only you would share yours with me.'

'Share what?' the man in the chair sobbed. 'You haven't asked me anything yet. What do you want?'

Saumerre suddenly changed his manner and stood up abruptly, stared at him icily. 'Don't play the fool with me, Brandeis. You've been expecting this for months. You've been a marked man since you turned police informant. London was hardly a good place to hide, was it? A pavement artist on the South Bank. Hiding in the crowd. It must be demeaning. You must miss the big time.'

'I don't know what you mean. I'm just an artist. A street artist. That's how I make my living. I draw people. Tourists.'

Saumerre took an iPhone out of his pocket and flipped it open, reading from it. 'Marcus Brandeis, formerly of Brandeis Gallery, Prinzegracht 3, Amsterdam.' He snapped shut the phone. 'Until recently regarded as Europe's premier broker for black-market antiquities. Special interest in art and antiquities stolen by the Nazis. Not, I might add, in returning art to its rightful owners, even fellow Jews. But a particular interest in finding art still hidden away, then selling it to the underworld. Art used to lubricate deals, drugs, arms, you name it. The Russian Mafia. Big names, your clients.' Saumerre tapped the phone. 'A very exclusive list. Names like the one who lent us those three gentlemen standing behind you. Names who like to see deals finished. Names who like to remain anonymous. Names who no longer appreciate your services, my friend.'

The man slumped, then gave a shuddering sigh. He looked up, deathly pale, his face wet but his eyes now defiant. 'Which one is it?' he said quietly. 'Ivankov? Labazanov? Which one do you work for? Just tell me. I can give you what you want. Anything. We can still do business. I know far more than I've told the police. I know where Nazi art is still buried. In bunkers, in mines. Fantastic treasures. We can find it together.'

'Now we *are* getting somewhere,' Saumerre said.

Brandeis peered at him, narrowing his eyes. 'I know that face. Politician, diplomat. French, I think? Algerian? Who are you?'

'It is of no consequence to you.' Saumerre gestured at the man standing beside him. 'But you know Professor Raitz?'

Brandeis stared, his face strained. 'Professor Raitz? This is Raitz? We never met. But yes. Of course. From the pictures. Professor Raitz, of the Courtauld Institute. What are you doing here?' He raised his limp hand, flinching with pain. 'Why, Professor? I gave you so much. *Why?*'

'Professor Raitz has been so kind as to show us several Nazi documents that were once in your possession. Documents you passed directly on to him when you turned informant, when the police used the professor as an expert appraiser. Documents he insisted on having direct from you, for immediate conservation treatment, of course. Professor Raitz is a man of great influence. Documents the police never saw. *Documents they will never see.*'

The man looked back and forth between them, his eyes clouded with pain, but suddenly wily, calculating, the eyes of an underworld dealer once again. 'I know nothing about documents,' he said. 'But look at him,' he added, nodding at the professor. 'He's nervous. He's in almost as bad a way as I am. It's him you should be questioning, not me. He's the one who's concealing things.'

Saumerre leaned forward, hands on one knee, staring into the man's eyes. He sniffed, and crinkled his nose. 'I don't think so,' he said quietly. 'I really don't think so.' He snapped his fingers again, and the Russian came forward.

'No,' Brandeis said. '*No.*' The Russian lifted the man's right forearm, then bent the hand back. 'Please God, no,' he pleaded. 'I'm an artist now. This is my livelihood. Not that hand. Please. *Not that hand too.*' The Russian took the little finger, and abruptly jerked it backwards. Brandeis howled in pain. Raitz turned away.

Saumerre put up his own hand, as if inspecting it, glancing at the Russian. 'Well, one can still draw without a little finger, no? And why this paltry way of making a living when you have secret knowledge of art stashed away in bunkers and mines around Europe, your very words, as I recall?'

'All right,' the man mumbled, wincing in pain. '*All right*. Which document?'

'What do you know,' Saumerre asked, 'about Der Agamemnon-Code?'

'The Agamemnon Code.' Brandeis tensed, his hand shaking, then slumped. 'That one,' he said. 'Of course. It had to be.' He paused, grimacing again. 'You will spare my hand?'

'Tell us what we want, and I give you my word. Your hand will be spared.'

The man took a deep breath. 'Der Agamemnon-Code. That was my best discovery. And my most frustrating. For years my private passion was to collect any information about Heinrich Schliemann's lost treasures, the gold he took from Troy and Mycenae. I always believed there must have been more hidden away by the Nazis, not only the known treasures, but other objects Schliemann himself may have sent back to hide in Germany. I *always* believed this. I made a special study of Schliemann's psychology. If you want to be a treasure-hunter, you must know the mind of the man who has hidden the treasure, yes? Archaeologists know this. Everyone thought I was a bit mad, you know, an enthusiast, my obsession. But then, after the fall of the Iron Curtain, those objects from Priam's treasure surfaced in Moscow, where the Russians had taken them from Berlin. People began to take me seriously. It was as if some clue to El Dorado had suddenly been revealed. Little red lights lit up on the art underworld map all over Europe, treasure-hunters, dealers, enthusiasts, each believing they had some small clue, something overlooked, something misinterpreted. But it all came to nothing. It was like looking at those faked grainy photos of UFOs. Every single clue could be discounted. But I still believed, as I always had. And then it happened. An old Jewish man who had once worked for me showed up at my apartment in Amsterdam one evening. He was down on his luck, needed money desperately. He was an uneducated man, knew nothing about Homer, about Agamemnon. So he hadn't made the connection between what he had and Schliemann until he saw the news reports of the St Petersburg finds, and realized what he'd been sitting on all those years.'

'Very good. *Very good.*' Saumerre gestured at the Russian, who dropped Brandeis' hand and stood back. The release of pressure made Brandeis wrench in pain, and he leaned over, retching. Raitz looked with concern at Saumerre.

'We can surely give him some water, can't we? He's talking now.'

'Of course. *Of course.*' Saumerre reached back to the table behind him and picked up a small bottle of mineral water. He unscrewed the cap and made as if to push Brandeis' head up, but recoiled at the last moment, not wanting to touch him. He looked at the Russian, who came over and roughly jerked the man's head up, then took the bottle and poured the water into his face. Brandeis spluttered and coughed, then swallowed a few times. The Russian let go and Brandeis lurched forward, snorting water out of his nose. He looked up.

'Let me go, please, I beg you.' He coughed, and retched again. His voice was hoarse. 'I just want to go. I won't say anything to anyone. Look at my life now. I'm little more than a down-and-out. My friends are all drunks and street people. Who would believe my stories anyway? Please, just let me go.'

'Finish what you have to say.'

The man looked towards the window, blinking the water from his eyes, then took a shuddering breath. 'All right. When the old Jew showed me the document, I saw at once that it was genuine. I saw those words. *Der Agamemnon-Code*. I couldn't believe it. *At last*, I thought. Surely a connection with Schliemann. That word *Agamemnon*, from Homer. But could it just be coincidence? The Nazis loved codes. Agamemnon was a hero for them. It was possible, though, just possible, that it referred to the hidden treasures of Schliemann. I paid the man for it. I asked him over and over to recount the story of how he had found it, every detail, and the story remained the same.'

'Which was?' Saumerre said quietly.

Brandeis panted, grimacing in pain. 'Okay. Near the end of the war, in April 1945, he'd been a prisoner near Belsen, in a nearby labour camp in a forest. He was there when survivors from Auschwitz were marched in. With them was a Luftwaffe officer, who'd come with them all the way from Poland. It was unusual, as the camps were run by the SS, not the air force or the army. At first I thought that maybe the officer had seen the writing on the wall with the Soviet advance, and accompanied the prisoners as an excuse to escape west himself, to give himself up to the British or Canadian troops in that sector. But I soon realized there was more to it than that. To this day I still don't know what lay at the bottom of it, but I believe he was on a mission.'

Saumerre leaned forward intently. 'This is important. Was he carrying anything with him? A package, a bag? *Anything?*'

'No. I asked the old man that too. Apparently they left in an enormous hurry from Auschwitz. Even the officers had to forage on the way.'

Saumerre stared at Brandeis. 'So no treasure was taken from Poland. Good. *Good*.'

Brandeis winced, and shook his head. 'No treasure.'

'And? The officer? What next?'

'It's a myth that the Luftwaffe and Wehrmacht officer corps were reluctant Nazis. There were fanatics among them. He may have been one. A British patrol arrived unexpectedly at the camp, SAS I think, a day or so before the actual liberation. The old Jew said it sent the officer into a panic. He shot at the British and tried to escape into the forest, but was gunned down. Maybe there was something secret there he had to get to, something he had to do, something to hide. Maybe he expected to be shown no mercy in that place, even though he was not SS. He was probably right. The Jew said the British officer in charge personally shot all the SS who tried to surrender. After the patrol had left, the Jew went to the German officer's body and found that document, a single sheet of paper with those words in red at the top. That's all I know. It's some kind of map. A map to something hidden, possibly underground. There are no labels, only a series of joined lines, and distances in metres. I have no idea where.'

Saumerre looked hard at him, then sighed and rocked back on his feet. He clicked his fingers. The Russian came up and grabbed Brandeis' right hand again. 'No,' the man begged. 'You promised. *No*.'

'What did you say? No idea where?' Saumerre repeated, drumming on his knee, then raising his own right hand in front of him, stretching and admiring his fingers. 'No idea? Really?'

'All right. *All right*. Please. Tell him to let go.' Saumerre nodded, and the Russian backed off again. 'I can't take much more of this.' Brandeis swallowed hard. 'The old Jew said he'd talked to some of the new arrivals, from Auschwitz. He asked about the Luftwaffe officer because it was so unusual. One of the prisoners was the sole survivor from a specialized labour camp near Auschwitz. An aero engine assembly plant. It turned out that the officer had been in charge there. It makes sense, an air force officer. They used Jewish slave labour. They'd shut it down as the Russians advanced. That was it.'

'Where?' Saumerre stretched his fingers again, inspecting them closely.

'Okay. Okay. This really is it.'

'I will keep my word. No more fingers broken.'

'I have a lot more I can give you. A lot more information. Hidden old master paintings. Gold. We can work together.'

'Let's finish this one first.'

'All right.' Brandeis lifted his broken hand, shaking. 'You'll get me a doctor?' He jerked his head behind him. 'And these Russians? I'll never see them again? That one?'

'Never again. And I'll see you get the best possible care. *But first.*'

'All right. The assembly plant. He said it was near Krakow. About fifty kilometres from Auschwitz. A salt mine. A huge underground salt mine.'

Saumerre looked at the professor, his eyes gleaming. 'We have it. *We have it.*' He turned to the man in the chair. 'Have you told anyone else about this? *Anyone?*'

Brandeis looked defiant again. 'Of course not. In my line of business, you never tell anyone what you know. Never. Unless you find mutual interests. Those you can trust. Future business partners. Like you. Your boss.'

He looked at Raitz, who instantly sensed something. He had spent all his working life dealing with people like this. He knew their minds better than anyone else in this room. These shady dealers were like the treasure-hunters of old. Some of them would talk, some would leave clues, but some would carry their secrets to the grave. He kept his eyes glued on Brandeis, and put his hand on Saumerre's arm. 'Saumerre. We need to talk. A moment.'

'*Not now*, Raitz. We have what we want.' Saumerre showed a flash of anger. He pushed Raitz away impatiently and leaned forward. 'The old Jew?'

'Dead.'

'His family?'

'Family? What family? Auschwitz.'

Saumerre straightened up. 'Thank you.'

Brandeis craned his head up. 'You'll never get deep enough into the mine, you know. I went there. It's the Wieliczka mine. The World Heritage site, full of salt sculptures. I managed to work out the German officer's map. I got to the deepest accessible part, the end of the tunnel complex open to tourists. Beyond that, the guide said it was totally inaccessible, underwater. It's flooded since the Nazis were there. Where the map leads, it's at least a hundred metres under water. There are only a few people in the world who can do that kind of exploration. You'll never get anyone in there.'

'Oh, I think we will.'

'You'd need technical divers. People with cave-diving skills. People who know how to hunt for treasure. Whatever's down there is probably booby-trapped. You know the Nero Decree? The Nazis even booby-trapped their hidden treasures, to destroy them. The thousand-year Reich, or nothing. And you'd have to involve the Polish authorities. You can't just sneak into that mine. You'd need exceptional people to search it.' He managed to jerk his head back. 'Not like these thugs. Not like that Spetsnaz.'

'Exceptional people,' Saumerre repeated, smiling. '*Exceptional people.*' He pulled on a pair of leather gloves. 'I believe your present predicament, your change of career, was caused by a girl? The black-market art tycoon becomes a police informant, and then a pavement artist? Yes?'

'You mean Rebecca Howard?' The man was hesitant. 'She came to see me in Amsterdam. About returning a stolen Dürer from the Howard Gallery. Raitz will know about that. She met him too. Actually, she didn't like him much. She said he was a nasty piece of goods. She thought he was weak, too. Pretty shrewd, if you ask me. That's kids for you.' He jerked his head at Raitz again, then looked conspiratorially at Saumerre. 'I'd ditch this guy if I were you. Don't trust him an inch. Never did buy that spin on his Nazi family past. He's still one of them. Look at him. You can see the weakness in his eyes.'

Saumerre said nothing, but did up his coat. Brandeis looked suddenly frightened again. 'I only turned informer because I was being threatened. A new Mafia boss, from Kazakhstan. Kazakhs don't know the etiquette. Not like you people. Your boss. Which one is he? Please tell me. They all owe me favours. With Russians, real Russians, I can do good business. *Just tell me*. But the girl helped me to disappear for a while. Got me where I am now, which is better than a prison cell or the bottom of a canal. Daughter of Jack Howard, the famous marine archaeologist.' Brandeis stopped, and stared. He went deathly pale. His voice was a whisper. 'Good God. You can't. Do what you like with me, but you can't. *Leave her out of this.*'

Saumerre nodded at the Russian, who had been in a barely restrained rage, his fists balled. His English was evidently good enough to understand what Brandeis had said about him. He came up silently behind the chair, pulling a small automatic pistol from under his jacket and holding it close to his leg, the long black silencer pointing down. He raised it, hesitated for a moment, then in one lightning movement reached his arm round Brandeis' neck and jerked it up and to the right, holding it there. Brandeis made a choking noise, and the Russian jerked again. There was a sickening crack, and he let go of the head. It lolled down, eyes open, blood and mucus dripping from the mouth. The Russian stood back, grunted, and held up the pistol, jerking his other thumb at the corpse. 'Less blood my way.'

'Take him away.' Saumerre waved his hand dismissively. The Russian shoved the pistol into his jacket and the other two came up to help him. They lifted the chair and carried it with the body out of the door. Raitz leaned one hand against the wall, feeling faint. It had all happened so quickly. He had never seen anyone killed before. He was sweating, shaking. He turned to Saumerre. 'He had more to tell us. More gold to find. He could have led us on a treasure trail. Isn't that what you want? You and your people? What is it with this single lead, this code?'

Saumerre looked at him pityingly. 'What, you don't have the stomach for this? For killing? You disappoint me, Raitz. Remember what your revered Führer said. This man was subhuman. He was a Jew. Now, to business. The Howard girl.'

Raitz had a cold feeling in the pit of his stomach. *If they could do this, what was in store for her?* He grasped Saumerre by the shoulder. 'She will not be harmed, right? Nothing like this. That was *not* part of the deal. This was *not* what I wanted.'

Saumerre pushed the hand away, and looked at him with contempt. 'What on earth are you thinking? You naïve academic. A kidnapping works this way: you threaten to kill your victim, right? You make them feel pain. You make their loved ones know they feel pain. And hey presto, you have a result.'

'And then what?'

'Then? Then? What *then*?' Saumerre spat the word out with scorn. 'You are a sentimentalist, Professor. Not a good Nazi.'

Raitz straightened up, wiping his sweaty palms on his trousers. 'You are wrong. I serve the memory of the Führer. The thousand-year Reich.'

Saumerre looked at him appraisingly. 'And everything else is dispensable?'

'Nothing is more important than the cause.'

'That is exactly how we think too. Maybe we can still do business, Professor. Maybe we can.' He flipped open his phone. 'You know this girl, correct? She will recognize you?'

'As I told you. She came to see me at the institute to talk

about the return of that Dürer to Germany. We had lunch. A good Aryan girl, on her father's side.'

'Forget that Aryan nonsense. Just remember this. A date, a time, a place. This evening, seven p.m., the County Hall Marriott. Her school group is assembling there. You will greet her like an old friend. Pure coincidence that you are there, some academic meeting in the hotel just finished. It concerns Nazi art, your speciality. And you happen to have something extraordinary, something you think her father would be fascinated to know about. She'll always want to please him. Use that. Tell her you have pictures of a Nazi bunker, full of ancient antiquities.'

'She'll have security. That was an issue when she came to see me before. She should have involved IMU security, but she didn't.'

'She has no reason to be suspicious of you. And you just said it. She doesn't like security. There are two entrances to the hotel. One is from Westminster Bridge Road, the main entrance. The other is Belvedere Road. You'll tell her your car is there. The pictures are locked inside. She only needs to step out on to the pavement. My men will take it from there.'

'Where will you take her?'

'Where will *you* take her. You wish to keep my Russian friends from doing her harm? It will be your part of the bargain. I remain anonymous. You will take her out of the country. I will give you instructions. Somewhere close to Dr Howard's heart. Meanwhile, he and his Greek friend will do a little job for us. *A job from which they will not return*. And I need to be ready to take what they find.'

'And we will both have what we want.'

'If it leads us to where I think it will lead us, then you will have your art, for your secret Führermuseum. And I will have my treasure.'

'And if not?'

'You doubt me?'

'I didn't trust Brandeis. I was trying to tell you. That story from the old Jew. Brandeis wasn't telling us everything. When you asked whether the German officer had taken anything else with him from Poland. I could see it in his eyes.'

'Are you weak, Raitz? Was the girl right? You've let Brandeis get to you. This is what he wanted you to think. Sow the seeds of doubt. Take your eyes off the prize. Divert you from the cause.'

'Saumerre.' Raitz eyed him. 'You may think me naïve, but I have a first-class mind. I insist that you tell me the full story. You told me enough to convince me to join you. But now we're playing a different game. There's been a murder, and I'm involved in it. I insist you tell me. If you want me to remain on course.'

Saumerre stood for a moment, then went over and peered through the door. He shut and locked it, then came back to Raitz and spoke quietly. 'When we met in the British Museum, I mentioned the story my grandfather told me. The reason I believe Brandeis' story is that the account he had from the old Jew chimed so closely with my grandfather's account. The Dutchman just couldn't have made it up. The camp is one and the same, the labour camp where my grandfather survived by working as a cook. That document I gave you with the swastika, with the Agamemnon Code stamp, came from the same Luftwaffe officer. My grandfather must have stumbled across his body just before the other man. He remembered other documents in the man's pockets, but this one looked important and he just took it and ran. He was a profiteer, and desperate, grabbing anything he might sell, or use as a bargaining chip. But this is what I haven't told you yet. Do you swear . . .'

'Of course,' Raitz whispered. '*Of course.* I swear on the soul of the Führer. I will tell nobody.'

'My grandfather went into the forest. He hid there. He said it was a fearful place, with SS guards and former inmates trying to kill each other. He was desperate for food. He found a bunker. He saw a man go in and out, not someone he recognized. He followed him once into the bunker, hoping to find food. What he saw there was beyond your wildest dreams. All of the great lost works of art are there. A veritable shrine to your Führer. But there was another room. That room contains what I want. In the door he saw an impressed swastika shape in a roundel. A reverse swastika. It was a keyhole. Some kind of magnetic key.'

'And you think the key is what's hidden in the mine,' Raitz whispered.

'My grandfather had only a few moments inside the bunker before he crept out. The next day he saw two Allied officers go in with the man. The door shut itself and they never came out. He thought he might have heard a gunshot inside. Then the weather got worse and he had a bad feeling. He had just reached the edge of the forest that evening when it began to rain bombs.'

'My God. The bunker is still there?'

'Buried under a NATO airbase.'

'Have you tried to see how we might get there?'

'That's the next stage.'

'This is wonderful,' Raitz said, his concerns about the Dutchman forgotten. 'This serves your cause. And my cause.'

'And what is that?'

'The thousand-year Reich,' Raitz said reverently, clumsily clicking his heels.

'*Jazaka Allahu Khairan*,' Saumerre replied, closing his eyes.

Raitz stared at him. 'What does that mean?'

Saumerre opened his eyes. They were burning with fervour. He stared at Raitz, then seemed to remember where he was, and relaxed. 'I was forgetting myself. I am a Muslim, you remember, on my father's side, Algerian. It means good luck. *May Allah reward us with good*. It's just an expression. Now, I can still smell that Jew. We have arrangements to make. Let's get out of here.'

16

Off the island of Tenedos, the Aegean Sea

The Turkish navy crewman opened the throttle on the outboard and the Zodiac boat roared away, digging a trough in the sea and then rising above it to skim towards the distant grey shape of the minesweeper. Jack grasped the railing and leaned out through the stern of *Seaquest II*'s internal docking bay, a hangar-sized space open to the sea below that allowed diving and submersible launch in virtually any conditions. Today the sea had been unusually calm, a sluggish low swell occasionally ruffled by the early-afternoon breeze, and Captain Macalister had kept the stern door open. Jack closed his eyes and took a deep breath, relishing the breeze, the tang of salt, the whiff of two-stroke exhaust. These were the smells he had associated with diving all his life, the smells that meant he was in the right place, doing the right thing. He felt a burst of adrenalin. It had been a frustrating morning, as they had negotiated the best way to remove the mine from the shipwreck. But now they were back on course, and he could focus again on what he was about to see on the sea bed, a find that almost beggared belief, the extraordinary remains of a galley from the Trojan War.

Costas came up alongside, wiping his oily hands on a rag, wearing torn working overalls with tools poking out of the pockets. He followed Jack's gaze, and looked wistfully at the Zodiac as it receded into the distance. 'It should have been me,' he said. 'Defusing that mine. It makes me feel empty inside.'

'Not as empty as you'd feel if it had gone off while you were hugging it.'

'Speaking of which.' Costas pointed out to sea, and Jack saw that the Zodiac had come to a stop, perhaps a mile from the minesweeper. Two men came up behind them, Mustafa Alkozen, the IMU Turkish liaison, and Ben Kershaw, the ship's security chief. Mustafa, a muscular, bearded man with a deep voice, had a two-way radio receiver clamped to his ear. He took it down. 'Captain Macalister has just been informed by the captain of *Nusbat*. One minute.' The ship's klaxon sounded to warn the crew to brace for impact. They were well outside the danger zone, but Macalister was taking no chances. Jack looked out into the haze off the bows of the minesweeper, two, maybe two and a half nautical miles distant, Gallipoli just visible in the background, the coast of Troy to the right. Suddenly there was a wobble in the sea and a white ripple that flashed outwards, followed by a geyser of spray. Seconds later he felt something, barely discernible, as if a ghost had passed through them. 'That was the shock wave, this far away,' Costas said, shaking his head. 'Imagine those guys in the Turkish minelayer in 1915, snagging one of those things. They wouldn't have stood a chance.'

Jack turned to Mustafa, smiled broadly and shook his hand. 'Thanks again. That was excellent liaison. I'd like to have some of their guys dive with us, once the excavation gets under way.'

'You have a standing invitation to the Turkish naval academy for dinner, you know that. You and Costas. You'll be very well looked after.'

'I know about Turkish hospitality. I'd be delighted. I've got some good friends there from my navy days, and now some more. Once we're up and running.'

Ben nodded at Jack. He was a small, wiry man, with a quiet voice, British ex-special forces. 'They should have let you take out that mine with the Webley.'

'You kidding? You should have seen me yesterday. All over the place.'

'I was watching from the bridge. Not a bad final shot.'

'Pure fluke. I'd given up trying.'

'That's often the key. It's what I tell Rebecca. Stop trying so hard, relax.'

'She's a better shot than me.'

Ben grinned. 'You better watch it, Jack. She'll be taking over.' He stood quietly for a moment, a little awkward. 'I meant to say. I really would have gone with her to London, you know. You just had to say the word. She's . . . a really good kid. Hard to think what it was like on board without her. My guys would do anything for her. You know that.'

'I know.' Jack put his hand on Ben's shoulder. 'And I appreciate it. Really do. She thinks of you guys, the crew, as an extended family. It's the best thing for me to see, especially after what she's gone through.'

Ben nodded. He patted a bulge in his jacket. 'I've done those reloads for you. Took the bullet weight down a notch, two hundred and sixty-five grains. That should do the trick. Wouldn't mind having a go myself.'

'See you on the foredeck after dinner?'

'You're on.' Ben waved, and he and Mustafa walked back through the jumble of equipment. Jack turned to Costas. 'So what's the story with my Aquapod?'

Costas exhaled forcibly, shaking his head. 'Can't work it out.'

Jack looked at him incredulously. 'I didn't hear you say that.'

'Jeremy and I spent half the night on it. He's got a real knack. Sees things like you do, sees the whole problem first and then deconstructs it. Too many engineers are the other way round, too logical. I can't really understand what made him leave engineering to study ancient languages, for God's sake.'

Jack grinned. 'Same kind of challenges. Just less oily.'

'The problem's not a safety issue. It's the external link on the intercom. We can communicate between the Aquapods, but you can't link to the outside. We think it might be pressure-related. Only way to find out is to take it down.'

'Fine by me. I never liked talking much underwater anyway. That's the problem with all these submersibles. Diving's about getting away from that. Just you and your breathing.'

'It's hard enough getting you to say anything at the best of times when you've seen something on the sea bed. Some fishermen holler when they've got a fish on. Some go silent, like a dog on a scent. You're definitely the silent type.'

Jack smiled, then turned back and leaned out, feeling the breeze again, watching the occasional spray of whitecaps on the swell. 'I was just thinking of Lanowski.'

'Don't. Please God, don't.'

'Seriously.'

'You mean out there? The ripple effect from that mine. The shock wave. What he said about earthquakes.'

Jack nodded. 'If something like that mine can produce a discernible shock wave two miles away, imagine what an earthquake might have done in 1200 BC. I don't just mean our shipwreck. I mean a huge wave, an actual wave of water, hitting Troy. And watching the Zodiac go made me remember what he said about horses.'

'When I nearly went to get a straitjacket.'

Jack shook his head. 'He was right. I knew he was on to something. I just had to let it gel. It's blindingly obvious. You remember he said the Greek word, *ippoi*, horses, could be used to mean waves, whitecaps, and also ships?'

'Sure.'

'Think of another horse.' Jack jerked his hand to shore. 'This place. Troy. Horse.'

'Well. The Trojan Horse, obviously. But . . .' Costas' jaw dropped. 'Holy cow.'

Jack turned to him, his eyes blazing. 'That's the point. That's what Lanowski was driving at. The Trojan Horse wasn't a horse. *It was a ship.*'

'But what about Homer?'

'Homer? The full story of the Trojan Horse isn't even in Homer. It's only known from those later epic fragments. No way was Homer going to include a story of a wooden horse in the *Iliad*. He was far too great a poet for that. The story demeans the Trojans, makes Priam look ridiculous. What kind of enemy worth fighting is going to be duped by a gift like that? To make a great epic poem work, the enemy must be equal to yourselves. But that's not to say the Trojan *ippos* didn't happen. It was a terrifying event, truly the linchpin. But it was part of a different story, the story of the fall of Troy, the *Ilioupersis*. A poem Homer wrote but never revealed.'

'But you're saying some fragment survived, with that word, and that we've got it wrong.'

Jack nodded. 'A fragment mentioning a "Trojan Horse". But those later poets, the ones who compiled the epic fragments, didn't know the imagery. They didn't have the imagination. They hadn't been there, seen what really happened, as I believe Homer had done. To them, *ippos* meant horse, the four-legged variety, full stop. So the story of the Trojan ship fades from history. And lo, the Trojan Horse.'

'That might disappoint the site custodian at Troy.'

'It's not debunking the myth. It's just doing what I've always done. It's doing what Heinrich Schliemann did. *It's making it real.* Imagine anything more ridiculous than the Trojan Horse. That's the ancient equivalent of a scene in a dumbed-down thriller. But then imagine anything more mesmerizing, more terrifying, more awful than the Trojan ship, driven up into the walls of Troy, a swirling, howling blackness behind it, disgorging the warriors of Agamemnon into the citadel to do their worst. It's fantastic. *Fantastic.*'

★

Fifteen minutes later they were strapped into the Aquapods, with the Plexiglas domes closed over them, running through the electronics and cross-checking with each other. The Aquapods were hanging from davits on either side of the ship's internal docking bay, facing towards the stern, and were lashed down to stop them swaying dangerously with the roll and pitch of the ship. Even so, Jack was feeling distinctly uncomfortable, a combination of queasiness and his dislike of being cooped up inside submersibles, especially ones that only just accommodated his tall frame. He knew it would all change once they were in the water, when the small size of the Aquapods made them feel almost like a diving suit. He saw Costas glance over at him, and heard a crackle in the intercom. 'Hold on, Jack. Only a couple of minutes until the ship's under way, once the control team have told the bridge we're secure.'

The Aquapods swayed close together and Jack forgot himself for a moment, as he saw Costas in his full glory. He laughed out loud.

'What?'

'Nothing.' Jack shook his head. 'Nothing at all.'

Costas was still wearing his white overalls, but it was the huge sombrero hat that made him look so garish, sitting in a state-of-the-art submersible about to go a hundred metres to the sea floor, dressed like a gaucho on the range in a very bad Western.

Costas glared at him through his dome. 'You'll wish you had one if we have to bob about on the surface in the blazing sun.'

'Nobody's going to catch me bobbing about on the surface,'

Jack replied firmly, swallowing hard as the swell made the ship roll again. 'If *Seaquest II* misses us, I'll be waiting on the sea floor. On solid ground.'

The ship's screws churned under them and the deck began to vibrate. 'Thank God for that,' Jack murmured, as the ship stabilized. 'How long have we got?'

'The current running from the Dardanelles has strengthened a fraction since Macalister briefed us. It's between fifty and ninety metres' depth, like an underwater river. Lanowski's modelled it, and done a best-fit for where *Seaquest II* should drop us. When we go, we go down like lead, full ballast. Macalister's just told me we've got about twenty minutes till we're green-lighted. So relax and enjoy the ride. You think about the treasure we're going to find. I'm thinking about another one of those excellent cocktails the Turkish cook made me at the excavation house at Troy last night. What I came on holiday for.'

'I meant to tell you,' Jack said. 'I was on the phone to James while the mine was being cleared. You remember Hugh, of course, don't you?'

'Great guy. I helped him have a go at diving in the IMU test pool. You were away with Maria somewhere. We got on together like a house on fire. You'd think we were chalk and cheese.'

'A bit like you and Jeremy.'

'So what's the score?'

'Hugh has opened up quite a bit about the Second World War. Very emotional. A bad experience in a concentration camp. James said he kept his cool when Hugh was talking, stiff upper lip and all that, but when he was speaking to me

James had a real tremor in his voice, had to stop for a moment. Never heard him like that before. I think it really hit him, all those years he'd spent with Hugh as a boy, not knowing what Hugh was struggling with every minute of every day.'

'I don't know how those guys who were there could handle it,' Costas replied quietly. 'My great-uncle, the Monuments Man, said there was quite a lot of killing of SS at those camps after liberation, American and British soldiers encountering guards. Can you blame them? Some of the worst guards were women. Whenever I see those pictures of Belsen and Buchenwald, it makes me wish I could have pulled a trigger. When I was a kid in New York, we used to go up to Canada for holidays, to a forest wilderness where there were some older Germans, ex PoWs who'd gone there to work as loggers after being released by the Soviets in the fifties. A couple of them were unreconstructed Nazis, Waffen SS who'd disguised themselves as Wehrmacht for the Soviets. Looking back on it, I don't see why they should still have been allowed to live.'

'If they hadn't been, you wouldn't have met them. Seen that they were real human beings. Seen how that could happen.'

'So did Hugh open up about this treasure story?'

'James was letting him tell it in his own way, in his own time,' Jack replied. 'He's worried about Hugh's health. Thinks he's putting on a brave face for Rebecca but is much frailer than last time. He's calling me again after the dive for an update. I did tell him what Maurice found this morning.'

'Huh?'

'You didn't hear?'

'Up to my neck in the innards of an Aquapod all morning, I'm afraid.'

'Another statue. Opposite the one Jeremy and Rebecca found.'

'*Two* statues.'

'Almost like gate guardians,' Jack said. 'And he's been in another tunnel. Just can't keep him out of them. This time it's the one the Austrians working at Troy a few years ago found leading from the citadel out to a spring beyond the walls. He got almost a hundred yards into it. Says he thinks it may lead to the chamber he believes is at the end of the passageway with the statues. He had one of our halogen dive torches with him and said he could see a long way ahead, well under the citadel. He got stuck.'

'Well, that makes a change.'

'Said it needs a more lithe, athletic form.'

'Sounds right up my street.'

'Thought we might nip over there after the dive for a little recce.'

'You're on.'

Jack heard a crackle in his headphone, and turned it down. 'That was Macalister,' Costas said. 'Ten minutes to go.'

'Roger that.'

'While we wait. Run me through the Shield of Achilles again. What we're looking for. The decoration.'

'Best guess? Wooden-backed, about a metre across, covered in beaten gold. The decoration? Maybe bands of black niello, red carnelian, though whether that survives underwater for three thousand years, who knows. The scenes might show a kind of cosmography, a bit like a medieval *mappa mundi*. It's for a hero, for display and swagger and appearance, but like most prestige weapons it's made as if for real combat, using the best techniques of the smith. So the five layers described by Homer were probably built up one on top of the other, leaving a progressively smaller outer ring visible for the decorative scenes, and the thickest part of the shield in the centre, at the boss. That's exactly how you'd make a real working shield, strengthening the centre where you fend off the blows, minimizing the weight around the edge. I think Homer had seen a shield like that being made, as he knew what he was talking about. The scenes he describes are plausible, everyday scenes of the world of heroes, the world before the apocalypse, scenes of hunting, contests between champions, the countryside, town life, the unending cycle of life in the Age of Heroes.'

'And what if the world had moved beyond?' Costas said. 'Remember Auden? The thin-lipped armourer, Hephaestos, hobbles away, and Thetis "cried out in dismay at what the god had wrought". We know the armour won't protect her son Achilles from death, and maybe Homer's audience knew that the shield as a metaphor wouldn't protect history from the rise of Agamemnon, from the destruction of Troy, from total war.'

'That's good. Very good. Actually, thinking of Hugh has made me ponder all that too. What he must have seen, at the end of the Second World War. What Auden saw, in the bombed cities of Germany. A kind of truth that no artistry can mask, where no metaphor or simile or symbol can stand in for stark reality. Auden even talks about it, doesn't he? "Of barbed wire, of weed-choked fields, of rape, of casual murder." '

'The age of heroes, the age of controlled violence, is gone. The age of men has come.'

'The history of our times. Maybe it all begins at Troy.'

The churning of the screws ended, and was replaced by the whirring noise of the ship's water-jet stabilizers coming on line. A green light flashed above the entrance to the dock. 'Okay. We're on,' Costas said. He gave a thumbs-up to the controller standing on the deck beside him. She raised one arm and pressed her headset against her ear to listen to instructions from the bridge, and then stood back and gave an emphatic thumbs-down. Costas repeated the sign to her and turned to Jack. 'Good to go?'

Jack took a deep breath. They always treated submersible dives like SCUBA dives, using the same instructions and hand signals, a deliberate reminder that it was people, not machines, that were diving, and that the safety of a submersible dive was dependent on human judgement more than machines and computers. But Costas also knew Jack's discomfort with submersibles and understood that treating the dive this way gave him a sense of control. Jack exhaled, then closed his eyes for a moment. *It felt right.* He looked intently at Costas, then put up his left hand and dropped the thumb down. 'Roger that. Good to go.'

The davits quickly lowered and released them into the water. They were immediately under the waves, plummeting at a rate pre-set by the computer that controlled the buoyancy chambers in the pontoons. Had they lingered for even a moment and been a few metres off, they would have missed the wreck, with nothing to do other than abort the dive and try again. Thirty-five metres down, they entered the current stream with a jerk that pressed Jack back in his seat, but once in the stream he had little sense of it, like being on a high-speed escalator walkway. Dropping out of it, though, was a fairly serious G-force jolt that threw him forward. Below that the readout showed a modest 1.5 knot current, reduced enough for the Aquapods to maintain position at the site using their water-jet propulsion systems. Nevertheless, they had agreed with Macalister that this was not a day to linger, and they would leave in no more than twenty minutes. Officially the dive was a second recce to confirm what they had seen on the first dive and allow an excavation plan to be formulated for the next day.

Five minutes after exiting *Seaquest II* they had reached the site, perfectly on target. Jack breathed a silent thanks to Lanowski. He scanned the sea bed, remembering the waymarkers of their dive yesterday, distorted slightly through the Plexiglas dome. He activated the magnifier, which brought the image through the thick flat slab of glass at the front of the dome close to his face, as if he were looking through a mask. He immediately felt more comfortable, a diver again. They had come up off the starboard stern side of the wreckage. He saw the stem post of the ancient wreck, still there, the shape of the lion of Mycenae. He had not dreamed it. *It was real.* In the decaying superstructure of the minelayer he saw the gap where the Turkish navy divers had attached lifting bags and removed the mine. He jetted forward a few metres and angled the Aquapod to peer below the starboard side of the minelayer's hull, where he had first seen the ancient timbers, some eight metres from the stem post. He was concerned to see how much more exposed the timbers were after only a matter of hours, with the increase in the current and the effect of his own rapid clearance by hand the day before. He could see several square metres of planking and frames on both sides, giving an exact image of the dimensions of the ancient hull as it converged towards the stem post. His pulse quickened. He had been right. It was a war galley, there was no doubt about it.

And there was more. As he sank closer, he saw other objects, close to where he had raised the pottery cup the day before. They were sticking out of the sand in bundles, having been buried in a grey anaerobic layer that was now exposed and being eroded away. Each bundle comprised several dozen wooden rods, with a concreted mass at the end. Jack knew what they were. It was astonishing. He tapped the intercom. 'Now I know exactly what Agamemnon's treasure was.'

Costas' Aquapod was directly in front of him, on the other side of the ancient hull, and had its camera arm extended, angled down at the objects. 'A bundle of wooden rods coming out of a ferrous concretion. Talk to me, Jack.'

'A bundle of arrows,' Jack said excitedly. 'And that corroded mass? Look closely. It's not one mass. It's lots of corroded lumps, joined together. That's iron, Costas. Iron arrowheads. *That's what Agamemnon's treasure was.* That's what gave him the edge. It's exactly what James suspected. The Greeks had discovered iron technology. Look, beside it, there's another bundle. And another. That's how Agamemnon won the Trojan War, not by contests of heroes, but with iron, iron for all soldiers, for all weapons, for total war.'

'Typical archaeologist, riveted on lumps of corroded iron, totally uninterested in the gold.'

'What are you talking about?'

'Between those arrows and the minelayer's hull.'

Jack looked over and gasped. It was astonishing. The object was circular, perhaps a metre across, buried under the sediment. Around the edges he saw a glint of gold. *Beaten gold.* He activated the miniature water jet on the Aquapod's arm and gently sprayed the shape, clearing the sediment from about half of it. It was all gold, shining, uncorroded. He could see a thin layer of darkened wood beneath. 'It's a shield,' he exclaimed, his voice tight with excitement.

'The one we want?'

'Look,' Jack exclaimed. 'You can see the bands, as you go from the outer rim to the boss. Five layers, just as Homer described it. You can even see the dark rings, where glass niello is still visible.' He stared at it, his mind reeling. 'No decoration. Just an awful lot of dents and bashes. It's odd. It hasn't been flattened by the shipwreck. It still has the concave shape. It could be battle damage, but this just isn't a shield you'd take into battle. It's a display shield, a prestige object. That much *is* consistent with Homer. Something a king or a hero mounts beside his tent. But a lot of gold, no ornament. Strange. I feel as if this is Troy yet again, Costas. Fabulous find, but more unanswered questions than we started with.'

'Take a closer look.' Costas had extended the video arm to within inches of the shield, and was watching his screen. 'Jack, I'm sure of it. You *can* see decoration. Only just. Vine leaves. An animal, maybe. It's all been beaten out of it, really crudely. Check out your screen. I'll feed it through.'

Jack clicked on his monitor and immediately saw what Costas meant. 'Incredible,' he murmured. 'Look at that. It's like a ghostly imprint. But why do it? Why?' He drummed his fingers, speaking slowly as he thought. 'The Shield of Achilles. Awarded to the victor in the funeral games. Claimed by Agamemnon. Let's say he takes it to the armourers on Tenedos, those ones churning out the arrowheads, and they crudely hammer out the decoration. Why would he do that?'

'Pride?' Costas said. 'Agamemnon was always having stand-offs with Achilles, right? Didn't he take Achilles' girl, and Achilles went off in a sulk? All that prestige display stuff you were talking about. Agamemnon acquires Achilles' shield, but shows who's supreme by stamping out the ornamentation people associated with strutting Achilles. Agamemnon's now the boss, the tough guy, no frills.'

'But still very odd that it was left this crude.' Jack stared. There was no time to ponder now. 'I'm going to take it. We don't leave this exposed on the sea bed.' Costas rose above to give him room to slide the two forks of the extractor arm beneath the shield. Jack worked the lever until it seemed to be in the right position, then clicked the intercom to confirm with Costas. 'You've gone quiet. You okay? Let me know how this looks from your angle. Over.'

'Jack.' Costas' voice sounded faltering. 'About those bumps and dents.'

'What is it?'

'My camera is angled directly down on the shield. You need to take a look. I think you'll agree it's sometimes good to take a step back.'

Jack clicked on his screen again. The image was fuzzy as the feed came through. He suddenly felt the Aquapod beginning to angle up, and quickly focused on the buoyancy control.

He had to remember he was not on autopilot. It was exactly why he disliked using submersibles to excavate. He trusted his own hands more than mechanical extensions. He came level again and engaged the motor to drive the arms slowly under the shield, until he was sure it would lift out and not slip off.

'Well?' Costas said.

'Just let me concentrate on this.' He lifted the shield inch by inch, injecting water into the rear buoyancy tanks to compensate for the weight, raising a cloud of silt as he did so, watching it quickly settle. It was exactly as Lanowski said, a coarse-grained sediment, overlying the grey anaerobic layer that had preserved the wooden backing of the shield. Slowly Jack reversed the Aquapod until the shield was clear of the sea bed, grey sediment now falling away from it in a cascade. He used another lever to slide a metal basket beneath it, lined with plastic cushioning material like bubble wrap. A cover with cushioning would be extended above it, designed to cocoon artefacts for raising to the surface. He slowly depressed the lifting arm through the basket until it was several centimetres beneath, leaving the shield resting on the cushioning material, then withdrew the arm into the Aquapod. He exhaled forcibly. 'Would you look at that?' he murmured.

'I think it's about time you did exactly that, Jack,' Costas said.

'My screen. Yes.' Jack saw a grainy video image of the shield from five metres above. The feed was still not working properly. He looked again. Then he saw it. 'My God,' he exclaimed. '*My God.*'

'Remember I told you my great-uncle took me to see that in the Archaeological Museum of Athens as a kid?' Costas said. 'Never thought I'd see it this way.'

'*So that's what Agamemnon did*,' Jack whispered in astonishment. He was barely able to register what he was seeing. 'That's what he had those smiths on Tenedos do. He must have had the golden mask to show them, the mask he later took back to Mycenae, where Schliemann found it.' He stared. He was gazing at a face. The entire shield was a face. *And it was the face of Agamemnon*. The bumps and bashes were where the smiths had made an impression, like a ghostly impression of the mask, not crude at all, but executed with enormous artistry, as bold as any art from antiquity Jack had ever seen. In shadow it would have looked extraordinary, the ultimate extension of one man's sense of his own power, stamped over the shield of the greatest of the heroes.

'So let me get this right,' Costas said. 'Homer saw this, but he must have seen it earlier, before it was remade.'

Jack was sure of it. *As sure as he had ever been.* 'Homer's story was about the contest of heroes. Nobody in that story saw the shield this way. This shield, as we see it here, was an image from after the fall of the heroes, an image of the terrible face of war, of Agamemnon himself. It was being shipped back to the plain of Troy from Tenedos for Agamemnon's final assault against the citadel when a seismic storm whipped up the sea and sank this ship, and pushed the galleys of Agamemnon from the beach into the very walls of Troy itself.'

'I think Maurice might owe James that crate of whisky,' Costas said.

Jack looked back at the bundles of arrows still visible in the background. Those would have to wait. Costas' Aquapod was fitted with the video and lights array rather than for finds retrieval. They would have to come back down here as soon as possible. He looked at the shield again. He wished he could touch it, hold it to his chest, grasp a spear, feel the tactile power he had felt holding the Webley on the deck the day before. He gazed at that face with its hooded eyes, staring blindly upwards yet all-seeing, as they had done through all the history that had passed this way, through the age of mankind that had been set in motion during those few days at the death-knell of the Bronze Age. He stared at the iron arrowheads, and in a flash he understood. He understood the temptation. The temptation of power, the temptation to swing the murderous pendulum of anger and retribution. War as a condition of life, without reason, beginning or end. *The temptation that had driven Agamemnon to take the tablet of war, to cast away the tablet of peace.*

'Jack. Reality check.'

'Okay. Let's get this topside. In that current, we're in for a joyride. I can't imagine anything worse than dropping this.'

'Roger that. I'll advise *Seaquest II*. Over.'

Jack activated the autopilot to maintain position three metres above the sea bed while he closed the basket down. He could already sense the pull of the current, edging both of the Aquapods beyond the stern of the minelayer wreck. He extended the upper cage over the basket, lowering it until the plastic wrap cushioned the shield on both sides and he could see only a rim of beaten gold sticking out. It was as secure as he could make it. He heard the rumble of ship's engines in the water and looked up, seeing nothing but a dark blue haze. Costas edged his Aquapod alongside. 'Okay, Jack. Do you read me?'

'Loud and clear. Over.'

'I've just spoken to Macalister. Here's the drill. That current's becoming more serious, four, maybe five knots. We're going to move apart, fifteen metres or so, then rise very slowly up into the current where it takes off about eight metres above us, and let it take us. *Seaquest II* has got us on sonar and they're going to track us, maintaining position above. Once we rise above the current at about fifty metres' depth, we'll assess the situation, but we won't ascend further until *Seaquest II* is overhead and the divers are in the water. Copy?'

'Copy that.' Jack took one last look at the wreck, staring at the rusting hulk of the minelayer over the ancient war galley, seeing that lion prow rising on the edge of the sand channel. He remembered that it was a war grave. *A grave from two wars.* He closed his eyes briefly, whispering the words he had spoken at every shipwreck he had excavated since finding a Viking longship in the ice off Greenland three years before: *Han til Ragnaroks*, 'Until Ragnaroks', the Old Norse hymn for passing warriors, that they should meet up again. He had only ever told Rebecca that he did this, and the reason why. His empathy for the past came at a price. He disliked excavating burials because he could feel the emotions of those who had stood by the graveside. And shipwrecks held the emotions of those whose final moments were imprinted here. But now he had said those words. He looked at the finds basket, at that rim of gold, and shook his head with astonishment. He was itching to return. *What else would they find?*

'Jack. I've just had Macalister on the com again. He's had a call from Maurice at Troy.'

'I read you. Over.'

'Apparently, it was mostly an attack of coughing. Macalister had a hell of a time making it out.'

'That sounds promising. Sounds like Maurice has been down his hole again.'

'Well, wait for it. You and Maurice might *both* be owing James a crate of whisky.'

'You're kidding me.'

'You've found the Shield of Achilles. Kind of. Call it the ghost of the Shield of Achilles. And Maurice, with that palladion thing. It's not that he's found it, exactly, but it's the same kind of thing. A ghost. As you say, that's Troy for you. Never gives you exactly what you want.'

Jack felt his Aquapod tilt alarmingly, and he quickly pressed the buoyancy control handle to inject compressed air into the forward end of the pontoons, compensating for the extra weight of the finds basket out in front. He felt the submersible level out, and exhaled in relief.

'Jack. You still with me? Over.'

'Only just. James nearly lost his crate of whisky from me. The autopilot doesn't like that weight at the front. I'm ascending on manual. Over.'

'I never designed these as heavy-lift vehicles. But it's another problem I can put Jeremy on to.'

'Just give me a moment.' Jack held the stick, then feathered the pedals to get as near to level as he could. On manual it was like flying a helicopter, with similar inherent instabilities that needed constant attention. He was having to ascend by bleeding air into the forward chamber in the pontoon, then quickly injecting a blast into the aft chamber to keep the Aquapod from tilting in the other direction, at the same time ensuring that both the port and starboard chambers were balanced. It was taking all of his attention, and his eyes were glued on the gyroscope and depth meter. He glanced out. The sea bed still seemed close, as if they were getting nowhere, but he knew that was an optical illusion, a function of the refraction of light through the Plexiglas that meant that everything outside looked thirty per cent larger. He glanced at the depth gauge. Ninety metres. He had achieved a modicum of stability with the controls. He glanced over and saw Costas in his Aquapod keeping a good distance away, about twenty metres to the north-west and five metres above him. The last thing they wanted was a collision. He pressed the intercom again. 'Okay. So what's he found? Over.'

'He made his way along the tunnel. His team had dug out where the entrance collapsed yesterday and they'd shored it up with timber. Aysha's arrived, by the way. She banned him from going anywhere near it, but he snuck back by himself over lunchtime.'

'That's my man,' Jack said, eyeing his screen. He had no sense of lateral movement, of their horizontal speed. He looked down and caught his last glimpse of the shipwreck, a black smudge in the gloom far off to the right. Currents were always disconcerting, barely discernible without waymarkers unless you tried to fight against them, but sometimes alarmingly apparent if you veered away from your dive partner in a separate stream. They were rarely uniform, more like a swirl of tendrils weaving around each other, and this one was no exception. At any moment the two Aquapods might be drawn towards each other by forces they could never hope to counter with the water-jet engines. He could see that Costas sensed the danger too and had edged further off, at least thirty metres distant now. Jack looked up, and saw the dark form of *Seaquest II*'s hull above. That was a relief. Macalister was a damned good captain. He remembered Lanowski's model for the current, suggesting that they should be out of the main flow at about fifty metres' depth. He glanced at the gauge. Sixty metres. Another ten to go. He tapped the intercom. 'I'm listening. Over.'

'Okay. Didn't want to distract you. So anyway, Maurice goes down the tunnel, and reaches this mass of ancient masonry that's fallen in such a way that it leaves a passage ahead. He sees those hieroglyphics on the wall. Other inscriptions. Different languages. That linear thing James was on about.'

'Linear B,' Jack exclaimed. 'Fantastic.'

'He says they're like dedications. He says it's like walking into UN Headquarters, as if lots of different countries have put in a plaque.'

Jack felt a lurch, like flying over a thermal in a light aircraft. He remembered Lanowski's warning that the sea here would be like that, with different water density and temperature caused by the outflow from the Dardanelles, little patches of the Black Sea expelled from the strait that continued outwards into the Aegean, eventually to meld with the more salty Mediterranean. He looked at the gauge. Fifty-one metres. He suddenly lurched again, this time more alarmingly, the back of the Aquapod lifting up, followed by a violent juddering. He saw only a yellow blur in the direction of Costas' Aquapod.

He compensated for the tilt but could do nothing about the juddering. They had reached the top of the fast-moving current and were breaking into the calmer water above. The juddering was caused as they bounced and skidded along the top of the faster current, while being slowed down by the water above. He saw the basket in front of him shaking, and decided to gamble on a big blast into the buoyancy tank. The Aquapod jumped upwards, leaving his stomach somewhere below, and then he was free, coming quickly back to the level. The basket was still there. Costas' Aquapod appeared close alongside him. 'Everything okay? Over.'

'Bit of a rollercoaster ride.'

'See? Submersibles are fun.' Costas grinned at him, then pulled on the sombrero he'd pushed off behind his back at the wreck site. 'Macalister's just been on again. They know we're ahead of them but into safer water, so we're to maintain this depth until they come overhead again. You copy?'

'Copy that. Maintaining depth. So, back to Maurice. He's got more inscriptions. Amazing. I think it's some kind of ancient meeting chamber. That UN analogy might not be so far off.'

'Wait for it. There's more. So Maurice crawls further along. He says somebody's been there before. He said it was the strangest thing. He found tools, neatly arranged. A couple of trowels, a mattock. Almost as if someone had left them.'

'Well I'll be damned,' Jack murmured.

'Then at the end, there's a door, metal. Made out of bronze. A door into a chamber. He thinks it's slightly ajar, but blocked up with debris. He's going to get his guys in there tomorrow and try to open it.'

'Incredible. I've got to be there.'

'There was one other thing. The thing that might save him a crate of whisky. Or that means he owes one too. In the door. A kind of keyhole. He really wanted you to know. He thinks it's the palladion. Well, not exactly. More like the impression of it. But he thinks that counts.'

'What did he say about it exactly? What was it?'

'That's what baffles me. He says it's in the shape of a swastika.'

Jack was stunned. He tried to think, talking as he did so. *A swastika. A keyhole. The palladion in the shape of a swastika.* 'Okay. Incredible, but not as bizarre as you might think. That's where the Nazis got the swastika from, a symbol used across the Indo-European area. It's found stamped on pottery at Troy. Schliemann even had it put as decoration on the house he had built in Athens. It didn't have a sinister meaning then, not until Aryan nationalists hijacked it a few decades later.' He paused. 'One question. Did he tell you which way around it was?'

'Reverse. Counterclockwise.'

That was it, then. The Trojan swastika. *The symbol of Troy.* The key to a chamber beneath Troy. Jack thought of that face again, the face that Schliemann had lifted from the tomb at Mycenae, the face that lay concealed in the basket in front of him, staring upwards, seeing yet not seeing. *The face of Agamemnon.* Had he, too, stood before those bronze doors? Had he locked that door seemingly for ever, and taken away the key? Had Schliemann found the key, and gone there himself? *What had he seen?* Jack had thought that the day before had been the most extraordinary day of discoveries in his life, yet today there was more, much more. It was incredible. Yet over it all still hung that elusiveness, that uncertainty, that particular quality of Troy, as if it were all just beyond their grasp; it was as if the mask of Agamemnon lay over the whole site, and to lift it might reveal untold treasures, or merely a void. The mask of Agamemnon. *The mask of Troy*.

'Jack. Are you getting *Seaquest II* yet?'

Jack pressed the com, but heard only crackles. 'Nothing. Another fifteen metres and I'll try the other channel. Over.'

'Okay. Ben's talking to me. Stand by.'

Jack looked up. He could see the safety divers in the water now, ready to attach the cables that would draw the two Aquapods into the docking bay. He would go up first, with the shield. They would be taking no chances with that. He craned his neck, seeing the entire form of the hull above him, distorted through the Plexiglas dome. He remembered the last time he had peered up from underwater like that, in the lake of Issyk-Gul in Kyrgyzstan six months before. Rebecca had been there then, waiting for him, and he had seen her long hair falling down as she peered over at him from the Zodiac, framing her face. Then, he had been yearning to tell her about the most extraordinary discovery in the lake bed, an ancient tomb glimpsed and then vanished beneath tons of silt. This time, he had something tangible, something she could see and touch. *One of the greatest treasures he had ever found*. He wished she were here now, looking down on him. He wanted to show it to her before anyone else. He took a deep breath. *Next time*.

'Jack. We're holding position here while they manoeuvre the cables into position.'

'Roger that.'

'Jack, there may be some worrying news. Rebecca seems to have disappeared.'

Jack forgot the shield. 'What do you mean, disappeared?'

'From her hotel in London. About an hour ago. Our security guy called Ben at once.'

'The County Hall Marriott? Have they checked the swimming pool?'

'Apparently there was some guy in the lobby she knew. He'd been at a meeting in the hotel. Happened to have something in his car she might like to see, something he'd just been doing a presentation on. She told the security guy it was really important, that you'd want her to have a look. She said she wasn't going beyond the hotel entrance. Our guy wouldn't let her go until he called Ben to check this man out. Someone from the Courtauld Institute, a professor.'

'You mean Raitz? Hans Raitz?'

'That's the one. Ben said they'd checked him out when Rebecca went to see him before. A Nazi specialist.'

'A Nazi, full stop,' Jack replied. 'Got the Gold Medal of the Royal Institute of British Architects a couple of weeks ago, probably in line for a knighthood. But I don't trust anyone with a Nazi family background who specialized in Nazi art. To me it looks as if he's furthering the cause.'

'At least he's legit,' Costas said. 'Whatever his views, he's hardly a gangster.'

'Rebecca would never willingly get into a car with him. She told me she thought he was a creep. Her words. I think he might have tried it on with her. I was going to drop into the Courtauld next time I was in London and have a quiet word.'

'Probably best let Rebecca handle that. He'd be on the receiving end of one of those karate chops Ben's been teaching her.'

'She's probably just gone out for a walk,' Jack replied, trying to keep calm. He could feel his hands going cold. 'Like any seventeen year old in London. Maybe we're wrong to put her on such a tight leash.'

'Ben's taking it seriously, Jack. I think he feels he should have flown with her to London. He's got four of his guys there combing the South Bank and Westminster, and he's prepped an old special forces buddy of his who runs a private security company in London, got him to put another half a dozen guys on to it. I just hope that when Rebecca comes back from her stroll, she's grateful.'

Jack tensed. They both knew Ben never overreacted. There must be legitimate cause for concern. Jack looked across and saw Costas peering up towards the divers. 'Okay,' Costas said. 'Cables ready. We're good to go.'

'Roger that.'

The Aquapods rose together, side by side, and soon passed the twenty-metre depth mark. Jack pressed the com, heard another crackle and then it was clear. 'I think I've got the external link at last,' he said.

Ben's voice came over the intercom. 'Jack, was that you? Do you read me?'

'Loud and clear. Fill me in.'

'There's been an ultimatum. Relayed to Macalister from IMU just minutes ago. You and Costas have to be ready to move. I've alerted the Embraer crew and the equipment team at IMU HQ. The ultimatum's very specific. It doesn't leave us any leeway. You're in the helicopter ten minutes after you step out of the Aquapod.'

Jack stared ahead. Suddenly his breathing, each breath he took, was his entire focus. Nothing else mattered. Everything fell away, the wreck, the shield, as if it had all disintegrated into sand. He sensed his hands. They felt heavy, leaden. He stopped breathing. He was utterly still.

He had felt like this before. It was like the final moment before a free dive. His body was in survival mode. He clicked on the com. His voice sounded different, distant. 'What's happened?'

'Brace yourself, Jack. Rebecca's been kidnapped.'

17

Wieliczka Salt Mine, Poland

Jack snapped off his seat belt as the Toyota four-wheel drive came to a halt, then tapped his fingers impatiently as the driver spoke a few sentences into his cell phone. A moment later the wrought-iron gates to the compound opened, and the driver accelerated inside. He drew up in front of a white building with a head frame above it for the mineshaft winch, and switched off the ignition. Jack opened the door and stepped out. The sky was leaden, and it was cold. He stretched, rising on his toes, extending his arms out with bunched fists, grateful for his fleece. He had not slept more than a few fitful moments since he and Costas had flown out of Turkey the night before. *Thank God they had used the Aquapods to dive on the wreck*. It had been Costas' call, and he had been right. Jack had initially wanted to dive using

SCUBA with trimix, but that would have meant a twenty-four-hour delay for decompression before they could fly. As it was, two hours after surfacing they had been in the Embraer jet on the way to the IMU facility in Cornwall in England, where the equipment they would need was already being prepared. Costas had flown out with it to Krakow in the early hours of the morning and was already here. Jack had remained in England a few hours longer to confer with the IMU security team. Ben had advised against informing Scotland Yard or the security service. But Ben would pull in every favour to uncover who was behind this. And meanwhile they would scrupulously follow the kidnappers' demands. *Almost*.

Jack let his body relax, but the instant of release made him tense up. *Rebecca. Where was she? What were they doing to her?* He balled his fists again and took a deep breath, letting it out slowly, watching it crystallize in the morning mist. Now more than any other time in his life he needed to remain focused. He needed to keep the rage inside him under control. He needed to forget that Rebecca was where she was because of him. Because of his relentless quest, his search for revelations that would pit him against people like this. Ben had told him to put that from his mind. The first reaction to kidnapping was always guilt. *What could I have done to prevent this?* The kidnappers knew that, knew the weakness of those first hours, would try to exploit it. Jack had to forget that. He remembered how Dillen had been when they had met at the airport in London. They had just embraced, and said nothing. James had already left a long phone message about Hugh's revelations that afternoon, and Jack had listened to it over and over again on the trip from Turkey, trying to distract himself with the amazing discoveries they now knew Schliemann had made. It was all there, an extraordinary thing, as if he could hear every word of Dillen's message, hear him speaking, yet it meant nothing, as if he had been staring for hours at a canvas in a gallery, imprinting it in his mind for some time in the future when he might actually be able to see it.

He had to use all his powers of lateral thinking to sidestep them, to stay ahead. He had to work with his team, with Costas, with Ben, the others. They would play the kidnappers' game for now. The rage, the helplessness must remain in check. Focus on the goal. Focus on when Rebecca would be found. On when the kidnappers would be playing *his* game.

'Jack.' Costas came out of the door to the building and walked quickly up to him. He was unshaven and unkempt, wearing a hooded fleece, but he had a cold determination in his eyes. Jack felt a sudden rush of emotion. Costas was solid as a rock. They had been everywhere together, had looked out for each other. This time, this place, was no different. *Just another dive.* Costas peered at him. 'You look how I feel.' He passed him a bottle, an energy drink. 'I bet you haven't had anything to eat or drink. Not good before a dive. Get this down you. Now.'

Jack unscrewed the cap and drank the bottle dry, then tossed it into the Toyota. He swallowed hard, and shook himself. 'Where the hell have they taken her?'

'Put it from your mind, Jack. They want you to think that. They want it to consume you. I know what's inside you. It's inside me too. There are three guys here now. Focus on them, but keep your cool until the time's right. We're a team. We come out of this place alive, we're one step closer to her.'

'Right.' Jack's voice was hoarse. 'What have we got?'

'I've just come back up from the mineshaft to wait for you. Everything's ready. Our three new friends are down there, kitting up. I can barely stand to be near them. You've got to stop me from going for them, Jack. Like I said to you on the phone, we've got to keep each other in check. Until the time's right.'

'Any more heads-up on them?'

'They're Russian. Just as Ben guessed. These aren't the kidnappers, they're hired heavies. They only speak basic English. I call the leader Chechnya, because that's what's tattooed in red across his hands. The European underworld's awash with ex-military thugs like these, a lot of them Russian veterans of the war in Chechnya who couldn't get enough of the blood and killing.'

'Naval tech divers?' Jack asked.

Costas shook his head. 'Not from what I've seen. Ben was right about that, too. Our kidnapper has found some heavies who've got basic diving skills, but you don't get ex-naval tech divers working as hit men. If you've got that level of skill, there's far more money to be made doing legit commercial diving on the oil rigs. Our gamble has paid off, so far. They understand the SCUBA gear we've given them, but not the rebreathers you and I are using. I've made a big show of adjusting and fiddling with those. Lots of doubtful muttering from me. I don't think they'll question it. Ben said to play on the macho aspect too. Get into their little world. They're the tough guys, with the tough old-fashioned gear. The stuff they saw their own navy divers use. We may be able to go deeper, but only by using fancy gear. They're the real men. The hard men.'

'Jesus,' Jack muttered. 'What a charade.'

'We'll use it against them, Jack. At the water's edge. I've got some theatrics planned. Until then, just keep cool.'

'Anyone else here?'

Costas nodded. 'Wladislaw's going to meet us up here, then we go down the shaft in the lift to the lowest level.'

'Who the hell's Wladislaw?'

'Guy I mentioned to you on the phone. Site engineer. I know him – I realized that he and I met at a conference a while back. Trained in America, speaks excellent English. He's straight up, I'm sure of it. He's thrilled by this. Doesn't have a clue about what's really going on. You're a star over here. Your book on Atlantis was a number-one best-seller in Poland. When the caller purporting to be IMU got in touch two weeks ago suggesting we wanted to look for Neolithic remains deep in the mine, Wladislaw was overjoyed. They promised to shut off the whole mine from visitors for the day of the dive.'

'*Two weeks ago?*' Jack exclaimed.

'Two weeks ago. The call came from someone claiming to be you. Whoever it was told him' to keep it top secret. Something to do with a clue to the exodus from Atlantis, at the dawn of civilization. Something that would really put Poland on the archaeological map.'

'Jesus,' Jack murmured. 'So they were planning the kidnap as far back as that. They must have been following Rebecca's every move.'

'Let's focus on the here and now.'

'So what's the dive profile?'

Costas flipped open a notebook. 'Lanowski gave me the

specs. It's all relevant stuff. No unnecessary science.' He paused, looking up. 'He's really upset about Rebecca, you know. Distraught. He wanted to come with us.'

'We don't need distraught people here,' Jack said coldly. 'We need people who can kill.' He put his hand up to his forehead, and shut his eyes for a moment. 'You know what I mean. Lanowski's a sweet man and Rebecca's made many friends. But we've gone to war. That's the only way I can think of it. The only way I can handle it. Rebecca's like Helen of Troy. We're fighting the Trojan War again. And if this goes belly-up, I swear to God those walls will burn. They'll burn like they've never burned before.'

'We'll get her back, Jack.'

'There'll still be hell to pay.' Jack's hands were balled into fists, his knuckles white. '*Hell to pay*.'

Costas put his hand on Jack's shoulder, then looked down at his notebook again. 'The mine. Folded saliferous Miocene deposits. It's a huge area of salt karst, fissures going deep underground where the salt has dissolved. That's how Neolithic miners would have got down there. Our kidnappers did their homework on that one. The actual mine workings date from the thirteenth century onwards. It's huge, unbelievable. Three hundred kilometres of tunnels, going down more than three hundred metres. The section open to tourists is only about one per cent of that. We're roughly one-forty to one-ninety metres above sea level, and the lower reaches are all flooded.'

'Is it pumped out?'

Costas nodded. 'The Nazis apparently pumped it out much deeper, to the depth we're going. Wladislaw thinks the aquifer has risen dramatically since the war, with renewed mining and those deep tunnels acting like siphons. Where we're going must have been accessible to the Nazis, but it's now at least a hundred metres underwater.'

'Have we got a route?'

'Wladislaw's been on it. Apparently, two weeks ago the caller purporting to be you specified a tunnel sequence, evidently something they'd found out about from the war. He has a 3-D CGI of the entire complex, with the fissure we're following waymarked. I've downloaded it into our helmet computers so we can see it on screen. It's a natural void, descending at about forty to sixty degrees from where we are now. The upper part's all been mined out, so it looks like man-made caverns where the rock salt has been extracted. Below the pool – our entry point – there are more flooded mine workings, but then as we go deeper it reverts to natural. Up here, it's all rock salt. Looks a little like grey limestone. Down there, a lot of what we'll see is natural salt crystals, some of it recrystallized since the original halite was taken out by prehistoric workers. Wladislaw's very proud of their dating for the salt growth, which shows we're on the right track for the Neolithic remains he thinks we've come here to find.'

'Okay. Tell me more as we go in.' Costas took off the bag he had been carrying on his shoulder, then reslung it more securely. Jack jerked his thumb at it. 'You managed to get that by your three stooges?'

Costas replied in a low voice. 'That's the other thing I need to tell you. Before we go in to Wladislaw. I've just got off the phone to Lanowski. He didn't just research the geology. He's also looked for any connection between salt mines and Nazis.

This place was used as an aero engine assembly plant, using Jewish slave labour. It's all very shady. It was shut down before the Soviets arrived and the Jews were sent to the death camps. We're only about thirty miles from Auschwitz, you know. He also researched other instances of salt mines being used for storage, and found an account of the Altaussee salt mine in Austria, liberated by the Americans in May 1945. They found thousands of looted paintings and crates of other treasures, belongings stolen from Jews. In April 1945, the local Nazi *Gauleiter* sent in some more crates, only weeks before the war ended. The *Gauleiter* was a fanatical Nazi and was carrying out the Führer's last orders, the Nero Decree. Each crate contained a five-hundred-kilogram bomb. I read the account at IMU before flying out, so I had time to raid my tool kit. I'm fully prepared.'

'That makes a change from last time.'

'There's more at stake here.'

'These characters security-check you?'

'They strip-searched me. Had all my tools out. Ham-fisted bunch of bastards. They wouldn't let me have my diving knife. But I got away with a few metres of detonator cord.'

'They didn't recognize it?'

'It's hanging from the front of my e-suit, masquerading as a lanyard with hose clips to stop my gear dragging on the cave floor. It's what you always say. People hide things in the most obvious places.'

'That was a risk.'

'What were they going to do if they found it? They need me too. They know we're a team. And det cord's not usually an offensive weapon.'

'Your man, Wladislaw, knows nothing of this?'

Costas shook his head. 'But how long we're able to keep it up, I don't know. I don't exactly see eye to eye with the Chechnya guy. It'll become pretty obvious to Wladislaw when we kit up. You make your own judgement about Wladislaw. Maybe there'll be a chance for a swift word before we dive. He could be our contact with IMU. But if our stooges think he knows what's going on, Wlady's dead meat. They're relying on his ignorance of all this to keep the mine closed off. They'd think he'd contact the police.'

'He's probably a marked man anyway. There's only one reason these guys are here: they've been sent to kill us once we've got what their paymaster wants.' Jack paused. 'What about our own gear?'

'Still bagged and locked up. I'll know if it's been tampered with. I doubt it will be, though. They want us to do the dive and get a result. They've been given strict instructions. Payout for them is when they show up with what we've found. And there are easier ways than fiddling with our equipment to make sure we don't come back up. Cruder ways. Come on.'

Jack followed Costas towards the door. He stopped for a moment before going in. Costas had mentioned Auschwitz, how close it was. Jack looked again at the leaden sky. So close you could almost sense it, in the air. It was strange. James had mentioned Auschwitz on the phone the day before, the story of Hugh and the girl who had done the drawing, the girl with the harp. The image of that girl had stayed with Jack, had been with him over the last twelve hours, like a piece of music that would not go out of his head. He knew it was to do with Rebecca, as if that image of the other girl, a girl he had never

332

even seen, was giving him something to hold on to. Something enduring, eternal, from a time of shock and horror, something like an old master painting, like one of those works of art the Nazis so coveted. He looked around. Everything here, the buildings, the ground, was pastel-coloured, washed out, and it was about as landlocked a place as you could find. It seemed inconceivable to be going underwater, let alone doing one of the most dangerous dives they had ever attempted. He took a final deep breath outside and stepped through the door.

Jack followed Costas into an office. A small, balding man was sitting behind the desk, writing. He looked up, smiled broadly and immediately bounded over to Jack. He was wearing jeans and a short-sleeved shirt, and had an open, intelligent face, suffused with excitement. Jack felt a jolt of discomfort as he saw him. *Someone else he was going to let down. Someone else he had put in terrible danger.* He dismissed the thought. Wladislaw offered his hand, and looked up penetratingly. 'Dr Howard. A pleasure to meet you. A *real* pleasure.' He pumped his hand. 'Everything is as you wished it. Dr Kazantzakis has seen to that. Anything else I can do, let me know. I'll accompany you down to the pool. But before we go, this.' He picked up a piece of paper and handed it to Jack with a flourish. 'Came through yesterday. The uranium–thorium results. They date the halite recrystallization to the early Neolithic. To exactly the time of the Neolithic exodus.' He slapped his hands together theatrically. '*To exactly the time of Atlantis.*'

Jack looked at the sheet. It was true. It was fantastic. He looked at Wladislaw, forcing himself to smile broadly, and put a hand on his shoulder. 'Brilliant. *Brilliant*. Now we know we're on the right track, let's get down there.'

'Of course.' Wladislaw put the sheet back on the table, picked up a ring of keys and led them out of his door. He pressed an alarm box on the wall beside his office and they heard the door lock behind them. 'That locks up the entire place, the main gates, everything. Exactly as you wished.'

Jack coughed. 'Very good.'

Wladislaw looked at Costas. 'Your three colleagues? They are ready?'

'Familiarizing themselves with some new gear, and kitting up.'

'New gear?' Wladislaw said with interest. They reached the sliding metal door of the lift shaft and he opened it up, then pressed a button on the side.

'State-of-the-art,' Costas replied. 'At IMU, the technology's always one step ahead of the diver. That's my department.'

'You're using trimix? Rebreathers? It's going to be too deep for compressed air, yes?'

'Rebreathers for Jack and me, to give us the safest option for very deep water, if we have to go below a hundred metres. The other three are going to be using nitrox from one tank, and then trimix from the other. They'll be fine to eighty, ninety metres. It's state-of-the-art too, but it's easily used by anyone who has used SCUBA. The rebreathers are a different matter. Only Jack and I are certified for them.'

'Got you. So the other three guys are back-up. Logistical support.'

'You got it,' Costas said.

Wladislaw nodded sagely. 'I suppose that's the reality. In Dr

Howard's books, it always seems to be you two alone.'

'It usually is.' Costas looked beyond Wladislaw at Jack. 'Health and safety, you know. Our board of directors have clamped down on us.'

'I know the problem. Running a tourist mine? Oh yes.' The lift light flashed green, and Wladislaw slid open the inner door, motioning them inside. 'Here in Poland, though, we still take risks.' He grinned, pulled the door shut behind them and pressed the down button, then pressed another button for level 2A. The floor jerked, and Jack could hear the machinery above straining and whirring as the cable paid out. Lifts were not his favourite places. *Flooded mines were not his favourite places.* It was something else he needed to forget. The near-death experience years ago in a flooded mine shaft, when Costas had saved his life. He needed to stay focused. The lift creaked to a halt, and Wladislaw opened the mesh door. 'We're just below the second level, a hundred and twenty metres deep. This route is normally sealed off. We'll walk through a series of chambers to the pool. It's faster this way, and there's a chamber I want you to see.'

Costas turned to Jack. 'I went with our friends to the base of the shaft, at a hundred and thirty-five metres. That's the deepest level of these workings. We carried the diving equipment along a shaft about two hundred metres to our entry point.'

Jack stepped out of the lift, followed by the other two. They were in a small cavern about the size of a car garage. Ahead of them a rusting railway track led to a tunnel, lit by a connected string of light bulbs that extended down the tunnel out of sight. Jack took a few steps inside the chamber and put his hands on the wall, feeling the damp. He could see pick and wedge marks, evidently old workings, though the floor and the walls at the lift entrance had clearly been shaped more recently. He looked around. It was the colour that was most unexpected, a dark grey, like wet concrete, with off-white streaks inside the gouge marks. It was almost sepulchral. He turned to Wladislaw. 'Presumably the man-made tunnels follow the seams?'

Wladislaw nodded. 'The grey colour is rock salt darkened by surface oxidation. You also get bronze-coloured salt, with iron, and green-coloured, with copper. And there are some crystal-clear patches, where the rock salt's been dissolved and reconstituted without mineral inclusions.'

'Those little stalactites,' Jack said, pointing up at the ceiling.

'That's secondary crystallization, from salt leaching out and then solidifying, in the years since this chamber was dug.'

'We're well above the water table here?'

Wladislaw nodded. 'That begins at the pool.'

Costas leaned against a rock pillar in the centre of the chamber, as if testing it, and then pushed hard against a timber support inletted into the salt. He looked sceptically down the tunnel. 'What's the structural stability of this place?'

'Sound enough, where the salt hasn't been completely dug out. Generally the miners didn't do that in case it created chambers that were wider than they were high. They always seemed to be mindful of safety. Must have been some terrible accidents early on. You can see there's been lots of shoring up with timber too. This particular tunnel follows the line of a natural fissure, which is another reason I wanted to bring you this way. It's the most likely route that Neolithic miners would have taken to get deep underground, and we know it extends off below the main workings beyond that pool. In the early Neolithic, the water level may have been considerably lower, and the deeper fissures and passageways more accessible.'

Jack breathed in deeply. The air had a distinctive heady smell that seemed to sharpen his senses, to revitalize him. He and Costas followed Wladislaw down the tunnel. They stopped at the entrance to another chamber, much larger. Jack took another deep breath, and Wladislaw watched him approvingly. 'Sodium, calcium, magnesium chloride. The air's full of it. Enjoy it while you can.'

'What do you mean, while you can?' Costas asked.

Wladislaw pointed up. 'Look at the roof of the cavern.'

Costas craned his neck. 'Either those are shadows, or it's scorched.'

'Before the development of a ventilation system, methane released from the rock would collect in pockets against the ceiling. The miners went round with torches on long poles and burned it off. We're all right in the main workings, but where you're going is a different story. You might encounter what look like pockets of air. Except they're not.'

Jack glanced at Costas, then turned to Wladislaw. 'Do the others know about this? Our colleagues?'

'I'll warn them when we get there.'

Jack shook his head. 'Thanks, but let Costas do it. That's what he's here for. Part of the safety briefing.'

Wladislaw nodded. 'Of course. You're the experts.' He led them into the next cavern, a space that rose above them like the interior of a cathedral, thirty metres or more in height.

'This will interest you.' He grinned. 'One for Jack Howard. The clue to a treasure.'

'Tell us as we walk,' Jack said, glancing at his watch. He had little interest in stories now. He could only focus on Rebecca. *On what they had come here to do.*

'Okay.' Wladislaw clattered down the metal stairs, producing an odd dull echo in the chamber. He gesticulated as he spoke. 'In 1944, the Nazis established an assembly plant for aircraft parts in this chamber. They used Polish Jews as slave labour. When the Soviets came close, the Nazis dismantled the plant and the Jews were sent to the death camps. But one of the Jews who survived came back here recently, and told me a story. He said they all knew the deeper chambers were used by the Nazis to hide treasures. They all assumed it was gold, stolen from the Jews of Poland. There was always a guard post at the entrance to the deep passageway to prevent anyone entering. Then, the night before the evacuation, several of the fitter prisoners were ordered to go down there, with picks and hammers, evidently to do some kind of manual work. They were accompanied by a couple of the Hungarian SS guards and a Luftwaffe officer, the boss of the factory. *Only the officer came back out.* He was carrying something in a bag. The survivor saw the officer again, because he accompanied the death march from Auschwitz of the Jewish survivors being sent to work on bomb damage in German cities. The officer remained with them until they entered the concentration camp where the survivor was soon afterwards liberated by the British, somewhere near Belsen.'

Jack suddenly stopped. He had only been half listening. 'Where did you say?'

'A camp, near Belsen. In Lower Saxony, Germany. One of many satellite camps, probably.'

Jack turned to Costas, who had also stopped and was staring at him. They both looked at Wladislaw. Jack felt a chill of certainty. *It all made sense.* An object secreted away here, in a place apparently impregnable from discovery, secure for ever in the heart of the thousand-year Reich. But then the unthinkable happened. The war was being lost. An ultimatum was activated. The object was removed, taken west. It was to be the signal for the worst horrors to be unleashed. Jack remembered the story Dillen had told him from Hugh. The document Hugh had found on the motorcycle courier, with the counterclockwise swastika. *The Agamemnon Code.* Jack thought hard, staring at the ground, his heart pounding. The people who had kidnapped Rebecca must not hear this story. They must not know that the object might no longer be here. The three men who would be diving with them. *At all costs they must not know.* He looked at Wladislaw. 'Did the survivor tell you anything else?'

'He saw the Luftwaffe officer when they entered the camp near Belsen, and said that he still had the bag with him. He never saw him again after that. He thought the bag must contain some great treasure stolen from a museum in Poland, hidden to begin with in this mine. They all thought that was what the Nazis stored down here. By telling me the story, he thought he was doing a service to Poland. There might be a chance of recovering the treasure, somewhere, somehow, and bringing it back home.'

Jack tensed up. 'Does anyone else know this? *Anyone?*'

'The man told me he'd never told anyone else. He spoke to

me in my office, where you met me. He insisted on locking the door. He told me he was old and dying. He'd come back to this place for the first time since 1945, had seen that we had a memorial to the Jewish prisoners. He'd asked to see me. I was very busy that day, but I remembered the story a few days later and phoned the place that looked after him. They said he'd died the day after coming here. Just slipped away.'

'Who else have you told? Your friends? Your family?'

Wladislaw shook his head. 'Nobody. It was the day we took that phone call from you, from IMU headquarters. When you said you wanted to come here to search for the Neolithic remains. I thought I'd save this story until you came. Icing on the cake for you.'

Jack looked intently at Costas, then at Wladislaw. 'A pact, just the three of us, right? We tell nobody about this. Not until we can take it further. *Nobody*. Not even our three friends waiting below.'

'Done,' Costas said. Wladislaw stared at Jack. 'Of course. You have my word.'

Jack slapped his back. 'Good man. Now let's move.'

'We should get you over to the IMU campus in Cornwall, Wlady,' Costas said as they clattered down. 'I invited you when we met at that conference, remember? I didn't know there was an archaeologist in you then. We need an IMU representative in Poland. What do you think, Jack?'

'Excellent idea,' Jack said.

'You really think so?' Wladislaw said. 'You would not be disappointed in me, I assure you.'

'Take it as a done deal,' Jack said. 'But for now, news blackout.'

'Total secrecy,' Wladislaw agreed.

Jack glanced at Costas as they followed Wladislaw off the metal walkway and on to a platform of wooden duckboards. They had reached the end of the complex that was open to the public, barred off with a mesh barrier but with a little door that Wladislaw swung open. It was cooler now, and damper. They crouched through and carried on. The way ahead was a narrowing void, the timber vaulting fitted into the wall becoming sporadic and then finishing altogether. The duckboards ended, and Jack could see where the boards had lain over a narrow-gauge railway line that carried on ahead down the tunnel. The ceiling was just high enough for the tunnel to have been used for pushing carts up from the deepest mine workings. After a few more metres the passage widened into a chamber the size of a small room, lit by a single bulb. On the sides Jack could just make out shadowy forms, half-finished sculptures in salt that seemed to leer out of the walls, inchoate. It was a macabre place, like a catacomb. Wladislaw pointed his torch at one of the figures. 'St Clement, patron saint of miners,' he said, his voice sounding strangely dull again, without any echo. 'This is not like the sculptures you see on the tourist route. These ones are the real deal. They were done long ago, hundreds of years ago, by the miners, not for visitors but for themselves. They show what the miners really felt, the terrible fear, the pact with God they made to come down here, the bargain they made to survive.'

Jack stared at the sculpted face in the torchlight. It looked like Munch's *The Scream*. Secondary recrystallization had clouded the features, obscuring the sculpted lines, as if the salt in the walls were reclaiming the figure, absorbing it back into a world of stone where humans were never meant to pass. Wladislaw went forward and they carried on. The passageway was now only just tall enough for Jack. It dropped at a steeper angle, dipping to follow the salt seam, the walls shadowy and deathly grey. He felt a tiny lurch, a tightness of the breath, then steeled himself. *If you feel fear, it is fear that you will let Rebecca down. It is not fear of this place.* He saw light ahead, another chamber. The light reflected off a pool of water, green and iridescent, as if it were full of algae. 'The colour's from copper,' Wladislaw said. 'The water might be like that ahead. Nobody's explored it for years, since it flooded.'

They entered the chamber. It was the very last one before the tunnel disappeared underwater. Above the pool was a string of suspended light bulbs, trailed down on the cord they had followed from the upper chambers. On the left side three men sat kitted up in diving suits and SCUBA twin-sets, filled with the oxygen, helium and nitrogen mix tailored for their dive by Costas at IMU the night before. They had their hoods on, so Jack saw only three constricted faces, barely distinguishable from one another. He made out the red letters tattooed on the hands of one of the men: *Chechnya*. He remembered what had happened in the war in Chechnya, to the children, and he felt physically repulsed. These men, others like them, were holding Rebecca. *There would be a price to pay.* He stared at them, and then followed Costas a few steps to the right, where their own equipment was bagged and locked. Costas gave the bags a quick inspection, then unlocked them. They quickly pulled out their gear and silently kitted up. Jack stripped down to his underwear and T-shirt and pulled on his e-suit, turning to let Costas zip up the neck seal, then he did the same for Costas in return. They helped each other don the rebreathers and yellow Kevlar helmets, each with a sealable visor instead of the conventional face masks the other three men were using. They hooked in the intake and exhaust tubes to the base of the helmets and then sat down by the water's edge, pulling on their fins and letting their legs dangle in the water. Jack looked into the green haze. He could barely see his legs. At least they had the 3-D navigation system, following the route Wladislaw had mapped in.

He activated his rebreather and helmet computer system, testing the mouthpiece and cross-checking with Costas, then strapped on the wrist computer he always carried as a back-up. He still liked to see his dive time and depth on his wrist, as he had been trained to do before the advent of dive computers and all the technology they were using today. He glanced at the time. There was no way of knowing how long the dive would last. If they were going to a hundred metres' depth, it would be twenty minutes, twenty-five maximum. The rebreather would minimize nitrogen intake and decompression problems, but they had no safety margin.

Costas glanced at him, then put up his hand. 'And now for the best part,' he bellowed. 'For the *real* men.' He sat heavily by the water's edge, then reached back ostentatiously to his bag, clanging together some glass bottles. He pulled one out, and held it up to the light. It was a half-bottle of vodka. 'Ah,' he exclaimed loudly, smacking his lips. 'Krepkaya. The best.' The three Russians watched in amazement as Costas knocked the cap off on a rock and put the bottle to his lips, gulping down half of it. He let out a long gasp, then passed the bottle to Jack, who put it to his lips, tasted it with relish, then drained it. He gasped, nodded appreciatively, then tossed the bottle into the pool, before turning back and checking his equipment. The Russian with the tattoo got up and took a few steps over to them, lumbering in all his gear. He pushed Costas' shoulder roughly.

'So,' he said, his English guttural and heavily accented. 'A little drink for the nerves, no?' He jerked his head towards the pool, then turned back to the other two Russians, smirking. 'A little too much fear, eh?'

Costas stopped adjusting his helmet and slowly gazed up at the man, a look of utter contempt on his face. He suddenly erupted in laughter, and turned to Jack, barely able to control his mirth. 'This moron thinks we're afraid of that little puddle.' Jack shook his head, snorting in derision. Costas turned back to the man. 'You idiot. We always drink alcohol before a deep dive. It dilates the blood vessels. Stops us getting the bends. Learned it from the old French navy divers. Really tough guys. They'd break a Spetsnaz like a matchstick.'

The man leaned heavily over and took Costas' chin in his hand, twisting it. 'I'll fucking break you before today is over.'

Costas pushed him away. 'So that's what your boss ordered? At least we know where we stand.'

The man reached back to Costas' bag, where two more bottles were visible. Costas shot out his arm and put it over them. 'Only one bottle for the three of you. Dr Howard and I are used to it. It's extra proof Krepkaya. You won't have the stomach for it.'

'Fuck you. We're Russian.'

The man pushed Costas' arm aside, and yanked out the two bottles. He broke open the caps with his teeth, first one, then the other, and passed one to the nearest of the other two men. Then he tipped up the other bottle himself, drinking deeply. As he wiped his lips, gasping, Costas spat on the rocks beside him. 'Hey. Chechnya. Don't drink too much. I don't want to swim in your vomit.' The man snarled at Costas, then tipped up the bottle again, nearly draining it. He gasped, then passed the remainder to the second man, who finished it, then did the same with the bottle from the other man. The air stank of alcohol. The Russians donned their face masks and put in their regulators, then followed the tattooed man into the pool, staggering and slipping on the salt. Costas shouted at them, 'Test your regulators. Go under the surface for three minutes.'

They all disappeared under the surface, leaving only a maelstrom of bubbles. Wladislaw came up quickly and knelt down between Jack and Costas, whispering urgently. 'What the hell was that all about? Sure alcohol dilates the blood vessels, but it also dehydrates. That *causes* the bends. What were you doing?'

Costas peered at him. 'What we were doing, Jack and I, was keeping hydrated.'

Wladislaw knitted his brows. He suddenly understood. 'You mean your bottle was *water*.'

Costas nodded. Wladislaw stared at him. He stared at the bubbles. 'So who the hell are these guys? What's going on here?'

Jack turned to him, speaking low, quickly. 'We didn't want to tell you. In case they realized that you knew. Your life would be in danger.'

345

'Knew what?'

Jack clicked on his visor monitor and paused. He saw that Costas was ready. He made the 'okay' sign, and Costas repeated it. Jack kept his visor open and turned to Wladislaw. 'Do you have children?'

'Three.'

'My daughter's been kidnapped. Whoever's running these three guys is extorting us. There's something down there they want.'

'*Your daughter*. My God.' Wladislow looked stunned. He spoke in a whisper. 'So this has all been a set-up? It wasn't IMU who contacted us after all. You're not searching for Neolithic remains.'

'Not this time.'

'This has something to do with the Nazis.'

Jack nodded.

'I knew it,' Wladislaw exclaimed. '*I knew it*. From what the old Jewish survivor told me, I knew something sinister had gone on down here.'

Jack spoke urgently. 'I was given instructions by phone yesterday after my daughter was abducted. They're using us to find a hidden Nazi treasure because they think it's down at the very base of the fissure, more than a hundred metres below water level. We're expert divers and know how to find treasure. They got hold of some old Nazi document. Their leader, the one with the Chechnya tattoo, knows the details. We're supposed to follow him, and he'll point the way. Costas thinks he knows where it is already, from his talk with the man earlier and from your plan of the mine he's programmed into our helmet computers, which shows only one possible route beyond this pool. Then they stay at the maximum safe depth for their breathing gear, and wait. We find what they want, then they dispose of us on the way back up.'

The head of a diver bobbed up on the surface, breathing noisily from a regulator, staring at them. Costas shut his visor and gave the thumbs-down sign, moving to the edge of the water and pushing off. The diver who had surfaced descended beside him. Wladislaw turned to Jack, helping him with his helmet. 'Quickly. Tell me anything I can do. I've got a pistol in my office.'

'Too late for that.'

'Do you have any weapons?'

'Costas has tools for bomb disposal. He thinks that whatever's down there might have been booby-trapped by the Nazis.'

Wladislaw nodded. 'The Nazis did that when they concealed stolen treasures, works of art.' He paused. 'Is that what this is all about?'

'I'll tell you. When we surface. Here's what I want you to do now. Take my phone. It's in my fleece pocket. Don't answer it if anyone rings. But there's a text message ready to send to our security chief. It says *Der Agamemnon-Code*. It means we've gone under, and everything is as planned. Go back to the surface, send it, then leave this place immediately. Don't call the police. Go home, collect your family and take them away somewhere safe, somewhere far away. Don't tell anyone where you're going. A sudden little holiday while the mine is shut. Then call IMU. They'll look after you. Use your own phone, not mine. Leave mine on your desk, where I can find it. It's my only contact with the kidnapper. If we escape this he'll know about it, and I'll need to speak to him.'

Wladislaw put his hand on Jack's shoulder. 'Understood.' He paused. 'Your daughter.'

'Yes?'

'What's her name?'

'It's . . .' Jack swallowed hard. The enormity of it suddenly hit him. *What were they doing to her, right now, at this very moment?* His voice was hoarse, a whisper. 'It's Rebecca.'

'Rebecca.' Wladislaw knelt up. 'Good. For Rebecca. You can rely on me.'

Jack reached up and squeezed Wladislaw's hand, then flipped down his visor, sealed it and clicked on the intercom. He heard Costas' breathing, a measured, reassuring sound. 'Costas. You read me?'

'Loud and clear. You okay?'

'Roger that.' He slipped into the water, feeling the pressure against his e-suit, his cocoon against the water. He made himself remember how much he enjoyed that sensation, how relaxed it made him feel, the beginning of a dive. He took a few deep breaths from his rebreather, and glanced at the readout inside his visor. Everything was good. He just had to stay in control. To forget about the tunnel, the walls. To stem his anger, his terrible fear for Rebecca, to let the adrenalin work for him, not against him. He would pay back those who had done this. He would relish it. *But not yet.* He took another deep breath, and clicked on the screen display inside his helmet, showing a 3-D lattice map of the labyrinth ahead of them, their route marked out in red. He dropped below the surface, watching the green water rise up his visor, seeing Costas' face in front of him. The forms of the other three divers were visible in the gloom beyond, the beams from their headlamps wavering in the water. He switched on his own headlamp, keeping it angled down to avoid it shining directly in Costas' eyes. Costas put out his right hand and turned his thumb down. 'Good to go?'

'Good to go.'

18

Troy, 18 March 1890

Heinrich Schliemann embraced his wife and left her standing on the grassy knoll at the highest point of the ancient citadel, staring out across the plain of Troy towards the distant waters of the Dardanelles. He took out his fob watch, scratched and battered after almost twenty years of excavating, in Greece, in Egypt, in Italy, here within the walls of fabled Troy, relentlessly searching. He slid it back into his waistcoat pocket. A quarter to seven. *It was almost time*. The delegates to the conference would be gone by now, departed for Çanakkale and Constantinople and their home countries, and the archaeological site would be barred to all comers except the three he had specially invited to join him this evening.

His pulse quickened, and he took a deep breath. The

terrible pain in his head, the sickening earache that had assailed him for months now, the ringing that had tormented him day and night like a thousand mosquitoes swarming round his head, all of that seemed to disappear the moment he stepped back into the citadel. Nobody knew whether it was real or imagined, none of the physicians he had consulted, whether the product of a fevered imagination or some dormant affliction he had released from an ancient tomb. All he knew was that the ache had begun when he knew the time was right to return to Troy, to bring back what he and Sophia had found that night in the royal grave at Mycenae, to return it to the vault of its founders where it might once again serve as a bulwark for the world against darkness and evil war.

He took a few steps along the rickety plank that served as a walkway over the open excavation, then glanced back towards the knoll. It was the last place on the upper citadel left to excavate, beside the great trench they had cleaved through the mound of Troy twenty years before. He had felt close to Homer on that knoll, closer than anywhere else at Troy. It would be the site of their final excavation, once the great task that lay ahead of them was finished, the excavation of the passageway that would now begin in earnest beneath the citadel. One day he would sit where Sophia was now standing, where he believed there was an unexcavated room of the great palace: a place where Priam might once have sat and looked out over the walls, where marauding Agamemnon had found him. Like Priam, he would not see the ravages of war but instead would soak in the bounteous richness of the land; not hear the battle cries and shrieks, but instead hear soft music of the lyre, soothing his ears, lulling him into a paradise where Troy was the city of heaven, a city of joy and love, and not a crucible of war.

'Heinrich,' Sophia whispered after him in Greek, her voice like sweet music on the wind. 'You must go now. Do you remember what you said at Mycenae, when we lifted the mask? *For the sake of our children.*'

Schliemann looked up at her, and smiled. 'For all the children.' He blew her a kiss. As she turned away, the gold that bedecked her shimmered, gold they had found here that night in the darkness seventeen years before, digging secretly at the bottom of the great trench. He turned and carried on along the walkway, passing that very spot, peering down. He had told the world they had found the treasure of Priam, but in truth he knew it was a thousand years too old, the treasure of a nameless ancient king who had ruled Troy when the citadel was still young, when bronze was still a modern marvel. He had wanted to divert attention from the truth, from the discovery they would reveal once all the pieces were in place. He remembered the other citadel where he and Sophia had dug secretly, when he had lifted the golden mask of the great king. Now he felt as if he were about to lift a mask off Troy itself. He felt the bulge beneath his coat, where Sophia had swathed the object in silk inside his satchel bag. He felt a rush of excitement, yet a tinge of apprehension. *What if it were all to no avail?* He thought of those he was about to meet. All that he had done, all that he had found, everything he had put his soul and his energy into, all of that was at stake. This was the most important day of his life. *There was no turning back now.*

He heard a rustle in the grass, and saw the silhouette of a man scurry up the slope of the trench and disappear over the top. It was Kemal, the site foreman, who had first shown Schliemann this place as a boy, whose ancestors had known Troy since time immemorial, descendants of Prince Hector himself. He could never tell Kemal to leave this place, nor did he wish to. Kemal was continuity, the future. And that was what this evening was about. The future. *The future of the human race.*

Schliemann turned east over the trench, then came down on the path that led around the citadel, from the excavation house towards the entrance to the secret passageway. Sophia had left little candles in tin holders to mark the way, and they flickered in the breeze. Around the corner another man came into view. He was large, wearing a fur-lined overcoat and a trilby hat, carrying a walking stick and one of the lanterns that had been left at the entrance to the site. He stopped and raised the lantern, peering. Schliemann saw the features that had cowed so many, the heavyset face, the bags beneath the eyes, the hint of a scowl, but he also saw in those eyes what those close to the great man knew, the humour, the thirst for knowledge, the humanity. 'Ah,' the man said gruffly, moving closer. 'Herr Doktor Schliemann.' He spoke in German. 'I was wondering where you were.'

Schliemann's heart raced. He replied in German also, holding out his hand. 'Your Excellency. I trust you had a felicitous journey.'

'Felicitous!' the man grumbled. 'Fortunately, the King of Greece lent me his yacht. The Ottomans would not let an Imperial German warship into the Dardanelles. *I ask you.*

There will be a war, you know, and the Turks need an ally, what with the Russians on one side, and Gladstone and the English baying for their blood on the other. *That infernal man.* I hope I never meet him in person. I would not answer for the consequences.'

'Ah,' Schliemann said.

'What do you mean, "Ah"? And what's the meaning of all this subterfuge? For years I've been asking you for a tour of Troy. Now I'm here, and it's too dark even to see it.'

'My dear Otto.' Schliemann took the man by the shoulder, and steered him on the path between the little candles. 'We were both awarded freedmen of the city of Berlin, yes? We are a rare breed. A secret society. And like all secret societies, we must have our little rituals, our indulgences.'

'Freedman of the city, yes, but I failed to convince those swine to make you a member of the Berlin Academy,' the man muttered. 'After all you've done for Germany. Donating your greatest finds to the Reichsmuseum. Even the unmentionable Gladstone had you made an honorary Fellow of the Society of Antiquaries of London, and all you gave them was a few miserable pots.'

Schliemann smiled. 'My dear old friend. If I were the type of man on whom academic honours were showered, I would not be the type of man who would have found Troy. And I already have the greatest prize a man could ever ask for.'

The man stopped. 'Where is she? Your queen? I wish to kneel before her and kiss her hand.'

'Sophia and the children await you with pleasure. The children remember your skill in woodwork, and I have promised them you will build them a model of the Trojan

Horse. But that must wait. Now, we have momentous matters to discuss. And others to meet. Others who may surprise you. Others with whom I fervently hope you will find a common cause, a cause that surpasses all the affairs of state at which you have so excelled. A cause that is greater than any in the history of mankind.'

'More subterfuge,' the man grumbled, but his eyes twinkled. 'Wherever you take me, Heinrich, there is sure to be excitement. I would not be anywhere else. Lead the way.'

They followed the line of little candles around the eastern edge of the mound, past exposed sections of earth where the excavations had revealed the eroded remains of limestone walls and mud-brick revetments. They rounded a corner where the grassy slope of the mound rose steeply in front of them, and dropped down a series of makeshift wooden steps into a deep trench that led back towards the centre of the mound. Schliemann went down first, then turned to point out a pile of shovels and baskets on the floor of the trench. 'Mind your step.'

'This is where you work?' the man asked, stepping stiffly down on to the earthen floor of the trench, leaning heavily on his stick.

'Just Sophia and me. We don't allow any of the other workers down here. My assistant Dörpfeld continues to work in the great trench, revealing the walls of the first citadel, early Bronze Age Troy. But this season, the Troy of King Priam, the Troy of Homer, is ours alone.'

Beyond the tools, the candlelight revealed a section of the passageway about three metres wide where the excavation appeared to be complete, with dressed stone walls on either side that sloped slightly outwards, rising at least five metres to the edge of the grassy mound above. The man stopped, leaning on his stick, peering at the alignment. 'Unless I am mistaken, these walls are of the same construction as the defensive walls I examined on the way in, just beyond the excavation house.'

'The walls of Homeric Troy,' Schliemann said excitedly. 'You are correct. I am convinced of it. These walls date from the same phase of construction. But they are not defensive walls. They line an entranceway, converging ahead of us, deep beneath the citadel. It is the most astonishing discovery.' He led the other man beyond the exposed masonry to a section where the sides of the trench were still not fully excavated, between rough earthen walls. He could see the final candle a few metres ahead, where the excavated trench came to an abrupt end. In the gloom he spied two other figures, both with canes, standing on either side of the floor, and his pulse quickened. *They were all here.* 'Gentlemen,' he called out. 'Welcome. Welcome indeed.'

He stooped down to where Sophia had left a gas lantern, quickly lit it and carried it forward, turning down the flame and placing it on the ground in front of the other two men. Then he stood back, and beamed at them. They were both old men, like the man who accompanied him, wearing dark overcoats with hats in their hands, both sporting the archaic long sideburns of an earlier age. One of them was taller, with craggy features and intense eyes. The smaller man was less forceful in appearance, wearing spectacles but with a determined stare. Schliemann sensed his companion stiffen at the sight of the taller man, and he quickly made the introductions. He gestured first to his companion. 'Gentlemen. Allow me to introduce Count Otto von Bismarck, Chancellor of Germany.' He spoke in English. His companion clicked his heels, and glared. Schliemann turned to the other two. 'Chancellor, I give you my dear friend Senator Hoar, the most distinguished elder statesman of my adopted country, the United States of America.' The two men bowed slightly, and shook hands. Schliemann turned to the taller man. 'And of course you will recognize the Right Honourable William Gladstone, Prime Minister of Great Britain.'

Bismarck glared, clicked his heels again, and shook hands. 'We are acquainted,' he said coldly in English. He turned to Schliemann, speaking quickly in German. 'This is unfortunate. *Most* unfortunate. My pleasure is in danger of utter shipwreck. You have brought me into the eye of a storm, Herr Schliemann. *Ein Tempest.*'

'Ever the Shakespearean, I see,' said Gladstone loftily.

Schliemann quickly stood between them and took both men by the arm. 'I trust Mr Gladstone too had a felicitous journey?'

'The Orient Express to Constantinople,' Gladstone said. 'A most extraordinary city. I touched with my own hand the column of Constantine the Great, and worshipped in Hagia Sophia. It is less desecrated by the infidel than I had feared.'

'Mr Gladstone has spoken out with a passion against the Turk,' Bismarck said in English. 'I am surprised he has made it this far.'

'I am travelling incognito. On Dr Schliemann's instructions. I own that rhetoric, in the heat of the moment, led me to write ill-advisedly against the Turkish people, whom I find to be both hospitable and delightful. For that I am contrite. But I remain as resolutely and strenuously opposed to the Ottoman campaign against the Bulgars as when I published that pamphlet.'

'And Mr Bismarck?' Senator Hoar asked. 'You have had an agreeable voyage?'

'I too was travelling incognito.'

'What? Chancellor von Bismarck?' Gladstone exclaimed theatrically. '*Travelling incognito?* As whom, pray?'

'As the Duke of Lauenberg. It is to be my new title. I fear the new kaiser will shortly oust me. I am to be a sidelined elder statesman. He thinks I will retire to shoot grouse on my estate in Poland. He is, I can be frank, a bellicose and stupid man. I fear for the future. He will make Germany into a monster.'

'A monster you nurtured,' Gladstone said haughtily. 'When you unified the country.'

'I unified Germany to yoke in a hundred warring states. It was realpolitik. Something that Mr Gladstone, the idealist, does not understand.'

'Unlike Herr von Bismarck, I would not aspire to be an Agamemnon.'

'Gentlemen,' Schliemann said. '*Gentlemen*. If you contine thus I shall insist, as Sophia does, that we speak entirely in ancient Greek. Then the affairs of this world will drop away, and we will inhabit solely the past. But it is a danger, Mr Gladstone, you have warned me against, of divorcing the two worlds entirely, ours and the ancient. And it is not my purpose here solely to present you with the marvels of archaeology.

My purpose is indeed the present. Events will move fast in our remaining lifetimes, and those of our children. Time is short, and we must act now.'

'You speak portentously, Mr Schliemann,' Gladstone said, looking intently at him. 'I trust we are not to hear a profound announcement, of a grave nature? Your health is well?'

'Mr Gladstone, your concern for my health has always been gratefully received, and is more efficacious than any course of medicine. But you need not tax yourself.'

'I *am* relieved.'

Schliemann paused. 'We are here today on common ground. Count von Bismarck is a man of the highest education and literary interests. Many times we have spoken together on ancient history. Mr Gladstone, in this regard as in all others, hardly needs an introduction. The author of three books on Homer, who did me the signal honour of writing the preface to my book on Mycenae. And Senator Hoar. Not just a statesman of the greatest esteem, but president of the American Antiquarian Society, regent of the Smithsonian Institution, trustee of the Peabody Museum of Archaeology and Anthropology. You three have been my greatest supporters, and to bring you here in person is the least I can do. But there is more to this meeting than that. I bring you here with a higher purpose. You are all men of the utmost probity, of the greatest moral resolve. I have come to know you personally, and I am convinced of it. In your hearts I know you are peacemakers, not warmongers.'

Gladstone snorted, peering at Bismarck. 'A sentiment that can hardly be ascribed to one whose governance precipitated the greatest conflict of our times. I refer, of course, to the

Franco-Prussian War of 1870. A war that upset the balance of power that had kept Europe peaceful since the fall of Napoleon.'

'It was not the war that upset the balance of power,' Bismarck replied coldly. 'It was the peace treaty. As you know perfectly well, I strenuously opposed the secession of Alsace-Lorraine to Germany. I saw in it the seedbed of the future. Of an even more calamitous war to come.'

'And then you took Germany on a colonial adventure in Africa. In deliberate and ostentatious antagonism towards the interests of my own government.'

'It deflected the French focus on Alsace-Lorraine. I believe in so doing I prevented a terrible escalation in Europe. And colonial adventures? Under the premiership of Mr Gladstone? I have not enough fingers to count them. War in Zululand, 1879. Afghanistan, 1880. The Sudan, 1885. Brave soldiers, yes, but bungled wars, all of them. Dispatching General Gordon to Khartoum, then failing to rescue him. I give you the Right Honourable William Ewart Gladstone, peacemaker.'

'Gentlemen.' Hoar held up his hand. 'We are not on the debating floor. And we all know that the morality of a man is not easily judged by the circumstances in which history envelops him, and for which history may yet hold him accountable.'

Gladstone and Bismarck both snorted and shuffled for a moment, and then stood still. Hoar lowered his hand. Schliemann looked at them, a sudden flicker of doubt in his mind. *Had he misjudged them?* Had he himself been too much of an idealist, blinded to reality? Were they all too old, too much immured in the rhetoric of politics, their morality calcified? *He needed to know*. He spoke quietly, almost whispering. 'What say you?' he began. 'What say you, gentlemen, on the subject of war?'

Gladstone looked hard at him, then glanced down. 'My detractors call me a pious pacifist,' he said, his voice less theatrical. 'And they are right. Herr Bismarck is right, too. I *did* let General Gordon down. It weighs heavily upon me. My Christian morality is at odds with war, and sits poorly when war is thrust upon me. I ask forgiveness from those dead warriors I did not have the courage to lead into battle like an Agamemnon.'

Schliemann turned to Bismarck, who had been looking shrewdly at Gladstone. Bismarck leaned on his cane, and put his other hand on his hip. 'I have proclaimed that the great questions of the time will not be resolved by speeches and majority decisions, but by iron and blood. To maintain the vote, I must appear to be a Prussian realist. But anyone who has ever looked into the glazed eyes of a soldier dying on the battlefield will think hard before starting a war.'

Schliemann slowly nodded. 'And Mr Hoar?'

Hoar spoke carefully, deliberately, without the flourish of the other two but holding their attention completely. 'I have never held the reins of supreme power, as have these two distinguished gentlemen, but I have made my voice heard over generations of presidents. I have seen the devastation of our own brush with Armageddon, the Civil War. I have watched with trepidation the hawks in our government who would bring America into the colonialist fray. Even where there is moral purpose in such adventure, we would slay thousands whom we would seek to benefit. We would bring home from war innumerable sick and wounded and insane to drag out miserable lives, wrecked in body and mind. We would make sullen and irreconcilable enemies the world over, possessed of a hatred that centuries will not eradicate. Our flag would become an emblem of sacrilege: of the burning of human dwellings, of the horror of torture. I do not like to think of America angry, snarling, clawing, but as an august and serene beauty. A beauty, gentlemen, perhaps a little pale in her cheeks, with a dangerous glint in her eyes, but inspired by a sentiment, *even toward her enemies*, not of hate, but of love. Gentlemen, I am implacably opposed to war.'

'We are resolved, then,' Schliemann said.

'We are resolved,' Hoar said, looking sharply at Bismarck and Gladstone. 'But pray tell, my dear Schliemann. Resolved to what purpose?'

Schliemann stared at the ground. Now was the time. He delved his hands into his pockets and held them out, his fists bunched as if concealing something. 'Mr Gladstone. You have written to me about ancient copper metallurgy. You were fascinated when I discovered that the age of heroes was an age of bronze. Well, it will delight you to know that we have found bronze arrowheads in the ruins of Homeric Troy. Arrowheads that I believe were fired into the citadel from the shoreline where the Greek ships of Agamemnon were beached. Arrowheads such as these.' He opened his left fist to reveal two tanged leaf-shaped barbs, green with corrosion. He proffered them.

'May I?' Gladstone said. Schliemann nodded, and

Gladstone dropped his cane, took the two arrowheads, then whipped out an eyeglass and examined them closely. 'Native copper is found widely and abundantly, I believe,' he murmured. 'But tin? Do you know where the tin in this bronze came from?'

'You will be astonished by my theory.'

'Nothing you say can astonish us now.'

Schliemann peered at him, his eyes burning with excitement. 'Here it is. At the dawn of the classical era, the Greeks wrote of their forebears going west, exploring the very limits of the known world. I believe these included survivors of Troy, fleeing apocalypse. One of them we know well: Aeneas, legendary founder of Rome. But I believe they were not the first. I believe they were following in the wake of earlier explorers, of the Bronze Age *before* the fall of Troy, ancestors of the greatest seafarers of the ancient world. You may guess of whom I speak. You are a biblical scholar as well, Mr Gladstone. *The Phoenicians*. The Phoenicians who sailed out into the Atlantic and far to the north, where they found a fabled archipelago, a group of islands the Greeks called Cassiterides.'

'The Tin Islands,' Gladstone exclaimed, removing his eyepiece and staring at Schliemann. 'I stand corrected. You *do* astonish me. Do you mean to assert that the Trojans, the Mycenaeans, acquired their tin from the Cassiterides?'

'By which I refer, gentlemen, to the British Isles, to the tin mines of Cornwall. It cannot be proved at present, but I am certain of it.'

Hoar put up a hand. 'I beg your indulgence. You are suggesting that the Phoenicians, the traders of the Old

Testament, were the metal-brokers of the Bronze Age? Those self-same Phoenicians who provided the Greeks with their alphabet?'

Schliemann nodded. 'Brokers in a commodity far more precious than gold. You are correct, Mr Gladstone. The question of the tin is a vexing one. It was the rarest of commodities, and its sources were few. And I perceive that your thoughts, Mr Hoar, bend on a convergent path to mine. The Phoenicians *did* provide the Greeks with their alphabet, but much earlier than we had thought. I believe it was traders of the Bronze Age who first brought the alphabet to these shores. I believe the scribes of Agamemnon were the first to use the alphabet to write Greek.'

'You believe they spoke Greek?' Gladstone exclaimed. 'You truly believe the Mycenaeans spoke *Greek*?'

'I believe that the language of Homer was the language of Agamemnon.'

'Mr Schliemann, I stand corrected *again*. My mind is in a perfect *hurricane* of astonishment.'

'Scholars will ridicule me for the idea, those same scholars who mocked my quest for Troy. But I am sure of it.'

Bismarck pointed at Schliemann's right fist. 'And your other hand? What treasure have you concealed there?'

Schliemann held out the hand, then hesitated. 'This, gentlemen, is truly why you are here.' His voice was tense with excitement. 'I knew I had to return to Troy. I believe, Mr Gladstone, that urgency, that feverish urgency, to have been the cause of my past illness. A mounting anxiety, with physical symptoms. Now that I am back here again, those symptoms have lifted. Two months ago, when we returned, we found this. To be precise, Sophia found it. She picked it from the spoil heap left beside the great trench we had dug through the site in 1871. I remembered seeing many of these, dozens, hundreds, but ignoring them in my thirst to dig deeper. I had been driven by a lust for gold, yes, but more than that, by a passion to prove that I was right, to find the Troy of Priam. And I *was* right. Yet in my enthusiasm I failed to see a greater truth that was staring at me. A truth that became my obsession in the years that followed, that vexed me day and night, that nearly overwhelmed me. Not *whether* Troy fell, but *how*. How mankind was toppled so quickly from brilliant civilization to the deepest well of barbarism. I talk not of Helen of Troy, not of the sophistry of poets, not of war caused by love and jealousy and rage, but of hard truth, the truth of power and bloodlust and the force of arms. A truth revealed not in gold and bronze, but in this.'

He opened his hand to reveal a shapeless lump about two inches across, discoloured with red and brown oxidation. Gladstone peered closely at it, bringing up his monocle again. 'Mmm. Ferrous concretion, unless I am mistaken.'

Schliemann nodded, then held the lump between his thumb and forefinger. 'This, gentlemen, is another arrowhead. But not an arrowhead made of bronze. An arrowhead made of *iron*.'

'Of the age that followed the fall of Troy, you mean?' Hoar murmured. 'Some great battle of the Dark Ages, unknown to history, fought in the ruins of Troy?'

Schliemann shook his head emphatically. 'These arrowheads were all found in the destruction layer of the seventh citadel. *Homeric Troy*. They were found intermingled with bronze arrowheads. After Sophia recognized this lump for what it was, we re-examined a section of the rampart we had exposed all those years ago. We found two bronze arrowheads and three of these iron ones, embedded at different places in the outer wall.'

'Arrows fired by an attacker,' Gladstone murmured.

'You follow my train of thought, Mr Gladstone.'

Bismarck thumped his stick down. 'Superior technology,' he exclaimed. 'That is what you have discovered, Herr Schliemann, yes? *Superior technology.*'

'He who possessed iron in the age of bronze possessed the advantage,' Gladstone said.

'As he who possesses the Maxim gun in the age of the musket is tempted to war,' Hoar murmured.

'An advantage not in the *quality* of weapons, but in their *quantity*,' Schliemann continued. 'We are speaking of the very cusp of the age of iron, when the technology was in its infancy. The quality of this iron, the edge, the strength, may not have been greater than the best bronze. But that is not the point, gentlemen. The point was made by Mr Gladstone. *Tin is exceedingly rare.* It was worth its weight in gold. But iron ore is found virtually everywhere. Once you have mastered the technology, you have an unlimited raw material. And if you are the first to master the technology, before it becomes widespread, then for a few years, for a few decades perhaps, *you reign supreme.* You are king of kings. *You are god.*'

'Agamemnon,' Gladstone breathed. 'You speak of *Agamemnon.*'

'Troy was felled not by a trick of Odysseus, not by a wooden horse,' Hoar murmured. 'But by another kind of cunning. By the cunning of Hephaestos. By the cunning of the forge.'

'Perfectly put, Mr Hoar,' Schliemann said.

'Herr Schliemann? You have a theory?' Bismarck asked, stomping his cane again. The three men looked at Schliemann expectantly. He pocketed the arrowheads, and took a deep breath.

'The twenty years since I first set foot on the mound of Troy have been a whirlwind for me. Some would say that I have been restless, unable to concentrate. Within two years of arriving here I announced the discovery of the treasure of King Priam. Then I went to Mycenae, and found the Mask of Agamemnon. Then I travelled around Greece, searching for the other great Bronze Age palaces, at Tiryns, at Ithaka, at Orchomenos. I went to Sicily, on the path of those western Phoenicians, the tin traders. Then I went to Egypt. I told them I was searching for the tomb of Alexander the Great, in Alexandria. The world thought I was on the hunt for yet more gold. Heinrich Schliemann, self-made millionaire, who made his fortune on the back of the California gold rush, had seen the lustre of gold at Troy and Mycenae and had fallen bewitched again, lured by Mammon. My critics shouted with glee. They were vindicated. I was no archaeologist, I was a treasure-hunter. *But they were wrong.*'

'They were wrong,' Gladstone murmured, 'because you were not in search of gold. You were in search of bronze and iron.'

Schliemann clapped his hands. 'Mr Gladstone!' he declared. 'You *do* understand me.' He stared at them intensely, then pointed down the passageway. 'The very last place where

Sophia and I dug all those years ago was right here, where we stand now. We found something extraordinary, something we knew would take weeks more, months more, to dig out. We sealed it up, intending to return. I went to Mycenae seeking confirmation, and seeking a key. And I found it, gentlemen. *I found it*. We uncovered the shaft graves, the Mask of Agamemnon. But we also found another tomb, the great beehive-shaped structure I called the Treasury of Atreus. I was elated. I went to the other palaces, and I found more of them, more so-called tombs. And then to Egypt. Beneath Alexandria I found not the steps down to the tomb of Alexander, but something infinitely older. And then in a blinding flash I knew what the Egyptian pyramids were for. Tombs, gentlemen, royal tombs to be sure, like the tombs of the Mycenaeans, *but something else*. The pyramids were erected at the beginning of the Bronze Age, with the explosion of power and wealth that bronze created. *The Bronze Age*, gentlemen. Structures meant to safeguard the treasures not just of the dead, but of the living as well.'

'The Treasury of Atreus,' Hoar murmured, the shadow of a smile on his face. 'I believe, Mr Schliemann, you have surpassed yourself. You have kept this trail you are on a secret, yet like any good explorer you have left clues, a safeguard, perhaps, against calamity, that some future-day archaeologist might follow. Clues in the names.'

'You chose not to call it the *Tomb* of Atreus,' Bismarck exclaimed. 'You chose to call it the *Treasury* of Atreus.'

'And not a treasury of gold,' Gladstone rejoined. 'But a treasury of *bronze*.'

'Herr Bismarck asked if I had a theory,' Schliemann said. 'So here it is. The advent of bronze technology, two thousand years before the fall of Troy, was the most revolutionary advance in human history. For the first time, people had good agricultural tools, ploughshares and sickles. They had tools for carpentry, and for masonry. And they had superior weapons.' He delved in his pockets, and produced a clear flint arrowhead in one hand, and a leaf-shaped metal one in the other. 'Stone points, like this one we found in the oldest Troy layer, little different from chipped tools made by their ancestors of the Stone Age, gave way to bronze weapons like this one. But there was a rub. The tin needed to make bronze was always in short supply. It was hugely prized. The power of chieftains rested on it. The smiths – the bronze-workers – were kept within the walls of palaces, of citadels. Supplies of tin and bronze were closely guarded. Great vaults were built, places that doubled as the burial grounds of kings. Vaults such as the Treasury of Atreus at Mycenae. Vaults such as the one that I believe lies before you down this passageway, gentlemen, dug into the limestone deep beneath the citadel of Troy.'

'You have brought us to see the treasury!' Gladstone exclaimed.

Schliemann held up his hand. 'There is another rub. A most extraordinary one. Bronze tools, carefully controlled, doled out by the king, their use supervised, allowed the city-states of the Aegean to flourish. A brilliant civilization emerged. But I know the question you are asking yourselves, gentlemen. You are politicians. You have seen what men will do. At Gettysburg, at Sedan. Give them weapons, and they will make war. And in the Bronze Age Aegean, men *did* fight.

We know about it from Homer. The clashes of arms, the bellows and taunts of the victor, the cries of the vanquished. But these are individual combats, not pitched battles. Why? Because there was never enough bronze to equip a city-state with an army large enough to take on another city, to lay siege to it and conquer it. And sheer force of numbers was never possible, huge numbers like the sweeping tides of men we know fought battles in the ancient Near East. The mountain-girt valleys of the Aegean did not have the population, the surplus manpower. Homer reveals it: individual kings in the Greek forces contributed all they had, but it was often merely a few ships, a few hundred men. He gives us a blood-soaked stage, true, but we watch his heroes just as Romans watched gladiators, or as the masses of our industrial age might view a sporting fixture. This was a world of *peace*, gentlemen, of peace that spawned a brilliant civilization, a civilization that grew so fast and so strong that it outstripped the ability of men to destroy it with the technology at their disposal.'

'There is a weakness in your theory,' Bismarck rumbled. 'A weakness we all know from our own age. Men hungry for power will form alliances, often to prosecute war, not to prevent it. And surely that is what we see in Homer. Agamemnon leads a huge alliance of all the Greeks.'

Schliemann paused. 'When I studied at the Sorbonne before embarking on my great quest for Troy, I had a thirst to know what the living world might tell about my long-dead heroes. I travelled to the islands of the Pacific, and observed the native peoples. Where their own limitation of technology and manpower prevented them from defeating each other, they ritualized their standoffs, in an *entente cordiale*. They exchanged gifts, women, cemented friendships. They held secret ceremonies in which the chieftains would confer, at one place recognized by all as a paramount meeting place. And whenever power was unbalanced, when a new technology was introduced, gunpowder, for example, when one chieftain had a brief ascendancy before the others had the technology as well, his first objective would be to conquer that paramount place where power had always been maintained, a balance of power that had kept the peace.'

'You speak in metaphor of Troy, I believe,' Gladstone murmured. 'You speak of Troy, and you speak of this chamber before us. Am I correct?'

Schliemann stared hard at them. 'Herr Bismarck spoke of an alliance. What of this? Agamemnon, already power-hungry in his own land, straining at the leashes that keep him in his citadel of Mycenae, learns of a new technology: the technology of iron. It is not yet perfected, but he sets his smiths to work. He knows he has no time to lose before others have it too. He gambles, and embarks on his path to war before the weapons are ready. He uses all his kinship ties and his strength and he summons an alliance, one that casts its net across the Mycenaean world. They are going to the place Agamemnon has gone to before in peace, as a broker of power, as a member of a council that kept war at bay. Yes, Mr Gladstone: *they go to Troy*. The alliance provides the manpower to lay siege to the citadel, but not yet the weapons. On the island of Tenedos, Agamemnon's smiths work day and night, experimenting, testing. For nine years, if we are to believe Homer, his army fought in the traditional way, individual duels below the walls of Troy, Achilles and Hector, Patroclus and Diomedes. For nine years Agamemnon bided his time, while the forges hissed and burned, while the technology he had secretly acquired was honed and perfected. One day, let us surmise, in that ninth year, some master smith discovered a way to forge a metal that was no longer brittle, iron that could be stronger than bronze. Suddenly the stage was set. The world groaned. Agamemnon unleashed hell. A thousand iron arrows flew into the walls of Troy. Then ten thousand arrows. Then ten thousand more. Forges, gentlemen, forges on the island of Tenedos, forges that once had wrought the finery of heroes, helmets and breastplates and spears of the finest bronze, burned and blasted day and night to produce these new weapons, weapons that overwhelmed Troy like a tidal wave, that unleashed the bonds on what men could do.'

'And all of this because a young Trojan prince kidnapped a Greek queen named Helen?' Hoar said.

'The spark of war,' Schliemann said. 'A spark created by Agamemnon, perhaps. A subterfuge. In a world where high-status women were part of the web of alliances, it could have been enough.'

'Some damned foolish thing in the Balkans,' Bismarck grumbled.

'What did you say?' Gladstone demanded.

'What I have said to the new kaiser, seemingly to no avail. I said to him that one day the great European war will come out of some damned foolish thing in the Balkans. That will be our Helen of Troy.'

'You see?' Schliemann exclaimed. 'We speak of a coming war as if it is inevitable. That is why I have brought you here tonight, gentlemen.'

'What would you have us do?' Hoar asked.

Schliemann pulled a little white book from his pocket. 'In Homer, the gods appear to shape destiny, and men are mere pawns. But that is because, before Agamemnon, the world is presented as an unchanging one, and thus one in which men appear to have no power. I believe the truth was very different. Just as it was an individual, Agamemnon, who brought calamitous war, so it was individuals before him, generation after generation of kings, who kept the balance of power, kept the peace. They were not pawns. *It was their free will to shape history*. We know some of their names. Atreus, father of Agamemnon. Minos, King of Knossos. Priam, King of Troy, an old king at the time of the siege, who, let us surmise, had seen Agamemnon as a young prince, had nurtured him perhaps, but then had seen something in his eyes, that smouldering fire that makes a prince an Alexander or a Genghis Khan, that only needs an extra spark to ignite and raze all before it.' He held up the book. 'Thomas Carlyle, our great political theorist, on how history is shaped by individuals. I have been reading him this very day. I look to our world, gentlemen, and I see a world where the power of the individual is under threat, with calamitous consequences. It is the individual who has morality, not the crowd.'

Hoar put up his hand. 'I speak as a citizen of the United States of America, where individual freedom, the rights of the individual, is enshrined in the Constitution. I look to Europe, and I fear greatly for the future. Mass movements, *Volk* movements, begin on a high ideal, on ideals of social justice, but they submerge the individual, and thus the voice of common morality.'

Schliemann nodded. 'We live at a time when the voice of the individual is needed as at no other time in history. We stand, gentlemen, we four, in front of history, able to shape it, able to throw off inevitability, to shake off those who would have us believe that fate is not ours to control, to show that men left to their own devices are not foredoomed to destruction and war.'

'And we stand at a time of changing technology,' Gladstone said. 'That is your point. That is why that iron arrowhead is so important.'

'The age of bronze ended with Agamemnon. The age of iron is about to end for us. We live in terrifying times. Contemplate the changes in our own lifespans, gentlemen. From muskets to machine guns. From black powder to nitroglycerine. From ships of the line to ironclads. From muzzle-loading cannon to giant breech-loading guns, capable of lobbing a shell fifteen miles. Veritable doomsday weapons. And men will fly, gentlemen. With my own eyes I have seen the "monoplane" of Monsieur Félix du Temple. Powered flight is a certainty. *Men will fly*. There are fearsome possibilities, gentlemen. *Fearsome possibilities*. The modern alchemy of science will produce wonders, but also horrors. Human guile may reawaken the oldest nightmare of them all. I speak of the plague. *The plague*. It may be the black death, or cholera, or a new deadly smallpox, or some frightful dormant virulence. If some necromancer can harness disease as a weapon, then truly, Mr Gladstone, the Christian God will have forsaken us, all of the gods will have forsaken us, and we will find no redemption.'

'Does anything give you hope?' Hoar asked.

'You three give me hope. In the Bronze Age, in the world of Homer, we are to believe it was the champions who were the heroes, Achilles and Hector and the others. But they were not the true heroes. The heroes were the kings, those who came before Agamemnon. Let us be modern-day kings. Let us be modern-day heroes. Let us ride above the tide of history. *Let us prevent another rape of Troy.*'

'You spoke, Mr Schliemann, of finding a key,' Hoar said. 'You spoke metaphorically, I surmise?'

Schliemann let out a shuddering sigh, suddenly exhausted. *He had said it.* He felt an indescribable sense of relief, but also huge urgency. The wheels were now truly in motion. He gave Hoar a tired smile. 'My dear senator. I am an archaeologist, remember? When I speak of a key, I mean a key.' He reached into his inside pocket, to the heavy object he had been carrying in the satchel, wrapped up by Sophia. He hesitated, then pointed with his other hand down the passageway. 'When Sophia and I dug here in secret all those years ago, I found a way through to the end, inside a natural tunnel created where blocks had fallen down from the top of the walls, forming air spaces. I saw inscriptions along the sides of the walls. *Inscriptions.* I could not make them out, but they seemed to be Bronze Age, pictograms, linear symbols unrecognizable to me, even hieroglyphics. And at the end, far ahead of my reach, I shoved my lantern forward and saw it. A great bronze door, the door to the chamber that must lie beyond. In the centre of the door above a metal crossbar was an angular shaped depression in a circle. A keyhole, gentlemen. And this is the key.'

He took out the package, and unwrapped it. They all gasped as he let the cloth fall away. It was a metal cross, about twenty centimetres wide, equilateral, with bars extending at right angles from each arm. It was gold, lustrous and dazzling in the flickering gaslight, with a silvery metal as the core.

Gladstone reached out and touched it. 'Of course,' he murmured. '*Of course*. The symbol you write about with such passion in your books. The symbol you found incised on pots at Troy. The symbol, as I recall, you had painted into the decoration of your house in Athens.'

'Schliemann the treasure-hunter, again,' Hoar said. 'Leaving clues for posterity.'

'This is the shape of the keyhole in the bronze door ahead of us?' Gladstone asked.

Schliemann nodded, flushed with excitement. 'I give you the *Hakenkreuz*, gentlemen. The hook-cross. What in Sanskrit is called the *swastika*. The symbol of the Aryan peoples, the first Indo-Europeans who came from the east, over the Black Sea, the people I believe were the first settlers at Troy. This was their symbol. The symbol of the first civilization. *The symbol of Troy*. And this metal is not just gold, but meteoritic. Some ancient sacred discovery, shaped in this way for the kings of Troy.'

Bismarck reached out, then let his hand drop. 'I know this symbol,' he growled. 'The *Hakenkreuz* has new meaning for the nationalists in Germany, the *Volk* movement. There are secret societies, those who hark back to an Aryan past. It seems,' he said, looking at it uneasily, 'to stand for all the possibilities of the past, and all the dangers of the future. Coming events cast their shadows before.'

'Where did you find this?' Gladstone asked.

'It was Sophia, not me,' Schliemann said. 'I lifted the mask, but Sophia led me there.'

'The mask?' Gladstone said incredulously. 'You mean the Mask of Agamemnon? *At Mycenae?*'

'Have no fear, my dear Gladstone,' Schliemann said, touching the other man's arm. 'Your eloquent argument in the preface to my book *Mycenae* still holds truth. I too am convinced that the shaft graves contain Agamemnon and his family. But when I raised the golden mask, it was not a skeleton I saw beneath. In my mind's eye I saw Agamemnon, yes, a spectral image that flashed before me, so when I told the world I had gazed upon the face of Agamemnon I was telling the truth. But what I found beneath the mask was this. The *Hakenkreuz*, the swastika. I give you the most astonishing find I have ever made. I give you the palladion, gentlemen.'

'The *palladion?*' Gladstone breathed, staring at the cross. 'But the palladion was a wooden statue, surely, in the temple at Troy? The statue of the goddess Pallas, stolen by Odysseus?'

'That story may well have been true. There are those who believe that statue found its way to Rome, and then to Constantinople, where it remains concealed to this day. The story would have suited Agamemnon. To steal the statue of the protecting deity was to steal the soul of a city. It meant Troy was doomed. But it would also have suited him that the story concealed the truth, that the palladion was not a wooden statue but this cross, the key to that chamber ahead of us. It may well have been concealed in the temple, in some underground repository, perhaps, a holy of holies, its whereabouts known only to the great kings who came to convene in that chamber to keep the peace.'

'Agamemnon had been one of those kings,' Hoar murmured.

Schliemann nodded. 'Yet years later, he stood here, at this very spot, that fateful night of fire and death, dripping with other men's blood, slamming down his great sceptre, his bloody sword hanging from his other hand, staring at that door ahead, remembering. All he wanted was that chamber shut for ever, and this entranceway buried. Shutting the door would close off the chamber of power that had thwarted his own ambitions, had prevented his ascendancy above all the others. He had killed Priam, and now he would seal off the chamber that had counselled peace, not war. Those fallen blocks of masonry ahead of us were not the result of some natural convulsion, but were deliberately caused. And having buried the chamber, he would find the key, take it from this place, and conceal it for all time. He stormed up to the temple ahead of his men, the fires raging around him, the cries of women filling the air, and found the palladion, then took it back with him to his citadel at Mycenae. And where better to conceal it than in the hallowed burial ground of his ancestors, behind a mask that showed his own face, the ultimate act of power. Then, standing over the grave of his forefathers, Agamemnon could feel as mighty as a god, could raise his staff to Mount Olympus and shake it with contempt. *The age of gods had ended. The age of men had begun.* And he is there some- where, his own burial, I am sure of it. What matters is that we have found the palladion. What matters is that we can turn back history, stand in front of those doors as all those kings before Agamemnon did, and reach up again with this key.'

'What would we find?' Hoar asked quietly.

Schliemann paused. 'I do not know what we will find. *I do not know*. It may be an empty chamber, a place where treasures of metal were once stored, a council chamber with empty seats. But even that could be enough to prove my theory, so that we may go forth with confidence and proclaim it to the world.'

'What would you have us do?' Bismarck said.

'A year from now, a year to the day, we will reconvene at this spot. The arrangements will be made with the utmost secrecy, and we must not speak a word of this until we are agreed to do so, when the time is right. We must have something to show. I must be believed, not mocked. A grand opening. The press gathered, as they were at Mycenae when I revealed the Mask of Agamemnon. God willing, by a year from now Sophia and I will have dug through to that door, and created a passage wide enough to open it. It will be the greatest moment of all our lives. An incalculable treasure, far richer than all the gold in the world. The key, gentlemen, to *the abatement of war*. Proof, somewhere, indeed in the very existence of that chamber, that men could once control the urge to self-destruction.'

'Do we few, so few, old men all of us, have the strength and morality to rise above the tide of technology, the monster of self-destruction humanity has created?' Hoar asked.

'The monster is within ourselves,' Bismarck murmured, still staring at the swastika.

'The world needs heroes,' Schliemann said. 'Not lords of war, not champions like Achilles, but heroes like Atreus, Minos, Priam of Troy, men willing to stand against the stream.'

'We need more treaties,' Gladstone murmured, tapping his fingers against his cane. 'Treaties, with redoubled effort. I will be prime minster once again. This has convinced me of it. I will stand for re-election.'

'We need a balance of power,' Hoar said. 'We will never prevent nations from having weapons, but if we maintain our strength we may prevent war through deterrence.'

'Much can be set in motion in a year,' Gladstone said. 'And then, if we can show to the world that it has worked in the past, there may be the vigour and strength of purpose to get it done.' He turned to Bismarck. 'Chancellor, you have famously said that history is more than mere written words. We are old men, but we need to make history, not write it.'

'It seems that after all we speak from the same page, Herr Gladstone.'

'Gentlemen,' Schliemann said, turning to them. 'There is an ancient expression of the Hittites. *I give you a tablet of war; I give you a tablet of peace.*' He held out his hands as he spoke, palm up, left hand then right. 'Which is it to be?'

Silently the others came up, first Gladstone, then Bismarck, then Hoar, and placed their hands one on top of the other, on his right hand. They remained still for a moment, and then Bismarck and Hoar withdrew, leaving Gladstone alone, staring into Schliemann's eyes, a look of concern on his face. 'My dear Heinrich,' he said softly. 'You have left your mark upon this age. *An undying name.* A name that I trust will be with us for many a year. You do not need to push so hard as to be injurious to your health, as is your wont.'

Schliemann squeezed his hand. 'Your solicitation is most gratefully acknowledged. But have no fear. My health is redoubled by this meeting. My energy is undiminished. Great days lie ahead.'

Gladstone withdrew, and stood beside Bismarck in the shadows. Hoar raised his right hand and pulled a golden signet ring off his finger. 'Gentlemen, I am humbled to be here. I feel a mere mortal among giants. This ring bears the crest of my forefathers, who signed the Declaration of Independence and the Constitution of the United States of America, the greatest affirmations of peace and liberty ever devised. Those documents, gentlemen, give us hope that the will of the individual can triumph. I give you this ring in solemn affirmation that I have spent and will spend my days in the pursuit of life, liberty and happiness for all mankind, and in observance of our pledge here today.' He knelt down stiffly and pressed the ring as far as it would go into the earth on the side of the tunnel, then pushed a potsherd over the top of it. He got back up, tottering slightly. 'And to you, Mr Schliemann, in your great endeavour to finish this excavation, I wish Godspeed.'

'And Godspeed to you too, Mr Hoar.' Schliemann turned to go, took a few steps and then turned back. The three men were still there, standing, but had receded into the gloom. For a split second he saw them for what they were, three old men already half into shadowland, looming like wraiths of long-dead kings, like the kings Schliemann imagined still pacing the halls and battlements above. He felt a chill wind, and wrapped his coat around him. Could these men still make history? Or had he deceived himself? Had his passion, his yearning for more and more discoveries, his endless delay in returning to Troy, year after year, made him push this day too far ahead? *Had he left it too late?* He shook away the thought, and raised his hand. 'Godspeed to you all. Until we meet again here, a year from now.'

Schliemann returned on the path past the point where he had met Bismarck, following the line of little candles, now spluttering and dying. Night winds at Troy were always disturbing, and he half imagined the rustling he heard was not the wind in the grass but the advancing Greeks parting their way through wheat on the plain below, and the sound of bare feet pattering over the smooth adobe of the streets and walls, the trembling sounds of that final night before the storm, a night when each breath could be heard. He reached the ramp up the western wall of the citadel, on the edge of the great trench they had dug through the site. He looked up at the stars and saw Orion, the hunter, his favourite. Far above him, close below Orion, he saw black birds flying silently, heading north.

He looked towards the grassy knoll on the northern edge of the citadel, and felt a rush of warmth. Sophia was still there, framed by the night sky, the wind blowing back her veil and revealing the golden belt, the bracelets, the headband, glistening in the starlight. But was it Sophia, or was he imagining another, Helen of Troy? Schliemann closed his eyes for a moment, feeling dizzy, a sound like the sea coming and going in his head. He opened his eyes and saw that Sophia had lifted up a tallow torch and lit it, sending wisps of smoke curling in the wind towards him. The flames suddenly erupted, illuminating her red dress, and for a moment it looked as though they would devour her, as if she herself would become a torch, a leaping, twisting beacon of fire, a signal into the night. Was that how it had all begun? And was the Trojan Horse real, or was it some dark force of the sea, raging, tossing its mane, turning to fire and bloody murder as it swept death towards the citadel, breaking over the beacon, carrying all before it?

He knew Homer off by heart. He thought he knew about the Trojan War. *A war fought for beauteous Helen, and the wealth she brought*. But had it been? He closed his eyes, and tried to conjure it, melding fragmentary images as they came to him. The sea, the colour of widow's tears, steel-blue. Grooms beside beached ships, whispering to tethered horses not to fear the sea, then kissing and releasing them. Harpies flying overhead, bronze and iron messengers of death. He looked at his hand, calloused as he imagined Agamemnon's might have been: the hand of Agamemnon, people-devouring king, battle-wise, lion-maned, he who knew war in all its bloody ways. The ringing in his ears became shouts, bellows, roars. Blood was everywhere, pounding in his head, cloying in his nostrils, its iron taste filling his mouth. Dark blood spurting from wounds cleaved by champions. Blood swept up from the plain and falling like a rainstorm, staining the ground black. Blood lapping against Scamander's shore, drenching the beach, drowning the plain below the battlements, seeping up over them. *Sophia, blood-red beacon, dripping fire.*

Schliemann gasped as if coming up for air, leaning against

the stone ramp. Perhaps Gladstone had been right. He was letting the past consume him. He looked up and saw Sophia turn and walk towards him, holding the burning torch. He pushed himself back up, and waved at her. He remembered how close he had felt to her that night years before, in the shaft grave in the far-off citadel of Agamemnon. He remembered the thrill of that moment, but also the fear, a tremulous, paralysing fear, just before he had lifted the golden mask. A fear that had been his greatest weakness, the fear of making a discovery that would cap his career but dim the light of his passion and infect the memory of all that had gone before, the exhilaration that had fuelled him. He feared a discovery that might diminish his yearning for more, and diminish the supreme fulfilment he had found with Sophia.

And there had been the other, deeper fear, a fear of what he might reveal, an awful truth about the human condition, about war. Those terrible images of blood, those dreams that always came to him up here, were more than just a vivid imagining of Homer. He remembered what Bismarck had said. *Coming events cast their shadows before*. Schliemann had finally realized why those images so unnerved him. It was as if the tide of the future were rolling back, and he was seeing the river Scamander not drenched in ancient blood, in the blood of heroes, but in fresh, red blood, in the blood of the children of today. It was not the past he was seeing. *It was the future*.

Sophia reached him, and they embraced. He held her tight, taking the torch and holding it away from them, the flame flickering in the breeze. All grim thoughts left him, and he experienced a supreme contentment. Their children were waiting. He felt a burst of the familiar adrenalin. Tomorrow he and Sophia would be here again, in the tunnel, at the crack of dawn, alone in secret with their trowels and shovels, just as they had been so many times before, knowing they were on the cusp of another discovery that they would one day reveal to an astonished world. What they found here could change history. He could hardly wait. *There was no time to lose.*

19

Wieliczka Salt Mine, Poland

At first all Jack could see underwater was a green haze, obscuring the forms of Costas and the other three divers in front of him. He sank to the bottom of the pool, only a few metres below the surface, and angled the headlamps on either side of his helmet, locking them in place once they had reached a convergence point about five metres in front of him. He had never seen water of this hue before. Green usually meant organic matter, algae, that would reflect the light from underwater torches, like using full-beam car headlights in a snowstorm. But here there was no reflection, just haze. He remembered what Wladislaw had said about the copper inclusions that caused the colour, evidently particles of very small size.

He could hear the suck and exhaust of the three Russians,

all of them breathing hard on their regulators. The rebreathers he and Costas were wearing only needed to be vented of excess gas build-up every ten minutes or so, so were effectively closed systems most of the time that produced no exhaust. Through the intercom he could hear Costas' breathing, calm, slow, reassuring. He knew his own breathing would conform to the same rate, a sign of a good buddy pairing. Only he and Costas would be able to talk to each other. Ben had not mentioned this to the phone contact when the arrangements had been made. The three Russians had been too concerned with understanding their own equipment, and they had evidently been briefed that he and Costas would have specialized gear. And each of them had just drunk a third of a litre of neat vodka. They were probably too drunk to care.

He feathered his buoyancy control, injecting air into his e-suit, then looked around and saw a dark smudge where the tunnel descended. He looked at Costas. 'You read me?'

'Loud and clear.'

'Let's move. They can follow, if they're able.'

'One of them's breathing like a steam engine. No way he'll last.'

'Shouldn't drink and dive.'

'You getting the map on your screen?'

'Roger that.' Jack peered at the lattice of red lines visible in three dimensions inside his helmet, to the left of his visor. 'Looks like we've got about fifty metres ahead where the railway track continues to a vertical shaft. The shaft drops way down, about eighty metres. Then at the bottom there's another stretch of tunnel angling down at about thirty degrees, evidently the line of the natural fissure. Looks like our target area's going to be a hundred and ten, maybe a hundred and twenty metres below water level.'

'My computer gives us about twenty-five minutes no-stop time. If the Russians stick to plan, they'll go no deeper than eighty metres. That means part-way up that shaft.'

'You ready?' Jack said.

'We're heading into a sump, completely submerged for a bit and then surfacing again near the head of that shaft. The railway tunnel must have collapsed at some point. I'll go first.'

'I'm behind you.'

They ignored the other three and swam down into the gloom, their headlamps reflecting off the walls of green halite, which had been hacked away to widen the tunnel. After about ten metres the salt gave way to bare rock, cracked and jumbled in front of them. 'Looks like someone got a little ambitious with the pick,' Costas murmured. 'Remember what Wlady said, that the miners tried not to dig out all the halite to keep the walls from collapsing.' He swam down, pulling himself along the rusted metal rails of the track. Jack could see a way ahead, with only a metre or so of clearance below the collapsed rock. He followed Costas, inching along. He heard the three Russians close behind, scraping and clanging their tanks as they hauled themselves along the passage, the exhaust from their breathing cascading along the cracks and fissures above Jack. He swore under his breath. If they caused another rock fall, nobody would be coming out of here alive. He concentrated on looking ahead, and saw that Costas had reached the end of the sump and had knelt up out of the water. Jack came alongside, and broke surface. They had come nearly to the end of the rockfall, and could see the end of the tunnel about ten metres ahead, half submerged.

'This must be where the vertical shaft begins,' Costas said. 'I'm looking at my atmospheric sensor. There's still oxygen here, but methane as well in pockets against the ceiling. Probably breathable, just.'

'Won't be like that below,' Jack said. 'From what Wlady said, we'll have to assume any gas pockets are methane.'

They crawled and waded forward, past a ledge that had once been some kind of loading platform. A massive rusted pulley mechanism hung down from the ceiling where the track ended. It was a winch for a lift, but the metal cable was missing, evidently cut off or rusted away and dropped down the shaft with the lift platform. He looked back and saw the first of the Russians haul himself out of the water, spit out his mouthpiece and wheeze heavily, his hands on his knees. Jack turned back, and saw Costas' fins sticking up. He pulled himself along, below the winch. The view over the edge was astonishing. Costas was hanging upside down, his headlamps aimed down a vertical shaft lined with timbers. The coppery green had gone, and the water was extraordinarily clear. Jack could see down a phenomenal depth, but still not make out the bottom. It was an awesome sight, spine-tingling, as if he were looking down a shaft into the centre of the earth. Costas craned his head up, looked at him. 'You good with this?'

'Good to go.' They had been in a mineshaft before, just like this, when Jack had run out of air and nearly died. But now was not the time for flashbacks. Survival instinct overrode that. He remembered Rebecca, why they were here, and steeled himself. He watched Costas drop head first down the shaft, and then followed him. The water was so clear that it was as if he were jumping into air, and he instinctively put out his hands and feet to catch himself on the wooden beams, to stop himself from falling headlong. He made himself straighten his legs and hold his hands ahead like an arrow, spiralling down behind Costas. They dropped quickly, twenty metres, thirty, forty. He was grateful for the automated buoyancy control, the computer that sensed their speed of descent and kept it in check. He tilted his head so that he could see directly ahead. Far below them, thirty or forty metres perhaps, he could now see the glimmerings of the base of the shaft, a mass of collapsed metal machinery lit up by their headlamp beams. Two minutes later they were nearly there. 'Let's go neutral,' Costas said. Jack pressed the manual buoyancy override and injected air into his suit, then tucked into a ball and rolled upright so that he came down feet first like a parachutist. He injected more air to stop just short of the coiled pulley cable and iron platform, coming to a halt alongside Costas. They both looked up. A confused mass of bubbles and light beams moving to and fro was visible far above, where the Russians were coming down.

Jack looked at his depth gauge. *Ninety-five metres.* He turned and aimed his beam horizontally into the passageway they were about to enter, the level that would drop at a thirty-degree slope towards their target area about a hundred metres ahead. Costas came alongside and did the same. An extraordinary vista opened up before them. It was clear that they were following a natural fissure in the rock, just as Wladislaw had predicted, with outcrops of halite crystals visible. The crystals shimmered and sparkled as they panned their headlights over them. The fissure had once formed a series of interconnected caverns, but the narrower spaces between the caverns had been hacked away to create a continuous tunnel wide enough for a narrow-gauge track to be laid, identical to the one they had followed at the higher level. Jack could see the track continuing for about thirty metres and then ending at a point where the rock had been left untouched, a much narrower gap. They swam slowly forward. On either side the indentations formed deep chambers, some crudely hacked into a rectilinear shape, one of them with a half-built wooden door and wall enclosing it. Tools lay strewn around, whitened by salt precipitate growing over them. At the end of the track they saw the railway car, a standard narrow-gauge hopper small enough to be pushed by miners, containing a wooden cradle as if some substantial piece of equipment had been carried in it to this point.

'This tunnel doesn't look like salt mining,' Costas said. 'It looks like someone was building a storage facility.'

'And then abandoned it halfway,' Jack replied. 'None of the side chambers are finished.'

'The Nazis?'

'It's difficult to see why miners might have come down here. This deep, it may often have been flooded, by changes in the water table like the one that causes the water to be so deep now. The odd thing is, it might make sense for Neolithic miners to have got this far underground when it was dry, making their way down the natural fissure where that shaft is. We know that Stone Age painters could get a long way into cave systems. And they may have been looking for especially prized halite crystals only found this deep. But for later miners with metal tools, there was a lot of salt still to be dug out much closer to the surface.'

They reached the end of the metal tracks. Jack rolled over and looked up, seeing the shimmering surfaces of pools where methane gas had accumulated. He looked back to the end of the shaft, where the first of the Russians had appeared. 'Christ. They've come all the way down. At least fifteen metres beyond the safe depth with trimix. About where nitrogen narcosis will really kick in too.'

'Drunk, narked and on a one-way ticket to hell,' Costas said.

'But dangerous. Did you see their knives?'

'Roger that. Let's get this done.'

They swam forward beyond the end of the track, through the crack in the rock. Ahead of them the fissure carried on as far as they could see, with a crudely cut pathway along the floor. On either side were shimmering crystal caverns, some with halite crystals five or six centimetres across. Costas was ahead, and after only a few metres he stopped and sank down to about a metre above the floor, over an area where the crystals seemed to be remarkably uniform in size, as if they had all grown from the same genesis. 'You remember Wladislaw and his dating of the salt growth to the Neolithic? Take a look at this.'

Jack peered down. Beneath the crystals was a shape, staring up at him. He had seen this before where calcium carbonate, precipitated minerals, formed stalagmites over bones, but never with salt. *It was a human skull*. He saw a ribcage, leg bones, arms laid over the chest. He could just make out chipped and polished stone tools laid alongside, hand axes and adzes, several still attached to wooden hafts. 'It's a burial,' he murmured. 'Maybe that's what these people were doing down here as well, using it as a burial chamber.' He stared again at the skull. The jaw had dropped, as if it were leering. He remembered the grim sculptures they had seen in the passageway with Wladislaw, the one that had reminded him of Munch's *The Scream*. Perhaps this was what those medieval miners had seen. Perhaps it was not their own mortality they feared, but some terrible demon of the depths they had encountered down here – in a place that perhaps was never broached again by the miners, and was only reopened when the Nazis decided to create a top-secret storage facility in these depths.

'My sensor registers almost zero oxygen in the water,' Costas said. 'That's why it's so clear. No life here at all.'

'Ten metres to go, according to my map,' Jack said, peering into the tunnel. 'I think I can see something at about that distance, ahead and to the right. A small cavern entrance, maybe. Something blocking it.'

'Jack, there's something strange about the floor ahead of us. Odd shapes.'

Jack dumped air from his suit and sank down, staring ahead. Too late he realized that he was going to hit the bottom, and he silently cursed. He prided himself on his buoyancy control. And in caves, silt could be stirred up with barely a touch and completely obscure visibility. He injected a burst of air into his suit and just avoided impact, but watched a pressure wave from his body ripple through the silt ahead. In a fleeting second he realized what Costas had seen. Bodies. *Human bodies*. Lying on either side of the path. But not solid bodies. As the ripple passed through them they disintegrated and exploded upwards into the water, a great cloud of white particles and flakes that engulfed Costas and wafted towards Jack.

'Thanks, Jack. A swim through disintegrated human flesh. That rounds off this little excursion nicely.'

Jack swam forward, dropping down into the haze. He saw skeletons, two, three along one side, picks and crowbars strewn haphazardly around, the bones wearing the remains of clothing. 'This looks a little more recent than our Neolithic friend,' he murmured. 'The shoes look pretty modern. Are you thinking what I'm thinking?'

'The story from Wladislaw? German officer goes in with Jews and guards, only German officer comes out?'

'They've all been shot in the head, execution style,' Jack said. 'You can see the holes, the shattered skulls.'

'Not these two.' Costas' fins were poking out of the cloud of white ahead, and Jack went alongside. The two skeletons below were more contorted, and had fragmented sternums and ribcages as well as holes in their skulls. 'Different clothing. Look.' Costas reached down and pulled up a collar. He rubbed it, and Jack saw the SS death's-head insignia. 'These must be the two Hungarian SS guards. Remember, the officer came out alone? He must have shot them too. Looks as if he had to catch them unawares, presumably after they'd executed all the Jews.'

Jack stared at the obstruction in the small cavern ahead. 'I think I know why the officer had to bring them down here. They were carrying something for him.' He swam closer, and his heart sank. The entrance to the chamber, carved out of the rock salt, was about a metre square, wide enough for a person to crouch inside. He could see a dark cavity beyond. But wedged into the entrance was an unmistakable shape.

It was a bomb.

He was looking at the tail piece of an aerial bomb, four sheet-steel vanes welded to a cone, reinforced with box-shaped struts of bar steel. The cone was striped red and blue, and the rest had been painted green, now streaked with rust. Beyond the cone he could see the extension cylinder with a fuse head, and beyond that the main body of the bomb, but the nose was out of sight inside the cavity. The bomb seemed to be about a metre and a half in length, maybe a little more. It was precariously wedged on the rim of the entrance, with nothing else obvious holding it up beyond.

'German SD-250, thick-cased fragmentation bomb,' Costas said, coming alongside. 'Seventy-nine kilograms of TNT, series five and eight fuses, usually. Huh. Never seen one of these live before.'

Jack shut his eyes. *This time, it was going to have to happen.*

Costas eyed him. 'Looks like we don't have any Turkish navy ordnance disposal divers around to help with this one.'

'I noticed.'

Costas pulled open a Velcro flap on his leg and extracted a hammer.

'What are you doing with that?'

'Well, I have to get at the fuse.'

'It's there, look.'

Costas shook his helmet. 'No. That's the dummy fuse. The actual fuse is further forward in the main casing, just beyond that rock lip, I reckon. It looks as if the bomb's been deliberately wedged that far forward to conceal the fuse head, yet left balanced on the rim so it could fall into the cavity or into the cavern where we are now.'

'Either way wouldn't make any difference, would it?'

'Boom.'

'*Boom.*' Jack shut his eyes. 'Okay. What next?'

'The guy was a Luftwaffe officer, right?'

'That's what Wladislaw said.'

'That makes sense. He knew what he was doing. This bomb's clearly been put here as a booby trap. In which case, there'll be anti-handling devices.'

'*Anti-handling devices.* This gets better every moment.'

'The Luftwaffe had used them since the 1940 London Blitz, for delayed-action bombs. But we're talking 1945 here. All the sinister genius of Nazi engineering designed to kill anyone trying to defuse this bomb.'

'That means us.'

'Okay,' Costas murmured, both hands on the bomb casing, leaning forward to see as far as he could into the chamber. 'Delayed-action bombs had a clockwork fuse. So you take that out, fine. The problem's what's underneath. The standard early anti-handling fuse was the ZUS-40. The jolt of impact would release a ball bearing, which would arm a spring-loaded firing pin. Or unscrewing the outer fuse would have the same effect, cocking the firing pin underneath. Or there could be another device entirely, a type 50 fuse with a mercury tilt switch that would arm itself when the bomb hit the ground, and then complete an electrical circuit if anyone tried to move it. Or there could be both devices.'

'Okay. Okay. Just what do we do?'

'Hold the tail unit.'

Jack backed off, then approached the bomb from behind and reached his arms carefully around the metal fins. He tried to stand on the base of the passageway, but the salt precipitate on the floor was viscous, slippery. He found a rock protrusion with his left fin and wedged it in. 'Okay.'

Costas lifted the hammer and hit the edge of the rock cavity. Fragments came tumbling down around Jack. He hit it again, harder. Jack was barely breathing. Out of the corner of his eye he saw the Russian who had come down the passageway, watching them, hanging in the water just beyond the white haze about ten metres back, his exhaust streaming up into the gas pocket in the ceiling above.

There was a sudden jolt, and Jack flinched. He thought he felt the bomb move. If it slipped in his direction, there was no way he was going to be able to stop 250 kilograms of steel and high explosive from falling to the floor of the tunnel, pinning him down. But if that happened, they were finished. Costas hammered again, producing a shower of fragments, and then slipped his hammer back in his pocket and took out a tool like a socket wrench. 'Okay. I've exposed the fuse pocket.'

'What do I do?'

'Watch our friend. I've seen him. He's as likely to blow as this thing.'

'How long?'

There was a ringing sound of metal on metal. Costas had taken out another tool. He was straining as he spoke, pulling the wrench. 'Guy who taught the bomb disposal course I did once defused one of these in Portsmouth Harbour. Took him twenty hours to clear the rust around the fuses.'

Jack looked at his gauge. 'We have ten minutes. Max.'

'I think I need my hammer again for this.'

Jack cautiously released the tail unit, then let himself drift back, staring at the Russian. He was coming down, approaching the haze of human decay in the water. 'Okay, Costas. I'm going to take him out.'

'Just keep him away from me. Any disturbance and this thing could blow. Above those first bodies the fissure rises into a chamber, and I saw a surface. Must be a gas pocket. I saw a couple of miners' picks on a ledge.'

'Okay. I'll be back.'

'You better be.' Costas' eyes were glued to the bomb, inspecting the surface minutely, selecting tools by touch from his pockets. Jack remained still. The other two Russians were nowhere to be seen. Maybe they were sticking to plan, waiting further up until he and Costas returned. The man coming for them might have no method, no rationale. His mission was suicidal, but could still be murderous. Jack saw the glint of a wicked-looking blade in the man's hand. He steadied himself. He heard the tap-tap-tap of Costas trying to free the fuse. He tried to remember Rebecca's face, but it was not there. What he was about to do now was pure instinct, survival. He felt the adrenalin course through him. Not just survival. *Rage*.

He suddenly swam towards the Russian as fast as he could, grabbed the man's jacket inflator and pulled it, sending them both rocketing upwards. He seized the man's neck in a half-nelson with his left arm and clamped his wrist with his right hand to keep the knife away. The man's eyes were wild, but his wrist was rock-hard and Jack knew there was no way he was going to move it. The tip of the knife was inches from his intake hose. They surfaced together inside the cavity in a welter of bubbles, creating a wave that sucked them down and then pushed them against the side of the chamber, ripping the left arm of Jack's e-suit down to the Kevlar mesh. They bounced down again underwater, then up. Jack's wrist began to shake, his grip loosening. The man had short, thick arms, massively muscled, and Jack's longer arm could not hold against him, requiring far more leverage than he could muster. He felt a spasm of pain go down his back as he put every muscle in his body into holding the knife away. It was no use. He had only one option. He kicked with his fins as hard as he could, driving them both upwards. The instant he felt they had risen as far as they could go, he let go of the man's neck with his left hand, reached up and pushed hard against the ceiling, forcing them back down deep underwater. He pulled the emergency inflate on the man's jacket and it ballooned outwards, forcing them both upwards again and slamming the man's head against the ceiling. Jack grabbed the head again with his left hand, let go of the wrist with his right and instantly balled his fist, ramming it upwards into the man's face. It was the killer blow Ben had taught him, a massive upwards punch at the base of the nose that would splinter the bone and drive the fragments into the brain.

The Russian went limp in Jack's hands. His mask quickly filled up with blood, his eyes still open behind it, like some ghastly avant-garde artwork. Jack ripped off the man's mask and hood, spraying dollops of blood everywhere. His nose was a mess of blood and mucus and protruding bone fragments, and his eyes were covered in a film of red. Suddenly they flickered and he bellowed, pushing back from Jack and scrabbling to the far side of the chamber. He still had the knife in his hand and he leapt forward, swinging. Jack swerved sideways and caught the man's head in a massive swipe with the flat of his hand, pushing it sideways into the wall. He had wedged his feet against the rock, and as he held the man, who seemed to hang there, limp again, he realized that the razor-sharp halite crystals on the cavern wall had driven into the Russian's head. The man lurched again, snorting blood, his eyes crazed, and dragged his head backwards as Jack pressed on it, leaving a smear of blood and skin along the wall of the chamber.

Jack let go, and drew back, panting. *The man would not go down.* The Russian heaved himself half out of the water and stood there, panting, his head a blood-soaked mess, still holding the knife. Jack remembered the miners' tools Costas had mentioned, on the ledge. He dropped down underwater, reaching blindly, and felt a handle. He wrapped his hand around it and pulled, releasing it from the salt accretion. It was a pick, with a flat, adze-like blade on one side, and a long, flat-ended spike on the other. He reared upwards out of the water, lurching sideways to give himself enough room to swing the pick in both hands. The man lunged again with the knife, missing and staggering back to the ledge. Jack swung the flat end of the pick, catching the man below the left ear, sinking it into his neck. He pulled the blade out and flipped the pick to the spike, bringing it back and swinging again, as hard as he could. The spike caught the man in the same place and went through his neck, protruding out of the other side in a geyser of blood. The man's tongue lolled out, dripping blood, and he made a terrible gurgling noise, his eyes rolling upwards in their sockets.

Jack shook and shook until the pick came free, the man's body flopping like a rag doll. He staggered sideways, finding a better foothold, and then drove the pick again into the Russian's head. This time it came away easily as the man's head split open. Jack was bellowing with rage. He struck again and again, until the head was unrecognizable pulp. *You bastard. You bastard. Nobody messes with my daughter.* He realized he was yelling himself hoarse, bringing the pick down again and again, slower now, his visor flecked with blood. He stopped, and dropped back into the water, panting. He felt sick to the stomach, exhausted beyond belief, but as if a terrible burden of guilt and anger had been released from him. The adrenalin was pumping through him like a massive painkiller. *It felt good.*

He sank back into the water, tensing his arms to stop them from shaking, and forced himself to concentrate on his equipment. He had to stay focused. He checked his hoses and helmet. The only damage was the scrape on his suit, and that had not punctured. He was panting hard, too hard, and he tried to calm himself. He looked at his helmet readout, and realized that a red warning light had been flashing, hardly visible with the blood all round. It was telling him that it was time to surface. The rebreather tanks were running low, and they were only a few minutes from crossing the decompression threshold. He checked his wrist computer, and did a swift calculation. Five minutes more would take him to the limit of the safety margin. He dropped back down, looking up to see the smudge of the body on the surface and a darkness in the water that seemed to follow him, swirling tendrils of blood that hit the rocky base of the tunnel and slowly pooled in cracks and fissures. He reached Costas, who was still entirely focused on the bomb, and came up slowly beside him, trying to control his breathing, to calm himself, to slow the sound of his heart, which was still pounding in his ears.

'Problem solved?' Costas said, without looking round.

'One down, two to go,' Jack said hoarsely.

'I heard it all,' Costas said distractedly. Jack saw what Costas was doing, and suddenly forgot about what had just happened. Costas had pocketed his tools and was in the final stages of unscrewing the fuse from the bomb. He released it, held it up and then pocketed it, keeping one hand pressed into the fuse pocket. 'For my collection.' He moved his head to get his lamp beam angled correctly, and peered into the socket. 'Yep, ZUS-40. God damn it. I knew it.'

'Three minutes, Costas.'

Keeping his fingers in the fuse pocket, Costas whipped out a handful of threaded plugs from his pocket, dropped several until there was only one in his hand, handed it to Jack, pulled out a socket wrench, took the plug back from Jack and leaned over, quickly screwing the plug into the fuse hole. 'Okay. What happens is this. When I push the bomb out of the hole, it hits the floor of the cavern and arms itself. If it moves again after that, if it's jolted, it goes off. It's the only way we're going to get it out of the entrance to the chamber.' Without waiting for a reply, he finned back and then upside down, wedging his feet against the ceiling of the tunnel and pressing on the tail fins of the bomb. It tilted, and then slid out of the opening, clanging sickeningly on the floor of the tunnel and coming to rest about five metres down the slope, sliding part of the way.

'That floor's slippery as hell,' Jack said. 'Anything could move it.'

'Okay. You're in, Jack, then we go.'

Jack pulled himself into the aperture where the mine had been. The chamber was roughly square, about three by three metres. He looked quickly round. There it was. In the centre of the floor was a black metal box the size of a small suitcase. He reached down to the handle, and pulled. It was unlocked. Someone had opened it. Inside, he saw another metal case, about twenty centimetres across, with a Nazi swastika emblem on the top. He opened it, and stared, his heart pounding like a jackhammer.

It was there. *But it wasn't.* He saw the shape, but only the impression, where the metal case had been formed to fit it. *The reverse swastika.* The palladion had been there, but it had been removed. The German officer. The story was right. *But the Russians, their controller, must not know.* He shut the smaller case, unrolled the mesh bag on his waist belt and shoved the case inside, then twisted around and powered out of the chamber, nodding at Costas and swimming hard alongside him away from the chamber, up the passage towards the lift shaft. Ahead of them he could see one of the other Russians, hanging in the water.

'Well?' Costas said, breathing hard.

'Not there. But it once was. I've got the case, which will look convincing. The Luftwaffe officer must have come down here to get it, using the prisoners to shift the bomb, then armed it, maybe to look convincing to the guards, before they executed the Jews and he killed them. He probably dumped the lift cable from the top of the shaft.' They were more than halfway back to the shaft now. Jack twisted on his back, still finning hard, and looked down to where they had been. The white haze in the water had mingled with the blood from the Russian. He twisted back, then realized he had seen something and turned again, stopping finning.

'Come on,' Costas said, pulling him. 'We have to keep going up.'

'Costas, something awful is happening.'

Costas stopped too, and they both stared. The body of the Russian was slowly sinking from the air pocket above, a dark shape in the dead man's float, arms and legs hanging down, a haze of blood where the head had been. It hit the floor, bounced upwards in a macabre slow-motion dance, and then stopped. 'Forget it,' Costas exclaimed. 'Now let's go.'

'No. Look.' Jack's eyes were glued to the body. To his horror an arm lifted up, as if the Russian had come alive again, and then very slowly flopped back. The body began sliding, barely perceptibly. *Sliding towards the bomb.*

Jack glanced at his gauges. 'We can go back. We can wedge it.'

'No way. Going back down there means going beyond our no-stop deco time. And if we had to do a ten-minute stop on the way up, we'd run out of air.'

'The shock wave from the explosion would kill everyone in the water anyway, right the way up to the top of the shaft.'

'At least by carrying on and getting out we have a chance. Our Russian might take a breather from his dance of death and stay put. Now come on.'

They turned and powered back up the tunnel. Jack felt that every pulse of water from his fins was pushing a current back to the corpse, edging it ever closer to the bomb. He dared not look back again. But now there was another problem. The second Russian was barring their way. Jack pointed towards the shape in the bag at his waist, and did a thumbs-up sign. The man took out his knife. *Not again*. This time there was something wrong. It was the one who had been breathing heavily near the surface. Jack had noticed that he was a terrible diver, useless at maintaining his buoyancy. The man kicked upwards and began to sink, and then injected too much air into his buoyancy compensator, rising up in front of them. He flailed and kicked, nearly hitting Jack, and then pressed his exhaust valve and bled off air from his jacket, sinking down between them again, hyperventilating. Jack glanced down and saw that the man's tank pressure gauge was less than 200 psi. That meant that his tanks were nearly empty. He glanced at Costas, pointing at the man's gauge. 'We may be about to lose another one of our valued colleagues.'

Costas craned his head up at the ceiling of the chamber, a good eight metres above them. It looked like quicksilver, a shimmering pool in reverse, reflecting his headlamp beam. The Russian's exhaust bubbles cascaded against it. The man stopped and swivelled round to look at them. He seemed to be staring past Jack, his eyes wide. Jack had seen that look in divers many times before, the look of hypoxia, of someone struggling to breathe, in this case compounded by narcosis and alcohol. Normally he would be unhooking his safety regulator to allow the man to buddy-breathe, but even if he had wished to do so, the rebreather system only had a back-up hose that could be hooked into another helmet, without a mouthpiece. The Russian suddenly turned towards Costas, grasping his arm, then began fumbling for Costas' hoses.

Costas held the man like a vice, staring at him, then pushed him away forcefully, pointed at his depth gauge, then drew a hand across his throat. He pointed up. The man looked, realized there was what appeared to be an air pocket at the top of the chamber and began to fin for it. Jack saw him press the inflator to bleed air into his jacket, buoying him up to the surface but emptying his tank completely of breathing gas. He watched him hit the surface in an explosion of bubbles, and then bob about. The Russian threw off his mask, which came tumbling through the water beside them to the floor of the cavern. He seemed to be struggling with his arms, and was kicking spasmodically.

'How was it the miners cleared methane?' Costas said. He had unravelled a length of detonation cord and crimped a blasting cap on to it. 'Should be just enough oxygen from his exhaust up there to give this a good helping hand.' He activated the time delay and let the cord loose in the water, then ducked under it and pressed the purge valve on his rebreather, sending the length of cord writhing like a snake towards the surface beside the man. 'Fire in the hole,' he said. There was a ripple of light and a crack as the cord detonated, and then a flash of orange as the gas in the chamber ignited. The man's legs trembled for a moment, and then went still. His arms slowly dropped down, hanging lifeless.

Costas glanced at Jack. 'Two down.' They swam to the base of the shaft, and looked up. The third Russian, the one with the Chechnya tattoo, was where he was supposed to be, clinging to the wood on the edge of the shaft about fifteen metres above them. 'I saw him down here at the base of the shaft to begin with,' Costas said. 'Bad idea. He'll be way beyond his no-stop time. And all that alcohol should help to give him some nice little cramps as he goes up.'

They began to rise, letting their computers take over and adjust their buoyancy to maintain the optimal ascent rate. Another minute down there and they would have been doing a ten-minute stop on the way up, impossible with the tank pressure they had left. Jack calmed his breathing, taking strong, deep breaths, sensing the change as the rebreather increased the proportion of oxygen in the gas mix, feeling it cleanse his blood. The last ten metres would be on pure oxygen, the critical time to avoid the bends. He looked up. The Russian was rising way above them, far too fast, close to the surface. 'He must have decided to take us out at the entry point,' Jack said.

'He won't be able to move, if he's still alive.'

Three minutes later they reached the ten metres mark, where the computer halted them for two minutes. Jack's mind had been blank for the ascent, as if he knew that contemplating what might happen at any moment with the bomb was simply a waste of effort, when his whole system, body and mind, needed to focus on the battle to keep him from succumbing to the effects of pressure and nitrogen build-up. But now, floating still in the water and seeing the shimmering pool of the surface above, he suddenly, desperately wanted to get out. The shock wave from the explosion would be virtually instantaneous, and they would die here as quickly as they would have done with the bomb beside them. He saw Rebecca's face again. *He had to survive.*

Costas signalled him, and they began to rise, coming out of the shaft into the pool in the chamber. Jack saw the man's fins where he had pulled himself out and was lying on the edge, one leg drawn up. They both rose out of the water, cautiously. The man was on his side, his tanks still on but his mask and hood pulled off. He was moaning, saying something in Russian. He tried to move, and groaned. Costas crawled up out of the water, snapped up his visor and leaned over the man's face. He was drooling, one side of his face collapsed, and he stared at Costas in desperation. Costas picked up the man's regulator mouthpiece, and sniffed it. He crinkled his nose and dropped the regulator, looking at Jack. 'This man's been drinking. Should never have gone diving.'

The man feebly raised one arm. He spoke in heavily accented English. 'My arm. I can't feel it. Help me.'

Costas leaned over him again, took his chin in his hand and twisted it savagely, raising the man's face close to his own. 'Remember what you said to me before we went in? I'll fucking break you before today is over. I remember that. I remember that well.' He jabbed his other hand at the water, wrenching the Russian's head so he could see it. 'Well, Chechnya. This is my world. That's why I'm walking out of here, and you're not. You trespass in my world, you die.' He let go of the man's head, backed into the water and made a show of wiping his hand on his suit.

'My leg. I can't straighten it,' the man continued.

'That's why they call it the bends.'

'Help me. Please. Help me.'

Costas paused. 'Well, Chechnya, you have a choice. With all that nitrogen fizzing in your bloodstream, another bubble will form, a big one, and go to your brain. Maybe it will kill you straight away, maybe not. Maybe you'll live for hours, screaming in pain, insane. And then you will die. Or you can go back down and join your friends. Going deep, the pressure will ease your pain. And you will drown, an easier death.'

The man pathetically waved his right hand as if to reach for his regulator, and flapped one fin. 'Help me get in. I can't move.'

Costas sighed. 'It seems you've made your choice.' He turned to go, wading towards the entrance to the sump, behind Jack. They both crouched through the hole created by the rockfall, and knelt in the water on the other side. They could see a glimmer of light through the water from the pool where they had entered, where they had left Wladislaw only forty minutes before. Costas felt the rock, peering at it, then looked at the man still visible in the background, groaning. He unhooked the remainder of the detonation cord from his gear, coiled it into a crack at the top of the rockfall and crimped a blasting cap on to it. Then he glanced at Jack. 'Ready?' Jack nodded. Costas kept one hand on the cap, and stared back through the jagged hole. The man was moaning, his eyes pointing in different directions, sightless.

'Hey, Chechnya,' Costas bellowed. 'Happy hangover.' He clicked the cap, snapped shut his visor and dropped down into the sump, quickly finning behind Jack up into the green pool. There was a thump and a rumble of falling rock. Costas came up alongside Jack, visor to visor, and they rose to the surface.

'Three down,' Jack said.

'Not for a little while yet, I hope,' Costas said grimly.

They broke surface. The light bulbs were still on. Jack quickly scanned the tunnel up the line of the train track. There was no one to be seen. Wladislaw must have followed his instructions. *Good*. He dragged himself on to the edge of the pool, then quickly unhooked his hoses and his rebreather unit, slipping it off. He unhooked his helmet and dumped it beside him, and took a deep breath. Costas did the same, then sniffed loudly. 'It smells better here than when we left. That vodka breath. Phew.'

'How's your deco?'

Costas glanced at his gauge. 'Fine. You?'

'Three minutes margin.'

'My guess is we're going to go flying. We'll have to go in the recompression chamber on the Embraer.'

Jack stood while Costas unzipped the back of his e-suit. He remembered claustrophic hours spent in that chamber, a long metal tube with barely enough room to kneel in.

'At least we can lie down,' Costas said, yanking on the zipper.

Jack grunted. He bent down and drew the neck seal over his head, then pulled out his arms. He saw that the suit was still covered in blood. 'Hard stuff to get off, blood,' he murmured, turning to unzip Costas.

'Forget it. What you did, you had to do.'

'I don't have a problem with that. I just mean a ruined e-suit.'

Costas pulled his own suit over his head and stepped out of the legs, and Jack did the same with his. They both quickly went to Costas' bag and got dressed, zipping up their fleeces. Jack went back and took the bag with the swastika box from his e-suit belt and tucked it under his arm. Costas delved in his bag and pulled out two small bottles of water and two energy drinks, and they both squatted on their haunches, drinking. Jack finished the water, then uncapped the other drink. 'I couldn't help noticing. Some good archaeology down there.'

'Jesus, Jack.'

'You had your fix. The bomb.'

'Jack, for all the Neolithic hand axes and little statues in the world, I wouldn't go back in there again.'

Jack took a deep swig, then stood up, nodding. 'Roger that.' He dropped the bottle in the bag. 'Right. We have to get cracking. Got everything we need?' He patted his pockets, feeling for his things. Costas did the same, then looked at him, and put his hand on his shoulder. Costas' hair was matted and his face lined with exhaustion, but his eyes were cold and determined.

'We can leave all this here. All we need is your phone.'

'I know where that is. We need to get in touch with the kidnappers and convince them that we've got what they want. They'll have been expecting Chechnya to have it, having disposed of us. But if they've got any intelligence, what's happened won't come as a complete surprise. Not the desired outcome, but it doesn't change the balance of power. They've still got what we want, and we've got what they want. We have to keep them thinking that.'

There was a sudden rumble, a deep vibration that sent a shimmer across the pool of water, a pulse of energy that coursed through the rock. They both stood silently for a moment, watching dust shake off the walls of the chamber. The rumble stopped. The tunnel ahead was still clear.

Costas coughed. 'Remote detonation. Always the safest way. I timed that perfectly, don't you think?'

Jack narrowed his eyes. 'Let's move.'

★

Ten minutes later they left the lift shaft and went straight into the office where they had first met Wladislaw. Jack found his phone on the desk pad, exactly as he had instructed. *Good man*. He picked it up and switched it on, tapping his fingers impatiently while it connected, and then he pressed the code for the IMU secure channel. It was picked up immediately. 'Jack.'

'Ben.'

'Status.'

'The Lions are at the Gate.' It was a code they had prearranged in case anyone might be eavesdropping on the line. 'I repeat, *The Lions are at the Gate.*'

'Copy that. Now switch off your phone and put it down.' Jack did as instructed. Seconds later there was a muffled ringing sound. He went round to the front of the desk and pulled open a drawer. It was another phone, evidently Wladislaw's personal phone he had left there. Jack picked it up. 'Yes?'

'Okay, Jack.' It was Ben again. 'Wladislaw called us when he returned to the office and I told him to leave his phone there. I'm using a disposable. We can't be too careful. In about two minutes you'll be answering your phone again. It's a pre-recorded message that will only come through once. It's essential that you listen to what I'm about to say now.'

'Copy that.' Jack did as instructed, staring hard at the ground as Ben spoke. After less than a minute he lowered the phone and clicked it off. Almost immediately his iPhone rang, and he answered it. There was a crackle, and then he heard a voice, educated English but with a hint of an accent. 'Dr

Howard. This message presupposes that you have found what I want but your diving companions are unable to bring it to me. As you will know by now, your people have been given our instructions. You will wish to speak to your daughter.' The crackle ended, there was a click and then a uniform hissing sound. He heard sounds of movement, a scuffle, then breathing close to the phone.

'Dad?'

'Rebecca.' *Thank God*. 'Are you all right?' Jack's mind raced. 'You must be tired.'

'Yes, but nice to stand here and imagine Orion.'

Jack's mind raced. *Night sky*. A time zone ahead of where they were now. And the constellation Orion. She and Jack had stood on the battlements looking for it two nights ago, then realized it was still below the horizon. He had told her that he had always thought of Orion as his guardian, ever since he was a boy. *So that was it. She really was there.*

'Orion's looking after you, even if you can't see him,' Jack said carefully. 'You don't need to worry.'

'It's kind of, um, creepy, though. I could really do with a double vodka.'

Jack remembered what she had called Raitz. *A creep*. And what the US Marines she had befriended in Kyrgyzstan called a Russian male. *A shot of vodka*. Professor Raitz, and two Russian thugs. 'You need to keep warm,' Jack said slowly. 'You should be inside.'

'Don't worry, Dad. We're going back in now. I found us a place. It's only just opened. You'd be amazed, Dad. It's so cool.' There was a sudden scuffling sound, then a guttural snarl, Russian, and another man's voice in English. 'Give it back to her,' the voice said. Rebecca came on the line again. She was panting. 'Sorry, Dad. I have to go. I love you. I just want to know. On the shipwreck. Did you find it?'

Jack was stunned. It seemed an age ago. A lifetime. He flashed back to the moment the day before when he had been carrying the shield upwards, imagining Rebecca looking down and seeing it. He swallowed hard. 'We found it, Rebecca. Costas and I found it. You'll be amazed.'

'When do I get to see it?'

'Tomor—' The phone was snatched away, and went dead. He hoped Rebecca had heard the word. He turned to Costas, who had gone out of the room and now returned. Jack clenched his hands, felt the energy course through him. He was beyond tired, but those few words with Rebecca had kept the adrenalin pumping. 'Okay. Here's the plan. Ben's got in touch with Wladislaw and he's coming to pick us up. The Embraer's fuelled and ready to go at Krakow airport. At Istanbul we transfer to the helicopter and then to *Seaquest II*. If all goes to plan, we should be there by about three a.m. Ben's going to have a security team ready, as well as a section of Turkish navy commandos from the minesweeper.'

'He's told the authorities?' Costas asked.

Jack shook his head. 'Too risky. The kidnappers want the Lynx to fly to international waters, where they're going to drop Rebecca in a Zodiac. They must have a vessel offshore. There's obviously big money behind this. We don't want an overzealous policeman jeopardizing the whole thing. But Ben's told the minesweeper captain we suspect we're being shadowed. Has to be kept top secret. The Turkish navy guys are fully prepped on the illegal antiquities trade and this is just what they'd love to get their teeth into. Officially it's a covert training exercise. Ben will tell them about the kidnapping once they're in position and you and I are inside.' He heard a car draw up outside. 'Here's our ride. We've got to move, now.'

'Where are we going?'

Jack looked at his hands. There was still blood in the cracks, under his fingernails. He thought of what he had just done, in the mine. He felt nothing. *Nothing.* He looked up, and gave Costas a steely look. 'We're going to Troy.'

20

Troy

Jack crouched low against the bank of the watercourse, training his night-vision scope on the overgrown mound about a kilometre away across the fields. It was the first time for fifteen years that he had seen Troy from this vantage point, only a few hundred yards from the spot where he and Costas had excavated the ancient beach with the galley timbers from the time of the Trojan War. The dykes and marshy fields looked like no-man's-land, an image of war. There was a hint of a breeze, and Jack remembered imagining Greek warriors standing silently among the rustling reeds, their spears black against the moonlight, waiting for the signal to move forward. Except they now knew it had not been like that. It had been a maelstrom of raging sea and hellfire, a wave of destruction that swept the warriors in their ships from this place up against the battlements, arrows storming down, engulfed in flames.

He never could have imagined being back here again in these circumstances, sighting the best approach route to confront the kidnappers who had taken his daughter. He put down the scope, took a deep drink from his water bottle, zipped up his fleece and slid down close to the river course where he could stand up without being seen from the mound. He had to keep moving. He had not slept while he and Costas had been on the Embraer from Krakow airport in Poland, cooped up for half the flight in the recompression chamber after their dive in the mine. His only thoughts had been of Rebecca. He knew she was out there. He had spoken to her on the cell phone the night before. And it might only be a matter of time before whoever was behind this determined that the palladion had not been in the mine after all, and that what Jack was doing now was a charade. If that happened, all bargaining chips were lost. Rebecca might became irrelevant to the kidnappers, yet too much of a liability to return alive.

He slithered along the mud bank to where Ben and Costas were waiting, just visible in the moonlight. He glanced at his watch. It was five a.m., and the time stipulated by the kidnapper was an hour from now. They had got here as fast as they could, with barely time to get their plan into action. Ben beckoned him over, and Jack and Costas hunched down, listening. 'I've got to get my team in position now,' Ben said. 'Here's the score. The kidnappers have come here because this is our turf. They know we've got carte blanche here from the authorities. We can clear the place, which we've done. There's nobody else anywhere near the site tonight. All our personnel, Hiebermeyer, everyone, are back on *Seaquest II*. And the kidnappers are using us for the getaway. The Lynx is going to land in the car park at 0530. They're going to leave in it, with Rebecca, once the exchange is made, and go directly to a vessel waiting for them beyond the twelve-mile territorial limit. Except they're not going to do that. Because Jack doesn't have what they want, only an empty box. So the only way they're getting out of here is in a body bag or in cuffs. Am I right?'

'Roger that,' Costas muttered.

'Costas has an iPhone. When he calls, my team goes in. Until then, you're on your own. Jack, Costas has what I promised you. All clear?'

'Copy that,' Costas said. Ben disappeared into the darkness. Costas reached in his bag and took out Macalister's Webley revolver. 'Ben said he's tested the loads. The accuracy's phenomenal, but aim low and to the right because there's an almighty kick. Something about a manstopper.'

Jack picked up the heavy revolver, weighing it in his hands, seeing that the chambers were loaded. He opened his khaki bag, took out the black box with the swastika emblem on the lid and put the revolver inside, in the space that had once held the Trojan palladion, with the impressed pocket in the shape of the reverse swastika removed to make space for the pistol. 'That would be the flat-nosed bullet designed for maximum damage on impact.'

'Sounds about right.' Costas pulled out his own Beretta pistol from a shoulder holster and snapped the slide, checking that a round was chambered, then holstered it again. 'Good to go?'

Jack closed the lid and put the box in his khaki bag, folding the flap over. 'Good to go.'

Ten minutes later they were at the entrance to the underground watercourse some two hundred metres south-west of the mound. It was a low dell, surrounded by trees and dense undergrowth, where a muddy trickle came through a narrow tunnel that went underground towards Troy. It had been found by the Austrian excavators several years before, and was part of a water supply system that allowed the ancient Trojans to tap into a spring beyond the city walls. Jack followed Costas to the iron grid door, shut but with the lock hanging to one side. He gave a silent prayer of thanks to Hiebermeyer for having left it that way. The two men had spoken on the phone from the Embraer on the way to Istanbul airport. Maurice had come down to this spot the previous morning, while the excavation was still ongoing and before Rebecca had been kidnapped, and had managed to make his way through the tunnel as far as a low portal blocked up with rubble. He had cleared that single-handedly and got into the underground chamber he had reached previously by its other entrance, the passageway Jack would be following shortly. And if Maurice could get through this smaller tunnel, then Costas could make it too.

Jack ducked his head away from the wasps that were swarming around the entrance. He flicked on Costas' headlamp and gave him a Mag-lite for back-up. They heard the helicopter approaching, clattering loudly over the citadel mound towards the far side, where it landed and powered down. 'Okay,' Jack said. 'That's the cue. It's 0535. I'm due to be in there at 0600. According to the time it took Maurice, you should be in position by then. Your entrance to the chamber will be on my right as I enter from the main passageway, and I'll be looking for you. I'll leave my bag outside and then return for it once I've made contact with the kidnappers. When you see me come back in and put the black box down, you might be taking a shot. I'll try to make eye contact with Rebecca, warn her something is about to happen. We'll have to play this as it comes.'

'I'm moving now. Good luck, Jack.'

'Good luck.' Jack watched Costas slosh down the tunnel and disappear around a corner, then turned and made his way back towards the mound, walking openly once he had reached the main path, where anyone watching might have assumed he had come from the helicopter. He entered the deep trench where Hiebermeyer had been excavating, where they now knew Schliemann had worked as well. He passed the two gate guardians, the statues of ancient kings of Troy, and then went into the tunnel through the rubble, enlarged to over his height and shored up now with timber. He found a place to hide his bag. Maurice had told him on the phone what they had found, but nothing could have prepared him for it. There was a great bronze door, half ajar. He remembered how Gladstone had argued that the Treasury of Atreus at Mycenae once had a beaten bronze door. And there in the middle was the symbol, the impression of the reverse swastika in a roundel, exactly as Dillen had told him, from the story recounted by the old foreman to Hugh and Peter. There were columns of green stone on either side, with meander pattern decoration, again exactly as in the Treasury of Atreus. He stepped through into a cavernous chamber, and switched on his diving torch, flashing it round. There was no noise, only a slight hollow echo, but he knew he was not alone.

'Rebecca?' he said. 'Are you there?'

Still nothing. He could only wait. He looked around. It was an astonishing sight. Just as in the Treasury of Atreus, the chamber rose in a beehive shape, with corbelled masonry, but it was what was on the floor in front of him that was so astonishing. It was a circle of stone seats, set halfway to the centre of the chamber, a dozen of them, all identical. They were like seats he had seen in Bronze Age palaces before, in Knossos on Crete, in Egypt, in the citadels of the Near East. *The thrones of kings.* He panned his light over them. Each chair had an inscription on the back. He saw hieroglyphs on one, cuneiform on another, Hittite, Linear B. *A council chamber of kings.* He glimpsed something lustrous behind the seats, around the base of the chamber, as if the lower courses of masonry had been gilded. He panned his light sideways, to the wall nearest him, and stared in amazement.

Ingots. *Metal ingots.* There were hundreds of them, stacked to his height and higher, row upon row, surrounding the entire circular wall of the chamber. They were copper, dull green in his torchlight. And there were ingots of tin, absolutely distinctive, their silvery surface covered in a fine white corrosion dust. Each ingot was about a metre long, with arms at the corners like flayed oxhides, just as he had seen them on shipwrecks of the Bronze Age. Ingots being brought to the great palaces of the Aegean, copper from Cyprus, from the Levant, from the west. He stared at a tin ingot on top of the stack beside him. It had a stamp that he recognized. A stamp of the Cornovii, the prehistoric tribe inhabiting south-west Cornwall. So it was true. *The Trojans were importing tin from the Cassiterides, the British Isles.*

He stared back at the thrones, his mind in a turmoil. A council chamber of kings. Kings who had kept the peace. Kings who controlled the supply of metals for weapons, who doled it out among themselves, keeping the balance of power. Until one came along whose ambition, whose lust for power, could not be contained within these walls. One who had found a new, more deadly weapon, a better metal, harder, which made all of this stockpile of copper and tin redundant. *Agamemnon, king of kings.*

A light shone blindingly in his face, and someone grabbed his neck in a lock, twisting his arm behind his back. He had been expecting this, and did not resist. He was pushed and kicked forward, and then his neck was released and he was frisked. A voice came from the other side of the circle of stone seats, somewhere near the light. 'Dr Howard.'

'Where's my daughter?' Jack snarled. The man behind him yanked his head back, and Jack strained against him. 'I want to see my daughter.' The man got his hand over Jack's eyes, then pushed him forward roughly, releasing him. Jack blinked hard, and saw three figures against the stack of ingots on the back wall. One of them was Rebecca. A man was holding a pistol to her head. The figure on her other side stepped forward, put his torch on one of the seats with the beam angled upwards and stopped a few feet in front of Jack.

'Dr Howard.'

Jack stared at him. 'Professor Raitz.'

'Fortunately Rebecca had her passport on her and we were

able to fly to Istanbul first class, a distinguished architectural historian and his new girlfriend. I told her we would kill you and Costas if she didn't behave.'

'Why are you doing all this?'

'Because you have something I want.' His voice was suddenly shrill. 'Where is it?'

'You can keep the Goebbels impression for the bathroom mirror, Raitz. It really doesn't work.'

Raitz clicked his fingers, and Jack was suddenly winded, on his knees on the floor, unable to breathe. He gasped, then struggled up, staggering forward, feeling the throbbing pain in his back where the man behind had slammed into him. As he got up, he scanned the other side of the chamber, facing south-west. He could see another opening in the wall, with rubble in front. That must be it. The entrance to the tunnel. Costas should be there by now. Jack would stall for another few minutes. Then he had to take a gamble.

'Now. Again,' Raitz said, bringing his face close to Jack. 'Where is it?'

'Why do you want it, Raitz? Your own private collection?'

'For the Führermuseum,' Raitz said quietly.

Jack pretended to stifle a laugh. 'The Trojan swastika? The palladion? What does that have to do with the very dead little Austrian?'

'It is the key to the greatest hidden art treasures in the world. I will find them, and they will be the centrepiece of my museum, to perpetuate the memory and vision of the Führer for all time.'

'And your colleague? The one I spoke to on the phone?'

Raitz looked nonplussed for a moment. 'Of course. He has

his own interests. Family interests. Gold, antiquities, not art.'

'You and I need to talk about that.'

Raitz snapped his fingers again, and the man in the shadows beside Rebecca grabbed her arm and shoved the pistol closer. Raitz took out his own pistol from his overcoat pocket, a small Walther that he fumbled with and cocked. 'Now. You tell me or Rebecca dies.'

'You're getting better at this, Raitz.' Jack gestured back to the entrance. 'You didn't think I was going to come in here with it, did you? I needed to see that Rebecca was here. I've hidden it outside. I'll go and get it. It's in the black box, as we discovered it in the mine.'

Raitz snapped again. The man behind Jack grabbed him by the neck and pulled him roughly back. 'Get it,' Raitz said.

'By myself. This man stays in here.'

Raitz gestured impatiently. The man let go of Jack, and then moved around in front of him. He was another Russian, like the ones in the mine, a thug. Rebecca had said there were two. The second one was holding the pistol to her head. Jack had seen no others. He turned back towards the entrance, making a show of staggering, still being in pain. He reached the edge of the rubble and pulled out the black box, and then turned and went back, holding it in front of him, displaying the Nazi swastika emblem. As he walked slowly towards the centre of the chamber, he saw out of the corner of his eye something in the dark entrance to the right. *It was Costas.* Jack looked hard at Rebecca, who stared at him, then he nodded his head, almost imperceptibly. She lowered herself to the ground until she was squatting on her haunches, hands pressed against her ears, head bent over and eyes closed, and began sobbing, loudly. Raitz stepped back towards her, waving his pistol. 'Shut up, Rebecca.' She kept sobbing and wailing. 'Shut up!' he yelled.

At that moment Jack saw Costas' Beretta aimed out over the stack of ingots towards the man beside Rebecca. He would have a perfect head shot, with no risk of hitting her as long as she remained crouched, hidden from Costas' viewpoint. They just needed to divert the man's attention, to get him to take his aim away from Rebecca, even momentarily. Suddenly Costas bellowed, 'Hey! Where's Chechnya!' The two men and Raitz spun round, and the man beside Rebecca instinctively raised his pistol, aiming it into the darkness. There was a deafening crack from Costas' Beretta and the man's head disintegrated, leaving his body slumping over the ingots, his pistol falling from his hand. In the same instant Jack slammed backwards, sending the man behind him reeling. He fell forward, kicked open the box and took out the Webley, rolling over and aiming at the Russian's chest, low and right as Ben had said. He pulled the trigger and the revolver kicked up, the massive report echoing through the chamber. The man remained upright, staring, a dark patch spreading over the front of his shirt, the hole where the bullet had gone through his sternum clearly visible. Jack saw that he had a Spetsnaz tattoo on his wrist. The man suddenly dropped like a stone, leaving a spatter of blood all over the stack of ingots behind him.

Jack turned, and saw Raitz staring like a scared rabbit, the Walther dangling from his hand. In one lightning movement Rebecca kicked upwards, catching Raitz full in the crotch. He howled in pain, doubled over and dropped the Walther, which Rebecca snatched up and trained on him. Costas was already there, aiming the Beretta at Raitz's head. He rolled on the ground, groaning, and then slowly raised himself. Rebecca had come round beside Jack, who took the Walther and lowered the smoking Webley. He hugged her briefly, then pointed her to the entrance Costas had come in through, away from any further bullets. As she went towards it, Raitz raised himself up on his knees. 'Don't shoot. Please. *Please*.'

'Nobody aims a gun at my daughter,' Jack said coldly.

'I didn't. I swear I didn't. I never would have harmed her.'

'Well then, I think we might have to let him live, Costas.'

'Right-oh.' Costas kept the Beretta trained.

'Let me see,' Jack said. 'Attempted murder, extortion, kidnapping. On Turkish territory. That means a Turkish prison.'

'No,' Raitz whispered. 'Not that. I'd rather die.'

Costas levelled the Beretta at his eyes, holding it with two hands and sighting it. 'You'd rather die? Really? Have you got the guts to die?'

'No, please.' Raitz fell forward on his knees, sobbing. 'Don't shoot.'

Jack held the Webley ready. 'Better still. We're in a military zone. That means you come under the jurisdiction of the Turkish military. At least it'll save you the public humiliation of a trial by jury. You'll get a tribunal of Turkish officers. They're good men. I know plenty of them personally. But I don't need to call in any favours. They'll see that justice is done.'

'Just outside Diyarbakir, isn't it?' Costas said.

Jack nodded. 'In the desert on the way to the Armenian border. Just about the worst place in the world. A sweathole in summer, freezing in winter. Maximum-security military prison. Murderers, psychopaths, homosexual rapists, that kind of thing. No human rights there, because the inmates barely count as human. You go in there, you don't come out. Throw away the key. Simple as that.'

'We can do a deal,' Raitz said hoarsely, craning his head up, his eyes desperate. 'I've got original documents, maps. Treasure maps.'

'Der Agamemnon-Code?' Jack said.

'I know nothing about that.'

Costas waved his pistol. 'We may as well kill him, Jack. This is getting us nowhere. Rebecca, block your ears.'

'No!' Raitz begged. 'Please. I'll tell you. In a safe in my house. Under the floorboards in the cellar. At the bottom of the stairs.'

Jack kept aiming. 'Only the one document?'

'Only one with those words. But there are more. Many more. Photos. Maps to bunkers. A treasure trove. Just don't hand me over to the Turks. Please God. I can give you the key to untold riches. All the lost treasures of the Nazis.'

'You mean in the other safe in the study? Or the one behind the bookcase in your office in the Courtauld? Our security guys are pretty adept lock-breakers, wouldn't you say, Costas? Both safes empty now, I'm afraid.'

'*Scheisse*,' Raitz muttered, staring at the ground. '*Scheisse*.' He looked up at Jack again, suddenly defiant, tapping his head. 'In here. Much more in here. I'll do a deal with the Turks. Just like Schliemann did.'

'Schliemann didn't mess around with the Turks. They were the ones who were using him. Anyway, they won't believe you, without documentation. And they won't listen to you where you're going. Just another insane Westerner babbling away in solitary confinement in a hellhole Eastern prison.'

'For the rest of his life,' Costas said.

'Not a very long life, I would imagine, especially if they ever let him out of solitary and the other prisoners get their hands on him.'

'What can I do?' Raitz sobbed.

Jack put the Webley in his fleece pocket, took out a small notebook and pencil, walked over and knelt in front of Raitz. 'Here's the deal. You'll do time, but I can keep you out of that place. I can even put in a word for repatriation to a British prison. And you know how lenient judges are in Britain. You're still a young man. You could remake your career. Even argue that you were forced to do this against your will. A British court would probably believe you. You have lots of influential friends, former students and colleagues, politicians.' Jack pushed the notebook towards him. 'All you have to do is write down one name. The name of the person who's been controlling you.'

'He'll find me and kill me. Whatever it is he wants in that bunker is too precious to him. He's got more of these thugs. Russians, mostly, but they call themselves *Totenköpfe*. Ironic, isn't it? I'm the one with the Nazi background, not . . .'

'Not who?' Jack demanded.

'He'll kill me. They'll hunt me down.'

'I don't think that should be a concern where you're going.'

Raitz was still for a moment, then put his hand on the notebook. He let it rest there, then picked up the pencil and scrawled a name. Jack quickly took the pad, stared at it, thought hard for a moment, then pocketed it. 'Okay,' he said quietly. 'Why? You wanted your absurd Führermuseum. What on earth did a man like that want?'

'Gold,' Raitz said. 'Gold, and works of art. Everyone knows he has Marseille gangsters in his background. The press love it. He's used it to his advantage. A charming Algerian intellectual, with a bit of rogue in his genes. The truth is, that wasn't just in the past. He's secretly in charge of the family crime syndicate. No longer just small-time gangsters. One of the biggest in Europe. Worth hundreds, hundreds of millions.'

'So he was interested in all your leads? All the material on hidden art you'd collected?'

Raitz shook his head. 'No. Only the Agamemnon Code. Only that one bunker in the forest.'

'He was playing you,' Costas said.

'You've been a fool,' Jack said to Raitz angrily. 'A bloody fool, duped into going along with someone who had no interest in your cause, let alone antiquities or art.'

'You're wrong. He said—'

'I don't care what he said. You're a naïve academic, Raitz. You've forgotten what real people are like.'

'What do you mean?'

'Look around you,' Jack said. 'All this bronze, all this raw material for weapons, enough to equip all the armies of the ancient Aegean world: the Mycenaeans, the Trojans, every one of them. *Yet all of it redundant.* It's because a new metal had been forged, iron. And then think of today. People are always on the search for the new weapon. Or the weapon that may already have been devised and then been hidden away. Think of the underworld since the fall of the Soviet Union. First they were on the hunt for nuclear weapons, components for dirty bombs. Then, with the revelation of what the Russians had taken from Nazi Germany, the lost treasure of Priam, and all the revived interest over the past few years in hidden Nazi art, their ears pricked up. They'd forgotten about the Nazis, about what might still be hidden. About the dreadful weapons that probably still lie in those bunkers today.'

'I know nothing of weapons,' Raitz mumbled. 'This is nothing to do with me.'

Jack picked up the empty black box and tapped it. 'In 1945, a Luftwaffe officer took the Trojan palladion from the salt mine in Poland to the bunker near Belsen you know about. He was a fanatic. He was one of those who had been activated, to be there, poised ready to fulfil Hitler's final decree. Not the Nero Decree, the destruction of the Reich. No. The Agamemnon Code. *Armageddon*. There were others activated, too. We believe at least one of them was there, in the forest, waiting, because of what happened. The officer took the palladion into the bunker, but a few days later, while he was waiting for the final order, he was shot by British soldiers. Then the SS guards at the nearby camp took a girl into the bunker and raped her. She saw the palladion. It was her drawing of it that gave us the clue. We knew it was there all along, not in the salt mine. We knew that two officers, one British and one American, were told about it, and went to investigate. Nobody knows what happened to them. But it is possible that the other fanatic was there, waiting for the final activation signal from Berlin, and they died together in a fight. Whatever was in there that was so lethal is still there today.'

'But the palladion was the key to opening a storeroom of art,' Raitz said weakly.

Jack waved his hand dismissively. 'Is that the story Saumerre sold you? Why have a special key for that, some sacred symbol? No. It was the key to something completely different, much more sinister. I believe the palladion may have been partly meteoritic, according to an ancient Trojan myth about its origins. The reverse swastika itself is hardly a unique key, but there could have been a unique magnetic signature that made it the only way of opening the door.'

'The door to what?' Raitz said.

'We can only guess. The worst the Nazis could come up with. Not nuclear, which they were never close to achieving. Perhaps not chemical, which might be difficult to propagate widely without aircraft or missiles. That leaves biological. And that's the worst. Typhus. Plague. Look what happened to the world with the flu epidemic in 1918. That would have been fresh in the minds of the Nazi scientists. They might even have had access to diseased bodies. They certainly had access to plenty of live humans for experimentation, in that camp. They could have reawakened the Spanish influenza virus, and even mutated it. If that's still in the bunker, if it was released, it could kill hundreds of millions. *Hundreds of millions*. It could wipe out civilization as we know it. Is that part of your Nazi dream?'

'My God,' Raitz said. 'My God. *What have I done?*'

'What you can do,' Jack said, kneeling down in front of him, 'is help us. We need to know whether Saumerre was operating solely for his own business interests. Such a weapon could be worth millions. Billions. We need to know whether he is interested as a middleman, or whether there was any other motivation. Did he say anything, did you hear anything? If I believe you, that's another mark in your favour with the courts.'

Raitz looked pale, and put his hand to his forehead. His voice was shaky. 'I can't think of anything. Anything at all. We only ever spoke about it in the British Museum where we first met, where he passed me the code document, and then in that ghastly flat in London where they murdered the Dutchman. It was only ever family interest with him. The family business. Marseille mafia. It was just money.'

Costas nodded at him, still keeping the Beretta trained. 'Just out of curiosity. What's Saumerre's religion?'

'Saumerre? Muslim, of course. His grandfather was from Algeria. So what? There are millions of Muslims in Algeria, in France. And look at him. He's hardly a terrorist.'

'Who is?' Costas murmured.

'He did say something. When we parted at that flat.' Raitz stared at Jack, clearly thinking hard, then sank down and put his head in his hands. 'Oh my God. *Oh my God*. Why didn't I see?'

Jack reached over and lifted his head up. 'What?'

'I said I was doing this for the Führer. For the cause. For a museum, God help me. He said something in Arabic, about Allah, but then seemed apologetic, as if he'd let something slip. I thought it was odd, as he'd been so adamant about this being all to do with gold and antiquities and money. But I thought he was just repeating a familiar phrase. I remember it. It was *Jazaka Allahu Khairan*. May Allah reward us with good. A perfectly normal expression for a Muslim. He even said so, when he explained it. But maybe . . . my God. *My God.*'

Jack leaned over and took Raitz's chin in his hands. 'Listen to me, and listen well. If you breathe a word of this to anyone, anywhere, my people will know. You'll be getting that one-way ticket to Diyarbakir. Play your cards right, and I'll see what I can do for you.'

Jack nodded at Costas, who took the iPhone from his belt and pressed it. Seconds later Ben appeared at the entrance to the chamber flanked by two IMU security men with handguns drawn, and then a team of black-clad Turkish navy commandos with MP-5 sub-machine guns, who quickly filed into the chamber, training their weapons on Raitz and the two bodies, and then kicking the bodies. Jack recognized the officer in charge, did a thumbs-up at him and pointed to Raitz. The officer gestured, and two of his men dragged Raitz to his feet, handcuffed him behind his back, and then pushed him through the entrance and out of sight down the tunnel. They could hear the clatter of a helicopter somewhere close by. Rebecca had come running from her hiding place, and Jack took her in his arms and held her tight.

'I hope I never see him again,' Rebecca murmured.

'Are you all right? Did they touch you? Thank God you're here.'

Rebecca shook her head. 'Don't worry, Dad. I'm fine. What about you?'

One of the security team, a woman, passed them each a small water bottle, and they uncapped and drained them together, then clicked the bottles together. Jack smiled at her. 'I'm fine. A little tired.' He gestured at Ben and the security team. 'Bet they're itching to hear your story.'

Costas came up to them, and eyed Rebecca shrewdly. 'Nice kick. Ouch.'

'Ben taught me that.'

Jack nodded at Ben, who had joined them. 'Yeah, he's pretty good like that.'

Ben nodded, and looked intently at him. 'Got a result?'

Jack handed him the notebook. 'Got a result.'

'I'm on to it.' Ben tapped his BlackBerry, Googling the name. 'Saumerre. Keynote speaker at a European Union cultural affairs conference in Brussels today.' He looked at his watch. 'Should be on the podium in roughly forty-five minutes.'

'Okay. He's going to be on tenterhooks waiting for a result from here. I imagine Raitz would have been planning to call him about now. Get Raitz's cell phone and try the contact numbers. I want to be on the phone with Saumerre before he makes that speech.'

'What are you going to say to him?'

'I'm going to tell him that I know everything about his criminal activities. Enough to destroy his political career. That career is undoubtedly crucial to his, shall we say, business interests, as well as to the bigger picture that may lie behind all this. He won't want to jeopardize his status and influence, as that's worth a huge amount to him, to the organization he may represent.'

'Fill me in.'

'We need to check any affiliation he might have with extremist terrorism.'

Ben peered at him. 'Okay. Got you.'

'What's the latest on the bunker?'

'We've been overtime on that one. My people have scoured everything they can get their hands on that's not under the Official Secrets Act, and called in a few favours to see some things we shouldn't have. We knew the site of the camp was under a NATO airbase built fairly soon after the war. The construction workers came across a pit full of hundreds of skeletons, all shot. We now think we can pin the likely location of that sector of forest with the bunker to an area well within the military compound, actually beneath the runway tarmac. That's good news as far as we're concerned, Jack. Nobody's going to go burrowing around there and it's about as secure a site as you could get. It's still an active base, two Luftwaffe squadrons flying Tornados. The question is, how long will that last, with the Cold War standoff finished and so many bases being mothballed?'

'Have you told anyone in the military about the bunker yet?'

'You said to hang fire, and I've done that. It's your call. When they built the base, there was no ground-penetrating radar, but any survey today in advance of new building work might reveal it. The runways get resurfaced routinely but are pretty old underneath, and at some point they'll redo them if the base is kept running. There's probably no structural issue with the bunker under the runway, as it'll be buried very deep, but if you're right, we may need to think about whether our NATO pilots should be taxiing and landing with JDAMs and who knows what other munitions with something just beneath their runway that may contain a deadly biological weapon.'

'Okay. Good work. I'll give you my decision when we're out of here. Meanwhile, let's catch Saumerre on the phone.'

'I'm on to it.'

Rebecca waved at the other security people she knew, then detached herself from Jack and went down the passageway. Jack watched her stop and stare at the rubble wall, and then turn back to him. 'Dad. I forgot to say. That ring Maurice found here, the signet ring? It was George Hoar. A famous American senator who knew Schliemann.'

Jack knew he had seen it before. 'Of course. Hugh has Hoar's copy of Schliemann's *Mycenae*. The bookplate with the coat of arms in the front.'

Rebecca waved, then turned and spoke intently to the others, gesturing. Jack remembered Dillen's account from Hugh of Schliemann's foreman, and the men he had seen here that night in 1890. What was George Hoar doing here? Had Schliemann invited him to see this wonder he had begun to uncover? Jack remembered reading Hoar's speeches to the US Senate against imperialism. Had Schliemann wanted to tell others what he thought had happened here, others who might find hope in this chamber for avoiding war in the future?

He looked at Rebecca again, and then at Ben, who gestured back, smiling and pointing at Rebecca and doing a thumbs-up. Jack returned the gesture. She was in the best possible hands. He and Costas were now the only ones left in the chamber, discounting the two bodies. Jack took out the Webley, clicked it open, ejected the cartridges into his hand and dumped them in his fleece pocket. Then he closed the Webley and held it tight. *It was over. He could let go*. He walked towards the ancient bronze door, and suddenly began to shake uncontrollably. He squatted down, then stood up, leaning against the door, the

Webley still in his hand, bowing his head, trying to control it. Costas put a hand on his shoulder. Jack nodded at him, then stood upright, taking several deep breaths, and tried to relax. He swallowed hard. 'Two days can seem like a very long time.'

'We did it,' Costas said. 'You did what you said you'd do. You got Rebecca back.'

Jack high-fived Costas with one hand. 'Right on,' he said, wiping his eyes. *Right on.* He looked at the door he was holding, and then moved round to glance at the extraordinary symbol, the keyhole, visible from both sides.

'I was thinking about the swastika, the meaning, the associations,' Costas said. 'On one side, the clockwise swastika, you've got war, horror, the Nazis. On the other side, peace, the balance of power, if you're right about this place.'

Jack stared at it. 'The ancient Hittites had a saying. "I give you a tablet of peace; I give you a tablet of war." It's the same thing, offering the same tablet, different sides. We make the choice. One side, war. The other side, peace.'

'Unless you're up against Agamemnon with ten thousand arrows of iron, or Hitler and the Nazis.'

'Or a bunch of Russian thugs.'

'No choice there.'

'None at all.'

A team of Turkish naval ratings in overalls appeared with body bags and went past them into the chamber, quickly bagging the two bodies and carrying them out. Jack looked back at the extraordinary place Hiebermeyer had found, that Schliemann had found, thinking of the days ahead when this discovery would be splashed across world headlines. Hiebermeyer would take the cake, but Jack would be there alongside him once the shipwreck excavation was finished and he could reveal the splendours of the Shield of Achilles and the other discoveries. He looked around again. Had Schliemann truly dug this far, and seen this? Jack fervently hoped so, hoped that in the days before his death Schliemann had been vindicated, had found what he needed to prove he had been right. This place now would be put before the world as Jack imagined Schliemann would have planned, not simply as an astonishing discovery but also for its place in history, to show a time when men might have found a way to curb war. He looked around one final time, and sniffed. He could smell the blood in the chamber. He thought of it for a moment, of all that this meant. The smell of blood. *The smell of iron.* He shook his head. He looked at his fingernails, and realized that they still had the dark residue of blood in them from the Russian he had killed in the mine. At Troy, killing was never far away.

'I think . . .' he said to Costas, rubbing his stubble. 'I think I might take a trip to Paris. Look at some art, you know. It's been a while.'

'While you've got a Trojan War shipwreck to excavate? No way. You mean you plan never to let Rebecca out of your sight again, ever.'

'You can come too.'

'Me? The Louvre? Dad and Uncle Costas? Accidentally in Paris, just when Rebecca happens to be on a school trip there? *No way* Rebecca will allow that. Let Ben deal with security. Anyway . . .'

'Let me guess. You've got a submersible to fix. And Jeremy's waiting.'

'Uncanny mind-reading ability.'

'What do you expect? That's how I've saved your life so many times.'

'Huh? What? Let's just get that right. Who defused that bomb?'

'You didn't defuse it. You activated it.'

'And what about in there? Covering your back like that?'

Jack put his hand on Costas' shoulder. 'Yeah, yeah. What would I do without you?' He cracked a tired grin. 'I need to get under the sea again. Let's get out of here.'

Epilogue

Oświecim (Auschwitz), Poland

James Dillen got out of the taxi, paid the driver and watched the battered old car reverse and speed back the way it had come, belching exhaust into the narrow lane. He waited until the noise had gone, then turned, pulling up the collar of his coat, tucking the folder he was carrying under his arm and shoving his hands into his pockets. It felt cold, like the cold he had felt that morning five months ago when he and Rebecca had gone to visit Hugh in Bristol, only this time it was not tiredness that made him shiver, but the real bitterness of an early November morning, cold enough for snow.

He smeared his foot over the light hoar frost that covered the lane. The air itself seemed to have frozen, reducing visibility to a few hundred yards. He took a deep breath, feeling the sharpness in his lungs, and then exhaled forcibly.

He smelled burning, the lingering fumes of car exhaust. He reached out and put his hand on one of the trees that lined the lane, wanting to feel what life felt like in this place. *Place of the beeches*, they had called it. *Birkenau*. The bark felt tough and carapaced, yet also strangely yielding and soft. He leaned over, and smelled a mossy smell. Close up, he saw the colours of vegetation beneath the frost, deep browns, dark greens. He watched a leaf detach itself from a branch and fall, spinning slowly down, brushing his leg and coming to rest in the wetness where his foot had smeared the frost. He watched it settle, absorb the moisture, lose its colour, suddenly flat and immaterial.

He straightened up, discomfited. He had expected to be overwhelmed by this place, not absorbed in detail. Perhaps it was the detail that gave definition to the enormity that lay just beyond, in the mist. He looked through the trees and spotted the disused railway track, bisected by the path to the house. He left the lane and walked towards the track, then knelt alongside it, listening. There would always be trains running along this track, lines of boxcars, frozen in time. He wondered if those trees had been saplings back then, whether they held some imprint of what had passed this way: crammed-together faces in boxcar doors, anxious mothers and exhausted children, moments of sudden fear. He looked up to where he knew the railway line was heading. The track cut across the image like a great tear through a canvas, and for a moment he felt as if he were a crouched figure in a painting, anonymous, insignificant. He stood up. He had come here to see Hugh, and the girl. And he had come to tell the others the final reckoning on Troy, the words of the ancient poet that he and Hugh had so painstakingly translated in the weeks since Rebecca had been freed and the excavation had ended.

'James!' He looked over to the house, startled. A figure was hurrying towards him, wearing snow boots, a grey school greatcoat, a multicoloured scarf and an orange hat, her long dark hair streaming behind her. She was rubbing her hands together, and gave him a quick hug when she reached him. 'Come on inside. You must be freezing.'

'Is Hugh here yet?'

'Dad and I flew in with him to Warsaw yesterday.' Rebecca blew on her hands again. 'We've only been here about an hour. The couple who run this place are really nice. Hugh's not very well, you know. It was a bit of a shock seeing him away from his room. He's pretty frail.'

'I know.' Dillen paused. 'But before we go in. How did you work out that this was the place?'

Rebecca shoved her hands in her pockets. 'After we came back from Troy, Dad decided to see if we could find out what happened to her. To the girl with the harp. He's been really preoccupied with that awful bunker, did you know?'

'I know that NATO has agreed to an excavation, and meanwhile the airbase is on complete lockdown. I know there's great excitement about the works of art and antiquities that might be there, but huge trepidation about what else they might find. It's going to be the big story next year.'

'And Saumerre,' Rebecca said grimly. 'When Dad had his little chat with him, the arrangement was that Saumerre keeps away from us, and we won't expose him. Dad said he only spoke to him about underworld dealings, his family business, and in no way hinted that we suspected any fundamentalist terrorist connection. The media already knows about Saumerre's family background, and if any of this stuff about stolen art and antiquities and the odd murder and kidnapping leaked out, then he could try to shrug it off as a media fantasy, meanwhile doubly securing himself against any personal implication. But if the idea of a fundamentalist backdrop leaks out, that's another story.'

'That's why Raitz's trial is so important.'

Rebecca nodded. 'Dad's hoping it can be stalled at least until the bunker excavation is finished. He thinks Raitz is a weakling and will spill the beans about Saumerre in his trial, even after what Dad said to him. If that happens, then Saumerre will disappear and become another Osama bin Laden. The security services don't want that. He has to be kept in play as long as possible, until his organization can be infiltrated. But Dad's worried that even before his trial, Raitz will break and try to plea-bargain. He's got influential friends in London, lawyers, politicians, who will be encouraging him to do this, and meanwhile painting his detention as a human rights issue. That's why the Turks are going to want to hold the trial pretty soon. They're only putting it off because of all the strings we've pulled. The security services know what's going on and why, but as far as public perception goes, it looks bad. Eminent architectural historian held for months without trial by the Turkish military for trespassing on an archaeological site. That's what it looks like.'

'Sounds almost as if a stray round should have got Raitz during your little showdown.'

'Dad says keeping him alive was essential to the game that's being played now, as Raitz is basically taking the fall for what's happened. But it's a pressure cooker and it's going to blow. Realizing that was what made Dad push for the bunker excavation. If we can find and secure whatever's in there, then at least that's one ingredient out of the equation.'

'Has Jack told Hugh about the excavation?'

'He's really torn about whether to tell him – because of Peter, how he might have died, that his body might still be in there. Anyway, Dad really wanted us to do this search for the girl. He said he'd spoken to you about it, and you'd decided we should do it straightaway, for Hugh's sake. So we started off at the Imperial War Museum in London, where the Belsen material is archived. Eventually we found reference to a satellite camp. Some sign-off forms for supplies by a doctor who'd gone straight out there from medical school at Guy's Hospital, and a tally form of new arrivals at the hospital the Red Cross set up at Belsen. The date was right. First of all we tried to find the doctor, but after the war he didn't return to finish his degree and there was no record of him. Then came the real scoop. A few years ago, one of the Red Cross nurses at Belsen recorded her experiences for an audio presentation at the museum, and we found her. She remembered another nurse, a friend of hers, who'd spent her first day out there at this other camp, the satellite camp. Next stop for us, Australia.'

'*Australia*.'

Rebecca nodded. 'The two women had kept up a correspondence. We found her in a nursing home in Brisbane. A lovely lady, Helen, very no-nonsense. But she wept so much when we spoke. It was like Hugh. It was the first time she'd really talked to anyone about it. She'd been in charge of the children at that camp. She remembered the girl with the harp, and the drawing. She was the one who gave it to Hugh when the SAS patrol came into the camp.'

'So she knew what had happened to the girl?'

Rebecca paused, staring at the railway line. 'Apparently the girl never spoke, but others who'd been at Auschwitz told the nurse the story. The girl and her parents were brought to the new Auschwitz camp at Birkenau in a cattle car in 1942, along this very line.' She faltered, and shivered. 'Her parents were immediately gassed, but she survived because they told the SS at the railhead that she was a talented musician. The SS put her in the camp orchestra, which played jazz and dance songs to the arriving Jews. Then they took her to the brothel. In early 1945 she was put on the march west, ending up in the camp near Belsen. Shortly before liberation, the SS camp leader, a woman, found out what the girl had been at Auschwitz and paraded her in front of the others, like an animal. Apparently, she screamed at the girl, *I will personally see that you suffer. Ich werde persönlich dafür sorgen, dass Sie leiden.* Helen said she always remembered being told that. It was only a few days before the liberation, and the SS knew the writing was on the wall, yet that woman could still be so cruel. Helen was told that they dragged the girl off into the forest, where she was raped by the guards in that bunker. She was left for dead but escaped into the forest, then went back into the camp when she saw the SAS patrol arrive. She was seventeen years old at liberation.'

'Have you told any of this to Hugh?'

Rebecca shook her head. 'Dad said Hugh would have a good enough idea. And we didn't want to upset him.'

'So the nurse in Australia, Helen, sent you here?'

Rebecca nodded. 'She'd worked here herself, in the 1950s. This is the last of these special houses, within sight of the Auschwitz-Birkenau camp. It's a closely guarded secret. There are benefactors, Jewish organizations, others. They still call them the children, even seventy years on. They're the ones who could never be rehabilitated. It's as if their lives ended that moment on the railhead, and the only chance of happiness is to bring them back here, because this was the last place before the train drew up at that ramp.'

'Hugh said that, when he showed us the drawing in Bristol. He'd spoken to the nurse.'

Rebecca nodded. 'She remembered him. That's why she agreed to tell us about this place. At first she wouldn't, but then Dad went back to her alone, flew all the way to Australia to talk to her again. She said it was for Hugh.'

'Okay. Let's go inside,' Dillen said.

Rebecca mounted the steps, then turned and held Dillen's arm. 'You said you knew? When I told you I thought Hugh wasn't well.'

Dillen paused for a moment, then looked at her. He took her hand in his, and held it. 'The day we visited Hugh, just before you were kidnapped, when I went back to Bristol to set him up with the translation, I went with him to the hospital. He wanted me to know. He'd known for some time.'

Rebecca was crying. 'I thought so,' she said. 'I thought there was something wrong when Dad and I picked him up. I just knew it. So Dad knew, too?'

'He didn't want to upset you. He thinks you've had enough already.'

Rebecca took off her glove and wiped her eyes. 'So that's what he went back to tell Helen in Australia. That Hugh was dying.'

'We don't know that. For sure.'

'He's ninety-two.'

'Come on.' Dillen took Rebecca in his arms, and gave her a hug. 'Chin up, as Hugh used to say.'

Rebecca sniffed, nodded and opened the screen door and then the heavier wooden door behind. It was very warm, and Dillen quickly shut the door behind him. His glasses steamed up and he took them off to wipe them. There was a fire in the room to the right, a warm orange glow, and at the end of the stone-flagged floor ahead he could see a kitchen with someone moving around, a kettle on the boil. Rebecca gestured to a doorway to the left. 'Keep your jacket on,' she said. Dillen followed her into a dining room with a partition wall and an open veranda. On the patio beyond he could see several rocking chairs facing a garden, partly obscured in the mist.

Jack was there, standing quietly at the entrance to the veranda, arms folded, looking out. He turned as he heard them, then put his finger to his lips and beckoned them over. Rebecca let Dillen go first. He nodded at Jack, and then peered round the open door on to the patio. Hugh was sitting outside in a wicker chair, swathed in a blanket, facing away from them. His thick white hair was carefully combed back. Dillen looked beyond, where Hugh was facing. The garden was long, narrow, shrouded in mist, enclosed on either side by high hedgerows. It was facing in the same direction as the railway line, which was visible through a break in the hedge to the left.

Dillen peered down the garden, straining his eyes for what he knew must be there.

Then he saw her.

She was sitting like Hugh with her back to them, bundled up in a thick coat and scarf. He could tell it was a woman, from her shape, from the long hair that tumbled down her back beneath her scarf, wavy and thick. It was white, but it could have been fair. He knew it was an old woman, but it could have been a girl. The image came in and out of view in the mist, sometimes sharply delineated, sometimes barely visible. Suddenly he saw her very clearly. She was sitting behind a musical instrument, large, unmistakable.

The girl with the harp.

Dillen couldn't see Hugh's face, or hers. He remembered his vision at the railway line, the image of himself crouched beside it. Here, it was two figures, but the image was the same, torn through by the line of the hedgerow, with the railway track beyond. He shivered, and took a step back. His breath crystallized, but he saw barely any breath in front of Hugh. He looked at Hugh's hands. They were white-knuckled, clutching at the arms of the chair, trembling.

There was a whinny and a stomp, and a white horse appeared, its head peering over the hedge, shaking its long mane, and then it snorted and cantered off out of sight. It had been the only sound he had heard outside, and it was startling. Jack put his hand on Dillen's shoulder, and then reached over and pulled the door to, leaving it slightly ajar. There was a sound of tinkling, and Dillen turned to see a woman place a tray of drinks and biscuits on the table. She was small, elderly, and was followed by a man of similar appearance. Dillen stepped forward and shook hands with them. The woman spoke English with an east European accent. 'Welcome to our home. Can I offer you tea? Coffee?'

'Thank you. Tea, please.' Dillen gestured to the patio. 'What about Hugh?'

'He's already had his hot chocolate,' Rebecca said, smiling sadly. 'Said it was the best he'd had since the war.'

'Did you tell him that she was here?'

'You can't keep anything from Hugh,' Jack said quietly, smiling. 'Former intelligence officer, you know. Had to have the full operational briefing before we flew out. But it's been a very big thing for him. He's been like that since we sat him out there half an hour ago.'

'And the . . . girl?' Dillen said. 'How long has she been there?'

'Every day,' the Polish man said. 'Every day, for as long as we have cared for her. She is the last of the children. Now that winter is drawing in, we'll bring her back in before too long. She has a hot-water bottle. She's warm.'

'Does she ever play?' Dillen asked. 'I mean, the harp?'

'We think she plays for her parents, in her mind, all the time. We think they loved to hear her play. We never hear it, but sometimes when you get close you can hear her humming quietly to herself, and you can see her fingers playing, nearly touching the strings. Children's songs, learning songs. The horse can hear it too, we're sure. It's got a beautiful mane, don't you think? It rises in the wind like the waves on the sea. We think she must have had a horse as a child. That horse is descended from the white horse that the camp commandant, Rudolf Hoess, liked to ride, when he played with his own children by the river here.'

'How . . .' Rebecca said, her voice little more than a whisper. 'How could he do that?'

The woman shook her head, and continued organizing the tray. Dillen thought of what Rebecca had just said. Apollodorus of Rhodes knew it. *There is no mighty bulwark against evil war.* Once total war was unleashed, once Troy had fallen, it was there always, tempting, beckoning. All that was left to hold it back was the will of the individual. And maybe Schliemann had known. It may have been his fervent hope. *Individuals have the power to shape history.*

Dillen opened his folder and took out a few sheets of paper. 'I've brought the *Ilioupersis*, the fall of Troy. It's a hundred and twenty-six lines, the entire text that Jeremy and Maria found in the lost library at Herculaneum,' he said. 'I want to read it to you.'

'Have you kept the Greek metre?' Jack asked.

Dillen shook his head. 'It wasn't written that way. It retains some of the imagery, the familiar epithets of the *Iliad*, but it's in a kind of free verse. Hugh and I found it disconcerting, at first. How could this be Homer, if it wasn't written in his famous iambic pentameter? But then we realized why. The pentameter of the *Iliad* was suited to the heroic cycle, to the story of men powerless to shape their fate, acting on a stage created by the gods, relentless, repetitive. And it was suited to memorization, to the beat of the bard, to the accompaniment of the lyre. But the *Ilioupersis* is different. The heroes are all dead. The gods are gone. Man is ascendant.'

'You mean the course of the story is no longer predictable, no longer familiar to the audience, time-honoured,' Jack murmured.

Dillen nodded. 'In the *Ilioupersis*, the poet describes what he sees, not a cycle according to some bardic formula. The *Ilioupersis* is shorn of ornament. For Homer, finishing the story of Troy that way, showing what he actually saw, was his poetic responsibility, just as it was three thousand years later for the poets of the First World War, for Graves and Sassoon and Owen and the others. The bardic tradition of the *Iliad* was for fireside stories of heroes, of clashes and contest, of strutting and shouting. Maybe Homer was afraid of this final truth he had written in the *Ilioupersis*, and put it away. Maybe his world crumbled around him as he watched and wrote, and the text was lost in the darkness at the end of the age of heroes.'

There was a low rushing sound outside, something flying overhead out of sight in the mist, the beating of wings. Jack peered out. 'We heard that before you came, and I asked our host. It's migrating birds, flying south from the Baltic towards Africa. Blackbirds, ravens, geese. It's a strange coincidence, but from here they fly south-east to Gallipoli, over the Dardanelles and into Asia. In a day or two's time, those birds will fly over Troy.'

Dillen listened, but they had gone. It was as if the birds were following a fault line, not a geographical fault but a rent in the fabric of civilization, between places that had become a terrifying crucible of death. He wondered whether Schliemann had looked up at Troy and seen those birds too, black ravens flying south, whether they had somehow brought to him a vision from the future, something so terrible it drove him to try to alter the course of history.

'So,' Rebecca said, cocking an eye at Dillen. 'You said

Homer actually *watched* the fall of Troy. Do you really think the *Ilioupersis* is an eyewitness account?'

'The evidence is all there, in the radiocarbon analysis of the papyrus, the textual analysis, the early form of the alphabet. If Troy fell in 1200 BC, this couldn't be much later than that.'

'You're not really answering my question.'

'Tell me what you think after I've read it out. It's for you to judge.'

'Archaeology can't tell the whole story of Troy, can it?'

Jack smiled. 'The pottery only sings if you know how to make it sing.'

'The immortal bard,' Rebecca murmured. 'That's what Alexander Pope called Homer.' She reached into her pocket and took out the copy of Pope's *Iliad* that Dillen had given her. She opened it, and Dillen saw the inscription. *To Hugh, with love and affection from Peter. Remembering our summer at Mycenae, 1938.* Rebecca looked towards Hugh, then suddenly cocked her head, listening. 'I think I can hear music. From the garden.' She listened again. '*The harp.*' Dillen craned his neck. All he could hear was an echo of beating wings. 'Don't go to Hugh yet,' she said. 'In case he can hear it too.'

'What music is it?' Jack said.

Rebecca turned to him, her face flushed. 'I thought I heard James play it, on his lyre at Troy.' She turned to Dillen. 'It was that last evening, when you went back up to your trench and thought nobody else was listening. I was on the path in Schliemann's trench, coming up to see you. It was a children's song. It was beautiful.'

'We should get cracking with the text,' Jack said. 'And Hugh shouldn't be out there much longer.'

Dillen smiled at Rebecca, then stepped forward to the doorway. Hugh was motionless, facing ahead. Dillen looked for the girl with the harp, barely seeing her through a shroud of mist, in utter stillness. It was as if they all were caught in the moment the girl was in. Then he saw flakes of snow falling, like ash. He remembered what else he had brought with him, and reached into his pocket, taking out the piece of pottery, black, crude, like a charred fragment, that he had taken from the ancient pyre in his excavation trench at Troy. He glanced at Jack. *The pottery will sing.* He put it to his nose and inhaled deeply, smelling the fires of Troy. In his mind's eye he saw another figure, sitting with a lyre on a rocky ridge above the battleground, watching the war-bent men of Mycenae surge forward, feeling the ground shake as the sceptre of their mighty king came crashing down. *Homer. Agamemnon.*

He saw Hugh slowly raise his right forearm, extend his finger like a pistol, and point it forward. Dillen knew that gesture, from the classroom all those years before. It meant *go for it*. He took a deep breath, then listened through the stillness, straining to hear the music that Rebecca had heard.

He looked down at the lines of ancient verse. *It was all true*. Homer had been there, had watched the fall of Troy. In the tenth year Agamemnon had stormed and raged, had crashed down his mighty sceptre, and his men had rained down a new horror, arrows of iron. The Trojan Horse had been a ship driven by the howling blackness of the sea against the walls of Troy, to disgorge Agamemnon's iron-girt warriors to do their worst. And Helen of Troy was no woman, but a flaming pyre, a beacon that lit up the night sky, a fire that he himself had touched, had smelled.

Like the Turkish boy who had watched Schliemann and Sophia almost three thousand years later, Homer had watched Agamemnon steal down a passageway under Troy, had seen him shut for ever the great bronze doors of a chamber where once kings had met to keep hateful war at bay, to keep down the beast inside the man that was now unleashed in Agamemnon himself, tempted by new and yet more deadly weapons.

The age of bronze had become the age of iron. The age of heroes had become the age of men.

Dillen lifted the paper and began to read.

Author's Note

I first visited Troy as an archaeology student in 1984, when the custodian allowed me to sleep under the eaves of the old excavation house next to the site. That night I wandered alone among the ruins, and knelt at the spot where Heinrich Schliemann uncovered the fabulous 'Treasure of Priam' in 1873. When I was there it had been almost half a century since the last excavations, and to visit Troy was to enter the world of Schliemann, to see the site as I imagined he had seen it for the last time in 1890 shortly before his death. I felt the same when I visited the site again while writing this novel, to view the results of renewed excavations: Schliemann's personality remains embedded in Troy like another layer in the archaeology. Without Schliemann, there might have been no 'Troy' in the popular imagination; it was his unique vision, his belief in the truth of the Trojan War and in Homer, that gives the ruins such power today.

Schliemann again followed ancient sources when he went to Greece to excavate the Bronze Age citadel of Mycenae, stronghold of Agamemnon in Homer's *Iliad*. The second century AD travel writer Pausanias wrote that Agamemnon had been buried inside the walls, and just within the massive stone ramparts Schliemann found the famous 'grave circle' with its shaft graves, containing a treasure that exceeded even his finds at Troy. Unlike the 'Treasure of Priam', which proved to be from the third millennium BC, centuries older than the likely date of the Trojan War – about 1200 BC – there was little doubt in Schliemann's mind that the treasures from the shaft graves were late Bronze Age, dating to the likely time of Agamemnon.

The excavations in 1876 were supervised on behalf of the Greek Government by Panagiotis Stamatakis, who was in frequent conflict with Schliemann over his methods. Schliemann's book *Mycenae* (1878) conveys his excitement: he found a rock-cut grave, the first 'sepulchre', but was forced by heavy rain to abandon it without – he claims – reaching the burials, only returning to it several weeks later after having uncovered other shaft graves and a huge wealth of gold, confirming that he had indeed found the tombs of royalty. In late November he reached the bottom of the first grave and found the famous 'Mask of Agamemnon', lifting it and claiming to see a skull which crumbled away on exposure to air. In the same shaft were two other bodies, one bizarrely deformed. Schliemann telegrammed the King of Greece to announce the discovery, later rendered in perhaps the most thrilling catch-phrase in the annals of archaeology: 'Today I gazed upon the face of Agamemnon.'

Whether or not Schliemann dug secretly at Mycenae is unknown. The fictional account in the Prologue draws inspiration from Schliemann's own account of excavating the Treasure of Priam at Troy three years earlier, when he claimed he saw gold, dismissed the workers and dug out the treasure himself, his wife Sophia by his side (*Troy and its Remains*, 1875). Schliemann felt compelled to defend himself against claims that he made a 'traffic' of treasures (*Mycenae*, p. 66). There is little doubt that he embellished aspects of his accounts, and that his excavation techniques sometimes did not meet the standards of the time. Schliemann's own story mirrors the uncertainties and fascination of Troy itself. Like the flawed ancient heroes he worshipped, like Agamemnon himself, Schliemann is best seen as he saw those heroes, as a character shrouded in myth but bedded in a brilliant reality, one that shines through from those extraordinary days of discovery in the 1870s when his vision entranced the world.

The present-day excavations at Troy in this novel are fictitious and unrelated to the renewed programme of investigations carried out at Troy since the 1980s. Those investigations have shed remarkable new light on Troy and its environs, and suggest how much remains to be discovered. The Bronze Age beachline in the Plain of Troy has been conjectured, as well as the likely location of the harbour for sailing ships at Beşik Bay, on the Aegean coast opposite the island of Tenedos (Bozcaada). The overlapping shipwrecks in this novel are fictional, but are based on my experiences diving on shipwrecks in the Aegean ranging in date from the Bronze

Age to the twentieth century. The shell-first construction technique of the galley is seen in a late Bronze Age merchantman excavated off south-west Turkey, and in Egyptian boats. The 1915 wreck is based on the famous Turkish minelayer *Nusret*, a full-scale replica of which can be seen at the Çanakkale naval museum. Unexploded mines and other ordnance from the 1915 Gallipoli campaign still litter the sea bed in the Dardanelles and have frequently been destroyed by Turkish navy disposal teams.

At Troy, I have imagined the fictional house excavation taking place close to the northern wall of the late Bronze Age citadel where structures may remain buried. The features of the house are based on other late Bronze Age buildings at Troy, including the sloping walls. Photographs of these structures can be seen on my website www.davidgibbins.com. The remains of the beacon pyre are fictional, though there is much destruction debris and evidence of burning. The wall-painting of the lyre-player is inspired by an actual fresco of a lyre-player found at the Mycenaean palace of Pylos in Greece, though without an inscription; as yet no inscription has been found to suggest a date for Homer as early as the late Bronze Age.

The passageway and chamber beneath Troy in this novel are also fictional. However, an extraordinary discovery in the 1990s was a water chamber and a complex of tunnels, totalling about 160 metres in length, beyond the south-western edge of the citadel. The idea of a large round chamber derives from the 'beehive' or 'tholos' tombs of the Aegean Bronze Age, the most spectacular of which is the structure at Mycenae that Schliemann dubbed the 'Treasury of Atreus'. My idea that structures such as these may have been used as arsenals is consistent with the highly centralized control over bronze-working evidenced in the Mycenaean Linear B archives, and the known example of a strongroom used to store ingots in the Minoan palace of Zakros on Crete.

Bronze arrowheads have been found at Troy, and the Mycenaean arrowheads described in chapter 3 can be seen in the British Museum. Iron-making spread across Anatolia and the Aegean in the final quarter of the second millennium BC, first producing high-status blades and eventually spearheads and arrowheads. The spread has been thought of as a slow process because of the expertise needed, but a perspicacious ruler could have seen the potential and seized on the technology to gain ascendancy in a long-standing conflict, potentially tipping the balance in a siege such as that described by Homer at Troy.

The story of the Trojan Horse does not appear in the *Iliad*, and is only mentioned three times in the *Odyssey*, in such a way that the reader was clearly expected to be familiar with it. The story that has come down to us is traditionally ascribed to the *Ilioupersis* – the 'Fall of Troy' – by Arctinus, thought by some to have been a pupil of Homer. Only a few lines of that *Ilioupersis* survive among the so-called 'Trojan cycle' of epic fragments, though it is possible that the Roman poet Virgil had access to more when he created Book 2 of the *Aeneid* – the account of the Fall of Troy that is the main basis for the story of the Trojan Horse in modern imagination, despite being written over a thousand years after the events it purports to describe. The fictional *Ilioupersis* in this novel fills the gap in

Homer's work; the fictional context of its discovery, a buried library at Herculaneum, forms part of my novel *The Last Gospel*. The idea that the horse should be understood less literally intrigued Homeric scholars in the late nineteenth and early twentieth century, including the possibility that it was a siege-tower or a ship, or an allegorical manifestation of Poseidon, horse-god as well as god of earthquakes and the sea; as we understand better the natural cataclysm that may have accompanied the Fall of Troy, these ideas may acquire renewed currency.

In ancient tradition the Trojan *palladion* (Latin *palladium*) was a small wooden statue of the god Pallas, equated by the Greeks with the goddess Athene. It was supposedly rescued from Troy and kept in the Temple of Vesta in Rome, and then removed to Constantinople by the emperor Constantine the Great and buried under his column there. The story is full of uncertainty; some in antiquity believed the palladion remained concealed at Troy and was only discovered there in the first century BC (Appian, *Mithridates* 53, following Servius). The idea that there were two palladions, a 'public' palladion and something hidden, derives from an account by Dionysius of Halicarnassos, writing in the first century BC: 'Arctinus says that a single palladion was given by Zeus to Dardanos, and that this remained in Ilion (Troy) while the city was being taken, concealed in an inner sanctum; an exact replica had been made of it and placed in a public area to deceive any who had designs on it, and it was this that the Achaeans (Greeks) schemed against and took' (*Roman Antiquities* 1.69.3, trans M.L. West in *Greek Epic Fragments*, Harvard University Press 2003, 151). The tradition that

Dardanos – the legendary founder of Troy – received the palladion from Zeus, that it had thus 'fallen from heaven', has led to the fascinating theory that the original palladion was meteoritic, consistent with the veneration of meteorites by other early cultures.

The shape that such an object could have taken, worked perhaps by early metallurgists into a powerful symbol, is a matter for conjecture. At Troy, Schliemann discovered many pottery items decorated with incised swastikas, a symbol well-known from India where it was seen as auspicious or generative – the Sanskrit word *swastika* means 'to be well'. The Troy finds were among the oldest swastikas known, and fuelled an association between these symbols and the theory of an 'Aryan' race which came to obsess German nationalists. On the Trojan pottery, both the right-facing swastika and the left-facing version – known in Sanskrit as the *sauwastika* – are seen, with neither clearly more prevalent. However, the most extraordinary find of a swastika from Troy, incised on the vulva of a female idol, is left-facing, and left-facing swastikas can be seen on the wrought-iron gates of Schliemann's house in Athens, among other emblems derived from Troy. And Schliemann did not only find them at Troy: digging into the first sepulchre at Mycenae, in the same grave where he was to find the Mask of Agamemnon, he discovered several small golden disks decorated with the reverse swastika – just as he had seen on pottery at Troy (*Mycenae*, p. 152). The swastika is visible in reverse through Nazi flags, but it was the right-facing version that had become the symbol of Nazi Germany by the early 1930s.

★

The Nazi camp in this novel is fictional, as are all the characters portrayed therein. However, the details are based closely on descriptions and photographs of the much larger camp at Bergen-Belsen in the immediate aftermath of its liberation by British troops on 15 April 1945. I have not intentionally used the words of eyewitnesses, though I have tried to convey the language of British soldiers and medical staff at the time. Of huge importance has been the Imperial War Museum, London, for its archive of Belsen and other Holocaust material, and for publications that continue to provide insights, for example into the emergency medical provisions in the first days after liberation and the special care of children. The fictional experiences of the 'girl with the harp' draw on actual accounts, including selection at Auschwitz to join the camp orchestra. The archives allow one to move from the sheer enormity of the Holocaust to the individual, not only the survivors and liberators but also the perpetrators. Among the shocking revelations in 1945 at Belsen was the role of the female SS auxiliaries. Numbers of SS guards were shot by a British SAS patrol that entered Belsen shortly before liberation, and in the days that followed British troops killed others who tried to escape. Three of the female guards as well as the camp commandant and six others were sentenced to death at the Belsen trial and hanged on 13 December 1945.

The camp at Belsen was liberated by elements of the British 11th Armoured Division, VIII Corps, 2nd Army, who with Canadian 1st Army formed the left hook of the Allied advance into Germany. In February 1945 the British and Canadians fought their last major battle in and around the Reichswald

Forest, experiencing conditions comparable to the American battles in the Hürtgen Forest over the previous months. The casualty toll of these battles is the backdrop to the insistence in my novel that a battle be avoided in the fictional forest beside the camp, at all costs. Even in April 1945 there were pockets of German resistance that were able to stall the Allied advance for days, not only remnant *Waffen-SS* and *Wehrmacht* but also fresh units such as the *2nd Marine-Infanterie-Division* (remustered *Kriegsmarine* sailors) as well as *Hitler-Jugend* and the *Volkssturm*, the boys and old men who were Hitler's last reserve. German officers interviewed after the war were derisive of the slow pace of the Allied advance along a wide front, and felt the war could have been won months earlier using spearhead 'Blitzkrieg' tactics similar to those the Germans had used in 1940. There is little doubt that one factor behind Allied decision-making was the need to discover Nazi scientific secrets and technology before it was destroyed, or used against them. The activities of covert units such as 30 AU – 30 Commando Assault (later 'Advance') Unit, the brainchild of Commander Ian Fleming, author of the James Bond novels – are still shrouded in secrecy, and there can be no certainty how successful the Allies were in revealing the Nazis' most deadly secrets, particularly biological and chemical weapons.

Among these units the 'Monuments, Fine Arts and Archives' men have been the subject of much interest, not least because their work highlights treasures stolen by the Nazis that remain missing. Among the most extraordinary discoveries in 1945 were caches of art treasures stored in salt mines at Merkers in Germany and Altaussee in Austria, the latter rigged by the local Nazi *Gauleiter* with 500-kilogram bombs – a particularly fanatical interpretation of Hitler's so-called 'Nero Decree', the order for the destruction of the infrastructure of the Reich. These discoveries inspired my idea that the famous Wieliczka salt mine in Poland could have been used for similar purposes, especially as it is known that one of the deep chambers was converted by the Nazis to an aircraft engine assembly facility employing slave labour. The underwater tunnels beyond the accessible mine in this novel are fictitious, but based on my own experiences diving in submerged mineshafts.

One of the greatest lost masterpieces remains Raphael's *Portrait of a Young Man*, stolen by the Nazis from the Czartoryski Museum in Krakow. Schliemann's 'Treasure of Priam', given by him to the Imperial Museum, Berlin, was stored during the war in the *Zoo Flakturm*, a vast concrete bunker built on the site of Berlin Zoo. The treasure disappeared in 1945 and was thought lost, but re-emerged in 1993 in the Pushkin Museum in Moscow. The possibility remains that other artefacts may have been secretly despatched by Schliemann for safekeeping in Germany or elsewhere, and that these may one day be discovered along with other treasures stolen by the Nazis.

An inspiration for the fictional meeting of the three statesmen in 1890 at Troy was my acquisition of a copy of Schliemann's book *Mycenae* originally from the library of Senator George Frisbie Hoar (1826–1904), one of the great American politicians and men of letters of the nineteenth century, as well as an ardent antiquarian. In his autobiography Hoar describes visiting England and the House of Commons, where he admired the oratory of the Prime Minister, William Ewart Gladstone (1809–1898). Friendship with Gladstone was a factor in Schliemann's fame; Gladstone arranged for Schliemann to speak at the Society of Antiquaries in London, and wrote the long preface to his book *Mycenae*. As well as his literary passion for Homer, Gladstone had a particular fascination with early metallurgy and discoursed with Schliemann on the subject. He was solicitous of Schliemann's health, and Schliemann himself eventually seemed to acknowledge his own mortality in his final letter to another supporter, the German Chancellor Otto von Bismarck (1815–1898). Bismarck had united Germany but would have been concerned at the new significance of the swastika, and the dark forces of nationalism it was beginning to represent; his famous premonition that the next European war would be sparked by an incident in the Balkans proved horrifyingly correct. These were men who saw archaeology through the prism of the nineteenth-century 'march of progress', for whom learning from the past was more than just a cliché. I have imagined them fearful of the future, but sharing with Schliemann a self-confidence and idealism that could have allowed them to stand together one night and imagine how they might prevent a repeat of 'the first hideous crime of civilized man', the Fall of Troy.

The quote at the beginning of the book is based on a clay tablet (RS 34.165) found at Ugarit in Syria, detailing the lead-up to a battle between the Hittites and the Assyrians in the late thirteenth century BC; the lower quote is from Alexander

Pope's *The Iliad of Homer* (London, 1806). The poems by W.H. Auden mentioned in the novel are in *The Shield of Achilles* (London, Faber & Faber, 1955). In chapter 18, George Hoar's declamation on war foreshadows his speech in the US Senate in 1902, arguing against war in the Philippines (Jennings, B.W. and Halsey, F.W., eds, *The World's Famous Orations. America III (1861–1905)*, New York, 1906). The cover illustration is based on the Mask of Agamemnon from Mycenae, now on display in the National Archaeological Museum at Athens. The illustrations in the text are a fourth century BC silver coin of the Greek island of Ios, legendary birthplace of Homer, showing the poet and the Greek letters OMEROU; a reverse swastika based on the decorations on Schliemann's house in Athens; and the bookplate of George Hoar in his copy of Schliemann's *Mycenae*. Other images of sites and artefacts in this novel, including a tour of Troy, Dillen's blackened potsherd, the books by Schliemann and Pope, shipwreck photographs and Jack's Webley revolver, are found on my website www.davidgibbins.com.

David Gibbins

The Tiger Warrior

The past may be buried. But it certainly isn't dead.

India. 1879. Lieutenant John Howard witnesses something so unspeakable it changes him for ever. His subsequent disappearance is never solved.

Egypt. Present day. Marine archaeologist Jack Howard makes an astonishing discovery on a deep-sea dive.

What's the connection?

Jack Howard doesn't know yet. But he's about to find out.

Jack's perilous journey takes him from the crumbling tombs of Ancient China and the Roman Empire, through India's vast jungles to the hostile terrain of Afghanistan.

This isn't just a treasure hunt; it's a desperate search for the truth. A truth that will unlock the mystery of Jack's great-great-grandfather's disappearance. A truth so compelling Jack's pursuit is almost unstoppable. *Almost*. A formidable enemy from Jack's past has appeared in his present, and this enemy will stop at nothing to protect its own earth-shattering secret.

Let the race begin.

David Gibbins masterfully fuses fact with fiction in his most thrilling novel to date.

Praise for David Gibbins, international bestselling author of ATLANTIS:

'What do you get if you cross Indiana Jones with Dan Brown? Answer: David Gibbins' *Mirror*

'Fascinating' *Daily Express*

978 0 7553 5438 2

headline

The Last Gospel

David Gibbins

JACK HOWARD IS ABOUT TO DISCOVER A SECRET. PERHAPS THE GREATEST SECRET EVER KEPT . . .

WHAT IF
– one of the Ancient World's greatest libraries was buried in volcanic ash and then rediscovered two thousand years later?

WHAT IF
– what was found there was a document that could shatter the very foundations of the western world?

WHAT IF
– you were the one who discovered this secret? And were then forced to confront terrifying enemies determined to destroy you to ensure it goes no further?

David Gibbins' electrifying new novel is the story of one last Gospel, left behind in the age of the New Testament, and of its extraordinary secret, one that has lain concealed for years. Follow Jack Howard, man of action and the greatest archaeologist of his day, as he unearths the mystery – and must prevent others from doing the same . . .

You won't be able to put THE LAST GOSPEL down. You won't be able to forget it.

Praise for David Gibbins, international bestselling author of ATLANTIS:

'What do you get if you cross Indiana Jones with Dan Brown? Answer: David Gibbins' *Mirror*

'Fascinating' *Daily Express*

978 0 7553 4734 6

headline

Crusader Gold

David Gibbins

THE HOLIEST OF TREASURES

The gold menorah, symbol of the Jewish faith, stolen by Romans who sacked Jerusalem's Holy Temple.

A HISTORICAL SYMBOL

Carried in triumph through Rome, it came to represent the Empire's ruthless conquests. When the Romans moved to Constantinople, the menorah went with them . . .

THE FINAL CRUSADE

. . . But it had vanished by the time bloodthirsty Crusaders pillaged the city in 1204.

AND TO THIS DAY NO ONE KNOWS WHERE IT IS.

Turkey, present day. In Istanbul's harbour, on a dive for lost Crusade treasure, archaeologist Jack Howard discovers something wholly unexpected. Meanwhile, in an English cathedral library, a long-forgotten medieval map is unearthed. Together they could alter history. Suddenly the clock is ticking for Jack – and the stakes are already too high . . .

What unfolds is a thrilling but lethal quest, stretching from Harald Hardrada, greatest of the Viking conquerors, to the fall of the Nazis and the darkest secrets of the modern Vatican.

An exhilarating blend of history, fact and fiction, CRUSADER GOLD is another unputdownable read from the author of the worldwide bestseller *Atlantis*.

'What do you get if you cross Indiana Jones with Dan Brown? Answer: David Gibbins' *Mirror*

978 0 7553 2424 8

headline

Now you can buy any of these other
bestselling books from your bookshop or
direct from the publisher.

FREE P&P AND UK DELIVERY
(Overseas and Ireland £3.50 per book)

The Tiger Warrior	David Gibbins	£6.99
The Last Gospel	David Gibbins	£6.99
Crusader Gold	David Gibbins	£7.99
Atlantis	David Gibbins	£7.99
The Life You Want	Emily Barr	£6.99
Don't Look Back	Scott Frost	£6.99
Sure and Certain Death	Barbara Nadel	£7.99
Vanished	Joseph Finder	£6.99
Plum Spooky	Janet Evanovich	£7.99
The Watcher	Brian Freeman	£7.99
The Unsung Hero	Suzanne Brockmann	£6.99

TO ORDER SIMPLY CALL THIS NUMBER

01235 400 414

or visit our website: www.headline.co.uk

Prices and availability subject to change without notice.